Praise for Cara Bastone's
Just a Heartbeat Away

"An utterly satisfying and delicious read. One for the keeper shelf!"
—Jill Shalvis, *New York Times* bestselling author

"Emotionally intense and real, *Just a Heartbeat Away* touches the soft place in your soul. Cara Bastone's debut novel will warm you from the inside out and stay with you long after you finish the book."
—Christie Craig, *New York Times* bestselling author

"Gorgeous, brilliant, with characters so unique and real they leap right off the page. It's a master class in achy breaky yearning. Don't start this one late at night unless you don't need to do anything the next day except for pre-ordering the next one."
—Sarina Bowen, *USA TODAY* bestselling author
of the True North series

"*Just a Heartbeat Away* is a beautiful slow burn romance. The chemistry between Sebastian and Via absolutely stole my heart!"
—Molly O'Keefe, award-winning author
of the Riverview Inn series

Also by Cara Bastone

Forever Yours

When We First Met (prequel ebook novella)
Just a Heartbeat Away
Can't Help Falling
Flirting with Forever

To learn more about Cara Bastone,
visit her website, www.carabastone.com.

flirting with
forever

CARA BASTONE

HQN

ISBN-13: 978-1-335-93597-7

Flirting with Forever

Recycling programs for this product may not exist in your area.

Copyright © 2021 by Cara Bastone

This edition published by arrangement with Harlequin Books S.A.

For questions and comments about the quality of this book, please contact us at CustomerService@Harlequin.com.

HQN
22 Adelaide St. West, 40th Floor
Toronto, Ontario M5H 4E3, Canada
www.Harlequin.com

Printed in Spain

For Ginia and Carolyn

flirting with
forever

CHAPTER ONE

MARY TRACE WAS one of those freaks of nature who actually loved first dates. She knew she was an anomaly, should maybe even be studied by scientists, but she couldn't help herself. She loved the mystery, the anticipation. She always did her blond hair in big, loose curls and—no matter what she wore—imagined herself as Eva Marie Saint in *North by Northwest*, mysterious, inexplicably dripping in jewels and along for whatever adventure the night had in store. Besides, it had been a while since she'd actually been on a first date, so this one was especially exciting.

"I was expecting someone...younger."

Reality miffed out Mary's candle. The surly-faced blind date sitting across from her in this perfectly lovely restaurant had just called her *old*. About four seconds after she'd sat down.

Sure, this apparent *prince* wasn't exactly her type either, with his dark hair neatly parted on one side, the perfect knot in his midnight blue tie, the judgmental look in his eye. But she'd planned to at least be polite to him. She'd had some great dates with men who weren't her physical ideal. She certainly didn't point out their flaws to them literally the second after saying hello.

"Younger," Mary repeated, blinking.

The man blinked back. "Right. You must be, what, in your late thirties?"

Mary watched as his frown intensified, his shockingly blue eyes narrowing in their appraisal of her, a cruel sort of humor tipping his mouth down.

A nice boy, Estrella had said when she'd arranged the date. *You'll see, Mary. John is a rare find in a city like this. He's got a good job. He's handsome, he's sweet. He just needs to find the right girl.*

Well, Mary faced facts. All mothers thought their sons were nice boys. And just because Estrella Modesto happened to be the kindest mammal on God's green earth didn't mean she didn't have one sour-faced elitist for a son.

"Thirty-seven," Mary replied, unashamed and unwilling to cower under the blazing critique of his bright blue eyes. "My birthday was last week."

"Oh." His face had yet to change. "Happy birthday."

She'd never heard the phrase said with less enthusiasm. He could very well have said, "Happy Tax Day."

"Evening," a smooth voice said at Mary's elbow. Mary looked up to see a fairly stunning brunette smiling demurely down at them. The waitress was utter perfection in her black vest and white button-down shirt, not a hair out of place in her neat ponytail. Mary clocked her at somewhere around twenty-two, probably fresh out of undergrad, an aspiring actress hacking through her first few months in the Big Apple.

"Evening!" Mary replied automatically, her natural grin feeling almost obscene next to this girl's prim professionalism.

Mary turned in time to catch the tail end of John's appraisal of the waitress. His eyes, cold and rude, traveled the length of the waitress's body.

Nice boy, Estrella had said.

Mary knew, even now, that she'd never have the heart

to tell Estrella that nice boys didn't call their dates old and then mentally undress the waitress. Mary was a tolerant person, perhaps too tolerant, but there were only so many feathers one could stuff into a down pillow before it snowed poultry.

"Right," Mary said, mostly to herself, as John and the waitress both looked at her to order her drink. How *nice* of him to pull his eyes from the beautiful baby here to serve him dinner. She turned to the waitress. "I think we need a minute."

Mary took a deep breath. She asked herself the same question she'd been asking herself since she'd been old enough to ask it—which, according to John Modesto-Whitford, was probably about a decade and a half too long. *Can I continue on?* If the answer was yes, if she conceivably could continue on through a situation, no matter how horrible, she always, always did.

She pinched the bridge of her nose. The answer to that question was going to come in the form of what shoes he was wearing, which she hadn't seen yet, as she'd arrived at the restaurant after he had.

In Mary's experience, men who wore wingtips were a lost cause. Not to mention men who wore wingtips to go along with their perfect hair, perfect tie and mean eyes. Wingtip shoes were some sort of inscrutable, masculine symbol, she was sure of it. Members of the wingtip club probably communicated with one another in secret, smirky eyebrow lifts, effortlessly transmitting information about the women in their general vicinity. She hadn't figured out the why of it; she simply knew it to be true. Men in wingtips were not compatible with Mary Trace.

She opened her eyes, ignored his coldly befuddled assessment of her behavior and flipped up one side of the tablecloth. Mary let out a gusting breath of relief. There they were, size-twelve glossy ocher wingtips, recently polished. Thank God. Now she didn't have to worry about whether or not she was doing the right thing when she carefully folded her napkin and set it aside. The wingtips were a clear sign from the heavens that it was time for Mary to get the hell out of Dodge.

Still obviously befuddled, John stood when she did. The only point in his favor so far.

"Thank you for meeting me," Mary said and meant it. The jerk could have stood her up, but he hadn't. "But this is not going to work out."

His eyebrows aggressively furrowed, changing his face from that judgmental smirk for the first time since she'd sat down. Now he just looked plain old mean. She paused for a moment, expecting him to say something. Anything. But nada, zilch, goose egg. His lips just pressed into a thin line as he glared at her.

"Have a nice night." She reached for her purse.

"You're just leaving," he said flatly, his eyebrows still in that aggressive V over his cold eyes.

She straightened her purse over her shoulder.

"You've got to be kidding me," he murmured, animating for the first time by tossing his large hands in the air. "What a freaking waste of time."

A waste of time because she wasn't going to sleep with him? Apparently, he'd gotten all dolled up, schlepped his way across town, and now he expected a cookie. *Her* cookie, to be exact. After he'd straight-up called her *old*.

She sucked in a deep breath and stepped closer to him, not wanting to cause a scene by raising her voice. He stiffened and pulled back from her as if age were contagious.

She didn't want to be rude, but she'd stopped allowing

herself to be bullied about a decade ago. Social niceties be damned. Mary tossed her hair back over her shoulders. "I'm not going to say anything to Estrella about this, don't worry. But she was wrong. You are *not* a nice boy."

John blinked at her, his face quirking up into an expression that told Mary that he thought she was a prize idiot.

She wasn't an idiot, but she *had* learned a lesson. This was the last time she was letting a mother set her up with a son. Even if she was one of the best local artisans Mary stocked at Fresh.

She turned on her heel and sailed out of the restaurant.

Mary was just unlocking the door to her apartment when the worst part of what had just happened really hit her. It wasn't the cruel and unnecessary commentary on her—apparently geriatric—age. It wasn't the sneer of the mean-faced man as he'd eyed her across the table or the way he'd looked at the waitress.

No. The worst part of it was right now. This very moment, standing in her own doorway, when she couldn't call Cora. Her best friend of all time. Whom Mary had only had ten short years with before Cora had been killed in a car accident. And that had been five years ago.

For the most part, Mary had found her peace. She'd done the requisite universe cursing, the wondering why something so useless and pointless and painful could possibly have happened. She'd had the drunken, teary nights with the other people who'd loved Cora. She'd cried the tears.

And most of the time, she was okay. But not tonight. Not tonight when she wanted to call her best friend so freaking badly. When she wanted nothing more than to hear Cora's rude, snarky, biting tone over the phone. Cora would have hidden in the bathroom so her son couldn't overhear her say something like "Give me that loser's phone number.

I'm going to tell him to sit on it sideways. I'm going to tell him that he just screwed up the best opportunity that he ever had. He had a date with Mary Freaking Trace and he screwed it up in the first sentence! What a moron. Don't give him another thought, Mare, unless it's to pity the fool."

But was it even the mean-faced blind date that Mary wanted Cora to tell off? No. Because, really, Mary had done a good enough job of that on her own. She'd left the restaurant, hadn't she? Wasn't it this voice in her own head Mary needed help dispelling? This voice that sounded suspiciously like her own mother. *Too old… Running out of time… You don't want to die alone, do you? Thirty-seven and single and what a shame that is.*

Her mother would view tonight's debacle as comeuppance for Mary. Comeuppance for years of having the audacity to think that she had plenty of time to live her life before she looked for love. If she ever told her mother this story, she'd purse her lips and give Mary a look very close to an I-told-you-so.

Mary closed her apartment door behind her and locked it. All the lights in her apartment were still off, which always made Mary feel like she'd just walked into an exhibit in a museum that had closed for the evening. *Behold: the life of Mary Trace.* She viewed the lumpy shapes of her furniture, the blank geometric grace of the rugs on her floor, the frames on her walls. And then, across the way, the shadowed, ghostly version of herself in the hall mirror.

She ached for Cora.

I was expecting someone younger, the disdainful voice said again, popping up out of nowhere, threading in with her mother's voice. How many times had her mother warned her that she was rapidly approaching an age when men would, in fact, wish she were younger? A hundred? A thousand?

"What an ass," Mary huffed and flipped on the lights, tossing her home into bright, sharp focus. He was an ass who didn't deserve her. An ass who'd sneered at all the years she'd lost just trying to say goodbye to the friend she couldn't call tonight.

"TOUGH LOSS THIS MORNING, Whitford."

John's shoulders tightened as if his muscles were connected by a string that had just gotten half a foot shorter. He swiveled in his creaky chair, careful not to bash his knees on the filing cabinet he basically had to sit on top of to make room in his tiny office. And there was Crash Willis, leaning in his doorway, smirking like the royal asshole he was.

Willis was an assistant district attorney and John's least favorite person in the borough of Brooklyn. Even within the confines of his own mind, John refused to refer to him as Crash. What kind of parents named their kid *Crash*, for God's sake? Rich parents, apparently.

John let his eyes trace Willis from the top of his blond head to the tips of his teal leather loafers. Everything from the two-hundred-dollar haircut to the matching teal pocket square in the breast pocket of his suit screamed money. No one invested in teal loafers unless they had at least five *other* pairs of work shoes already.

"Wouldn't count it as a loss yet," John said, stretching his legs out and crossing them at the ankles, just because he knew his nonchalance would piss Willis off.

"Your girl gets indicted on all counts? Pretty big hit to the game plan, pal."

John took a deep breath. It was true that one of John's state-appointed clients—Hang Nguyen, first-generation Vietnamese-American, seventeen years old and officially tried as an adult in the state of New York—had been in-

dicted on three different counts of solicitation and one egre-
giously heinous count of sex trafficking that morning. But
that was to be expected. Everyone got indicted for everything in Brooklyn. But not everybody got sent to jail in
Brooklyn, and that was where John's job came in. He was
a public defender and proud of it.

He considered it a matter of course to sneer at the ADA
smirking in his doorway. Though defense attorneys and
district attorneys tended to be cut from different cloths,
there were plenty of ADAs that John respected, some who
he even counted as friends.

Willis wasn't one of them.

They weren't enemies by nature, he supposed, but more
by endgame. They were born into different worlds and
wanted to end up in different worlds too. Crash Willis,
with his pocket squares and butter leather shoes, wanted
the prestige and notoriety of someday becoming Brooklyn's
DA. He chewed through cases as fast as he could, tough on
crime and celebrating every indictment he could smooth-
talk out of unsuspecting grand juries.

John just wanted to keep minors out of prison. Willis
and John weren't exactly bosom buddies.

Besides, Willis was one of those assholes who insisted
on shortening John's last name from Modesto-Whitford to
just Whitford. John hated that.

In his mind, it was Willis's way of intentionally reminding John of his father. A small way of insinuating that
John's crusade to defend the innocent rang hollow. At least
in Willis's eyes.

"Well, next comes the fun part," John said amiably,
knowing that Willis had come in here attempting to get a
rise out of him. "The fun part" being the hours and hours
of underpaid, stress-inducing, nail-biting research, writ-

ing, negotiating, coaching, performing and defending of a kid who, in John's opinion, did not deserve up to thirty-five years behind bars.

"Hey, Crash," Richie Dear said as he skirted around Willis in the doorway and entered the office he shared with John. "My grandma called — she wants her shoes back."

John snorted with laughter, pulling his legs back to let Richie pass the eighteen inches he had to go to cram himself at his own desk.

Willis glared at both of them. "Whatever," he grumbled, turning on his heel and stalking away.

"They don't call me The Exterminator for nothing," Richie gloated, leaning across the small room to slam their door closed. "I know how to get rid of pests."

"Yeah. No one calls you that."

They both laughed. Richie Dear—his God-given last name— was bottle blond, about a foot shorter than John and always a little bit disheveled. His files often found themselves in messy piles on John's desk or chair. Two years ago, when they'd first started sharing this broom closet the state called an office, John had been positive that the very boisterous Richie Dear had been sent from hell to torture him. Now they were friends.

Plus, John had discovered noise-canceling headphones and that had significantly improved their working relationship.

"What was *Crash* doing here?" Richie asked with all the disdain of a thirteen-year-old mean girl.

"Just coming by to taunt me about my life choices. The usual."

"Ignore him. He's just salty that you have more courtroom charisma than he does."

John's cell phone buzzed on his peeling wooden desk,

spasmodically sliding a few inches to one side. John grimaced when he saw the name there and silenced it.

"Hiding from Mommy today?" Richie asked, eyeing John's phone.

John loved his mother dearly, but the woman loved to chat during the workday. He'd call her back on his walk home from the train. Or...not. He had an unusually heavy stone of dread in his gut when he thought of talking to his mother this time. "She's calling to find out about that date she set me up on."

"That was last night!" Richie realized, nearly pouring an entire mug of tepid coffee all over his pants as he swung around to face John. "How'd it go? I'm guessing if you're dodging your mother's calls, it was a bust. Didn't Estrella swear this was going to be a love match? Your future wife?" Richie slugged back half the mug of stale coffee without even a wince, something that all good public defenders learned how to do at some point or another.

"It was a waste of a swipe," John grumbled, referring to the MetroCard fare for the two trains he'd taken to get to that ridiculous restaurant.

"Why?" Richie asked nosily, slugging back the rest of the coffee. "Was she boring? Rude to the waiter?" He leaned in and theatrically whispered, "Was she one of those horrible people who blow their noses into cloth napkins?"

John laughed and shook his head. "No. No. There was nothing wrong with her." As far as he could tell. Actually, as far as he could tell, she was pretty much the most gorgeous woman he'd ever seen in his life. He'd spent the whole forty feet of her walk across that restaurant attempting to believe that she was actually there for *him*. It couldn't be. Mothers didn't set up their sons with movie-star beauties. And then that *smile*. Gah. His heart barely beat that hard when he went jogging. He'd considered it a miracle that he hadn't upended his water glass onto his pants or something idiotic like that. No. He'd made a fool of himself in a different way. A considerably worse way. Him and his clumsy freaking mouth. Guilt lanced through him. "It's just   Dating is a waste of time for me right now. I'm not in the position to…do that."

"For someone who is so unbelievably articulate in the courtroom, you sure have a *lovely* way with words when it comes to yourself," Richie said drily.

John pushed the pads of his fingers against his forehead as if he could massage through the bone and straight into the headache that always seemed to brew right there. "I play enough mind games at work to want to do that in my free time."

"Ah," Richie said with a sage nod. "Say no more. She was one of *those*."

Richie had already turned back to his desk, and John usually took every opportunity of averted attention from his chatty officemate to get as much work done as possible, but something about Richie's words made him pause.

"One of whats?" he asked Richie's back and then silenced another one of his mother's phone calls.

"A game player. Someone who has their own set of rules. Who sets traps and then greedily rubs their hands together when they watch you fall ass-first right into them. Trust me, I know the type. Sounds like you dodged a bullet."

Still a little stymied by his friend's assessment, John turned back around and woke up the twelve-year-old monitor that sat like a heavy, judgmental toad on his desk.

John considered himself to be an excellent judge of character—you kind of had to be in a courtroom—and that had not been how Mary Trace had seemed to him. But at thirty-one years old, with a grand total of one and three-quarters girlfriends in his entire life, John wasn't exactly an expert on women. Maybe Richie was right.

His computer belched an error message at him and John groaned, his mind getting pulled back to the task at hand.

Seven hours later, he emerged from the Brooklyn Supreme Court onto Jay Street, his messenger bag over his aching shoulder and his suit coat over one arm to keep it from getting wrinkled. It was that fleeting time of year in Brooklyn when there was very little difference between indoor and outdoor temperatures. The eight o'clock breeze kissed him through his cotton dress shirt. *Welcome to the world, John.*

Unfortunately, most of his world existed within the walls of the building behind him. These brief, warm-breezed, pre-sunset moments were simply the garnish at the edge of his plate. The real meat and potatoes lived inside the messenger bag slung across his hip. He strode purposefully toward the subway, ignoring the siren's call of Shake Shack, and jogged down the dingy yellow-painted stairs to his train.

Forty minutes later, he emerged in his neighborhood, the sun already down and a deep regret lodged in his gut that he'd talked himself out of fast food. All he had waiting for him in his fridge were salad fixings and half of last night's veggie stir-fry. Oh, joy.

John thought about calling his mother on the walk to his apartment but decided to wait until after he'd fortified himself with dinner.

He had just let himself into his third-floor apartment when a colorful blur snagged his attention. Actually, it was two colorful blurs. John's mother, in a bright purple dress, her salt-and-pepper hair piled up on her head, stomped out from his kitchen, holding John's cat, Ruth, who scrabbled and wheeled in Estrella's arms, attempting to get away.

"Ma," he said in surprise. "What are you doing here?"

She narrowed her eyes at him.

His stomach plummeted.

She'd found out what had happened on the date.

CHAPTER TWO

"Kylie, grab those two pink boxes from the storeroom, will you?" Mary called over her shoulder as she attempted to balance two armfuls of paper flowers she was about to place in the window of her homegoods shop. Mary had owned and operated Fresh on her own for almost five years now. And today was the day she got to put up her June window display, maybe her favorite of the entire year. She loved the chintz and glitz of the Christmas display as well, but in June she really let her flower flag fly. She let the colors clash and the fake greenery overfloweth. Mary loved the unabashed cheer of it.

"Can't find them!" Kylie, her teenage part-time assistant, called from the back of the store.

"Maybe they're purple boxes?" Mary shouted back. "They're filled with the...you know...whatever you call those thingies."

Mary lost every word in her head as one of the most devastatingly beautiful men she'd ever seen in her life walked past the front window of her shop. Tall, wiry and broad-shouldered, he had light brown hair and was wearing a construction vest to boot. He looked like he'd walked out of a porn that Mary herself had cast. The man did a double take at Mary checking him out through the shop window, shooting her a cheeky grin as he walked.

Damn. "Better than a shot of Red Bull," Mary muttered to herself.

"Do you mean the red boxes filled with the fake grass?" Kylie called.

Setting the paper flowers down in a heap in the window, Mary walked back to the storeroom to help out Kylie. After half a minute of searching, Mary found what she was looking for.

"Ah," Kylie said drily. "You meant the blue boxes filled with the mason jars. How could I have possibly misunderstood?"

Mary laughed. "Sorry. Got distracted by a hottie walking past."

Though there was more than twenty years of an age difference between them, Mary and Kylie were closer to friends than they were boss and employee. When Kylie had come to live with her half brother, Tyler Leshuski, one of Mary's best friends in the world, around last Thanksgiving, Mary had offered her a job in the shop. Both as a way to discreetly keep an eye on her when Tyler was at work and as a way to get to know Kylie. She hadn't expected the kid to be so freaking helpful. Seriously, Kylie worked less than fifteen hours a week and got more done than Mary's other two employees combined.

Mary's phone dinged in her pocket and she tugged it out to make sure it wasn't one of her artisans contacting her. It was just an email from her mother. The subject line was "Time Sensitive, Please Read Immediately." Mary clicked into the email and was surprised when her molars didn't crack down their meridians. It was an article about the drastic drop in a woman's fertility after the age of thirty. Apparently her mother meant the phrase *time sensitive* in the cosmic sense. She deleted the email without reading the article.

The front bell on the shop jingled and Kylie peeked her head out the storeroom door. She ducked back in. "Was your hottie wearing a construction vest?"

"Eep! Is he out there?" All thoughts of her meddling mother evaporated away.

"Sure is. I'm gonna…grab lunch for us." Kylie scampered toward the back door.

"Charge it to the company card!" Mary hollered before she smoothed her hair, sat a box of the jars on her hip and left the storeroom with a big old smile on her face. "Hi there, can I help you with anything?"

The man, who'd been leaning over to inspect a series of ceramic clocks that Mary had arranged along one wall, straightened up and grinned at her. Damn, he really was attractive. Tall and smiley. Just like she liked.

"Just, ah, looking. I guess," he said, his eyes quickly tracing over her.

Mary smiled harder. She wore tight jeans, a white V-neck T-shirt with flowers embroidered over both shoulders and brown high-heeled boots up to her knees. Her hair, naturally wavy, was behaving nicely today. "You're welcome to look," she said, setting the box of mason jars down at the window display and starting to arrange huge handfuls of mismatched paper flowers into them.

"Never seen your shop before," the man said in a smooth baritone. "You been here long?"

"Five years now. You must not live in the neighborhood."

"Guilty. We— I'm up in Queens." He had his hands shoved in his pockets and a slightly chagrined look on his handsome face when Mary turned back around.

She hadn't missed the accidental "we." She clocked him

at about thirty-five years old. Definitely old enough to be married.

"You and your wife?" she guessed.

His cheeks went pink. "Ah. Ex-wife. Force of habit to say 'we,' I guess."

"Oh. I'm sorry." She meant it too. She'd never been married, but she'd seen enough of her friends' marriages dissolve to know just how much it could screw up somebody's life.

"Don't be." He shrugged. "Long time coming. The name's James, by the way."

"Mary."

"Well, Mary, pretty cool selection of, um, these thingies you have here."

She laughed, finding his bumbling, blushing manner to be pretty freaking cute. "Those are napkin rings."

James puttered around the shop as Mary worked on the window display, the two of them idly chatting about the knickknacks that she sold and his construction work on a brownstone three blocks over. He was glancing her way an awful lot, and Mary was starting to feel a little blushy. He was just so dang good-looking. A buzz started in her gut.

In her early twenties, she never, ever used to ask a man out. Her mother's training had been clear. It was a man's job to do that. Being too forward would only emasculate him.

Cora was the one who'd helped her see that if a man was emasculated, that was his problem, not hers. In her mid-twenties, Mary had started to ask people out. That didn't mean that it was any less scary now than it used to be.

Her cheeks went hot and so did her palms as she turned to James. "I was wondering, James..."

He turned to her, a complicated expression on his face.

The bell jingled on the front door, but Mary didn't turn around to see who'd come in.

"Would you want to grab dinner with me sometime?" she finished, hoping her voice didn't carry to whoever had just entered her shop.

"Oh," James said in that same smooth voice that had been making Mary's stomach flip for the last fifteen minutes. He took a step closer to her and tugged a hand through his hair. It was then that Mary saw the flash of gold. On his left hand.

Right. *Rightrightrightrightright.*

"When I said ex-wife," he mumbled, his eyes flicking behind her toward the newcomer in the shop, "I probably should have said soon-to-be ex-wife. But we're, yeah, in mediation and I probably shouldn't…"

She refused to be the one who was embarrassed. He should be embarrassed. But she still couldn't stop the flood of heat in her cheeks. And sure enough, here came the underboob sweat. Like freaking clockwork.

"Oh. Okay." She rose up from where she'd been crouching to arrange the flowers, still holding a few of them in her hands. "That's fine. Good luck with all that."

James stepped forward. He seemed to be purposefully ignoring the other shopper. "I didn't mean to mislead you or anything. You're just so pretty and I was having such a bad day until you smiled at me."

Ugh. Did he have to be so cute? "It's totally fine. Good luck with everything!" She gave him a bright smile so that he wouldn't continue this apology that was only allowing embarrassment to dig its claws more forcefully into her.

"Right," he mumbled. "You too." And then he ambled out of the shop, shooting Mary a fairly miserable look through the shop window as he went back the way he'd come.

Mary resisted the urge to crumple up into a raisin and die and turned to the new customer with a sunny smile on her face.

She'd once stood on a curb when a cab had driven past and splashed muddy puddle water all over her new Anthropologie skirt. This was pretty much the emotional equivalent of that.

Because standing in her shop was a sympathetic-looking Estrella and a bitingly disdainful-looking John, his elbow firmly in his mother's grip.

The smile vaporized off Mary's face and she just sort of stared at them. If there had been one person on God's spinning earth that Mary would not have wanted to see her ask out a married man and be rejected, it would be John Modesto-Whitford. The memory of his surly judgment two nights ago was painfully fresh in Mary's mind. She didn't let that kind of thing get too under her skin, but this one definitely hadn't quite healed over yet.

"Mary!" Estrella said brightly, obviously determined to ignore the romantic crash and burn they'd just witnessed. "How are you? The shop looks beautiful as always. You know John, my son. He was taking his mother out to lunch around the corner and I wanted him to see your lovely shop."

Mary's eyes flicked over to the man in the black slacks, white dress shirt and dark blue tie. And yup, shiny wingtips. It was Saturday, for God's sake! How deep into the wingtip cult did a man have to be to wear wingtips on a Saturday?

"Hello," she said.

"Hello," John returned in a voice that was a bit scratchy, two-toned almost.

"I'm going to quick run to the USPS up the block,"

Estrella chirped. "Mary, do you have a second to show John your shop?"

Estrella didn't wait for an answer before she ducked toward the front door, nudging her son forward at the same time.

And then there was nothing but echoing silence in the wake of Estrella's departure. John blinked at Mary. Mary blinked at John.

"Well," Mary said, gesturing around her with the flowers she just now realized were still in her hands. "This is my shop. You're welcome to take a look around. Let me know if you have any questions."

Mary felt his eyes on her as she turned back to the window display and started messing around with the bouquets she'd already put together. They'd been bright and haphazard and happy only moments before, but suddenly they looked messy and lazy to her. Maybe she should start over.

She could tell that John hadn't moved from where he stood in her front entryway, and she could still feel his eyes on her back.

"Mary," he said a moment later in that double-layered voice of his. How had she not noticed his voice the other night? It was so distinct. "My mother and I weren't eating lunch around the corner."

Mary instantly decided that each vase of flowers was utter, cheery perfection exactly as they were. Screwing with them too much was bound to wring the magic out of them, like water from a sponge. She picked up an armful of the jars and began to set them around the shop. The rest she'd arrange in the window. "Oh?"

John cleared his throat. "She told me that the two of you talked about our, uh, date."

Mary whirled and was lucky that none of those jars

actually had water in them because she would have been soaked down to her toes if they had. "I didn't rat you out or anything. I just told her that—"

"That you didn't have a good time. I know. It's fine, Mary. You were honest with her. And she showed up at my house last night, spitting mad, because she says that Mary Trace always has a good time, no matter what she's doing, and if she didn't have a good time, then it must be my fault. And if it's my fault, then I owe you an apology." John traced his wide hands outward, palms up. "So, here I am."

Mary frowned. "Your mother dragged you to my shop to apologize to me?"

He grimaced, and for just a flash, that surly face had the grace to look a tiny bit chagrined. "I came willingly."

"She had you by the elbow when you came in here," Mary said, arching an eyebrow.

His mouth turned down. "I wanted to wait outside the shop while you had another customer. My mother didn't have any qualms about that."

Mary blushed, embarrassed all over again about James the married man. "Right."

John glanced out through her front window, his eyebrows furrowed down, though not as aggressively as she knew he was capable of. His hands were pushed into his pockets.

"Look, Mary. You were more right than my mother is. I'm not a nice boy. Although at thirty-one, I like to think I've graduated from not a nice *boy* to not a nice *man*."

She cocked her head to one side as she studied him. He seemed older than thirty-one. His dark, neatly parted hair was so shiny that she realized it gave the illusion of silver, but it was actually just a full head of black hair. And the lines around his eyes were more likely from fatigue than they were from age.

He cleared his throat, those bright blue eyes stuck on her face. "I'm busy and grumpy and preoccupied and…rude. But none of that is an excuse for making you feel bad. So, I apologize. Really, I do. I'm sorry, Mary. I'm sorry for the mess I made of the other night. And I'm sorry I was rude."

Oh. That was actually a good apology. None of that fast-dancing, zero-vulnerability, I'm-sorry-if-your-feelings-were-hurt-by-my-actions crap. That was a real apology. He'd admitted he was rude.

He stood, without moving, in the same spot. His hands were in his pockets, his eyes on hers, his mouth frowning, his eyebrows pushed down and mean.

"Well," Mary said as she stamped her foot. "It might be easier to forgive you if you hadn't just seen me strike out like that."

John smirked, a grunt coming out of him that might have passed for a laugh in another dimension. "Yeah. That was…hard to watch."

Mary glowered at him. "It's not my fault he was married."

"No. It wasn't."

"And honestly, I consider it a win that I didn't find out he was married *after* I'd gone on a date with him. I can't tell you how many times that has happened to me." She turned and continued to set the vases around her shop, positioning them this way and that until they were perfect. "Apology accepted, by the way."

"Oh. Good."

The bell to the shop jingled and in walked Estrella. She and her son exchanged eye contact, communicating silently, and Mary gathered that John was forgiven in his mother's eyes.

"Estrella, I'm glad you're back. I wasn't sure how to display the pots you brought over yesterday."

Estrella was one of the artisans that Mary featured in her shop, which was how they'd first become friends a few years ago. The woman was a true creative. She'd started out with these intricately embroidered throw pillows that had immediately triggered Mary's drool reflex the moment she'd first seen them. From there, Estrella had started into her tapestries phase, which rolled into the stained-glass windows phase, and now they were here, with these lovely pots that Estrella threw in a ceramics studio and glazed to perfection. Mary couldn't have loved them more. And she couldn't have loved Estrella more either.

The woman, unlike some of Mary's other artisans, was even-tempered and realistic. If Mary couldn't sell some of her pieces, Estrella traded them out, her pride uninjured. Mary deeply valued their professional relationship, but nowhere near as much as their personal one. It was almost once a week that Estrella stopped by for a lunch with Mary or just a quick chat. It was a miracle that she'd known Mary for so long before she'd tried to set her up with John. Mary had been weighted down with a full-body dread to tell Estrella that it hadn't worked out between them. She didn't want anything to damage her relationship with her friend. Apparently, though, it hadn't caused too much damage, considering that Estrella was smiling as she marched across the floor and gave Mary a little side-hug.

"You could display them over there, with the other pots." Estrella pointed.

"Never!" The idea was absurd to Mary. "Those pots are nothing compared to yours. No. I want yours prominently displayed, but I was wondering what you thought about me buying some plants to stick into some of them, to give the customer an idea on how to use them practically. I could put one or two in the front window and then the rest… Oh, I'll have to unpack them and figure it out as I go."

"Are they in the storeroom?" Estrella asked.

"Mmm-hmm. In the same box you brought them over in."

"John," Estrella ordered. "The box has blue painter's tape on it. Bring it out here, will you?"

Moments later, the women were unpacking Estrella's pots from the packing material and fussing with their placement around the shop. Kylie returned with a sack of tacos in one hand, adeptly realized that they were not taking a lunch break and took over dealing with any customers that came in while Mary and Estrella finished setting up the displays.

John dutifully followed his mother's directions on where to put this and that, though he said next to nothing and scowled coldly the entire time. When half an hour had passed, and the task was over, he stood at the far wall, his hands in his pockets, looking like he'd gladly walk through the gateway to Lucifer's private torture chamber if it meant getting the hell out of here.

Some of the friendly glow Mary had started to feel in the wake of his apology faded. Did he have to be so unpleasant? He was like a sinkhole for good feeling.

"Are you working next Saturday?" Estrella asked Mary.

"Hmm? Oh. Always."

"Not in the afternoon, though," Kylie called. "Right? I thought I was overlapping with Caleb next Saturday."

"Oh. Right. I should be out of here around two o'clock if you wanted to come by earlier than that, Estrella. Will you be bringing more of your work or is it a social call?"

"Neither," Estrella said, giving her a mischievous grin.

"Ma." John's tone was part warning, part admonishment, his voice gravelly from not having spoken in so long.

He seemed to know exactly what his mother was up to and didn't appear to approve one bit.

Estrella ignored him. "My block has a party this time in June every year. You should come. There's plenty of our neighbors there you could meet."

"Oh." Mary loved parties, she always had. Especially outdoor ones in the summer.

"She doesn't want to come to the block party, Ma," John groused. That aggressive V between his brows was back.

Well, if Mary hadn't wanted to go to the party, she certainly did now, if not just to prove Frowny McIceberg wrong. "Sounds fun. Is it a potluck? Should I bring anything?"

"Maybe a cake?" Estrella leaned in, ostensibly to cut John out of the conversation. "And dress up a little. There's a few nice boys there that I'd like for you to meet."

Mary held her smile in place, because she loved Estrella so dearly. But she was simply mortified to have the topic of dating brought up in front of John. Apparently the universe felt that Married James hadn't been punishment enough. "You got it," Mary said with a wink she hoped covered her true feelings on the matter. "I could be there around three thirty?"

"Perfect." Estrella stopped just long enough to kiss Kylie on the cheek. "Goodbye, my loves." She waved at both of them, grabbed John by the elbow again and tugged him out of the shop.

"Bye!" Mary called, shaking her head when she realized that John didn't even look back as he left the shop. He certainly didn't say goodbye.

CHAPTER THREE

MARY FOLLOWED ESTRELLA'S directions and dressed up for the block party. It was a perfect June day, warm in the sun, cool in the shade, with just enough of a breeze to keep the sweat from sticking. Mary wore a cap-sleeve floaty blue dress with yellow suns stitched onto the hem and her favorite pair of high-heeled boots. Once Caleb arrived at her shop to relieve her, she ducked into the back room and dabbed on some pink lipstick and a little mascara. Her hair had been a bit bashful that morning, so she'd straightened it and let it fall down her back.

Estrella had promised there'd be some cuties at the party and the thought made Mary's stomach flip. She liked cuties. She liked flirting. She liked men. She liked parties. Yeehaw.

She stopped at a bakery three blocks down and picked up a cake, then emerged from the train twenty minutes later in Estrella's neighborhood. As well as they knew one another, Mary had never been to Estrella's house before. She lived on a cute little block of Crown Heights, too far east to have been completely overrun by gentrifiers as of yet. The huge green oak trees touched hands where they loomed over the street, and one corner sported a Japanese cherry blossom tree, a few weeks past its May explosion of color but still gorgeous.

Estrella's block was cordoned off with blue wooden sawhorses warning cars away but inviting anyone who wanted to party. There were about a hundred more people there than Mary had expected. One end of the block was inundated with children, all vying for a turn on the ten-foot-wide trampoline that had been dragged outside. The other end of the block was muzzy with barbecue smoke. In the middle sat four tables pushed together with mountains of food. Mary slipped her cake onto the dessert table and immediately lost track of which one she'd brought.

"Mary!" And then there was Estrella, beaming up at Mary and grabbing her by both hands. "You're a vision. Come. You can stow your purse at my place."

Estrella, practically dragging Mary down the block, led her up a stoop onto the garden level of a blond brick town house, a little shabby but in a friendly way. Estrella kept a scattered assortment of flowers in a window box under one window, and a snow shovel, never put away from the wintertime, leaned up against the mailboxes in the front vestibule. Estrella's apartment was dim from a lack of natural light, but somehow still cheery. Colorful paintings and photographs covered all the walls, and a long, horrible rug led down the front hallway, instantly charming Mary. The kitchen was as snug as the bedrooms they passed, but it had flowers in the window and rice in colorful glass jars.

"I love your space," Mary said, and meant it.

"I hardly notice it anymore," Estrella replied. "I've been here almost thirty years. Your purse will be safe there. Come along."

Estrella pulled Mary back out onto the street.

"Ooh, punch." Mary stopped and got herself a glass, which was surprisingly flavored like white grape, even though it was a burnished pink.

"I have the most wonderful man for you to meet," Estrella said. "His name is Samuel. He's in computers or something, I never know. And he's quite handsome." She pointed across the block toward a shorter man with dark skin who was indeed quite handsome. "I've known him since he was in diapers. He's like a nephew to me. I'll get him."

And then Mary was alone, sipping her punch and looking around, watching three teenage girls holding hands in a chain and weaving through the crowd, watching a group of older women reclined in deck chairs in the sun, watching men elbow one another out of the way at the grill, each one reaching for the spatula. She got a funny tingle between her shoulders and knew she was being watched as well. She turned and halfway down the block was John, holding a beer and scowling at her. He ducked his head in hello and she did the same. Her eyes traced down John's form, and she almost rolled them. Though he'd foregone the tie, he wore a white dress shirt, black trousers and the ever-present wingtips.

What a party animal.

"Mary, this is Samuel. Samuel, Mary."

Mary turned in time to watch as Estrella two-hand shoved the shy-looking Samuel forward. Mary had to grab his elbow to help brace him.

"I'll leave you two alone!" Estrella toodled her fingers and was gone.

"Hi," Mary said with a laugh. "Estrella's quite…enthusiastic."

Samuel grinned at her. "That's one way to describe her."

He had round, handsome features, a clean shave and a hugely warm smile. Mary liked him instantly. "So. Estrella tells me she's known you since you were in diapers. Though I've always thought that was a strange way of explaining how long you've known someone."

His eyebrows quirked, apparently deciding to leave her

last comment alone. "Yeah, I grew up down the block from John and Estrella. In that red town house down there."

"It seems like everyone knows each other on this block."

"Oh, yeah. One big family."

Mary thought she detected just a trace of sarcasm in his tone but couldn't think of how to ask about it. "Think you'll play any of the games?" Mary asked, nodding her head over to where little girls were challenging one another in double Dutch, a basketball hoop was set up, and three full-grown men were each attempting to blow the largest soap bubble they possibly could.

"You happen to be standing next to the Lincoln Place hopscotch champ seven years running." Samuel blew on his fingernails and shined them on his T-shirt.

Mary laughed at the teasing glint in his eyes. "I wasn't aware I was in the presence of greatness."

"Sammy," a distinct voice said from behind her. "Your aunt is looking for you. She said your wife is on the phone."

Samuel grimaced, glancing quickly at Mary and then away. "*Ex*, John. Ex-wife."

"Oh, is it official now?" John asked blandly, taking a sip of the beer he held in his hand as he came to stand next to Mary. He let his cold eyes wander the crowd.

"Mary, I'll be right back," Samuel said, taking a few steps backward. "Don't go anywhere. I'll be *right* back."

Mary sighed as she watched him disappear into the crowd. "Is his wife really on the phone?" she asked John, one eyebrow raised.

John shrugged, unrepentant, bored. "You mentioned that you had a problem with married guys shooting their shot with you. I thought I'd help you out."

Mary was quiet as she stood shoulder to shoulder with John, watching two kids with water guns chase each other down the street, their mothers hollering after them. The line for the buffet table was three people wide and five sidewalk squares long. Loud, tinny music played from speakers jammed against the screen of someone's open windows. Across the way, Estrella laughed and leaned her head onto the shoulder of a humongous redheaded man.

Mary's grape punch was down to just pointy shards of melting ice. She stared into the bottom of her glass. She liked going to parties by herself. Of course, she'd never had a problem with that. But she really, really liked going to a party with a date. Maybe it made her old-fashioned, but she liked having someone who cared about whether or not her drink was full.

"So," John said, reminding her that he still stood on the curb next to her. "You're, like, really desperate for dates or something?"

"*Okay*, then," Mary said crisply, turning on her heel and marching away from John. A white sheet of blank disbelief had fallen over her, snuffing out her party glow. What an *ass*.

"Wait! Mary. Shit. I didn't mean— That was a terrible thing to— Please wait." Two heavy fingers tapped roughly at her shoulder. He appeared at her side, palms out, fingers looped around his beer bottle. "I'm an idiot."

"Has anyone ever told you that you're a complete sinkhole for happiness? Where good feelings go to die? *Desperate?*" she quoted him with a scowl. "Being thirty-seven and flirting with a good-looking man at a party does not make me desperate. Wanting to meet someone does not make me *desperate*. Jeez! You're like the human manifestation of the sad trombone sound."

John scowled at her, his bright eyes shadowed by the pull of his brow. "To answer your question, yes, people have told me that before. Never quite so…creatively. But yes, I've been known to bring the mood down."

"It's annoying." She scowled at him.

"Yes," he agreed immediately. "It really is."

"Mary," Estrella said, huffing and puffing a little, as if she'd stridden quickly across the party. "Where'd Samuel go?"

"Ma," John cut in. "Sammy? Really? You're setting her up with Sammy? He's not even divorced yet."

If looks could have turned someone back into a nine-year-old boy and sent him to his room, the mug that Estrella was shooting at John certainly would have done it. "Samuel is a good boy. But fine. He wasn't your taste, Mary? There's more. Come with me."

Estrella tugged on Mary's elbow.

John got in his mother's way. "Who's next in the lineup?"

"None of your business."

John followed his mother's gaze and made a sound of disbelief. "*Jonah?* Oh, for fuck's sake, Ma!"

"Estrella, I'm going to run to the bathroom. Be right back!" Mary tried to shoot both of them a bright smile, but she had the feeling that it might have come off a little canned. She appreciated what Estrella was doing, she really did. But setups were awkward enough without them being loud and confrontational and causing half of a block party to crane their heads to stare at the new girl.

Mary ducked back into Estrella's house, found the bathroom and washed her hands. She'd go back out there, get something to eat, chat with some people and head home. She didn't have to overthink this.

She walked back through the house and found John sitting on the front steps to his mother's house, passing his beer back and forth between his hands.

"Hi."

He looked up at her, rising quickly. Mary realized that due to some optical illusion, sans his perfectly knotted tie, he looked both taller and wider. Like his open collar and the triangle of gold skin it revealed had allowed his body to stretch out to its true size. "My mother has terrible taste in men."

Mary couldn't help but laugh. "I'm starting to learn that."

"Besides Cormac, really, just terrible."

"Who's Cormac?"

For the first time since she'd met John, his face truly softened. It was still a very far cry from friendly, but some of the ice had defrosted. He nodded his head across the block party toward the large redheaded man that Estrella had been leaning against before. "My mother's live-in."

Mary's mouth fell open. "Estrella has a partner? She never mentioned. Not once..."

"It doesn't surprise me. My mother is old-fashioned. Officially, she doesn't believe in premarital sex."

"Yet she has a live-in boyfriend?"

"Ah, ah, ah," John said with one finger ticking back and forth. "He's not her boyfriend. She refers to him as her tenant. I think I was about twelve when I finally realized that most tenants don't share your mother's bed with her."

"They've been together that long?"

"Almost as long as I can remember." Something pained flicked across John's face, but the scowl resumed almost immediately.

"Why don't they just get married?"

"My mother also doesn't believe in second marriages," he said with a roll of his eyes. That striking gaze flicked down to Mary. "She does, however, strongly believe in gray areas."

Mary laughed, despite her surly company. "So. What's wrong with Jonah?"

"Hmm?"

"The apparent next on Estrella's list. You said his name is Jonah. What's wrong with him?"

"Oh. Let's see. Midthirties, lives with his mother still, dates barely legals he meets on Tinder. Plays it fast and loose with deodorant. And I know for a fact he still shoplifts from Gristedes."

"Wow. Does Estrella even *have* criteria?"

John grunted. "I've never seen her quite so determined to set someone up before. That's really what I meant. Before. When I said that thing about you being desperate." He mumbled the last part. "I guess I just wanted to know why my mother was pushing this so hard."

Mary, of course, knew the exact answer to that question, but she'd rather eat the entire tube of Chanel lipstick she kept in her purse than explain it to John. "Maybe she just wants a project." Mary cleared her throat. "Maybe she knows just how great I am and wants to see me happy."

John grunted again.

What a lovely man.

"I'm going to grab some food, I think."

She was ten steps away when those two heavy fingers tapped her shoulder again. "Look, Mary, let me make it up to you."

"What do you mean?"

"My mother is going to keep trying to set you up with guys. Chances are, I'll know them." John took two steps to one side and chucked his beer bottle a few feet into a recycling can, came back and shoved his hands in his pockets. "I love my mother, and I can tell you do too, but we both know her definition of 'nice boy' is prohibitively inclusive. All you need to qualify is the Y chromosome and a pulse."

Mary couldn't help but laugh.

He blinked at her for a second and cleared some gravel out of his throat, although it didn't make that two-toned voice any less hoarse. "I put my foot in my mouth earlier, but you can trust me to give it to you straight. If there's one thing I'm good for…"

"You won't sugarcoat anything for me."

"Exactly."

"You want to help me weed through candidates?" she guessed.

"Here, take my number and you can text me the names of the guys she wants you to meet. I'll let you know whether they're worth your time. Or email. Whatever."

"My phone is in your mother's house." She eyed John for a moment. He had a thin mouth made thinner by the way he was pressing his lips together. He had the shadowed look of dark-haired men who shave their beards but never lose that bluish shading about the jaw. His eyes were startlingly bright, and cold, and surly, but the judgment that she'd seen at the restaurant was absent. He was rude, but he'd apologized for that, and apologized well. And she definitely trusted his taste in men more than his mother's. She made a split-second decision. "But you can have my number and text me so I have yours."

His eyebrows flicked upward from their typical downward V, but only for a second. He seemed surprised that she would volunteer her number. He pulled his phone from his pocket, a smaller iPhone model that had been new about seven years ago, but the screen was completely smudge and scratch free. He typed in her number as she told it to him and sent off a quick text to her.

"Have a good rest of the party," he told her.

"You too."

Luckily, Estrella held off on the parade of men for the

rest of the time, and Mary was able to enjoy herself. Samuel never reappeared. Mary assumed he'd been summoned home by his wife. She caught a few more glimpses of John through the crowd and then she thought he must have left.

She got all the way back to Cobble Hill, unzipped from her boots, had leftover Indian food heating in the microwave, before she finally checked her phone. She had a voice mail from her mother, who considered texting to be juvenile. "Mary, love, did you get my email? It was a forwarded invitation to Meryl Overshire's singles event on the Upper East Side next week? It sounds like a classier version of speed dating. Now, I'm sure you'll be one of the older participants, but Meryl assured me that—" Mary deleted the voice mail. She moved on to the three texts from her friends Fin and Via on a group chat they had together. And then there was one text from an unknown number.

She opened it up.

John Modesto-Whitford, the text said. Mary laughed at it. How boring! Not even a salutation. She hadn't ever known before that someone could have a frowny name, but she could practically *feel* the scowl coming off of each letter. She was almost tempted to text him back a blur of flower emojis. Thirty-five party horns, confetti fireworks, sunshines and trumpets. She pictured him receiving a colorful emoji-filled text from her and scoffing, the V of his eyebrows pulling down so far his nose disappeared.

Instead, she just saved his number into her contacts, ate her Indian food and went to bed.

CHAPTER FOUR

FIVE DAYS AFTER the block party, John did a confused double take at his cell phone as he sat in his office slogging through paperwork at 6:00 p.m.

Elijah Crawford.

Why in God's name was an unknown number texting him the name of his childhood bully? For one confused second, John thought that maybe Elijah Crawford was texting him and identifying himself. But from a Connecticut area code?

"Oh," he muttered to himself once he'd entered the text and saw that he and the number already had a thread going. Well, not so much a thread, but a single other text that had just his own name. It was Mary Trace.

He blinked. Took a deep breath. He was a grown man. With a law degree. His heart should not be shivering in his chest just because he'd gotten an unexpected text from a pretty girl. A very pretty girl. Okay, the *prettiest* girl.

And the sweetest one. She'd have to be if she was willing to forgive him for his multiple social faux pas that he'd already committed. He hadn't saved her number into his phone when she'd given it, simply because he hadn't thought she'd ever actually text him. His conscience, poking at him after all the rude things he'd accidentally said to her, had made him offer up his services, but he hadn't bothered to hope that she'd take him up on it. What woman wanted further contact with a man who'd already effectively called her desperate and old?

But there she was, sending him a text that was already two minutes old. Then the meaning of her text filtered down onto John. If she was texting him the name Elijah Crawford, then that meant that his mother was considering setting Mary up with that douchenozzle.

"What?" John whispered to himself. His mother was a reasonable woman usually. What was with this psycho matchmaking thing she was doing?

He typed his response out. Veto.

He tossed his phone back down and got through one more page of paperwork before she texted back.

Why?

John sighed and typed out, Because he intentionally spilled apple juice on the crotch of my pants in third grade, tripped me down the stairs in fifth grade and stole my prom date in high school.

He stared at his unsent words, the cursor still blinking on his screen. A flush of embarrassment rose hot out of his collar as he pictured sending those words to gorgeous Mary Trace. He immediately erased them. He'd botched his chance with her, he was very clear on that point, but that didn't mean he needed to inform her just how much of a nerd he used to be.

He's a bully, John texted. He thought for a second and texted another line. And not a good listener. You won't have fun.

Okay, she texted back a minute later. I'll tell Estrella I'm busy. Thanks!

As John was reading, one last text came through, an emoji of a shiny, smiling sun, its rays waving at him, reminding him of Mary's sunny, wavy hair. A weird jolt went through him as he looked down at the little image. It should be meaningless. It was just something she'd absently clicked on and sent. But for some reason, for a split second, John wondered if it was personal. If she purposefully picked it and sent it his way, actively wanting to send him a little sunshine.

He found himself frowning down at his phone screen. It was nice of her to send, he supposed. But what the hell was he supposed to text back? The only person who ever texted him emojis was Richie, and John ignored each and every one of them. Was it rude to ignore Mary's emoji?

Deciding, on principle, that he couldn't afford to care, John turned his phone to silent and exited out of the text strand.

Juggling anywhere between thirty and forty cases at a time, John found he didn't often have the time for indulgences like texting pretty girls. Especially not when he had two separate murder-one cases in his caseload plus that sex trafficking case that was keeping him up at night.

But none of those cases were where he needed his brain to be today. Today was all about Serge Raoul. He was a thirty-eight-year-old charged with felony assault who John had to prep for court. Normally, he'd meet with a client four or five times before the big show. He'd have clocked anywhere from ten to twenty hours of face time with them. But Raoul was rougher around the edges than most people. This would already be John's seventh time meeting with him and lately the meetings had more the feel of a play rehearsal than they did a legal meeting. Raoul seemed almost passionately committed to perjuring himself on the stand. If he didn't stick to the talking points that John had painstakingly prepared for him this time, John might have to go the rare route of not letting his client testify. Raoul had a motor mouth and a very twisted way of viewing the truth. There was no telling how the jury would perceive him.

He didn't usually like to overprepare his clients, because then they could come off as rehearsed, like the truth was something they'd had to memorize. But in this case, as John carefully packed the flash cards he'd made into his messenger bag, he figured that might be the lesser of two evils. He refused to let Raoul run roughshod over the stand and get himself sent up.

John didn't allow himself another look at his cell phone before he slipped it into the pocket of his trousers. He had work to do. A man's freedom to salvage.

IT WAS FRIDAY NIGHT, when he was out at a bar close to the Brooklyn Supreme Court with Richie on the barstool beside him, that John got the next text from Mary.

Michael Fallon.

"Oh, for fuck's sake," John muttered. Michael Fucking Fallon? Was his mother playing some sort of sick joke on Mary?

Hard veto.

Why?

Drug dealer.

You're joking.

Wish I were.

Which kind of drugs?

John gaped at the text, trying to interpret her response. Does it matter?

Well, sometimes people have good reasons for doing bad things, she texted back after a few minutes. In my opinion, there's a difference between selling dime bags and selling heroin.

John barked a laugh into the palm of his hand. He'd expected blonde, obviously rich Mary to go screaming toward the hills at any mention of the *D* word. Huh. Maybe she'd gotten really into *Breaking Bad* or *The Wire* or something.

Besides, she texted again. Innocent until proven guilty.

He shook his head at his phone, feeling weird. Maybe he should stop at one beer tonight; he was already a little bit light-headed. He flagged down Marissa, their usual bartender, and ordered a basket of fries while he one-handedly texted Mary back.

As a criminal defense attorney, innocent until proven guilty is obviously a core tenet of my belief system. But trust me on this one. I've seen him deal with my own eyes. And as for Michael Fallon having good reasons for what he does? He's 34 years old and in the middle class. His parents paid for his bachelor's degree in social theory, for fuck's sake. Date him if you want but just remember that I voted to veto.

"Jeez, Estrella's got you worked up tonight, huh?" Richie, who'd been chatting up the guy on his right, finally turned his attention back to John, his eyes narrowing at the phone.

"What? Oh. I'm not texting with my mother."

Richie's expression fell. "Oh, Lord. What did Maddox get himself into now?"

John laughed bitterly, nodding his head at Marissa when she came back with his fries.

"He wants mustard, not ketchup, Marissa," Richie reminded their bartender, who rolled her eyes and slid a bottle down the countertop toward them.

"You know," John said, "I do, in fact, text people who aren't my mother and my emotionally stunted younger brother."

Maddox was John's younger half brother, connected through the father that Maddox had grown up with and John hadn't met until a decade ago. Maybe emotionally stunted was a tad harsh. But John couldn't help but wonder if growing up with access to all their father's money had kept Maddox from developing certain survival skills that the rest of the world seemed to have. Survival skills like caring about keeping a job and knowing how to do more in a kitchen than call up expensive delivery.

John, who'd grown up without their father, had come by those skills quite honestly.

Richie squinted his eyes into the beyond, theatrically raising his fingers one by one. "Estrella, Maddox and me. But hold on, I'm sitting right here. Who in God's name is this mystery fourth texter?! I demand to know!"

John shook his head and stuffed some fries in his mouth, buying himself a moment. For some reason, he didn't want to explain the arrangement with Mary to Richie. Or why he was texting with her. It was simple, innocent, but there was no telling how Richie's perverted mind could twist it.

"Evening, girls," a deep, borderline rude voice said from behind them, two meaty paws clapping over their shoulders.

John wasn't often thrilled to run into Hogan Trencher around town, but right now he was relieved for the interruption. He slipped his phone back in his pocket and hoped that the appearance of Richie's unrequited crush would squash any residual attention on who John had been texting.

"Evening, Hulk," Richie said, a light blush washing over his cheekbones.

He called him that in reference to his first name, not because Hogan was built anything like a ripped, green monster. In truth, Hogan was a little chubby, all shoulders and spread legs and thumbs tucked into his belt. He even had the mustache to complete the picture.

John observed Richie's bashful expression, his eyes looking everywhere but at Hogan. A gay defense attorney with the hots for a straight cop. What a hopeless situation. It wasn't the first time that John had felt bad for the predicament Richie had found himself in.

Hogan Trencher wasn't a crooked detective by any means, but he had a healthy disdain for the defense attorneys he felt put his collars back on the street. And John had seen too many detectives bend the truth on the stand to ever truly want to break bread with Hogan Trencher. And so had Richie. Maybe, John reflected as he polished off his beer, that was part of the appeal. People often had feelings for those on the opposite end of the opinions spectrum. It probably made the sex more combative.

Either way, this bar, only five blocks from the Brooklyn Supreme Court, had become a sort of neutral ground for defense attorneys and ADAs, and, occasionally, Hogan Trencher. Who seemed to almost get a power-trippy charge out of prodding at defense attorneys in his off time.

"Haven't seen you around recently, John," Hogan said

after sending Marissa a wink and pointing at John's beer to indicate he wanted one for himself. "Keeping busy?"

"Yup," John grumbled. Talking to cops always made him feel like he was being interrogated. "Those meth labs don't start themselves."

Richie laughed into his beer, inhaling half of it and looking utterly mortified to be snotting foam in front of his crush.

"Just making conversation," Hogan replied easily. "Thanks, darlin'."

The big man slid money into Marissa's palm and held her eye contact as he took the beer from her. Marissa tucked her lips into her mouth and ducked her chin, looking up at Hogan through her eyelashes, a slight flush on her pretty brown skin.

Hogan reached forward, stole a few of John's fries and tipped his chin down at the two lawyers, a smirk firmly in place beneath his mustache. He sauntered away to a far corner of the bar.

"What the hell is it about that guy?" John wondered aloud.

"What?" Richie asked, his cheeks still pink, peeling the label from his beer bottle.

"Why is everyone so into him? From where I'm sitting, he's just a cocky asshole."

"You just answered your own question, John," Marissa said, taking his empty beer bottle away and replacing it with a water. He'd thought that she'd preternaturally predicted his reticence to have a second beer, but then he realized that happy hour was now over and Marissa knew that John categorically refused to purchase full-price beer. "Cocky assholes are irresistible."

"I have not found that to be true in my own experience," John replied, comfortable with these kinds of conversations with Marissa after almost five years of coming to Fellow's on Friday nights. "I'm a cocky asshole and women pretty much flee from me."

Sometimes literally. The image of Mary striding out of the restaurant flashed through his mind. He'd felt like such an utter dolt standing there, watching her go. But could he blame her? He could not.

"You're not a cocky asshole," Richie chimed in, apparently recovered enough from his unexpected interaction with his crush to be able to speak again. "You're a self-assured dick. Whole other animal. Highly repellant."

"I'm a self-assured— What the hell is the difference?"

"The difference is that a cocky asshole knows he's an asshole and uses his assholish swagger to charm and otherwise assert sexual dominance," Marissa said, pushing her glasses up her nose. She'd once told John that she'd studied anthropology at SUNY Downstate, and John could suddenly see that aspect of her intellect sparklingly clearly. "Self-assured dicks don't even realize they're being dicks until after they've hurt everyone's feelings."

"Oh." John frowned. "That…actually sounds pretty accurate."

"It's like the difference between watching a circus dude juggle fire and watching a dragon breathe fire," Richie mused. "One of them is doing it for a show and one of them is doing it because he was born that way."

"Are you telling me that I was born a dick?"

He felt his phone buzz in his pocket but ignored it.

Richie tipped his head from one side to the other. "Well, the jury's still out on nature versus nurture. All I know is that scowl of yours isn't there by choice. You're a dick, John. Accept it."

John shook his head good-naturedly and let the conversation move on to bigger and better topics.

I was expecting someone younger.

His own words played in his head and he was grateful that Richie and Marissa had one another's attention and didn't see the grimace his face pulled into when he remembered what he'd said to Mary when he first met her. What an idiot.

John wasn't sure that he'd ever had reason to talk to someone like her before. Women of her caliber were rare and exotic, spotted occasionally hailing cabs in DUMBO or brunching in Park Slope. Everything from the gold of her hair to the cut of her dress had screamed money. No. Not screamed it. Screaming implied gaudiness and she was anything but gaudy. No, Mary's appearance merely whispered money. It was the quiet, soothing melody behind her entire countenance. People as rich as Mary seemed to move through the world with their own soundtrack.

He was obviously not worthy of the brilliant gold gloriousness of someone like Mary Trace. He'd known that the second she'd walked into that restaurant. And he'd known that she would know it soon enough as well.

But he'd have liked to have lasted more than a single sentence before he'd ruined his chances. Pleasant conversation and a good-night kiss on whatever picturesque stoop led up to her home would have been nice. It wouldn't have been long before she realized that dating a defense attorney who lived in a studio in Bed-Stuy meant weekend trips to see his aunties in the Bronx, not ones that landed them on the beach in the Hamptons. She was sharp, so it wouldn't have been long before she realized that his desire to cook for her would have been fueled mostly by his inability to pay for fancy Brooklyn brunches. She would have no doubt tired of waxy carnations and started to wish for lilies and orchids.

His phone buzzed one more time and he ignored it again.

Texting her back when he was in this mood was a bad idea. No. Better to just leave it alone.

No question the whole thing had been doomed from the beginning.

Still. He wouldn't have minded that good-night kiss.

"GOT ANYBODY GOOD on the line?" Mary's best friend Tyler asked from where he lay on his living room floor, a couch pillow under his blond head and his feet crossed at the ankles. He had his eyes closed, so Mary wasn't positive how he'd even known she was texting someone.

"No. Just struck out again, actually. My friend set me up with this guy, but apparently he's a drug dealer."

Tyler cracked a navy blue eye. "Some friend."

Mary laughed and waved a hand through the air. "She's well-meaning. Just a little…out of touch. I think she's probably late fifties and a little bit on the optimistic side. She's one of my artisans."

"Who are we talking about?" asked Serafine St. Romain, or Fin for short, as she sauntered in from Tyler's kitchen. Fin was a singular presence. She was tall, spooky-eyed and blazingly beautiful. Plenty of people doubted Fin's skills as a psychic and energy reader, but Mary wasn't one of them. She fully believed in Fin's clairvoyance.

Fin plunked down on the floor next to Tyler, curling up like a clumsy kitten next to him. He hummed in pleasure, eyes still closed, and absently played with Fin's long dark braid.

Mary smiled at the sight the two of them made together. Preppy Tyler and hippie Fin. Such a strange pair, made all the more interesting by how blisteringly in love they were with one another. Mary envied them in a good-natured way. Though it might have bothered some people that her

entire group of close friends had paired off together, first
Sebastian and Via and now Tyler and Fin, Mary was just
happy for everyone.

Mostly.

She'd originally been friends with Sebastian and Tyler.
If it was unusual to have two male best friends, Mary had
never thought much about it. They were good friends, caring,
funny, kind. Sebastian had fallen in love with Via, a counselor at his son's elementary school, and Fin had come along
into their group as Via's best friend and foster sister. Tyler
and Fin had had a long road toward finally being together, but
when it had happened a few months ago, Mary had breathed
a big sigh of relief. She'd suspected all along that the gorgeous and enigmatic Serafine St. Romain had the power to
truly wound her goofy, preppy, crude, generous best friend.
She was glad it had worked out the way it was supposed to.

It didn't pass her notice, however, that both of her forty-
something-year-old best friends had ended up with women
a decade-plus younger than they were. It wasn't until she'd
learned that Fin and Tyler were truly together did it really
hit her. She might be on the losing end of a certain social
equation. Because it seemed to her that once over thirty,
men rarely dated women their own age. And even less
dated *older* women.

She'd just started toying with the idea of starting to date
older men, much older men, when Estrella had come along
and proposed her thirty-one-year-old son.

Mary frowned. Her thirty-one-year-old son who found
her age so repellant it was literally the first thing he'd commented on. And now Mary was on this strange waterslide,
where around every bend, there was Estrella shoving some
young thirtysomething guy in her path. She wasn't going

to complain, but maybe she should hedge her bets a little bit and date some older guys on the side as well.

"Hmm?" Mary pulled herself from her thoughts to answer Fin. "Oh. Estrella."

"I love that woman," Fin said emphatically.

"Me too. I just wish she had better taste in men. She's been trying to set me up lately to varying levels of failure."

"Weren't you going on a date with her son?" Kylie asked as she ambled into the room and tossed herself into the overstuffed armchair.

This was one of the many things that Mary loved about coming over to Tyler's house these days. Used to be, in the past, his condo was homey but a little too quiet. It was one-note. Only influenced by Tyler and his presence and his choices. These days, though, since he'd gotten custody of his fourteen-year-old sister, Kylie's backpack overflowed with textbooks in the corner, her sweatshirts hung on the coatrack. She looked utterly at home as she draped her feet over the opposite arm of the fluffy chair and shoved her face into her phone, barely waiting for the answer to the question she'd just asked.

Mary liked to see Kylie acting like a teenager. When she'd first come to Brooklyn around Thanksgiving, she'd been like a mini adult, all her corners tucked in and nothing-to-see-here-folks. But the other day, Kylie had even been five minutes late for work, and it had thrilled Mary to her core. Not that she rooted for her employees to be late, but that Kylie was *comfortable* enough to be a little late. That was real progress.

"What's that?" Fin asked, bolting upright and smiling when Tyler tugged her back down into his side. "You went on a date with Estrella's son?"

"*Date* is a relative term in this case." Mary sighed. She

hadn't told anyone about her mishap with John, but she figured this was as receptive an audience as any. "I arrived at this super fancy restaurant in Greenpoint, he told me he'd hoped I'd be younger, I picked up my jaw off the floor and left. End of date. Not exactly a love story for the ages."

"You've got to be freaking kidding me." Tyler sat up, a rare anger burning in his eyes. "That's the rudest freaking thing I've ever heard. Mary, I hope you shook it off immediately."

Mary avoided Fin's light gaze, knowing that her intuitive friend was going to see both what she did say and what she didn't. "It got me down for a few days. But I'm back in the swing of things. Anyways, he came to the shop to apologize, and I think he really meant it."

"Oh. That's who that guy was?" Kylie asked, looking up from her phone. "The mean-looking one with Estrella?"

"Yup."

"What is *wrong* with men these days?" Tyler groused. "If they aren't hitting on women in the subways, they're telling them they look old in fancy restaurants. Would it kill my species to have a little common *decency*?"

Fin and Mary exchanged wry eye contact. Dating a woman as beautiful as Fin had opened up Tyler's eyes to some of the cruder ways that men treated women. Especially in a city as anonymous as New York. But Mary suspected that most of his incredulous griping had to do with the fact that Kylie had apparently announced a few days ago that she was going to homecoming with a date. A male date. Tyler had yet to recover.

"You're a prince among men, my love," Fin said drily, kissing her boyfriend on the cheek.

"Ty," Kylie said, rolling to one side, "you're telling me that you never, not even once, hit on a woman on the train?"

Tyler responded, and Mary let the noise of the bickering

siblings fade fuzzily into the background. She picked up her phone and reread the text that she'd gotten a few minutes ago from John.

She pursed her lips. The part about his belief system and innocent until proven guilty, she actually liked. But it was the last line that really irked her. *Date him if you want but just remember that I voted to veto.*

What a grouch. The surliness rose off each word like curlicues of smoke. She frowned at his text.

Your warning is duly noted, counselor. Consider your duties in this matter to be fulfilled.

She sent off the text with a twisting flourish of her pink-polished finger. There. That would show him that she could be just as snappish as he could be.

But...

The truth was that she *couldn't* be that snappish. Not with any level of comfort. She flipped her phone over so that she wouldn't have to look at it anymore. Mary smoothed her hair down and grimaced when she found one of her thumbnails between her teeth. No, no, no. She'd just gotten a manicure. She wasn't going to give in to that old habit.

Ugh. She picked up her phone and glared at the lack of a response from him. But what had she been expecting? Him to immediately respond to a rude text from her? Just because he was naturally rude didn't mean that he was any good at receiving rudeness from others.

Mary set the phone down again, let a few more minutes pass and then finally gave in to temptation. She opened up their thread, carefully selected a sunshine emoji and sent it off, instantly feeling a little better.

CHAPTER FIVE

"MARY, I HATE every single one of your employees besides Kylie," Fin groaned as she leaned dramatically against the checkout counter at Fresh.

"I have to say that right now I agree," Mary replied. Her part-time employee Sandra was currently a no-show for her shift, and Mary was stuck behind the register for the third Friday night in a row.

"Need tacos! Was promised tacos!" a voice, comically weak, called from the floor at Mary's feet, hidden from view behind the register. It was Via, Fin's best friend and one of Mary's favorite people on earth. Mary had invited Fin and Via over to her apartment for a girls' night complete with at-home pedicures, the aforementioned tacos and—the silver bullet—the promise that she'd let them help set up her new dating profile on an app mostly featuring older men.

They'd both sprung at the chance like hyenas on a limping gazelle. As a member of the chronically single club, Mary had learned that if there was one thing that happily coupled people could never resist, it was playing on the dating apps of their single friends.

"Just let yourselves in upstairs, order some tacos, make some margaritas in my new blender, and I'll be up in a couple hours when I close up the shop."

"Yeah, right," Fin scoffed, resting half of her beautiful

face on her closed fist and making her cheek stretch. "No woman left behind. We'll hang here until closing time."

"Here, here," Via called from the ground. "But my feet have swollen from a week of hell at work, and I can't get my heels back on. So, I'm just going to participate from down here."

The bell on the door rang and Mary looked up. But it was just a late-night shopper in a long silk scarf, who seemed to be browsing, though Mary would bet a hundred bucks that the woman had already picked out whatever she was there to buy on the website.

Right on the woman's heels, though, happened to be Estrella. Her face brightened when she saw Mary. "Mary! I didn't expect to see you here on a Friday night. I thought for sure it would be Sandra."

"She didn't show up for her shift," Mary said gloomily. "What can I do you for, Estrella?"

"Fin, my love," Estrella greeted her before she turned back to Mary. "I'm just here to drop off those picture frames I told you about." Estrella held out a tote bag to Mary and grinned over the counter at Via. "I didn't realize you had a stowaway back there."

"Hi, Estrella," Via said with a big grin on her face. "We're supposed to be having a girls' night where I'd ideally be draped across Mary's couch, but I'm settling for the floor until Sandra gets here."

"I'm sorry your girls' night is ruined."

"Oh, it'll still be fun. Let's order the tacos now and eat them behind the register while we hide from customers," Fin said with a little grin on her face.

The one customer in the shop sniffed and didn't smile from where she stood comparing the embroidery on two separate pillows.

"You wanted tacos from Ish, right?" Mary asked, absently watching the snooty customer. "They don't deliver, unfortunately. But Rocko's does."

"Rocko's?" Via piped up from below. "No! I refuse! I got food poisoning from there once. I'm on a Rocko's strike."

"Ish is that place down by Borough Hall, right?" Estrella asked.

"Yup."

"Oh, they'll deliver to me." Estrella had a glint in her eye that Mary couldn't quite interpret.

"You've got the magic touch?" Fin asked with a wry expression on her face.

"Let's just say I've got connections all over this city." Estrella wasn't doing a *Godfather* impression, but Mary felt she might as well have been.

They told Estrella their order and then Mary worked her own particular brand of magic on the customer. She could clock what kind of shopper a person was from a mile away. And she knew that this particular lady was not one who wanted to interact with the sales staff. But she also knew that once she'd arrived at the shop, she'd started second-guessing which of the side lamps she actually wanted to purchase.

Mary made some subtle changes to the lighting in the store and decided that now was the perfect time to unpack those afghans that an artisan in Boulder had finally shipped to her. Their tones were deep and rich, not her usual summer decor, but they would set off the ruby lighting of those lamps and help make her sale, she predicted. And sure enough, not ten minutes after she'd draped one of those afghans over the armchair next to where those lamps were sold, Mary was ringing up and carefully wrapping the five-hundred-dollar purchase.

Not too bad for a Friday night. If it weren't for the aching cavern in her belly where food should be, she'd almost be glad that Sandra hadn't shown up for work. The girl was as likely to people-watch in the picture window as she was to actually try to sell anything.

Once the woman left, Mary briskly folded up the afghans again and readjusted the lighting.

"Didn't you just set those out, Mary?" Via asked.

"Our sly Ms. Trace did that just to make a sale," Fin observed, never missing a trick. "You must have known how those colors would perfectly offset the lamps?"

"Mary's mother didn't raise no fool," Estrella called from where she leaned against the counter.

Mary laughed, but that simple turn of phrase made something ancient twist a quarter turn inside of her gut. Because according to Mary's mother, she had, in fact, raised a fool. An aging, single fool who was going to wake up one day soon and realize that she'd prioritized her life in the wrong direction.

The thought threatened to sour the good mood she'd been brewing, her blood still thrumming from the sale, two of her good friends ready and raring to go for a girls' night. Mary smiled absently and hefted the box of afghans back into the storeroom, where they'd wait until fall, when the colors were more appropriate.

She heard the bell on the door jingle and Via's faint cry of "Tacos!" Smiling, she emerged from the room. But that smile immediately quirked into a look of confused curiosity.

"John?"

An annoyed, exhausted, semi-rumpled John stood in the front area of her shop holding an enormous sack of tacos.

Mary realized what had happened all at once. "Estrella, you didn't!"

"Oh, she did," John grumbled in that two-toned voice of his, a little more hoarse than usual.

"You sent a civil servant to pick up tacos for us?" Mary gave Estrella a hard time.

"He was a taco delivery boy before he was a civil servant, and my son long before either of those occupations. It won't break his back to bring food to a group of pretty women."

Aware of Fin's and Via's avid interest in the newcomer, which Mary was sure actually had very little to do with the tacos in his hands, Mary strode over to John, her hands out for the food. He handed it over and took a quarter step backward, like he wasn't sure if, sans tacos, he was officially invited to be inside her shop.

"John, these are my friends Serafine St. Romain and Via DeRosa. This is John Modesto-Whitford." She strode back over to the counter and could feel John hesitate before he followed her.

"You can call me Fin." Fin waved her hand, but Via, having hefted herself off the floor at the arrival of the tacos, leaned over and gave him a handshake.

"Nice to meet you two. Hi, Ma," John said, leaning down and pecking his mother on the cheek.

There really was something charming about a grown man kissing his mother, despite the fact she'd just cajoled him into delivering tacos.

Mary studied John as Estrella and Via fell into conversation. He really did look exhausted. He was still shaved and trimmed fairly immaculately, but his black hair had started to tumble forward out of its neat side part and onto his forehead. There were dark circles under his eyes. He wore his usual uniform of a white button-down, black slacks and wingtips, but the sleeves were rolled to the elbow and his midnight tie was loosened at the neck.

"Didn't mean to turn you into a delivery boy," Mary said in a low voice to John, hoping he could read the apology in her eyes.

He shrugged. "I often pick up food for my mother."

"Did you really used to be a taco delivery boy?"

"Chinese food. And yes. Paid for a lot of my undergrad that way, actually."

He practically swayed on his feet.

"Long week?" she asked, setting the tacos aside and leaning against the counter.

John's blue eyes, which had been flitting around the shop, taking in Fin and Via from their heads to their toes, finally landed on Mary, full force. "The longest. And it ended on a real low point."

She grimaced, absently reaching up to smooth her wavy hair over one shoulder. "Sorry about that. I really didn't think that your mother's taco connection was her grown son with a full-time job and better things to do on a Friday night."

To her surprise, he chuckled. Well, it was more like a forced exhalation of air, but she figured that that was about as close to a chuckle as John Modesto-Whitford ever really got. "I didn't mean that the tacos were the low point, Mary. I lost a case today. And lost a key witness on another." He pressed a heavy hand to his forehead and Mary was certain that he had a headache. "And both clients are people I care about."

"Oh." Mary blinked at him. In that moment, in her mind, his job stretched and grew wings and became more than his button-down shirt and fancy shoes and the messenger bag at his hip. Her imagination charged forward and his job had an office, coffee in chipped mugs, John standing in the middle of a courtroom and pointing one of his blunt fingers at the *real* perpetrator. She knew that very little of a lawyer's life was actually spent gesticulating in a courtroom, but still, it was fun to picture him that way. And more than that, John's job suddenly had people's lives in the balance, resting on those tired, wide shoulders of his. His scowl made a bit more sense to her. There were years of people's lives in that scowl. Their freedom. And not just random people. People John cared about.

"I'm so sorry," Mary whispered. She wasn't exactly sure what else to say, but she really did feel sorry.

"Thanks," John said back in that hoarse voice, his blue eyes looking almost kind in his complete exhaustion. She figured he didn't have the energy to look quite as off-putting as he normally did.

"Estrella," Mary admonished, "tell me you at least ordered some tacos for your beleaguered son."

"I'm not a *monster*," Estrella sniffed and made all the women laugh. John, however, just looked more irritated.

"Oh, you did, Ma?" He immediately reached into his pocket and pulled out a thin, ancient wallet. "Who paid?"

Mary waved her hand through the air. "I did, but no worries. I'm happy to buy you dinner."

Now John looked more than irritated. He looked downright angry. His eyebrows were pulling down into that V, his lips were thin, his wide shoulders, even in their fatigue, were pulling back. He opened up his wallet and fished through for bills.

"Seriously, John, you did all the work of picking them up. Let me at least buy you— Ow!"

Mary winced when Fin landed a swift kick to her ankle. She looked over at her clairvoyant friend and received some very meaningful eye contact. Mary frowned. She couldn't directly interpret Fin's wide eyes, high eyebrows, pursed lips, but she had the distinct impression that she wasn't supposed to be refusing the bills that John stuffed into her hand,

"Will you stay and eat with us, John?" Via asked. "Mary's gonna close down the shop in a bit and then we can eat."

"Oh. Ah…" John looked to Mary.

Flustered, John's money in her hand and at least a half an hour before she normally closed the shop, Mary smoothed her hair again. "Let's just eat now. You should definitely stay, John. I'll close the store down early tonight."

She felt her friends' eyes on her back as she hurried over to the door, flipped the sign and the lock and dimmed the front lights. Mary ignored their eyes as she pulled out her phone and sent a quick Tweet on the store's Twitter feed saying that she was closing up a bit early. And by the time she got back to the counter, with everyone leaning over their tacos, her friends were too busy eating to point out that she hadn't closed the shop early for them, but she had for John.

IT WAS A week later when John finally realized what was happening. He was in the middle of a date with a very nice woman named Tilli, who seemed just as confused about why his mother had set them up as he did.

John got a text from Mary, but he waited until pretty, brown-haired Tilli was in the bathroom to open it.

In their typical way, the text said two words and two words only. A name. Only, this time, it was a name that made John nearly choke on the very life in his throat.

Maddox Whitford.

Another text from her sat below that fateful name. Any relation?

"Yes, there's a fucking relation," John muttered angrily to his phone, slouching over it. His mother had set up Mary with Maddox? With his train-wreck half brother, who was just as likely to wind up hungover on a train to Niagara Falls as he was to actually make it into work on any given day? It had been just two months ago that Estrella herself had shaken her head at the *Page Six* article about his father's other son, outlining the fall of the drunken, high-society rich kid. And now she was magically deciding that Mary should date this guy?

"What the *hell*, Ma?"

John knew what Maddox did with women on dates. He used his trust fund to wine and dine them, promptly fell in mad, out-of-control love with them, got bored and either dumped them or sent himself spiraling on a bender of the first degree.

It was one of the many reasons that John was actually glad he hadn't grown up in Maddox and his father's world. He might not be the smoothest when it came to women, but at least he wasn't reenacting *The Wolf of Wall Street* whenever he found one he liked.

"Everything all right?" a nervous-voiced Tilli asked as she slid back into her seat, shaking her napkin out primly.

John looked up, his eyes focusing on his dinner companion. It all went painfully clear. Like HDTV on a sportscaster's rosacea type of clear.

Tilli was a nice woman his mother had met at the Crown Heights branch of the Brooklyn Public Library. She was slight and shy and had laughed nervously at almost everything that John had said tonight. They had less than zero in common with one another, besides the fact that John had grown up in Crown Heights and Tilli currently lived there. This date had all the explosive chemistry of milk stirred into flour. There was not a chance in hell that his mother had actually thought this would go well for John.

All the while she was setting Mary up with Maddox.

Sammy at the block party. Elijah Crawford. Michael Fallon. Maddox Whitford. The freaking *tacos*. He finally understood the game. And was beyond frustrated that it had taken him damn near two weeks to catch on to the sly scheme of his mother's.

"Ah. Yes. I just sort of realized that my mother was up to something." He put his phone away and directed his attention back to Tilli.

She seemed to immediately wither under his gaze. "Is it very important?" she asked timidly. "Because I don't mind if you have to go deal with it. That's okay. It's getting a little late anyhow."

It was roughly eight fifteen on a Friday night, and another thing became painfully clear to John. Tilli didn't want to be here any more than he did. "Um, right," he tried to say gracefully. He lifted up and pulled out his wallet, leaving cash on the table for the burritos they'd both eaten. His mother really needed to stop figuring out ways to get him to waste cash on food he could barely afford. "I'll walk you to the train."

Looking like she had absolutely no idea how to say no to that, Tilli nodded meekly. The two of them walked quietly to the train, John's mind traveling inexorably back to his devious mother.

He shook Tilli's hand at the top of the train entrance and tried not to take her look of utter relief personally when it became clear that he wasn't going underground with her. He knew he had a mean mug, but timid Tilli made him feel like he was the Grinch who stole Friday night.

He strode away and immediately pulled out his phone. His brother answered on the fifth ring. "Hello?" Maddox said fuzzily.

John frowned. It was a Friday, so it was equally plausible

that Maddox would either be shit-faced or already sleeping it off in some woman's bed. "It's John."

"Hey. Hold on."

John heard some hushed mumbling and then the sound of a door closing. "What's up?"

He wondered where his brother was. John knew better than to ask at this point. There was only a ten percent chance he'd get the truth anyhow. Maddox and John were only eleven months apart in age, but there'd been times in the last decade since they'd gotten to know one another that John had felt more like Maddox's father than he did his slightly older brother.

John and Maddox were night and day. Both in demeanor and physicality. Maddox took after their father, light complexion and dark eyes. John's swarthier skin and shockingly blue eyes didn't fit into Maddox's family one bit. Maddox was lanky and loose, always laying his head on someone's shoulder or falling asleep on the train. John was stocky and wide-shouldered and self-contained. He kept to himself, while his brother kept to everyone but himself.

"Have you talked to my mother lately?" John asked.

"Not since her New Year's party. Shoot. I should probably give her a call, huh?"

"Do me a favor and check your texts and emails right now. See if she's reached out in the last week or so."

There was a weighted silence on the other end of the line. "I've checked my email in the last week, John. I would know if she's reached out to me."

Now John was the one who was silent. Did he appease his brother's pride and agree with him? Or did he trust his own experiences with Maddox and assume that his brother could easily have let a correspondence or five slip through the cracks? "Will you just check for me?"

His request was met with stony silence, and honestly, John couldn't blame him. He considered himself to be a good influence on his little brother. Hell, he was the only reliable family member the guy had, but that didn't preclude him from also being a dick.

"Oh," Maddox said sarcastically. "Would you look at that? Absolutely no emails or texts from your mother. Just like I told you."

"All right. Didn't mean to doubt," John said briskly. "Look, if she reaches out to you in the next few weeks, about anything, just let me know, all right?"

"Is everything all right?"

For a moment, Maddox sounded just like John himself, that hoarse voice that had apparently originally belonged to their grandfather, though John hadn't met him before he'd died.

"Yes. She's just being a pain and trying to manipulate me into something. Using you."

"Okay..." Maddox laughed and there was a current of pain injected into the sound. "At least your mother cares about you enough to manipulate you."

It was true that Maddox's mother, Melody, was less than attentive.

"True," John agreed carefully. He and Maddox had muddled their way through the last decade, never quite sure how to talk about the many dissonances in their family, their separate childhoods, the awkwardness of their age difference. But they did all right.

"Dinner next week?" John asked.

"Can't. I'm out of town."

John heard muttering again, a woman's voice. He sighed and didn't ask any questions.

"All right. Call me when you're back in town."

"You got it."

John hung up the call and tapped his cell phone on his thigh. It was a nice night. The sky was still streaked a reckless pink from the sunset and the air was heavy with the potential of a thunderstorm.

Maybe he should take the train to Cobble Hill and explain to Mary in person about all of this. He knew that at least last Friday she'd been working this late. He thought of how her shop had glittered like a lantern once the sun went down. Warmth and light spilled from the window onto the sidewalk, banishing the bad moods of any who dared enter there.

He felt pulled toward her shop and her neighborhood. But he'd walked half a block toward the F train when he registered just how much his shirt was sticking to him. He'd come from work and his dress shoes were pinching his feet after a long day. He was a week past needing a haircut and he probably had guac breath.

He'd once watched *The Little Mermaid* and the image of the poor unfortunate souls trapped in Ursula's lair popped up into John's head. He pictured himself walking, disheveled and sweaty, into Mary's glowing, lovely shop and just sort of shrinking down into a big-eyed worm creature, blinking in the light of her goodness.

Yeah. It would be better just to give her a call once he got home.

John turned on his heel and instead caught the G train. He didn't interrogate himself too closely as to why he brushed his teeth and showered before he sat down at his kitchen table and called Mary. Maybe he was tired of feeling like a grouchy schlub where she was concerned.

Ruth, John's cat, jumped up onto the table and roughly pushed her forehead into the palm of his hand. He knew that plenty of cats had reps for being flirty and aloof, but Ruth was not one of them. She was a straight-up floozy, giving it up for free every day of the week. And she was the only cat John had ever met who had bad balance. She regularly miscalculated and tumbled off the back of the couch in a yowling, furry heap. He scratched under her chin and listened to his phone ring.

"Hello?" Mary answered, a thread of surprise in her voice. She probably had never expected to see his name on her caller ID.

"Mary, it's John."

"Hi."

He liked the way she said that one simple word. Her voice so bright it reminded him of the first delicious spoonful of lemon gelato on a hot day.

"Hi," he said back to her and grimaced, feeling like a doofus. He hadn't managed to inject the same magic into the greeting. He stood when he felt a bead of sweat travel down his spine and pinched the phone between his chin and shoulder, muscling open his kitchen window and hoping for a breeze. It was hot enough in his apartment that he was wearing only his boxers and an undershirt. He sat back against the windowsill and stretched his legs out in front of him. Ruth stared him down from the tabletop, her tail flicking back and forth.

"There is a relation," he said without preamble, but he'd accidentally talked over something Mary had said. "Sorry, what?"

"Nothing. I was just asking if everything was all right. What did you say?"

She wasn't actually asking if everything was all right, he knew. She was just trying to find a polite way to ask him why the hell he was calling her.

"I said that there *is* a relation between me and Maddox. He's my little brother."

"Oh, I didn't know that Estrella had two sons. She'd never mentioned him before."

"He's not related to Estrella. We're half brothers. Through our father." John plummeted on because he knew how awkward some people could get when confronted with information like that. "Listen, Mary, is there any chance that you told my mother that I offered to screen her candidates for you?"

"Hmm? Oh. Yes. At the block party she apologized for your behavior on our date again, and I told her it was bygones. I explained that you were even trying to make it up to me by making sure that I was getting the cream of the crop in terms of blind dates."

"And what was her reaction?"

"Oh, you're worried that she was offended? No, the opposite, actually. She seemed thrilled that you'd do something so nice for me."

"I'll just bet she was thrilled," John said darkly. "Mary, we're getting played by Estrella."

"What? What do you mean?"

"I mean that once my mother found out that I was screening your dates, she chose the three people that would probably set me off the most. My elementary school bully, a known drug dealer in our neighborhood and my problematic little brother. And then to prove a point, she set *me* up on a date with the human version of a cup of weak tea."

"Ouch. You had a date tonight?"

"Yeah."

"It didn't go well?"

"Mary, it's nine fifteen on a Friday night and I'm calling you to talk about my mother."

She laughed and it sparkled. An unexpected gem on a dark beach. "Point taken." Mary was quiet for a second. "But why is she torturing us like this?"

"Because she's still trying to get us together."

"Oh. *Ohhhhh.* She thought you'd come riding in to my rescue once you realized who I was going to be spending my time with. That's kind of sweet. Your mother is a romantic, John."

"She's a wily little trickster is what she is."

Mary laughed that gem-on-the-beach laugh again, and John raked the back of his knuckles over the window screen. The night air was a touch cooler than inside and ambient voices from the bus stop three floors down floated up to him. He absently moved toward his cabinet and pulled out a can of Ruth's cat food, smiling down at her when she galumphed off the table and then jammed her forehead into his ankle bones.

"So, should I tell her the jig is up?" Mary asked. "I was thinking that she was choosing men who were too young anyway. I've been meeting older guys on this dating app and was thinking I should put my focus there."

John frowned, a little taken aback by that information.

I was expecting someone younger.

He pictured Mary on a date with some rich retiree in a swanky Manhattan restaurant with a wait list half a year long. He pictured a cigar in the guy's shirt pocket and a Maserati glowing like an ember in whatever lot the valet had parked it.

"Oh. Right. Sure." He had no idea what else to say to that. If she wanted to date older guys, that was her prerogative. He just hoped that the dumbest five words he'd ever said in his life hadn't impacted her decision on who she was trying to date. "Well, if you wanted to tell her, you could. But I was also thinking it might be fun to make her sweat a little bit."

"How so?" There was reticence in her voice. "I should let you know right now that I am terrible at tricking people. I can't even stay hidden during hide-and-seek. I always get too panicky and jump out and forfeit."

John chuckled. He could picture that very clearly. "Been playing a lot of hide-and-seek recently?"

"Actually yes. I babysit for my friend's kid a lot. He's way better at it than I am. Anyway. What did you have in mind for your mother?"

"You should tell her that you changed your mind about one of them. Well, not Maddox. Pick one of the other guys she suggested and tell her that you want to go out with him next weekend. Make her sweat a little bit."

"But what if she actually takes me up on it? Then I have to go on a date with a bully or a drug dealer? How did he bully you, by the way?"

John ignored her question about Elijah Crawford. "I want to see just how far she'll go. And if she follows through with a place and time, you can always cancel at the last minute."

"Not my style. I don't stand people up. Even if they… tied your shoelaces together?"

He chuckled. "Not even close. If you end up having to go on the date, then do you have someone who could go with you?" He thought of the two pretty women he'd met at Mary's shop. "A girlfriend you could pretend to bump into at the bar? Something like that?"

"People have lives, John. I'm not going to tear one of my friends away from their Friday night just so you can see how far your mother will take this thing."

An offer to be the one she bumped into trembled at the tip of his tongue. He almost, *almost* volunteered to be her

In Case of Emergency. No. Terrible idea. She'd see right through it immediately. He was positive that the second the words left his mouth, a mystical spotlight would shine on him and somehow, across town, she'd be able to see the stupid smile on his face right now, his undershirt and boxer shorts and studio apartment and lack of air-conditioning. No way. If he offered her that, he'd show his ass. And she'd know everything.

"But maybe *you* could be there?" she asked after a second and successfully stopped the world from spinning, like she'd firmly pressed a finger to a twirling globe. "You're the one who's curious about this after all." She paused and he could practically hear the trepidation start to creep into her voice. "I mean, unless you're busy. Or you think that the guy would recognize you and blow the whole operation—"

"No, no," he said quickly. *Blow the operation.* Like they were spies. So cute. "I could be there." He couldn't believe that she'd been the one to suggest it. "We can choose a place where I can sit at the bar and not be too noticeable. If you need to pull the rip cord, I'll be right there. I'll, I don't know, pretend to run into you and invite myself to sit down to dinner. I'll be your buffer. And then you can go home. Or whatever else you'd want to do on a weekend."

He immediately felt like a nerd for suggesting that she'd head home. Just because he packed it in and spent the night in his boxer shorts after a bad date didn't mean that Mary would. He could picture her dancing the night away in some red-cushioned basement club, or strolling along the glittering water at Brooklyn Bridge Park, a slim cigarette between her fingers. No. Strike that. Something about that image was wrong. He mentally replaced the cigarette with a big red sucker. That was better.

"Okay. That sounds good." She paused for a second.

"Do you have any time constrictions or neighborhood preferences?"

For one semi-dizzying second, John felt like they were arranging a date between the two of them. She was asking him where and when they should meet. He cleared his throat. "I'll be free anytime after seven. I can meet you anywhere."

"I'll set it up with Estrella, then, and text you when I know what's what. You're sure you want to do this? Trick her like this?"

"The woman deserves it." And John really wanted to see Mary dressed up for a date again. Though he didn't say that last part out loud.

CHAPTER SIX

"WEIRDLY, I'M ACTUALLY free right now. Via's getting Matty from basketball practice and the two of them are going on a date. Wanna grab a drink?"

Sebastian Dorner leaned against the cashier counter at Mary's shop, one eye still on the gorgeous dining room table he'd just dropped off. He was a furniture maker, mostly custom, but every once in a while, he built something on spec and let Mary take a crack at selling it.

"Jeez, I can't remember the last time you were spontaneously free," Mary mused. "If ever."

Sebastian had been a single dad since Cora had died five years ago. Any time that he spent with friends was carefully orchestrated with babysitters. And considering that Mary and Tyler were usually those babysitters, it was often a thing of great difficulty to go out on the town with Seb.

"One of the wonders of having a live-in girlfriend," he said with a small smile on his face.

Though Mary had been best friends with Cora since they'd met in undergrad, she'd never been particularly close to Sebastian while Cora was alive. Always just known him as the guy who'd accidentally knocked up Cora and then married her a few months later. After college Cora and Mary had visited back and forth between Mary's hometown in Connecticut and New York, always making sure to keep in close contact even though they were a state away. Cora had begged Mary to quit trying to make her mother happy and just get the heck out of Connecticut already. But Mary had never quite been able to pull the trigger on the move. It had been Cora's death that had ultimately spurred Mary's move to Brooklyn; she'd found herself unable to turn away from Cora's bereft husband and three-year-old son. She'd inserted herself into their lives, feeling like it was the last real gift that she could give to her best friend. It hadn't taken long for Tyler, Sebastian and Mary to become a tripod. The three adults who kept Matty's life running. Who kept Sebastian's life running if they were truthful about it.

But the help hadn't been one-sided. Mary would never have been able to get Fresh up and running if it hadn't been for Sebastian's handiwork around the formerly dumpy shop. If it hadn't been for Tyler dropping off late-night food and helping her go over the books, charming the pants off of any female customer who happened to find her way in.

They'd become a family. One that, if she was being truthful, Mary missed very much. She knew it was the proper way of the world that Sebastian would fall in love and find a partner who could help him raise Matty, and Via was truly the jackpot of all jackpots. And Mary had been beyond thrilled for Tyler and Fin's budding love. But she also had more nights to herself lately than she was used to having.

And thus, she was grabbing her purse and shouting to Sandra in the back room that she was cutting out of work early. If Sebastian had a free evening, Mary fully intended to occupy it.

Mary bobbled her small leather purse and Sebastian bent down to grab it off the floor. "Hey, somebody left an ID down here."

He straightened up and handed it over.

Mary laughed aloud when she saw whose ID it was.

And the absolutely terrible picture of him. Of course John Modesto-Whitford wouldn't smile in his driver's license photo. Of course he'd glower at the camera like it had just hit him with a your-mama joke. What must it be like to live inside his surly mind?

She pictured the flustered way he'd ripped bills from his wallet the other night. It must have fallen out in the scuffle.

"What a doof," she murmured to herself, eyeing the glowering image of him one more time before sliding the ID into her purse.

"You know him?"

"Yeah. Have you met Estrella? He's her son."

"Ohhhh. The one who called you old on your date?"

They stepped out onto the sidewalk and into the sticky air. There were always one or two days in June that portended the dog days of August. When the humidity opened its mouth around you and the cigarette butts and banana peels sweated in the trash cans. Mary picked up her pace, leading Seb to her favorite bar in the neighborhood where they had plenty of cold beer and plenty of A/C.

"How'd you know about that?" she asked with a quirk of her brow and a smile on her face.

"Tyler has a big mouth." Seb shrugged his big shoulders, towering over Mary as they strode down the sidewalk. "And it really bothered him that someone would say that to you. Especially since you haven't been dating much since Doug. Or before Doug."

She felt Seb's gray eyes on the side of her face. Neither of them had to explain to the other how much time had been required after Cora had died for the two of them to get back on their feet. For a long time, Mary just hadn't had the energy to date. And then, after the Doug debacle, maybe she'd just realized that she didn't even know how to go about it without Cora in her corner. Cora had been her true north for so many things. Without her, it had just been easier to stand still instead of trying to regain her bearings.

"Tyler's worried you took the age comment to heart."

Mary glanced up. "It's the kind of thing that gets under your skin, you know? When someone pokes at an insecurity like that."

"But, Mary, you're not old. Not by a long shot."

"Oh, I know." She waved a hand in the air and smoothed her hair down. "But I'm definitely too old for *him*."

Seb held the door open for her at the bar, and they both sighed into the air-conditioning. At 5:00 p.m., it was still early enough that there were seats at the bar, and they collapsed side by side onto the tall stools.

Mary ordered a shandy and a water, and Seb ordered the same.

"And you're…bummed to be too old for him?" Seb asked carefully. It wasn't the first time they'd talked about their dating lives with one another, not by a long shot, but still, Sebastian always dealt with these matters with a ridiculously endearing delicacy.

Mary considered his question with surprise. Was she bummed that John thought she was too old for him to date? "No. Not at all. We'd never have worked out. He's too judgy. He's growing on me as a friend, though. I like him."

"You like everyone, Mary."

She laughed as she and Sebastian clinked beers. "True."

"So, if it wasn't a love connection, then why did you let his comment get to you?"

Mary sighed. "I think it was kind of John in one ear and my mother in the other."

"Ah. The root of the problem."

"Exactly. She's been even more on my case lately. Depressed because my thirties are over."

Sebastian scoffed. "Over? You're thirty-seven. My God." He scowled into his beer. "What a warped sense of reality."

"Well, that's my mother. Warped. She still wears her beauty pageant tiara every once in a while."

"You're kidding me."

"I wish I was."

"Like, around the house?"

"Only in her bedroom with the door closed, but I've caught her doing it three separate times."

"Somehow that's way, way worse than wearing it where people could see it."

"I know."

Sebastian thought for a second. "If she's so stressed about you being single in your thirties, then shouldn't she be thrilled that you're getting back out there and dating again? It's been a long time since Doug."

"Shh!" Mary clapped a hand over Sebastian's mouth. "Don't say his name in this bar! It's like Beetlejuice. He lives around the corner and might show up!"

She had less than zero desire to see her cheating ex tonight in this bar. But she also had less than zero desire to let the ghost of his infidelity chase her away from one of her favorite bars in Brooklyn. She made it a point to come here at least once a month.

"And to answer your question, I have not mentioned to my mother that I'm dating again. First of all, she's horrified by the idea of me dating anyone younger than I am. Oh, the *indignity* of it." Mary rolled her eyes. "And second of all, she'd give herself a heart attack finding me acceptable suitors. She'd have me on the train up to Connecticut every weekend for stodgy dates with men who have roman numerals after their names. Pass."

"Yeah. That sounds…not fun."

"I'm headed there tomorrow for the night, though."

"In the middle of the week?"

"It gives me an excuse to get back here faster. I have to mind the shop." Mary sighed. "Which is just another thing my mother refuses to understand about my life."

"What does she have against your shop?"

"Oh, it was Aunt Tiff's before it was mine, and she never approved of Aunt Tiff living alone in Brooklyn and running a 'hippie store.'" Mary rolled her eyes. "She doesn't like the decor that I stock either. She thinks I'll get wrinkles working there. She thinks men aren't attracted to women who work for a living. She thinks it pulls my attention away from finding a husband and making babies. Take your pick. The list goes on."

"And I thought I had problems."

Mary laughed and raised her eyebrow. "What problems do you have, Seb?"

He opened his mouth, thinking for a second while he caught a few metaphorical flies, and then clapped it closed. "Actually, now that you mention it, all's good in the hood." He sat back, looking a little bemused. "Wow. I honestly never thought I'd be able to say that again after Cora died."

Mary was grateful that Sebastian was at a place where he could bring up Cora in a casual way. There'd been a long time when they'd barely been able to say her name aloud. The best friend and the husband, both of them feeling like half of themselves had been beheaded after Cora's death. So many things had changed in Mary's life after that. They'd never really gone back.

It encouraged her to see that though Seb's life hadn't

gone back to the way it had been either, he was happier than ever. He'd become a more dynamic, kind, thoughtful person because of the pain he'd endured.

Mary only hoped the same could be said for her.

IF HE RAN, as in sprinted, he'd have time to grab a falafel sandwich from a halal cart before he had to jump on the F to the Q100 to make it to Rikers. Technically, if he took a cab, he'd be reimbursed, but public transportation was just as fast, and this way he didn't have to worry about the fossil fuels he was wasting.

John bounced on the balls of his feet as he waited in a crowded elevator of the Supreme Court building, resisting the urge to shoulder past his colleagues and various anonymous jury members whose time was apparently sweeter than his. Finally, the way was clear, and he sprinted in his dress shoes across the lobby, nodding to his friend Carlo, who worked the long, snaking line of security that all visitors had to pass through to get in.

John had his cash in hand and soon had a falafel sandwich in his life. He attacked his lunch like a raptor pouncing on a wounded triceratops as he strode back into the building to grab his bag and paperwork from the meeting room. He'd just met with an ADA for a blistering three hours, trying to slog their way through plea deal negotiations.

"Jeez, John, give it a chance to defend itself," Richie said with a laugh as he jogged to catch up, his messenger bag bopping his hip and his ramen knotted up into a neat take-out bag.

"No time," John said through an entire falafel ball, scraping food off his mouth with a napkin. "Gotta make it to Rikers by three. Got a client on limited visiting hours."

"Shit, man, you gotta run!"

John raised his eyebrows and turned to do just that when a sunny laugh echoed down the visitors' section of the security line, sounding very familiar.

John craned his head around to look as he flashed his clip-on ID to Marguerite, the security personnel member who handled the staff line. He'd taken three more steps when he saw her. Richie careened into John's back when John abruptly came to a halt.

Lettuce and tomato and hummus slopped to the ground with a wet splat from John's wrap.

"What the hell, John?"

Just then, Mary looked up from her conversation with Carlo, who was looking like a man who was exactly where he wanted to be at that particular second, and spotted John, mouthful of falafel and all.

"Look! There he is!" she crowed, pointing a finger at John and looking utterly delighted. "John! Come over here and prove you know me."

John strode forward, wishing he were eating carrot sticks or a hot pretzel, anything but this messy glob of food. He felt Richie at his back still, curiosity pulsing off of him in waves.

"Mary. Hi," John said, scraping at his mouth with the napkin again. "What're you doing here? Jury duty?"

She laughed and, as usual, it freaking sparkled. Her hair was brushed to a high shine, she smelled like coconut sunscreen and there were large, bug-eyed sunglasses in her hair. She looked like a different species than the bored, irritated New Yorkers who were staring at their phones and inching up the security line.

"No! Ha. I'm not here for jury duty. I've never been selected. Though I always wish I would be. Sounds like fun."

"Fun," Richie said dimly, standing beside John. He was apparently as dazzled by Mary as Carlo was.

"Hi, I'm Mary Trace." She shook hands with Richie.

"Richie Dear. I'm John's officemate."

"Wow. That's a *great* name."

"I get that a lot. So, if not jury duty, then…" Richie trailed off, glancing between John and Mary, shamelessly tossing logs onto the flame of his curiosity.

"Oh! Right. John, I found this in my shop yesterday and I wanted to return it to you. I was going to leave it at your office, but when I got to the public defender's office over on Fulton, the receptionist told me that you were here for the day, so here I am. I would have brought it up to your meeting room, but, rest assured, the security here is very good." She grinned at Carlo, and Carlo went a shade of peach that John had never seen him go before.

"Ah." John reached out for his driver's license, concluding gloomily that there was very little chance that Mary had identified its owner *without* looking at the photo of him. The photo where he pretty much glowered like a clean-shaven Blackbeard. Ah well. "Thanks. I hadn't even noticed it was missing yet."

"Well, I'm going out of town until tomorrow night, and I wanted to make sure you had it before I left." Mary checked her phone. "Actually, I'd better get going to Penn Station if I'm going to make my Amtrak."

"John," Richie said in a voice that was decidedly not his normal speaking voice. "Aren't you going to catch the train right now as well?"

John swallowed, his eyes narrowing on Richie's mischievous expression. "I'm taking the F, not the A."

"But the A takes you to the E, which will get you to the

Q100 just as fast as the F," Richie said helpfully, his voice as sickly sweet as a Coke stirred with a sugar straw.

"Maybe even faster," Carlo cut in, laughter dancing in his eyes.

Considering himself boxed into a corner with no graceful way out, John turned to Mary. "I have to go up and get my bag and paperwork before I can head out. Do you have five minutes?"

She checked the time again. "I have up to fifteen minutes, if I'm feeling crazy."

"Be right back." He silently willed Richie to come upstairs and leave Mary alone, but of course his nosy friend started chatting her up the second John took a step away. He sighed and made his way to the elevators, scarfing down his lunch on the way up. He had just enough time to wash his hands, steal a breath mint from the front desk and grab his things before he headed back downstairs. Richie, Carlo and Mary still stood in the same formation, all three of them laughing as John approached.

"Ready?"

"Ready. Bye, Carlo. Bye, Richie!" Mary waved at them both and turned just in time to miss Richie sticking his fist underneath his shirt and making his heart beat like a cartoon. Carlo, a bit more subtle, merely looked at Mary's back with the moderate wistfulness of a man who was actually very happily married.

John rolled his eyes at both of them and headed toward the train alongside Mary. "So. Where out of town are you headed?"

It always baffled John, who'd been born and raised in New York City, when people left the city. He knew the world was wide, but what could possibly be happening out there that wasn't already happening in here?

"To see my parents for the night. Which is why I'm dressed like I'm applying for a bank loan." Mary scrunched up her nose as they swiped into the train station.

John's eyes skated down Mary's form, taking in the overnight bag she had tucked against her hip and her navy shift dress and sensible heels. He hadn't noticed when she'd been standing in the security line. He'd been too distracted by her bright hair and brighter smile. But now that he really looked at her, she did seem a little muted.

"You dress up to see your parents?"

She shook her head. "I dress *tame* to see my parents. They're neutral-palette people."

He wondered briefly how neutral-palette people could have spawned such a colorful, exotic creature as Mary. He thought of the oft-stilted brunches with his own father in fancy restaurants. Once a month like rusty, resentful clockwork. He supposed lots of parents viewed their children as blocks of ice they could eventually chip into shape. "I'm not getting the vibe that you enjoy visiting them."

"Um. I like being in my childhood home?" Her tone of voice suggested that she was searching for something that she did actually enjoy about visiting her parents.

"But…" John prompted.

Mary sighed, her shoulders sagging a bit. "But my mother isn't the most accepting person. She has lots of opinions. And no grasp on the concept that her opinions aren't, in fact, facts."

John chuckled. "I know a great many people like that."

"As a lawyer, you probably do."

The train came riding into the station on a puff of stale air, and luckily there were plenty of seats available. Their conversation veered away from her parents and more toward the plan for the date on Friday. She'd told Estrella that she'd changed her mind about Elijah Crawford. So far, Estrella had not come clean, even going so far as to say that Elijah would be there at the restaurant at eight o'clock on Friday.

John could only shake his head at his mother's audacity, wondering if she was somehow going to track down his old classmate and talk him into showing up for the date. As they rode and talked, John became uncomfortably aware of a glowing warmth in his chest. Like an ember he wasn't sure how to put out. There was a panicky kind of momentum attached to it. Like if he paid too much attention to the feeling, he'd end up blowing on the ember and making it burst into flames. He really, really didn't want it to burst into flames.

When their train was only a few stops away from Penn Station, John started to sweat in his dress shirt. When he'd agreed to ride with her, he hadn't thought about Mary leaving the train. How did they usually part ways? A handshake? No. Should he stand? No. That was weird and formal for a train ride. He inwardly shuddered as he imagined publicly going in for a hug.

He'd settled on a wave and a tight-lipped smile as his safest bet when the train rolled into Penn Station.

"All right!" she said brightly. "See you on Friday. Don't be late!" And just like that, like it was the easiest thing in the world, she placed one hand on John's forearm, leaned over and pecked him on the cheek.

Before he could even stiffen in response, she was bouncing up with a final wave and striding off the train. John blinked after her. He ducked down to watch her weave through the crowd on the platform. If he hadn't known it was crazy, he would have sworn there was some sort of traveling spotlight over top of her head, constantly setting that sunny hair of hers aflame.

She disappeared from view and the train pulled out of the station. John adjusted his messenger bag at his feet and pulled out the ream of paperwork he probably should have been doing while he'd been chatting with Mary instead.

Still, he couldn't get the glowing warmth in his chest to just cool down already. It was distracting in its heat.

Then a thought occurred to John. He laughed humorlessly to himself. They'd ridden the train together, sure. But, the whole time, she'd been on her way to visit her rich parents in Connecticut and John had been on his way to Rikers Island. Mary's world was so much more similar to John's father's world than it was to John and Estrella's world. Part of him tsked unbelievingly at himself for this position he found himself in. Trying to catch a lingering glance of a woman who he firmly needed to remember lived in a different universe than he did. John hadn't been born into that sparkling, designer-clothes tier of humanity. His father had made sure of that. John had always viewed that as an unintentional favor, the lesson his father's abandonment had taught him about money and the doors it firmly closed in certain people's faces. It was part of the reason why John was currently headed to a prison to meet with a client. Because everyone deserved to enjoy the privileges of the constitution. Not just the rich. It was part of the fabric of John's very belief system. And yet here he was with a glowing warmth in his chest for Mary.

He needed to stay in his lane.

Connecticut with a Prada overnight bag over her shoulder. Rikers Island with a ratty, decade-old messenger bag he'd stowed at his feet.

If that didn't say everything about the differences between them, he didn't know what would.

"Do YOU HAVE to be so hard on her, Naomi?"

Mary blinked at her father in surprise. He rarely spoke up during one of her mother's passive-aggressive tirades. Actually, he rarely spoke up at all. He'd clearly learned the hard way that no good deed went unpunished. But about once a year he reached some private, internal limit and actually plucked up the courage to defend his only child. This dinner, apparently, was the annual event.

"I'm not being hard on her, Trevor," Mary's mother snapped. "I'm being realistic."

"Actually, Mom," Mary cut in, "it's possible to be both at once."

Naomi glowered at Mary. "I'm just attempting to get you to be honest with yourself."

Mary sighed and talked herself out of a theatrical yawn. That was something a younger, less emotionally mature Mary would do. Mature Mary simply pushed her carrots to one side of her plate and set her fork down. "You want me to be honest with myself about my hypothetical egg viability?"

"It's not hypothetical. A woman's fertility plummets at forty! PUH-LUM-METS," Naomi keened, practically forming the outline of each letter with her lips as she said it. Her pretty green eyes filled with tears. "I'm scared for you, my love. I'm scared you'll wind up lonely with none of the things that actually matter in life."

Mary took a deep breath. How could something possibly be so heartfelt and so freaking annoying at the same time?

"Single doesn't equal lonely, Mom."

Naomi pressed her eyes closed in a move that was the

emotional equivalent of an eye-roll, though Naomi believed eye-rolling to be juvenile and would never engage in such behavior. "Maybe not today or tomorrow, while you're still beautiful and have all those friends of yours. But someday, Mary, single does equal lonely. What about when your father and I aren't here anymore? What about when you're old and frail and sick and there's no one there for you?"

"Yes," Mary grumbled. "Life is scary, Mom."

"Don't patronize me! Like you know so much more than I do. When I'm the one who watched it happen to my own sister!"

And that was Mary's hard limit. She rose up and cleared the plates into a tall stack, then marched everything into the kitchen. She wasn't going to be ungrateful. She'd still clean the kitchen. But the minute her mother started reducing Aunt Tiff's life to something lonely and frail and sick was when Mary couldn't sit at the table a second longer.

"Mary," her mother called. "You can't just—"

Mary heard the quiet tone of her father interrupting. She knew what she would see were she to poke her head back into the dining room. Her father would be whispering in her ear, and Naomi would be pressing her hands to her brow bones, careful not to wrinkle her skin, even while upset.

As she set the plates in the dishwasher and slid the leftovers into containers, she heard her parents leave the dining room. She knew that her father would be depositing her mother into her favorite after-dinner spot on the couch. She knew that he would press a glass of brandy into her mother's hand and turn on an episode of *Downton Abbey* for her. If it had been the wintertime, he would have flicked on the gas fireplace as well.

Just a few moments later, he was there, in the kitchen with Mary and silently taking over at the sink with the pots and pans. Mary wordlessly did the rest, wiping down the countertops and brewing two cups of ginger tea for her and her father. It was something he did every night after dinner, and when Mary was there, she did as well. She knew that he'd always liked the tradition, and she liked the fact that something so small could make her father happy.

When the kitchen was set to rights, the two of them held their steaming mugs in their hands and eyed one another.

"Is it even worth it for me to try to explain her behavior?" her father eventually asked with a sad smile.

"Do you understand it?" Mary asked glibly.

"Yes, I do. We've been married for forty-odd years, and if there's one thing in this world I understand, it's your mother. Maze of emotions that she is."

"I know she's still sad over Aunt Tiff. Scared that I'll end up just like her."

"Sad? Mary, love, sad doesn't even begin to describe it. I'm not sure she'll ever be the same."

Mary frowned. But her mother had been so crisp and curt in the wake of her older sister's death. She hadn't even cried at the funeral. There'd been a constant air of so much to do and so little time, and not once had her mother just sat down and grieved. That Mary had seen, at least.

"I think..." Trevor said slowly, thoughtfully, his eyes squinting behind his thick horn-rimmed glasses. "I think that she wants to honor Tiff's memory by making sure that you don't suffer the same things that Tiff suffered. And she's terrified that you want to honor Tiff's memory by being exactly like Tiff."

Mary flushed with pleasure. "You think I'm exactly like Tiff?"

Trevor smirked. "Mary, if I hadn't been in the room at your birth, I might have sworn you were Tiff's daughter.

Your looks, your manner, even your voice. Not to mention your personality. Tiff was just as upbeat as you are. The only difference is that she never let your mother get her down. She'd just laugh and hug Naomi and remind her that there was more than one way to slice an apple."

Mary smiled fondly, even though a sheen of tears had sprung up in her eyes. That sounded just like Tiff.

"But the thing is, sweetheart, your mother is not naturally inclined to look at the world that way. She's in the school of thought that there is one right way to slice an apple and all you have to do is figure out which one it is. But while Tiff was with us, your mother was more flexible, kinder about it all, more understanding. Once Tiff died, though…" Trevor sadly shook his head, rubbed his fingers underneath his glasses. "Your mother took it as a sign that Tiff had been wrong all along."

"That doesn't make any sense, though! Tiff died of cancer. What does that have to do with Mom's fears over me being single?"

Her father gave her a brief, meaningful look. "You know that Tiff's death was more complicated than that. It was more than just bad luck. Just because you agree with Tiff's choices doesn't mean your mother has to. Besides, grief rarely makes sense, sweetheart. Your mother drew her own conclusions, and to her, the only way to square all the corners was to decide that Tiff had been wrong all along. An orderly, expected life was the only way to protect oneself against the random pain of the world."

"But—"

"Are you coming to watch with me?" her mother's quiet voice cut into their conversation. Mary looked over at her mother and felt an unexpected swell of affection for the woman standing there. Her hair was stylishly short, dyed dark blond at the roots and lighter at the choppy ends. She'd changed into an after-dinner housedress, long and silken like a kimono. With one manicured hand, she clutched the overlapping collar of the robe and looked nervously between Trevor and Mary.

Mary knew that look on her mother's face. The closest to chagrin and apology that her plastic surgeon allowed her to get. The brandy had softened her, but so had the distance from the dinner conversation. She was regretful of her vehemence, Mary was certain, though not of her message. But still, Naomi didn't want to sit alone at night in a room watching television by herself, and who did? Mary didn't blame her.

Who didn't want companionship?

Mary sighed and gripped her cup in both hands. "On our way, Mom. Be right there."

CHAPTER SEVEN

AT SEVEN FIFTY-FIVE on the dot, just as they'd planned, John watched Mary stride into the Brooklyn Heights restaurant. Mellow was a relaxed, darkened establishment that had a curved, shadowed bar on one end, which was why they'd chosen it. Mary had reserved a specific table near the window where she could see John back in the corner, but Elijah, if and when he showed, wouldn't likely notice him.

John sighed as he watched Mary speak to the hostess, a huge smile on her face. Of course she'd worn yellow pants. And a buttoned shirt and her hair in a high bun. The outfit was stylish and ridiculous and looked utterly perfect on her. On any other woman, John would have thought it made her look sunny-side up. But Mary just looked…good.

He groaned to himself as he watched her sit down at the table and then immediately peer through the gloom to seek John out. She shot him a little secret smile that made John groan again. Twice in about ten seconds.

"You all right, buddy?" the bartender asked.

"What? Oh. Yeah. Just kicking myself for something. Sorry." John nodded back at Mary. The bartender looked between them. "There a story there? One worth groaning over?"

For a moment, John considered confiding in this stranger. Maybe it would be a relief to explain it to somebody. But what would he say? *I'm a grown man who screwed up a*

*date with a beautiful woman, and now I have a crush on
her and I somehow orchestrated a situation where I get
to watch her date someone else, when all I really want to
do is go sit down in that chair across from her and start
the hell over?*

It sounded dangerously transparent to his own ears, so
he just shook his head and the bartender took the hint,
sauntering away.

But now John was thinking.

He'd told himself, and her, that he was here, in this restaurant, playing bodyguard for Mary on a bad date because
he wanted to know just how far his mother was willing to
take this whole thing. But that wasn't the truth. The truth
was that he'd wanted to go to a restaurant with Mary. Have
a reason to see her on a Friday night. She'd been the one
who'd suggested that he be her wingman, but hadn't he
been moments away from asking it himself? Wasn't this
exact scenario *always* going to be the way he made sure it
played out? John and Mary in a dark, sexy restaurant on
a Friday night in June? Who was he trying to fool? His
mother didn't play into this one bit.

He toggled his knee up and down and risked a glance
at her. She was looking out the window of the restaurant,
looking a little nervous herself, probably hoping like hell
that Elijah Crawford wouldn't show.

Maybe, John thought, he was making this situation
harder than it had to be. He pictured the names John, Mary,
Elijah and Estrella all starkly blinking in a Word doc, black
on white. He pictured highlighting and deleting *Elijah* and
Estrella. Easy as pie. With a few decisive strokes, it could
be just John and Mary. No subterfuge, no interferences.

Maybe it was as simple as going to sit in that chair across
from Mary, whether Elijah was really showing up or not.

Maybe all he had to do was plunk his ass down and say, *Mary, I'd really like to kiss you good night.*

His pulse beat woodenly at the hinge in his throat. For a man who was regularly brave in the courtroom, he honestly couldn't remember the last time he'd taken a real chance with a woman.

A few times a year, he'd start having sex dreams multiple nights in a row and he'd know it was time to find a hookup. When it was time, he did one of two things. Either he called up Stephanie Ortega, who he had an eighty percent chance of hooking up with—she'd been his three-quarter girlfriend about a decade ago and, if she wasn't involved with anyone, was usually pretty receptive to a booty call. Or he went to the same dance club in Lower Manhattan that he'd been going to since law school. It was dark, a little grimy, and the only dancing that anyone really did there consisted of the sweaty grinding of soft parts against hard parts. All John had to do was knock a few drinks back at the bar and then slide onto the humid dance floor. There too he had about an eighty percent success rate of going home with someone.

But that wasn't what he was talking about here. No. This move, this sitting down in the chair across from Mary, was a whole different thing. He sipped at his beer, which was warm because he'd gotten here so early to try to make sure he got the right seat at the bar.

He had two legs. He could stand up right now, walk over there and sit down. *Mary, screw Elijah Crawford. I'd really like to kiss you good night.*

He could do it.

He was going to do it.

John reached into his back pocket, pulled out his wallet and threw cash on the bar. He took a deep breath that tasted metallic in his throat. Shiny with nerves, he was about to stand when his phone vibrated in his pocket. He pulled it out and rolled his eyes when he read the text.

Whatever. His mother could wait. Right now, he had a chair to sit down in, he had a beautiful woman to be crystal clear with. He was nervous and unsure, but he was doing this. He was—

"Did she text you too?" A warm hand landed on John's elbow and all thoughts of the chair across from Mary died an immediate death. Because Mary stood beside him at the bar and the hostess was already clearing away Mary's used water glass from the table.

"My mother?" he asked hoarsely, trying to catch up and clear the nerves from his throat all at once.

Mary held up her phone to show him the text she'd just gotten at 8:00 p.m. on the button.

Mary, dear, so sorry but Elijah won't be making it tonight. Sorry you had to get all dolled up! Don't walk home alone, love. I'll see if John is still at work.

The restaurant wasn't actually far from John's work and he laughed as he showed Mary the text he'd just gotten.

Mary was just stood up by Elijah Crawford, she's at that restaurant Mellow. I'm sure you're still at work, so be a dear and head over there to see the poor girl home.

John watched Mary mouth the words *poor girl*.

"Your mother is ruthless!"

He tucked in his smile. "I told you so."

"I know, but I just couldn't picture it. She actually made sure I'd get stood up so that you would have a reason to walk me home. Either she's the greatest wingman of all time or she should see a therapist."

John, still trying to contain his smile, raised his eyebrows. "Could be both."

"Wow. I mean *wow*. I can't believe she went this far. For all she knows, I'm completely crushed right now."

"Well, in her defense, if you were crushed, she *had* just sent her charming, handsome son to pick up the pieces."

Mary laughed. "John, you're many things, but charming isn't *quite* one of them."

It was silly for his stomach to swoop at the fact that she hadn't refuted the handsome part of his teasing statement. Was it possible that she thought of him as handsome?

"You're all paid up?" she asked.

He nodded, all different strains of adrenaline racing and twisting through his system.

"Shall we? No reason to stay if Elijah isn't coming."

No reason. No reason. No reason.

Give her a reason! he internally shouted at himself. There was an empty stool next to him. Getting her to sit on the stool was just as good as sitting down at the table across from her, which was no longer an option. But…wait, was it as good? Buying her a drink and telling her he wanted to kiss her somehow seemed sleazier and less romantic than physically and metaphorically taking Elijah's seat.

Besides, she was already walking across the restaurant toward the door. Was he really going to sit there and watch Mary Trace walk out of a restaurant again? Hell no.

He nodded at the bartender, left the second half of his beer and hurtled after her.

"Which train are you catching?" she asked as they fell into step down the sidewalk.

"Oh." He cleared his throat, nerves and adrenaline playing his heart like an accordion. Every other beat talked him into and out of saying what he wanted to say. "I'll walk you home. I can catch the train from there."

Mary grinned up at him. "Estrella would be so proud."

He frowned playfully. "We can never tell Estrella her plan worked."

"Actually, I think it was technically *our* plan."

"Well, either way, she got exactly what she wanted. We can't reward bad behavior, Mary."

She laughed that sparkly laugh, but after a moment of strolling, it kind of rolled into a gusty sigh. "What a way to spend a Friday night."

"What do you mean?" he asked carefully.

"Fake stood up by a former elementary school bully, no dinner, and now I'm getting pity-walked home by a man who's already been crossed off the list. It's enough to make a girl feel a little pathetic."

Despite the balmy evening, John felt the blood prick coldly out of his face, his fingertips tingling in his pockets. His heart was no longer an accordion. It was simply a kicked-in shoebox vibrating idiotically in the empty hole of his chest.

Crossed off the list.

Ouch.

Welp, it wasn't going to get much clearer than that.

"It's NOT A pity walk," John said stiffly, glaring down at Mary. She internally sighed.

Apparently, they were back to the surliness. He'd already been a little bit aloof, his manner a bit distant and his eyes refusing to settle on her. But now that V between his eyebrows was back, his mouth turning down. Had she offended him? Was he bored with this whole thing? Was he resenting the obligation to walk her home?

Deciding she was not going to make decoding the complicated manner of John Modesto-Whitford her full-time job, Mary merely took his statement at face value and decided not to dwell. If he wanted to stew, he could stew. He was a grown man.

"Okay."

Mary's phone gave a short little bark in her purse, making her glance quickly up at John, hoping he hadn't heard it.

"Did your phone just woof?"

No such luck.

"Yes," she admitted, a little embarrassed. "It's a bark. I think it's supposed to sound like a fox. It's a notification for an app I just started using."

"Do foxes bark?" he asked, squinting seriously down at her as she played with the zipper of her purse, refusing to check her phone.

"Beats me."

Her phone barked again into the silence that had fallen between them.

"What's the app?" he asked after a minute, as if determined to keep the conversation going. She wasn't sure why things were so stilted between them right now. Maybe he really, truly hadn't wanted to come tonight.

"It's called Silver Fox." She blushed profusely. "It's for meeting older men."

She felt those alarmingly blue eyes on the side of her face. He didn't say anything for a beat. Maybe he was thinking about how great it was that she'd started dating in her own age bracket. Maybe he was thinking how pathetic it was to date through an app.

"You know," he said after a minute, a strange twist in

his two-toned voice, "I never got into the dating app thing. Although, now that I'm thinking about it, that might be the explanation for my oh-so-stellar track record with women."

"Never?" She gaped at him, glossing over the track-record comment. They could come back to that later. "You live in New York City and you've never used a dating app? How do you meet women?"

"Apparently through my mother," John answered drily. "If the last few months are anything to go by."

"Has she set you up with a lot of women?"

"Just you and Tilli."

"The cup of weak tea?"

"The very one."

"And nary a love connection." Mary shook her head in mock sadness. "For all her conniving plans, I'm starting to think your mother isn't very good at this."

"She's not," John said with a cold laugh that didn't reach his eyes. "She doesn't have so great a track record herself, except for Cormac. And she's kept the poor guy in no-man's-land for twenty-five years. I don't think either of us should be taking dating advice from Estrella."

Mary and John's pace had slowed just a bit, going from a brisk stride to a medium-paced stroll. His shoulders were still tight, she could see, and his eyes were on the ground. But the silences weren't quite so stifling. "Why won't she marry Cormac? Is it really because she doesn't believe in second marriages?"

"Yeah. And the divorce from my father definitely hit my mother hard. But there's more to it than that." John glanced at her, as if mulling something over in his mind. "I guess there's no reason to put my best foot forward anymore, huh?"

"Your best foot— What do you mean?" She was confused. In her mind there was always a reason to put your best foot forward. She had no idea what he was talking about.

"I just mean that I'm not trying to impress you or anything, so there's no reason to hide it, I guess." He scowled, his frowny eyebrows and turned-down mouth back in full force. "My father isn't exactly a stand-up guy. He's a sleazeball. He left my mom right after she gave birth to me. Got another woman pregnant before he and Estrella were even officially divorced. Maddox is only my little brother by eleven months."

"Wow."

John was telling this story like it was someone else's, like it didn't have a hugely personal effect on him, his hands in his pockets, his strides long and easy. But Mary looked at the lines on his face. The same way she'd once seen the lives of his clients in the surly lines of his expression, now she saw the weight of his father's betrayal there as well. Estrella's inevitable pain at having been left.

"Yeah. He married Maddox's mother and by all accounts was a pretty active father. At least in the public eye. And I think that my mother always just kind of thought that getting remarried herself would sort of put an all's-forgiven stamp on what he did, how he left us like that. I think she wears her single status with a sort of pride. That he left and she carried on as a single mom just fine. Even though she paired up with Cormac when I was a kid."

"What do you mean 'in the public eye'?"

John grimaced. "Yeah. He's, uh, John Whitford."

Mary stopped walking. "Your father is John Whitford, the mayoral candidate?"

"The *former* mayoral candidate."

"Oh, my gosh. I'm such a dummy. You even have his

name. John Modesto-Whitford. I never put two and two together."

"The Modesto tends to throw people off the scent. If it were up to me, I would have just gone by John Modesto, but my mother hyphenated it, out of defiance, I think. She wanted to remind my father, in some small way, that he had a responsibility to me."

She thought of the airbrushed subway ads she'd been subjected to for months during Whitford's mayoral run. His smarmy expression and light brown hair. He looked like the exact person who would show up for a newscaster casting call in some B-level movie. His teeth were too white, his jaw too sharp, his smile ever present and dishonest. "Gosh. The two of you don't really look much alike at all."

"And therein lies the problem."

"What problem?"

"It's why he left my mother."

"Because you don't look like him?"

"Bingo."

Mary stopped walking, her hands covering her mouth. "He thought she'd cheated?" *Oh, Estrella.* She could only imagine how devastating that must have been.

"Yeah. I have blue eyes. Both my parents have brown eyes. He thought it was clear that she'd cheated."

"I didn't think that brown-eyed people could have a blue-eyed baby."

"It's rare, but it depends on your genetics. I've got family members on both sides of my family tree with blue eyes. It was a pretty slim chance that I'd end up the family Sinatra. But here I am. John Whitford's blue-eyed son."

"That's awful," she whispered.

"It's not quite as dramatic as it sounds, at least not anymore. He and I reconnected a while ago. Laid a lot of it to rest. That's when I met Maddox."

"How did you reconnect?"

John groaned and pushed heavy fingers to his forehead, like he was kneading away a headache. "Can't believe I'm telling you my whole sad story."

"You don't have to if it's too private or something."

"No. It's not that. It's just…usually something I ease people into as they get to know me. But yeah, it's not a secret. We reconnected after I had dug into our family tree when I was eighteen and showed up at his office one day, prepared to bully my way inside."

"You wanted to prove you were his son?"

"More than anything I wanted to prove that my mother hadn't cheated on him. I'd convinced myself that I didn't care that he'd left me. I was just royally pissed that he'd besmirched Estrella's name like that."

"So, what happened?"

"I stormed in without an appointment, all the paperwork in my hand, ready to make some big courtroom-style scene." He smiled, an unexpectedly sweet mixture of wry self-deprecation and bashfulness. "I even practiced my speech. The way I was going to pace back and forth, the exact moment I was going to point my finger at the genealogy paperwork that proved that it was perfectly genetically possible to be his blue-eyed kid. That Estrella hadn't cheated or lied."

John laughed, knee-deep in the memory at that point. "Turns out, all that practice was a waste. Because I walked into his office, introduced myself, and he about fell out of his chair. I'll never forget how big his eyes were. The size of Ritz crackers. Turns out his father had died the week before, and then in I walked, looking and sounding a hell of a lot like the deceased. My father's campaign website might have had him listed as a Presbyterian like his wife, but he was raised as Catholic as my mother was and that man can hold on to a superstition. Apparently, it was like his father was communicating from beyond the grave. Either way, he stopped ignoring my existence."

John cleared his throat, obviously embarrassed that he'd just unloaded that much onto Mary. "Anyway. Tell me about the app."

Mary took a few more steps, still wading through John's story in her mind. She could think of a million and two questions for John. What was his relationship with his brother like? How often did he see his father? Hell, she wanted to know whether or not John had voted for him in the last mayoral election. But she looked up at the lines in John's face, surly, tired and…sad? She felt the curiosity leech out of her. For some reason, he'd popped the cork and let her in on this part of himself. And now he was looking a little bit like he regretted it? She couldn't tell. There was a defeated tilt to his mouth that Mary hated to see. Not wanting to push him too far, Mary allowed him to change the subject.

"The dating app?"

"Yeah."

"You want to talk about the dating app?"

"Sure. Something light. I didn't mean to go into my whole history."

"Right. Okay. Um, here. You can just check it out." She dug through her purse and handed him her phone once she'd opened the app. "It's one of those kinds where the guys can't reach out to me unless I reach out to them first. You cruise them there on that page. And if you want to connect, you can either write them a message in that box there, or you can tap them using these emojis."

"This app is my personal nightmare."

"Why? All the hot older-man action?"

He laughed. "No. The idea of a woman reaching out to me with just an emoji and then me having to try to figure out what to do next? I'd never sleep again. I'd just spend all my time trying to guess the difference in meaning between a waving-hand emoji and a cat with hearts for eyes."

"I'd never send the cat with hearts for eyes! Are you nuts? The man would think I was a psycho. You send that emoji as an icebreaker and you're practically showing up at his house with a boom box held over your head."

John laughed. "See? I'd fail. I don't speak the language of the emoji. I think I'm too literal minded."

"Most of the guys don't use the emojis. Most just respond with words."

"Are these your chats up here?"

"Yes. You can look, but I'm warning you, I haven't screened them yet today."

"Screened them?"

"Take a look for yourself, if you're feeling brave."

John clicked into her messages. Apparently, Ritz-cracker eyes were hereditary. He nearly choked as he took in the dick pics from four separate guys. There were three other perfectly nice chats as well. Kind, considerate men who hadn't replied to her "Hi, I'm Mary, how are you?" opening line with a horrifying photo of an erect penis.

"Good *Jesus*," John murmured, slamming his eyes closed and pinching her phone between two fingers like it was suddenly contaminated with perv germs. "That's awful. You have to screen those out *every day*?"

"Yup. I just forward them to the customer service concierge and then block the guy."

"What is wrong with people?"

She shrugged. "They're lonely? Horny? Depressed? Looking for a way to feel alive? Scared of the life unlived? Desperate? Sad? Overzealous? Proud? I think there're a lot of reasons why."

"Mary, you might be the most compassionate person I've ever met in my life. I would have just said they were all dirty perverts and left it at that."

She laughed. "And this from the public defender? Takes more than an unsolicited dick pic to send me running home."

He squinted at something at the top of the app. "Mary, you said this app was called Silver Fox."

"Right. See?" She pointed at the logo.

"That isn't an *o* in *Fox*. It's an asterisk."

"So?"

"So, asterisks usually indicate the vulgar spelling of a word, right?"

Her brow furrowed. Then a look of horror transformed her face. "You think this app is pronounced Silver Fux?" She buried her face. "Oh-my-God. No wonder I've gotten so many dick pics. This is not a dating app. This is a *hookup* app."

She might have shriveled up into a dust bunny and let herself be blown away on the breeze right then and there if John hadn't laughed. And not that airy exhalation of a chuckle that she'd heard him do before. But a real laugh. Deep and quiet and rolling and, actually, quite charming.

When she gaped up at him, he looked like he was trying to hold it back and couldn't. His lips were pulled over his teeth and his face tipped away, like he didn't want to show her what he looked like unarmed and open. But there was no hiding a laugh like that. It was utterly infectious. The CDC would have rated it highly contagious.

Mary couldn't help but laugh as well. "That's the last time I buy an app without reading the reviews."

He laughed harder. "It was an honest mistake."

Her phone chose that moment to bark, and she jumped about six inches in the air, making John laugh harder.

She shoved her phone in her purse.

"You're not going to check that notification?"

She did her best to glower at him, but she was so charmed by his laughter that she only ended up smiling. "I'll pass."

"You can't leave them hanging, Mary. It's rude. The barking dicks await."

She burst into laughter again, and it was half a block before they'd wound down, a silence settling over them again, but this one wasn't tense like when they'd left the restaurant.

"Mary," John said softly after a moment, his hands in his pockets and his eyes focused dimly on the night in front of them. "Did I ruin everything?"

"Ruin everything? When?" She was taken aback by the quiet tone of his voice, the set of his shoulders. She had the almost unquellable urge to knock her shoulder into his, try to cheer him up.

"On our first— On our date. When I said that stupid shit about expecting someone younger. Did I absolutely ruin any chance of us ever being—"

"Friends?" Mary cut in, horrified that he thought he'd ruined the chance to become her buddy. Maybe she'd been mad at him at the beginning. But those days were long gone and John had proved himself to be a kind enough person. A little rough around the edges, but he was looking out for her, she knew that. She'd never withhold friendship from someone as worthy as John on the basis of one stupid comment. No matter how much it had hurt her feelings. No matter how alone she'd felt in the wake of it. "Of course you didn't ruin it! I think we're actually becoming pretty good friends. Don't you?"

"Ah. Yeah." She watched his profile as his eyes dropped from the middle beyond to the ground. He watched his own wingtips as they walked another half block in silence. She tried to get a bead on his mood, but he was so mercurial, she gave it up as a lost cause.

"Look, don't beat yourself up, John. You could have been a lot nicer to me that night, sure. But, truly, when I look back on it, you did both of us a favor."

"I crossed us off each other's lists?" he asked, lifting his eyes to hers. She was relieved to see a self-deprecating humor flash there for a moment. Even if it gave way to his usual cold expression directly after.

"Exactly. Because sometimes you date someone for a while before you realize that you're not what they're looking for or they're not what *you're* looking for. With you, we got that part out of the way immediately. So, we're not meant for each other. No big deal. We're friends now. Even better."

"Even better," he repeated dimly.

"Well, this is me," she said, wishing they had a few more blocks to walk, feeling like she was leaving in the middle of a conversation.

John blinked up at her front door. "Oh. You live above your shop?"

Mary caught Sandra's eye through the big window of the store and gave her a friendly wave. Sandra waved back, sneaking her phone back in her pocket, obviously hoping that her boss hadn't seen her Tweeting when she should have been manning the register.

"Yup." She turned back to John in time to see that judgmental expression on his face. She hadn't seen it since the first time she'd met him, not in full force like this, and she'd forgotten how much it could sting.

"Wow," he said tonelessly. "You have an apartment on Court Street. Fancy."

She leaned forward and, with her two pointer fingers, forcibly drew his eyebrows up out of their judgy V. He jolted at her touch, his expression quirking into humor for just a flash. "What was that for?"

"I didn't want you to pull a muscle while you judged me."

His face collapsed into a soft chagrin. "Busted. You're right. It's an asshole move to judge where you live."

"I'd never judge where *you* live."

His eyes bounced back and forth between hers. "You really wouldn't, would you?"

"Nope."

"Even if I told you I live in a studio in a crappy building above a bus stop?"

"I hope I get to see it someday."

He did that choppy exhalation of a laugh and shook his head, his eyes on his shoes again. "You're something else, Mary."

"Something good, I hope."

"The best."

CHAPTER EIGHT

JOHN TOOK A break from Mary for the next two weeks. It was necessary. A matter of survival, he felt. Two things had become extremely clear the night of the fake date. John wanted something more with Mary, and she, decidedly, did not.

He figured it wouldn't take too long to get over her, as long as he wasn't forced to see and interact with her in the meantime. Which meant that John had to clear things up with his mother. The morning after the fake date, he called Estrella.

"John? Is everything all right?" she asked as she answered the phone. "You're calling so early."

He blinked in confusion at the clock on his microwave. "It's 9:00 a.m., Ma."

"Yes, but I thought you might…be sleeping in this morning."

John groaned, her meaning so clear it stung. Despite her public stance on premarital sex, she'd apparently hoped he'd spend the night and morning with Mary. "Ma, enough. *Enough.*"

"What?"

He'd have to remember to have her come in and coach his clients on how to affect innocence so effectively.

"You know exactly what. You have to stop trying to push me and Mary together."

"John—"

"No. Ma, we both know what you're doing, with the dates, with the terrible guys and getting me to walk her home and the tacos. We tried it out. It didn't work. And now you pushing us like this is just getting—"

He cut himself off because he wasn't sure he wanted to say the word *painful* out loud right now.

"Oh," Estrella said after a quiet moment. "Oh, John, I hadn't realized…"

With a mother's twenty-twenty vision, Estrella had seen to the heart of his words immediately. John sighed.

"You have feelings for her," Estrella guessed after a moment.

"It doesn't matter."

"And you don't think there's any chance that she…"

"We're friends, Ma."

"Right." There was a long pause. "Cormac wanted to know if you'd come help with the backyard this weekend."

Cormac was a strapping beast of a man, but he was getting on in years and had had trouble with sciatica recently.

"Of course. Why didn't he text me himself?"

"Because he doesn't think he needs the help," Estrella said sharply.

John laughed. "Is there any business you won't stick your nose into?"

"Plenty. But you and Cormac *are* my business. It doesn't count as nosy if it's about you or Cormac."

Even as he rolled his eyes at his mother, he enjoyed the enveloping wave of her palpable love. Mary's parents were neutral-palette people, expecting her to wear boring navy and grit her teeth through spending time with them. Maddox's mother hadn't even visited him when he'd been in rehab a few years ago. John was lucky to have a mother who loved him enough to mother-hen him.

"I'll be over this afternoon."

"John?"

"Yeah."

"It's good you have feelings for her. Even if it didn't turn out. It's been a long time since you thought about much other than work and family."

John grunted. "Woulda been better if she'd had 'em back."

Estrella sighed. "Maybe so."

AND THUS BEGAN the Mary fast. It was sort of like when, a few times a year, John allowed himself to splurge on a quart of fresh-squeezed orange juice. He would literally set his alarm fifteen minutes early on those mornings so that he could sit down with a cup and truly enjoy it. It was such a bright way to start his day. But then, inevitably, the quart would run out and he was back to his lone cup of black coffee. It wasn't that the black coffee was bad; it was just that juice was better.

"Mary's funny," Richie said with a laugh one afternoon while John stabbed at a soggy salad he'd brought from home.

"Yeah. Wait, what?" John swiveled in his chair and blinked his eyes a few times. He'd been staring at his computer screen for an hour and real life was hard to bring into focus, literally and metaphorically.

"Your friend Mary," Richie said, waving his cell phone at John. "She's funny."

John frowned, eyeing the cell phone. "You're texting with Mary?"

"No, I'm chatting with her through this game we both

play. She's the only person I've ever played who can beat me. Which would bother me, but she also talks some pretty hilarious smack while she's at it."

"How the hell did you connect with her on that app?"

Richie lifted an eyebrow. "We talked about it that day she came by the Supreme Court."

"And you've been playing ever since?"

"Is this a problem for you, John?" Richie asked drily.

"No." John frowned even harder. "I just didn't realize you two were becoming friends."

"She's pretty easy to like."

With that, John swiveled toward his computer screen and gave up on his soggy salad, packing it back into his bag. Maybe he'd splurge today and get some fries from the halal cart.

"You know, you've been extra crabby lately." The sound of Richie's voice told John that he was still facing him. John knew that if he turned around, he'd see Richie with one leg crossed over the other, his foot bouncing, an expression on his face that John had once dubbed The Untrained Psychologist.

"Is that so?" John was going to play dead in the hopes that Richie would get bored and stop poking at him.

"Yeah. I think you need to get laid."

Undoubtedly. "That's not the issue." Yes, it was. It was absolutely the issue.

"Oh, so you admit there's an issue?" Richie's voice took on a predatory, victorious edge, and John, still facing away, pressed his fingertips to his forehead to smooth away the headache.

Damn it.

"Richie…"

"All right, how about just a night out, then? I won't even try to get you laid. Just come out for a beer."

"It's a Wednesday."

"You know, in the state of New York, it's actually legal to drink beer on Wednesdays."

John swiveled back around, his arms crossed. "If I agree to get a drink with you tonight, will you let me get some work done?"

Richie grinned, pushing his stylish, white-blond hair up off his forehead. "I won't make a peep for the rest of the day."

"I have court at three, so we better make it seven to be on the safe side."

"Perfect."

Finally, Richie swiveled to face his own computer, and John, with a sigh, dug back into his bag for his salad. If he was paying for a full-price beer tonight, street fries were out. He winced through a wet bite of lettuce, gritting his teeth as he listened to Richie chuckle at something else Mary had messaged him.

John groaned as he looked at his notes on Hang Nguyen's case. He was old-school. He liked to get his thoughts organized with a pen in a spiral notebook. But his cramped chicken scratch had already filled half of one, and he was no closer to clearing this young woman's name.

Seventeen and being tried as an adult. Three different solicitation misdemeanors slapped onto her list of charges. But the doozy, the reason her case had been assigned to a hard hitter like John, was the sex trafficking charge. This young woman faced up to twenty-five years in prison— thirty-five if the misdemeanors stuck.

John had to prove that the money she accepted from various men was not, as the state claimed, in exchange for sexual favors. And, most importantly, he had to adequately show reasonable doubt that the rides that Hang Nguyen had given to various other women various other times did not amount to sex trafficking. No matter the age of those other women and what they were compelled to do once they arrived at their destinations.

For the most part, John was laser focused on his cases. He didn't let the greater themes of the world bear down on him. The world was a complicated, messy place, but here in his cramped office, Richie scratching away at his own notepad behind him, John was being *active*. Inside the walls of this crumbling but noble building, he was never passive. He was doing something about that complicated world. Each hour of concentration he lent to his cases he was making the world a more just, fair place.

Normally, it soothed him.

But there was something about this case that was under his skin. Technically, in the state of New York, a seventeen-year-old could be tried as an adult. He'd long ago accepted the crazy-making nature of this idea, this assumption that a child could have the same scope and understanding as a fully formed adult. There was nothing that John could do besides defend these people with his entire intellect, determination and passion. But this case? He just wanted to take the judge by the collar and shout, "Can't you see that she wasn't there willingly? Can't you see that she was scared for her life? Can't you see that she and her mother were one step up from homeless and in no position to turn away the cash that men were throwing at Hang after they did whatever the hell they were going to do to her?"

But were those men on trial? No, they were not. Had they been tackled by cops and slammed to the ground, handcuffed and tossed in the clink while their mothers scoured hospitals, thinking they were dead, making frantic calls to 911 dispatchers in Vietnamese only to get hung up on?

John sighed. Hang and two other young girls were the only people arrested in the prostitution bust in the East New York neighborhood.

"Hey, there." Sarah Riley, dyed brown hair and a blue pantsuit making her nondescript looks even more nondescript, poked her head into John's office. "You left a message about a case?"

"Yeah. I've got a sex trafficking case that's similar to that one you worked last year. You free this afternoon to consult with me?"

Sarah Riley was John's direct supervisor and someone he very much cared about impressing. She offered no compliments on a job well done, expected perfection and seemingly cared absolutely diddly about morale in the workplace. She was, however, a damn good public defender and one of the few who regularly stayed after hours putting in work on other people's cases. She was kind of his personal hero.

She nodded. "Come by in half an hour. Don't be late."

She was gone out the door, and the second it closed behind her, Richie pretended to shiver. "Hope you brought your snow pants to work."

"She's not that bad," John replied. "And I can't get my head on straight about this case. I need the help."

"You better have your head on straight when you go into her office or she'll chew you a new asshole."

"I know. I was gonna go check with Naya about that sex trafficking case she worked last month before I went to Riley's office."

Richie nodded. Conferring with colleagues was commonplace and one of the best tools in a public defender's arsenal. John had learned immediately that pride always, one hundred percent of the time, had to be shelved when it came to better serving a client. He helped absolutely no one if he didn't ask for help when he needed it, and he wasn't about to let his arrogance get in the way of exonerating someone.

Knowing he had only a few minutes if he wanted to catch Naya—he'd heard her say she had court that day— John quickly checked his email on his desktop and frowned. There was one personal email from his father, and it was addressed to both him and Maddox. Email threads with the three of them were historically…not great.

John opened it and groaned. His father wanted the three of them to "get out of town" at the end of August. "Just a week somewhere cooler," the email suggested. John scrolled down the links his father had taken the time to copy and paste. There were two rentals on Martha's Vineyard and one rental on a lake in Colorado. He did some quick pricing math.

If they were splitting a vacation like this evenly, John would owe roughly $168 a night. Just for lodging. And that wasn't counting the amount it would cost to even get to these places.

"Why in God's name do people like leaving New York?" he grumbled to himself.

Money sat like a stone at the heart of this email. If John had accepted money from his father, the way he'd tried to get John to do countless times, John would easily be able to afford a vacation like this. As it was, John couldn't even afford the week off of work, let alone an ungodly expensive week off of work. Which also meant that he wouldn't be spending a week with his father and brother. Who were doing their best to include him in their lives.

John supposed it wasn't their fault that they had such expensive taste. Just like it wasn't his fault that he didn't. A beach house for a few days on Fire Island? Maybe John could swing that. He'd pay to stay for a weekend or so and maybe commute back and forth one or two other days he could take off of work. That wouldn't run him more than five hundred dollars total. A wince-worthy sum, but doable in the name of family, he supposed.

But John Whitford Sr. was never going to go for a week on Fire Island. Nope. It just wasn't his style. John wondered if it even occurred to his father how expensive an ask this vacation was. If he'd even paused in sending out this email, reflecting on how John would feel upon receipt.

Was it even fair to wonder that, though? Because when John had rejected the trust fund from his father, hadn't he effectively been saying that he wanted his father to stay out of his financial life? Was it fair for John to want it both ways? For him to expect his father to take his money and shove it but also to painstakingly consider John's finances whenever he wanted a week of vacation with his sons?

John clicked out of the email. This was hurting his brain. And he had Hang Nguyen to think about.

JOHN BLINKED AT the basket of fries that had just been slid underneath his nose. He looked up to see Richie upending a bottle of mustard into one end of the basket.

"I thought you might be hungry."

John felt some of his crusty mood finally crumble away. He was out with his best friend, who was only trying to cheer him up. There was no reason to scowl into his beer and waste the whole evening.

"Thanks," John said, swiping a few fries and then pushing the basket between the two of them so that they could share. "You were right, by the way. I've been in a bad mood."

"Are you finally gonna tell me why?"

John twisted his beer in one direction and then the other. "Had a crush on Mary. She just wants to be friends. But I'm taking some time away from her, and that's helping. I should be over it soon. Sorry I've been a dick."

John looked up at his friend and was surprised to see that Richie had gone sheet white. Very uncharacteristic. "Shit. John. I didn't know. I should probably tell you that—"

"Hi, guys!"

John froze on his barstool, the two friends exchanging lightning-fast eye contact.

You didn't, John's eyes said.

Sorry, dude, Richie's eyes responded.

John broke the eye contact in time to turn and see Mary swing toward them on those long legs of hers, her hand still raised in a wave and the smile on her face bright enough to make a planet orbit.

He was dimly aware of almost every head in the bar turning to watch her walk past.

He was also dimly aware of every single one of those heads watching her toss her arms around him and press a kiss to his cheek. "John! Richie didn't say you'd be here too. I'm so happy to see you!"

She pulled back and gave Richie the same treatment, a hug and a kiss, and John tried very hard not to look like she'd just smashed a water balloon over his head, even though that was kind of how he felt. He let his eyes rico- chet over the other faces in the bar, and he watched as his colleagues and peers all bounced their eyes between John, Richie and the new girl.

This was an after-work bar, and Mary, in her white sundress and blue heels, her sunny hair down her back, stuck out glaringly among all the sweaty rumpled suits and pant-suits.

"How have you been? Oh, thanks!" Mary gracefully accepted the barstool he'd just vacated for her. She pointed at his beer. "Yours?"

"Yeah. I've been pretty good. Mostly just busy with wor—"

He cut off as he watched Mary take his ice-cold beer and bring it to her lips. He felt heat rise up along his back, making his shirt stick to his skin. That was the cheapest beer on the menu, which meant that Mary had essentially just swallowed a gulp of watered-down frat beer. Why couldn't he have sprung for some expensive foreign beer for once in his life?

"Mmm," she said, pressing her eyes closed for a second. "That's so perfect for a hot day. Makes me want to go to a ball game." She waved her hand at Marissa, who'd been pretending to wipe the counter four feet away while eavesdropping on the newcomer. "Hi! Can I have one of these?"

"Sure thing."

"On second thought," Mary said as she cocked her head to one side. "Do you have any lemonade back there?"

"Yeah."

"Could I have three-quarters of this draft and one-quarter lemonade?"

"Oh." Marissa blinked. "Sure. Totally."

Mary handed John's beer to him.

"Beer mixed with lemonade?" he mused.

She nodded. "It's the perfect summer drink. You'll see."

Marissa came back with Mary's drink, and John caught Marissa's eye. He pointed at himself and Marissa's eyes widened. John never, ever paid for other people's drinks.

Except on Richie's birthday. John held back his sigh, knowing that he was in for a full interrogation from Marissa the next time he was in here.

"Here. Try." Mary held out the neon-yellow concoction.

John felt a bead of sweat trace down his spine. He was positive that every person in the bar was watching him turn the back of his shirt transparent while he drank out of this beautiful woman's glass.

The flavor burst over his tongue, and he was surprised that he actually liked it. "Wow. That's pretty good."

"I know. Not too sweet." She offered a sip to Richie, who smiled and shook his head.

"Not a fan of shandies," he told her with a wink.

John had never even heard that word before. He made a note to look it up at home.

"So," John said in a gruff voice. "You two made plans to hang out tonight?"

Richie studiously avoided John's eye contact. "Yup. I figured after a few weeks of getting my ass handed to me online, I should see if this girl can dish it out in person as well."

She blushed and laughed. "I don't make a practice of talking smack in real life. Just on that one app." She paused. "And sometimes in the bathroom mirror if I need to pump myself up before a big date."

John burst out laughing. He couldn't help himself. Just picturing Mary rude-talking some confidence into herself, *8 Mile*–style, was too much for him. She looked up at him in surprise, her eyes on his mouth, almost as if his laughter had startled her.

"Who's your friend, Richie?" a low, familiar voice asked from behind John, and for a moment, he considered not moving to one side and just boxing Hogan Trencher out until he got the picture and left.

"Hulk," Richie said, a blush on his cheeks and a miserable look in his eye. "Meet Mary Trace. Mary, meet Detective Hogan Trencher."

John stepped aside, wanting to stand with one shoulder behind Mary, but going to stand beside Richie instead. Hogan slid into place effortlessly, one hand wrapped around Mary's and already saying something that made her chuckle.

John and Richie made eye contact again. This time it was John's eyes that said, *Sorry, dude*.

"Serves me right for inviting her without telling you," Richie muttered so only John could hear. "Karma is a bitch."

Richie and John both tried not to watch their crushes flirt with each other. Five minutes passed and Hogan and Mary were still chatting. John and Richie started up a conversation with Beth Herari, the one cop John actually considered a friend. Beth was Marissa's sister-in-law and occasionally found her way into Fellow's. Currently, she and Hogan were the only two cops with the stones to spend the evening in a lawyers' bar. She was just showing him pictures of her new puppy when John felt a sharp kick to his shin.

He jolted and looked up at Richie, who he'd assumed had been the one to kick him, but Richie was busy texting someone. He felt another sharp kick and John's eyes slid over to Mary, who he could see was smiling rather hollowly at Hogan. She caught his eye for half a second, and he could easily read the help-me signal.

Ignoring the balloon of pride in his chest at being the one she'd asked for help, he tapped Beth on the elbow and steered her toward Mary.

"Hey, Mary," John interrupted whatever cocky asshole thing that Hogan was saying. "Have you met Beth Herari? She's actually a beat cop in your neighborhood."

Hogan scowled at John, and John had to resist the urge to smirk at him.

Mary jumped on the chance. She slid off the barstool and took a few steps toward Beth, leaving Hogan behind and jumping into conversation with the other woman. John slid back onto the barstool, leaving Hogan nowhere to go but back to his original seat. He figured it wasn't a coincidence that the second Hogan's overbearing presence receded, Richie dragged his nose out of his phone and took a deep breath.

They finished their round, said goodbye to Beth and left the bar as a trio. "Jeez," Richie said glumly, once they were out on the sidewalk and headed toward the trains. "Next time I'll have you meet me at a gay bar, Mary. That way you won't cockblock me so hard."

Mary burst into that sparkly laugh of hers. "Who was I cockblocking you from? Oh, not Hogan?!"

"The very same," Richie said with a sigh.

"He reads as very straight to me," Mary said in a careful tone.

"Straight as an arrow," Richie agreed with an even bigger sigh. "Hence the need for a gay bar. I spend too much time with this guy—" he tossed a thumb toward John "—and not enough time with my own people."

John bristled. "Hey! I go to gay bars with you." He'd always been very conscious of making sure his best friend felt supported. John had no desire to stifle Richie's identity.

"Yeah, and then *you're* the one cockblocking me," Richie griped. "They eat up the tall, dark and grumpy thing he has going on," he informed Mary.

"Well, you should know better than to go cruising for guys with your hot friend in tow," Mary scolded Richie. She cocked her head to one side. "Either way, I can't imagine you have much trouble finding interested men, Richie. You're a babe."

Richie and Mary laughed and chatted back and forth, and John bobbed along behind them. His brain was still frozen on the moment when Mary had called him hot.

"Oh, are you free, John?" Richie's voice pulled John out of his blurry reverie.

"Huh?"

"Mary invited us to a party at her house this weekend. Saturday afternoon. Can you make it?"

"Oh. Uh." John made a show of pulling out his phone and looking at his calendar app when he already knew for certain that his day was glaringly, depressingly free. Richie knew him well enough to know that there was almost no way that John had plans on a Saturday and was likely asking him to give him a chance to figure out if he wanted to go, regardless of his schedule.

Hot. Hot. Hot.

Beer and lemonade. Ball games with Mary.

Crap.

"Yeah. I'm free," John said gruffly.

Richie narrowed his eyes at John. "We'll be there, Mary."

"Great! I'll see you then. You don't have to bring a thing."

She, again, kissed both men on the cheek. She waved her hand through the air, had a cab screeching to a halt and then was whisked away, back to her fancy Cobble Hill apartment.

John and Richie stood on the sidewalk and watched the cab disappear.

"Shit," Richie sighed.

"Yeah," John agreed, feeling that Richie had just pretty much perfectly summed it all up.

CHAPTER NINE

FRIDAY AFTERNOON, MARY muscled her way up the flight of stairs to her apartment. She was laden down with bags of goodies for her small get-together tomorrow, and her spirits were higher than they'd been in a long time. She blamed it on the hot, soggy weather they'd been having, but Mary had been a little down for the past couple of weeks. It had been so good to hang out with John and Richie on Wednesday night that Mary had resolved then and there to have a party this weekend. She wanted them to meet her friends. Because her friendships were what was bringing light to her life right now.

She froze when she realized that her apartment door was unlocked. She never, ever did that. She was the only person who lived in this building, it was just the one unit over top of the shop, and she was always careful to lock up after herself. She set the bags of groceries down and grabbed her cell phone, pulling up 911 just in case. Mary creaked the door open.

"Hello?"

And then she smelled the Estée Lauder.

"Mary, love, your tulips are wilting," her mother said as she stepped out from the kitchen, the corners of her mouth as wilted as the tulips apparently were.

"Well, they're a week old already. Hi, Mom." She kissed her mother on the cheek and went back into the hallway for the groceries.

"Good heavens, that's a lot of food!" Only her mother could make one sentence mean so many different things at once.

Fifty shades of judgment. How kinky.

"I'm having a party for some friends tomorrow afternoon."

"Here?" Her mother looked around. "Won't it be a little cramped?"

Only someone who *didn't* live in New York would think that a two-bedroom with a full living room and eat-in kitchen would be too cramped for a party. In Connecticut they threw parties in event spaces large enough for the party-goers to have to speak to one another through bullhorns.

"It'll be perfect," Mary said crisply, starting to unpack the groceries. "I didn't expect you today. Just in the city for some shopping?"

It was a ridiculous question considering not once in her mother's life had she come to Brooklyn for shopping.

"No." Naomi looked down at her hands for a second. "I actually came to see to Tiff's gravesite."

Mary froze, a twelve-pack of seltzer in one hand and a ring of shrimp in her other. If visiting Tiff was something her mother ever did, Mary had never heard boo about it.

"Really?"

Tiff was buried in Green-Wood Cemetery, a hilly peaceful oasis that sprawled kitty-corner from Prospect Park almost out to the water. Mary went there often to visit Tiff's grave, but as far as Mary knew, her mother had been there exactly once. The day that Tiff had been interred.

"Yes. I go about once a year to make sure that everything is being cared for." Naomi sniffed and wandered to the kitchen window, her arms crossed over her chest. "She was my big sister after all."

Something about the word *big* threw Mary for a loop, forcing her to view stiff, proud Naomi in a different light for a moment. A little girl tagging along after her older sister, wanting to play. Tiff had insisted that there'd been a time she and Naomi had been close to one another. Mary tried to picture them sipping wine and watching trashy television the way she herself used to do with Aunt Tiff. Nope. Try as she might, she couldn't insert Naomi into the image.

"Have you gone yet? I'll go with you if you're headed over there now. I try to go every few weeks."

Something in Naomi's expression folded down, whether with disapproval or softness, Mary couldn't tell.

An hour later, the two women were walking the windy, paved path to Tiff's grave. They arrived side by side, her mother as sure-footed in the path as Mary was, and Mary wondered if maybe she came more often than she was letting on. The gravesite was well cared for, as all the plots were in Green-Wood. The stone itself had lost that devastating crispness that new graves had and was starting to give way into a softer dignity. It had been six years after all.

Mary pulled a sprig of dried lavender from one pocket and laid it atop the gravestone, removing the sodden one she'd left there two weeks ago.

"Tiff's favorite," she said.

"I know," Naomi replied, reaching out to touch the lavender for just a moment. They stood side by side for a long while until Naomi shifted next to Mary. Mary realized, with a start, that her mother was crying, pressing a handkerchief to her face.

"Mom."

"This is what you want?" Naomi asked, pointing to either side of Tiff's grave. "Buried between two strangers?"

Mary's eyes grew into round coins, shock making her

mother's words move in slow motion. There was no way—it wasn't possible—no one would drag their daughter to her beloved aunt's grave in order to guilt her over being single.

Mary turned on her heel immediately, striding back down the path and toward the main road. She'd catch a cab by herself, and her mother could get her own ass back to Connecticut.

"Mary!"

Her mother sounded more shocked than angry.

A moment later, there was the swift clicking of sensible heels and then a strong hand at Mary's elbow. "Where are you running off to?"

It didn't help that her mother still had tears gathering in her eyes.

"I cannot believe that you'd use Tiff's grave as a prop to guilt me for being single."

"I— *What?* No!"

Naomi stopped walking altogether, but Mary kept on going. A moment later, she was back at Mary's elbow.

"Mary, stop. Mary!"

She skidded to a stop and swung around to face her mother.

"That is not what I was intending to do," Naomi whispered fiercely, her eyes red, her eyelashes clinging to one another.

"Mom, you get me all teary and then just zing me like that? *Buried between two strangers?* That's not a question! That was an accusation. What do you want from me, Mom? You want me to marry someone I don't love just so that you can sleep better at night? That's really what you want?"

"Mary, I felt terrible after your visit last month. Your father— It seems that I was too hard on you. I know we aren't close. But...you bring lavender to Tiff's grave because of how well you knew her. And I am just trying to understand you."

"By accusing me of wanting to be buried next to strangers?"

"It…came out wrong."

"No, Mom. I think it came out exactly as you intended it to. You're just unhappy with my reaction to it."

Naomi's mouth worked open and then closed. Her eyes filled again as she half turned from Mary and looked up at the bright blue sky, as if she could make her tears dry in the sun.

Mary stood there, breathing hard, wishing it weren't so bright, so hot. Wishing that she weren't fighting with her mother in a cemetery. Wishing that Tiff were here to referee.

And most horribly, part of Mary wished that she could still be that young-twenties version of herself that her mother had so adored. The apologetic, shrinking, soft-spoken girl she'd been. The one who'd let the world walk all over her, tell her what to do. Well, that girl had met Cora. And spent time with Tiff. And now this woman, the woman that Mary was now, was all that she had left of either of the strongest women she'd ever known. She wasn't going to let some crocodile tears make her regret who she'd become or the women who'd helped her get there.

"Mom, I'm getting in a cab and going home. If you want to share that cab with me, then you'd better come now." She turned on her heel and strode back toward the entrance to the cemetery. For some reason, the sedate clopping of her mother's heels behind her made sharp tears spring into Mary's eyes.

BY THE TIME her first guest arrived on Saturday afternoon, Mary figured she was as recovered as she possibly could be from her mother's hit-and-run of a visit. She'd had no choice but to just shove the whole encounter to the back of her mind, which was where it should have been anyway, considering there was a very good chance that she'd never fully understand her mother.

Either way, Mary swung open her apartment door and grinned at her neighbors from down the block, Josh and Joanna Coates, and their daughter, Jewel. "You made it!"

"Wouldn't miss it!" Josh chirped, nearly bowling Mary over in his quest to get indoors.

"Our air-conditioning is out," Joanna explained with a wink.

"Gimme the baby, Jo," Josh called from where he stood over the air vent in Mary's floor, his shorts billowing in the breeze. "I'm just gonna post up right here."

"Not a baby," Jewel grumped, a pattern of lines pressed into her cheek from where she'd obviously been sleeping not long ago. But even so, she toddled over to her dad, her arms up, wanting to be cuddled in the cool air.

"Sorry, we're not..." Joanna started to apologize for her family and then sort of gave up, shrugging. She laughed. "It's been a long few days with our A/C out."

Mary tugged Joanna inside, took her by the shoulders and pointed her toward the kitchen. "Please, my climate control is your climate control. Plus, there are yummy drinks and snacks in the kitchen. And, I might add, a guest bedroom down the hall if you want to stay with me while your air-conditioning is out."

Hot on the Coateses' heels were a handful of other neighbors, most of whom had bucked Mary's rules and indeed brought food and drinks of their own. Next up the stairs echoed a loud-shoed clomp that Mary would recognize pretty much anywhere. She waited for him in her open doorway, her hands on her hips and a huge smile on her face.

"My man," she said as soon as Matty Dorner made it to the top of her staircase, a mutinously grouchy look on his blunt face. Mary knew that Sebastian and Matty were practically carbon copies of one another, everyone said so, but Mary couldn't help but see Cora when she looked at Matty. Sebastian's face, though just as blunt, was always open and generous, his personality showing through. Matty's eight-year-old face was usually set in stubborn or humorous lines, just like his mother's always had been.

In the way of young children who teetered on the cusp between two phases of life, Matty high-fived Mary like a teenager might and then leaned his cheek against her hip, looping an arm around her leg like he used to as a toddler. "They didn't let me eat anything on the drive over here."

Mary laughed at the look of affronted injustice on the kid's face.

"Matty," a firm voice said from the top of the stairs. "Just because we didn't let you pick at the chips and dips we brought doesn't mean we were starving you." And there Via was, holding a tray of food that Mary should have known she'd bring and giving Matty a stern eye that told him to behave himself at the party.

Via was nothing like Cora in most ways, forgiving where Cora had been unrepentant, thoughtful where Cora had been brash, observant where Cora had been the center of attention. But when it came to handling Matty with a firm hand, Via actually really reminded Mary of how Cora had been. Loving and stern and confident with the kid who'd take a mile every single time an inch was up for grabs.

"Is there snacks inside?" Matty asked, looking up at Mary.

Sebastian sighed as he too came up the stairs, still standing two steps down but drawing level with Via all the same, such was their height difference. "Tell me he at least said hi to you, Mary."

"He was a perfect gentleman," Mary lied, winking at Matty as she swatted him on the butt and pushed him inside. "Shoes off and then there are snacks in the kitchen. But put them on a plate. Don't just eat out of the bowls."

She kissed Via on the cheek and then Sebastian. "So glad you're here!"

"Us too, Mare. And I'm so freaking glad this party is inside. It's brutal out there." Sebastian had the beads of sweat on his forehead to prove it. "I'm melting."

"Cold drinks. Air-conditioning. A cold shower in the guest room if worst comes to worst." She beckoned her friends inside and was just closing her front door when she realized that another guest was standing on her landing already.

"John!"

"Hello." His frown was in full force, his hair immaculately parted on one side and smoothed back. He wore the party version of his typical outfit, meaning no tie and his shirtsleeves rolled to the elbows. Mary glanced down at his wingtips and suddenly felt a rising, unexplainable glee that John was going to take those ridiculous shoes off. It would be her first time seeing him without them.

"I brought you this." He shoved a paper bag into her hand. "You said not to bring food or drinks, but Estrella would keel over if she ever found out I came empty-handed."

Mary looked into the bag and felt that glee rise a few more inches. He'd brought her crappy beer and expensive lemonade, presumably to mix together. "It's perfect! Thank you so much. Here, come in, come in."

As he was stepping through her front door, though, Mary stepped in front of him and reached forward, pressing two fingers to his eyebrows the way she'd done once before, changing his expression from judgmental to neutral. "I wouldn't want you to strain yourself while you look around my fancy Cobble Hill house for the first time."

Color rose to his cheeks as he looked down at her. For the first time, she caught a familiarly masculine scent from John. Aftershave. The old-school kind. She thought of barbershops and shaving strops. Her eyes dropped from his pink cheeks to his freshly shaved jaw, smooth but shadowed blue by his dark hair. "I'm not going to judge you, Mary."

They were standing a bit closer than she'd previously realized and Mary's fingertips sort of buzzed where she'd just touched his brow. "Richie's not here yet," she told him, just to say anything at all.

John smirked. "I don't expect him for at least another hour. He's only on time for court."

His eyes flicked over Mary's shoulder and his frown came back. It was then that Mary saw something else in those ever-present lines in John's face. It wasn't just his job and his past that he wore there. It was nerves as well.

He was nervous to meet new people at a party.

Cute.

John carefully took off his shoes and set them aside. Mary surreptitiously glanced down at his feet and almost rolled her eyes when she saw his crisp, predictable, perfectly black dress socks. She should have known.

She closed the door behind him and immediately swept him along to her kitchen, fixing him a drink and then herself one as well. She parked John next to Sebastian and Via, where she knew he'd be in safekeeping, and then went to answer the door, where Fin, Tyler and Kylie all waited, laughing. Richie stood on the landing with them as well.

She greeted them all with hugs and kisses and closed the door behind them.

"This has got to be some sort of New York City record," Mary said to Richie as they walked into the kitchen together. "One hundred percent attendance at a party in the first hour?"

Mary looked around for John, wanting to check and see if he was still nervous, and not finding him where she'd left him. She craned her neck and found him in the living room, sitting on an ottoman, but hunched forward over the coffee table, where he and Matty were chatting over a puzzle that Matty had just started. Matty loved jigsaw puzzles more than anything and Mary always kept a few for him at her house. Apparently he'd been able to rope a grown-up into helping him. Matty's signature move.

"Don't worry about him," Richie said over Mary's shoulder. "John generally finds the kids' table pretty fast at a party."

"Really?" Mary laughed.

"Oh, yeah. You should see him at his family's Thanksgiving celebration. He spends an hour or two coloring with a billion of his little cousins. Does a requisite half an hour playing hide-and-seek. Eats dinner, does a few dishes and waves at the grown-ups on his way out."

Mary looked back at John, a little mystified at this new information. "Why?"

Richie shrugged. "Family is really important to John, but small talk is not his thing."

"You two have been friends for a long time?"

Richie's hand toggled back and forth in the air. "A few years."

"Really?" Mary said in surprise. "It seems like you've known each other your whole lives."

Richie grinned. "That's just John. Once he decides to get to know somebody, he really gets to know them. When I first got assigned to be his officemate, I thought, *Great, of course they pair me with this buzzkill.* But not three months later, I realized he'd become one of my closest friends."

One of her neighbors caught Mary's attention and the party unfolded from there. She loved the energy of a party. She loved watching the web of her life become more intricate and stronger as the people in it spoke and laughed and got to know one another.

A few hours later, a group of them sat in Mary's living room, Mary perched on the arm of the chair where Fin was sitting.

Jewel was playing with some toys her parents had brought for her, piling plastic scoops of ice cream on top of one another and bringing them around for the adults.

"Yum yum," Mary said, pretending to take a bite of the strawberry ice cream. Jewel smiled and nodded and prepared some for her mother, and then for Via.

She brought a pair of chocolate scoops over for John to try, where he sat on the floor, his legs stretched out and his drink in his hand.

She held out the ice cream to John, who leaned forward and pretended to take a bite. A moment passed before he screwed his face up into a look of scowling disgust. "That is the worst ice cream I've ever had in my life," he informed Jewel. He stuck his tongue out. "Yuck."

At first quite shocked, the little girl glanced back at her mother, who was chuckling. Jewel turned around and started giggling at John's disgusted face.

"Bring me a different flavor," John demanded.

"Say pease."

"Please bring me a different flavor at once." John knocked a fist firmly against the floor beside him, making Jewel jump and laugh a little hysterically.

She ran back to her pile of ice creams and came back with a strawberry and a vanilla. Again, John pretended to sample them, his face smoothing into almost a smile before he screwed it up in disgust once more. "Blech. That is *terrible*! Just awful! Who makes this ice cream?!"

By now Jewel was fully belly laughing, which made everyone who was watching the exchange laugh as well.

She came back with pistachio in a bowl with a spoon. He sampled the ice cream, gave her a full smile and then let his face dissolve into horror and disgust. "That's the worst one yet! I want a refund! I demand to speak to the manager!"

Jewel was beside herself with giggles.

"You're catching flies," Fin muttered to Mary.

"What's that?" Mary tore her attention from John and Jewel and looked down at her friend who was peering, almost smugly, up at Mary.

"I said, you're catching flies in your wide-open mouth while you stare at John."

Mary pursed her lips. "I was *watching*, not staring."

"Sure." Fin tucked her smile into her drink.

Mary glanced back at John. His black hair, white shirt, black pants, black socks. Everything black and white. Except for the man himself, who was turning out to be quite a complicated pattern of color.

She wrinkled her nose and looked down at Fin again. "So, maybe I was staring," she admitted.

Fin laughed. "You catching feelings for him?"

"No," Mary said resolutely, shaking her head. Then she

thought of his aftershave. How happy she'd been to unexpectedly see him in the bar the other night. "Maybe."

Fin laughed again. "He's cute. In an unexpected way. Not your usual style."

That was true enough. Doug, Mary's last serious boyfriend, had been as quick to smile as she was. He was social and gregarious and a blur of sound and motion.

"We're not going to date. He thinks I'm too old," Mary reminded Fin.

Fin glanced back and forth between Mary and John. "Maybe you should check on that, Mary. Because I'm not getting many she's-too-old vibes from that one."

Then why would he have said it in the first place? Mary watched John continue to play with Jewel for a while and then rose up to check on the levels of food and drink in the kitchen.

Ten or so minutes later, John himself appeared at her side, refilling his glass, this time with just lemonade and ice. She peered at his cup, realizing she hadn't yet seen him with a plate.

"You haven't eaten yet, have you?"

Interestingly, the tips of John's ears went pink. "Uh. No."

"Nothing looks good?" She turned to cast an eye over the extensive spread of platters she'd gotten from the deli.

"It all looks delicious."

And when Mary turned around, it was to see John practically licking his chops at the food.

"But I ate before I came," he said as he cleared his throat and turned away.

"You've been here for a few hours already. Aren't you hungry again?" She wasn't sure why she was pushing him, other than the fact that she was almost certain he was hiding something and she wanted to know what it was.

"I'm, ah, I'm vegan." His ears went pinker. "I forgot to mention that on Wednesday. I should have brought my own food. It was dumb. I'm new at this."

She blinked. She'd seen him eat fries and falafel. Street food. But technically vegan. "You're a new vegan," she repeated.

"Yeah. Half a year or so."

"Why?" she asked, completely confounded. She lived for soft cheese spread on a cracker, a perfectly ripe raspberry poised on top. Paper-thin prosciutto. Ugh, eggs Florentine, extra-crispy bacon.

John laughed at whatever expression was crossing her face. "Carbon footprint, mostly. My New Year's resolution was to see if I could cut mine in half. Lot of fossil fuels get burned in the meat industry. At first, I was just going to be vegetarian. But as I read up on it, a lot of the animal cruelty stuff started to get to me, and now, yeah, I guess my reasons are a mixed bag."

Mary blinked at him. He was a scowly, rude-faced vegan. Somehow she couldn't make the pieces fit together. She thought of him sitting on the floor with Jewel, making the little girl laugh. Maybe she couldn't fit the pieces together yet because she still hadn't seen a lot of the pieces. He seemed so simple. Judgmental man in wingtips.

He wasn't simple.

"Well, I guess it explains your bad mood," Mary said, making a joke to cover her confusion. "You haven't had a decent meal in six months."

John laughed, and it startled her the same way it had the other times. It was a deep, rich laugh, but layered and two-toned just like his voice. Some people's laughter lingered on their faces, echoed for long moments. But John's laughter was always brief as a meteorite and then it was gone, leaving no trace to show it had ever been there.

"Hey, Mary?"

Mary jumped, as though she'd been caught doing something much more embarrassing than simply studying John. "What's up, Joanna?"

"Was that a real offer? To let the three of us stay in your guest room tonight? Because our A/C should be fixed by tomorrow, and it would be awesome if we could actually get Jewel to sleep tonight. She's been miserable in our sauna of an apartment."

"Of course!" Mary was thrilled. She loved having guests. "I'll make sure there are sheets and towels in there. You're welcome to stay as long as you like."

"Thank God. Josh almost cried when I told him it was time to go home. But we'll be back in a few hours with our overnight stuff."

Mary laughed and said goodbye. She turned to John. "I'm gonna go get their room set up."

She was glad for the short reprieve from the party. First Fin had planted ideas in Mary's head, and then John had been so pink-eared and cute in the kitchen. She smoothed sheets onto the guest bed and quickly folded some towels.

Was it possible that John had changed his mind about their age difference? Was it possible that if he'd changed his mind, Mary no longer cared that he'd said that in the first place? First impressions were important, but they weren't everything. Maybe John and Mary were outgrowing their first impressions of one another.

The thought was intriguing and made her heart gallop a little as she stopped into her own bedroom and checked her hair and makeup. She wore a blue-striped dress that swished at her knees, bare feet with a new red pedicure and her hair down her back. Mary didn't think she looked *old*.

Maybe John didn't think so anymore either. She smoothed her dress over her hips and took a deep breath.

Okay. If things were changing between them—which it kind of seemed like they were   then what happened next? Probably not anything today, because they were unlikely to get a moment alone together. Not with the Coates family staying over. But maybe she should secure a date in the calendar when they *could* be alone together?

A date? Her stomach took a quick tour around her midsection before settling back half an inch higher than it had been before. She pressed a hand to her gut and took a deep breath. A real date. Not one where she waited for a man who wasn't going to show up and John waited at a dark bar. Not one that was set up by Estrella in the most awkward fancy restaurant of all time. Not one where her friends watched her watch John eat—apparently vegan—tacos.

A date with just John and just Mary and whatever this was that was growing between them.

She let out a long breath through her mouth and lifted her chin on the way out of the bedroom. The first chance she got to catch John, she was just going to ask. *Would you want to go on a date with me?*

Simple as that. Piece of pie. Easy as cake. Or whatever the phrase was. Her underboob sweat made itself known. So, she was nervous. It was normal to be nervous!

Mary was just about to round the corner into the kitchen when she heard Tyler and John chuckling together over something. John said something in that hoarse voice of his and Mary strained to hear it, out of sight of the men.

"So," Tyler responded in a decidedly big-brotherly tone. "You're interested in Mary, then?"

"Ty!" Mary whispered to herself, her hands going to her cheeks as, still hidden, she waited for John's reply.

"Oh. Ah…"

"Because she was pretty sure you weren't interested after your date."

"Our date. Right."

Silence dragged on. What the heck? That was it? He wasn't going to actually answer the question? She was dying over here! She would have given her favorite pair of Jimmy Choos to see John's face right now. Though, an educated guess told her that he was probably frowning, his brows in a V.

"Sorry," John said after a minute, not sounding sorry at all. "Are you and Mary…?"

"No," Tyler answered immediately. "She's my best friend, though."

Another silence descended. Mary did a frantic pantomime of an awkward, screaming melt against the wall. "Someone say something," she mouthed to the heavens.

"I'm just looking out for her," Tyler said after a minute. "Seb and Mary and I, we've been through a lot together and she's been through some pretty miserable dating stuff in the last few years."

She was going to shave Tyler's eyebrows while he was sleeping. Why was he saying this to John? *Why?*

"And I guess I just wanted to say that she's a great person, and she doesn't deserve to get jerked around or negged or whatever."

There was a long pause.

"I agree that she's a great person," John said. "I've actually never met anyone else like her."

Long pause.

Mary was actually shocked her heart was still beating.

"So, you are trying to date her?" Tyler asked, point-blank.

"Okay," Mary whispered to herself, "maybe I'll only shave *one* eyebrow."

"Ah…" John started. "Mary and I—I think we're in really different stages of life."

Stages.

Of.

Life.

Mary had never before been aware of the oxygen in her bloodstream until it all evaporated at once. She shrank an entire coat size, feeling dizzy. If it was possible for words to bludgeon a person over the head, these ones just had.

Stages of life? Stages of *life*? Good God, he made her sound like she was two chess moves away from a nursing home! They were both in their thirties, for shit's sake, and he was acting like he was still a spring breaker, while she spent her weeknights knitting with the gals.

Stages of life?!

Mary turned on her heel and strode back to her bedroom, quietly closing the door behind her.

A memory came back to her. John's eyes sweeping up and down their pretty young waitress at the restaurant. His eyes sweeping up and down Via and Fin when he'd met them the night he'd brought tacos.

Had he ever looked at her that way? Mary didn't think so. Men weren't slick about these things. One could always catch them in the act. But she'd never once caught John checking her out. Always his eyes were looking squarely into hers or down at his own shoes. Never did they dip to her chest or ass or lips. Not that she really wanted him to ogle her. But still, it made something extremely clear. He wasn't attracted to her.

Maybe he didn't actually think she was too old, but Mary was certain that he was *more* attracted to younger women. Twenty-two-year-old waitresses with high ponytails. And why wouldn't he be? He was young and hot. She was sure that he wanted to be young and hot with other young, hot people.

Mary knew she was beautiful. But she'd never felt more out of touch. More single.

This is what you want? Buried between two strangers?

Mary winced and pressed the heels of her hands to her temples.

"No," she said aloud. "You don't get to make me doubt myself."

She wasn't sure if she was talking to her mother or to John.

She gave herself one long moment to picture the hug that Cora would have given her at that moment, so tight it hurt, her chin digging into Mary's shoulder, her voice in Mary's ear.

Mary Freaking Trace. That was what Cora had always called her in moments like this. MFT for short. She wouldn't let herself be cut down by the perceptions of others. She was MFT.

It would have been great if John had reciprocated. Dandy. But it hadn't happened and, in the end, that didn't really change anything at all. Because she'd been MFT long before she'd met John, and she was still MFT now.

Mary took one more deep breath, fixed a smile onto her face and went back out to her party.

CHAPTER TEN

"YOU KNOW, IF you hadn't refused Dad's money, you could be doing this disgusting little performance in your own penthouse."

Maddox leaned lazily against his kitchen island, watching John take a bowl of preheated pasta straight to the dome. Despite the towel John had wrapped around his waist, water was pooling at his feet where it dripped from his bathing suit. He swallowed a huge bite and glugged half a glass of seltzer that Maddox had just made him in his seltzermaker thingy.

John rolled his eyes at his brother's words, but he didn't deny them. When he'd first come back into his life, his father had repeatedly tried to reimburse him for the trust fund he would've gotten access to at age eighteen, like Maddox had. But John had refused over and over again. Maybe it was the same stubborn streak that Estrella had, the one that had kept her from marrying Cormac after all these years. But John had felt that taking the money would be too transactional. As if his father were paying to exonerate himself from the guilt of abandoning John and Estrella.

Besides, there was something symbolic about a trust fund. It was something you set up for a kid you acknowledged as your own. Like Maddox. It wasn't just a blank check from an overstuffed bank account twenty-odd years later. The whole thing offended John.

Still, principles had limits and John's stubborn streak didn't stop him from coming over to his brother's house and swimming in his saltwater pool and eating the food his housekeeper stocked the fridge with.

Finally, John finished his food and grabbed a dish towel to mop up the pool water at his feet. "Thanks, man. I needed that."

"The food or the swim?" Maddox asked, his arms crossed lazily over his chest, his head lolled to one side.

"Both. All. It's been a hell of a summer so far."

"Big caseload?"

"Always. And my clients have had some shit luck with grand juries lately. Everything has been getting indicted. And I mean everything."

"You're seeing a lot of court time?"

"No." John shook his head. "Lots of plea deals and kissing ADA ass to keep these kids out of court." John sighed, suddenly feeling ten years older than he was. "Sometimes I wonder why I even do this whole Sisyphus thing."

Maddox laughed. Now he was the one rolling his eyes. "John, are you kidding me? You'd never be happy if your job was even a smidge easier. You feel like Sisyphus rolling the boulder up the hill? Well, did you ever stop to think of what would happen if you actually got to the top of the hill?"

John opened his mouth, closed it and cocked his head to the side, looking a lot like his brother in that moment. "Good point. I guess if you get to the top of the hill, there's nowhere else to go."

"Or you're like Dad, and you make yourself a new hill." It may have sounded like a compliment, but Maddox's face was tight when he said it.

"You're talking about ambition."

"You don't become the DA of Manhattan without it."

"Yeah, well, apparently you don't become the mayor of NYC with it."

The two of them cracked into a grin. It was petty that they both still got so much joy out of their father's mayoral disappointment. But yeah. As different as their upbringings had been, Upper East Side versus Crown Heights, they were both still New Yorkers to the core and neither of them had believed that their father's proposed changes to policy would have been good for the city.

Plus, their dad was an ass who pretty much got everything he wanted, and it had felt good to see him lose one.

"So, that's it? That's the whole reason for your mood? Work?"

John shrugged and strode over to the small bag of clothes he'd brought to change into after the swim. Standing in Maddox's living room, he started changing under the towel, thoughtfully looking out at Maddox's—literal— million-dollar view of the East River, Queens and Brooklyn.

"I always thought it was ironic that the richest people in New York are forced to have the working class in their view at all times," he said after a minute. "All the money in the world and you still live in New York City, surrounded by all walks of life."

Maddox grunted. "You're feeling philosophical today."

John tugged track pants on and his T-shirt over that. He wore his nice work clothes almost every day of the week, wanting to look respectable and put-together no matter what he was doing. But it gave him a perverse thrill to look shabby and tossed-together whenever he visited Maddox's penthouse.

"Do you know what negging is?" John asked, sitting down on Maddox's couch.

Maddox looked slightly surprised, whether it was because John seemed to be extending their hang or at the question itself, John wasn't sure.

"Um. Yeah." He took his own seltzer and spread out on the far side of the couch. "It's when you say negative things to a woman about her appearance or her personality. Backhanded compliments. Like 'your hair is pretty, but it would look better long.' That kind of thing."

John screwed up his face. "What's the point of it?"

"Well, I think the idea is that if you're a little bit mean to her, it intrigues her. She seeks your approval."

"That's—"

"The dumbest shit you've ever heard? I know. It's just some stupid pickup-artist shit. Misogynistic crap."

John's eyebrows rose. He'd never heard Maddox refer to misogyny before. But then his stomach fell as he considered the concept of negging. "I think I accidentally negged this woman recently."

Maddox laughed, loud and boisterous, so unlike his brother. "John, you can't accidentally neg someone. The whole point is that it's a calculated move to knock her off her game and get her to lean on you. If you said something negative to her, it's not because you were negging her. It's just because you're a—"

"Dick, I know. I've been told." John leaned his head back and looked at Maddox's high, perfectly white ceilings. No water damage for the penthouse. "I accidentally told her I thought she was old, when what I really meant was— Ugh. God. Never mind."

Maddox laughed again. "Well, is she old?"

"No! She's only five or six years older than I am."

"And I take it she didn't immediately seek your approval following the negative comment?"

John raised an eyebrow at his brother. "Of course not. She left the restaurant and I spent the next few weeks trying to convince her that I'm not an utter—"

"Dick."

"Right."

"And?" Maddox prompted.

"And now we're friends."

"Ouch."

"Yeah." John rolled his head and looked out at the view again, but in his mind's eye, he was back at yesterday's party. "There are a million reasons it'd never work out. I just expedited the process. You should see her apartment. Huge two-bedroom right on Court Street. Skylights in every room. Fancy furniture. Whole bunch of copper kitchen stuff. Candles the size of my head."

"Rich?"

"Yeah." John messed around with the buttons at the side of his crappy track pants that he'd had for a decade.

"Money isn't everything, John," Maddox said after a quiet moment. "It doesn't have to draw lines in the sand the way you think it does."

John rolled his head to look at his brother. *That's something rich people say*, John's face told Maddox.

Maddox read his expression, and his own tightened in response. No longer was he resting easily on his gigantic couch. He was stiff and uncomfortable, looking angrily away from John.

They'd been here before, with the disparities between their upbringings sitting between them like a rock wall.

It had taken years for them to see over it even enough for John to come and swim and eat spaghetti.

Once, Maddox had shouted at John, *"You think I wouldn't choose your life over mine, John?"*

It had only fortified the wall between them. The idea that Maddox had romanticized John's life with Estrella had infuriated John. Maddox saw their rented brownstone, Estrella's artwork, John's determination and drive in his career, and thought that all that simply came from good old-fashioned elbow grease. Thunderbird gang members snapping their way down the cobblestone streets of a plucky upbringing.

Maddox didn't see the fact that both Estrella and Cormac had worked two jobs for years. That John himself had worked since he was twelve. He didn't see the emotional toll that took on a family. He didn't see the nights of worry over bills, the tears in Estrella's eyes.

John's work as a public defender perfectly positioned him to see what advantages those with money actually had. The kinds of advantages the rich come to view as rights. And maybe they were rights. But they were rights that the lower class had no access to. Maddox didn't see that.

John supposed that he couldn't see over the wall any better than Maddox could, but he wasn't going around wishing to switch lives either. That was just naive.

Normally, this would be the part of the afternoon when Maddox got up angrily and said something about having plans and John would go home. John was surprised, then, when Maddox simply continued to sit there, his face drawn in lines of mutiny, but his dark eyes pinned on John.

"I'm just saying that the money thing probably isn't the line in the sand that you think it is, John. Not for her anyway. There's a chance that it hasn't even occurred to her that there's a disparity."

John masked his surprise at his brother's stolid attempt at reigniting the conversation. "At some point she's going to notice that I only ever take her to restaurants with a single dollar sign on their Yelp pages."

"And if she cares, then she's not the right person for you."

John's eyebrows rose and then his eyes narrowed as he looked at his brother. His lawyerly mind started putting the pieces together. "Misogyny, wealth disparity, you didn't storm off in anger just now... Maddox, did you *meet* somebody?"

Maddox pursed his lips, but there was a small smile to hide there. "You think a woman is the reason for my sudden self-improvement?"

John just waited.

Maddox crossed his arms and grumbled. "Fine. Yes. I met someone. She's great. She cares a lot about social issues. She pushes me. I'm a better man now. Blah blah blah."

John had mixed feelings about this. He would love for his brother to meet a good, steady woman, but Maddox had such a crappy track record with relationships that John couldn't quite muster the mustard to get excited about it. Maddox had at least two epically dramatic and public breakups a year, the kind that catapulted him toward a bender of some kind.

"And, just like with your girl," Maddox continued, a genuine frown on his face now, "she won't date me."

Now, *that* John could get behind. Women tripped over their Manolo Blahniks to date Maddox. Any woman who was lecturing him about misogyny and refusing to date him was bound to be a good influence.

"Really?"

"Oh, put that smug look away." Maddox scowled.

"Who is she?"

Maddox winced, looking out the window instead of at John. "Sari's new nanny."

"Oh, Maddox." John's heart fell again. Sari was Maddox's daughter, and though they weren't estranged, they were definitely not regular fixtures in one another's lives. Dating her nanny was not a good idea. In fact, it was an epically bad one.

"I know, I know. It's terrible. And if Lauren ever found out, she'd castrate me on the spot. Apparently it took her a year to find somebody good enough with Sari that she could actually justify going back to work. If I screw this up for them…"

Maddox's ex wasn't exactly the kill-'em-with-kindness type. She was more the kill-'em-by-any-means-necessary-but-preferably-with-a-rusty-shank type.

Maddox finally turned back to John. "You think I *want* to be the deadbeat dad who resurfaces just long enough to date her nanny?"

"No," John answered honestly. "But you have to admit, this kind of thing just sort of happens to you. Enough that it's probably not a coincidence."

"What's that supposed to mean?"

"I mean that your dating life reads like bad porn scripts, Maddox. Two years ago, you were screwing a widow who you met when she came to your door literally asking to borrow sugar. Before that it was the flight attendant in various exotic locales. Somewhere in there was your secretary— which you should have gotten sued for, by the way. And then there was—"

"I get it. My life is awesome, and you're totally jealous."

John couldn't help but laugh. "Don't date the nanny. Spend time with your daughter. Keep it in your pants until she's not Sari's nanny anymore. The kid's already in fourth grade. How long does she need a nanny for?"

"That's already the plan. I told her I'm going to ask her out in two years. Because that's the length of her contract and that's how long Lauren thinks that Sari needs someone to be around after school. And until then we can be friends."

Now, that was a genuine surprise. "Really?"

"Really. Well, that was after I asked her out and she said no. Then I let her know about the two-years-from-now plan."

"And what'd she say?"

"She rolled her eyes."

"You're fucked."

They both laughed.

John rose and gathered his things, not wanting to wear out his welcome. Maddox followed him to the door, and the brothers quickly embraced. They made a plan to see one another in a few weeks, but John knew that there was a good chance Maddox would cancel in the meantime.

He walked to the train and thought about old money. How, like anything, if it was ever present in your life, you barely thought about it. Mary must have spent a couple hundred bucks on the food alone for her party. A party she'd thrown just because she'd wanted to have a party, celebrating nothing but summer and friends and life. He thought about the difference between Mary's party and Estrella's annual block party. Both parties were for the same reasons, and both were jovial and lively. And strangely enough, Mary had looked at home in both settings.

MARY'S HOUSE FELT empty after the Coateses left just shy of a week after they'd arrived. Their air-conditioning had taken longer to be fixed than they'd thought, and Mary hadn't minded the company.

She didn't want to feel vulnerable after the conversation with her mother and John's words at her party. She wanted it to roll off her back. But for whatever reason, her mother and John had served up a one-two punch that was still smarting five days later.

Mary had taken the opportunity to give Jewel a million cuddles, to bring home dinners for Josh and Joanna, to laugh and fill her time with company.

But now they were gone, and her apartment felt much too large for one person. Mary was normally a good sleeper. Good enough that even after thirty-seven years of life, 3:00 a.m. still felt like an unfamiliar and vaguely creepy betrayal of the daytime. She wasn't ever comfortable at the witching hour.

She rolled in her sheets and wondered whether John was a good sleeper or not. She could easily picture him as an insomniac, red eyes cracked and the sheets twisted at his hips. But then, he was so intense and focused in his waking life, maybe he was one of those people who just passed out cold the second his head hit the bed. She could also picture him dead to the world, his face finally relaxed and slack in the kind of sleep that restored a man.

And therein was the problem. Mary didn't *know* John. She didn't know him well enough to predict his propensities or inclinations. If she'd known him well, maybe she wouldn't have been so shocked by his words to Tyler. So appalled. So embarrassed.

She tossed and turned for another hour before she started to drift.

A noise brought her back, dimly, to the surface of sleep. She sifted back down, warm and soft. But then the noise came again. She opened her eyes.

Sat up.

That sounded like it was coming from downstairs. From her shop. There! The tinkling of glass. Scuffling.

Mary scrambled to the end of her bed and grabbed her

phone, tugging on her robe over her nightshirt, even though sweat had sprung up down her spine.

She was frozen. Call the cops? Go down there by herself? She walked carefully across her bedroom floor, avoiding the creaky spots. She stopped in her tracks and listened for more sounds. Nothing.

Then a crash so loud that she couldn't help but yelp. She covered her mouth with her hands, staring into nothing, her heart's fists beating against the glass pane in her chest. Oh, God. There was someone in her store and they were destroying things. She had to call the cops.

Mary made it to the kitchen, somehow feeling unsafe in her own bedroom, and once again froze solid.

The sound of footsteps on the stairs that led up to her apartment was unmistakable. Mary peered out toward her front door and saw that she'd pulled the chain and cocked the dead bolt before bed. They would have to break down her door in order to get in. Even so, she scampered back toward her bathroom, the only other lockable room in her apartment, and locked the door behind her. She sat down hard on the edge of the bathtub and called the police.

CHAPTER ELEVEN

IT WAS A two-shirt kind of Friday. John had fully sweated through the button-down he'd worn to court that morning and was in the bathroom across the hall from his office, shirtless, and swiping cold water over the back of his neck, when he heard Richie's voice in the hallway.

"Hey! What're you doing here?"

A woman's voice, more muffled than Richie's, echoed back and then faded away as they stepped into the office.

Wondering who it was, John dried off with paper towels, reapplied some of the deodorant he kept in his bag and quickly buttoned himself into his clean shirt. Now he had to get out of this sweltering bathroom before he melted again.

He shouldered into his office, absurdly grateful for the measly five-degree differential provided by their wheezing, ancient window unit.

"Beth!" He was surprised. He'd never known Beth Herari to pay a house call before and he rarely saw her in her dress blues. He wondered if she was here in an official capacity. It was exceedingly rare to see a cop in a public defender's office. They didn't, in general, play nice. After all, public defenders built their careers around their abilities to pick holes in a cop's procedure and even, occasionally, their character and credibility.

John's eyes bounced to Richie, who wore an expression that John had rarely seen him wear before. Shock and chagrin.

"What's up?" John asked Beth.

"I've been calling you all morning," Beth told him.

"I had court. My phone's off." He pulled it out of the pocket of his black slacks as if to prove his point. He turned it on. "Seriously, what's going on?"

"Your girl's shop got broken into last night. Trashed pretty bad."

His mind stuttered on the word *girl*. Whose girl? His? And then his thoughts tripped over to the word *shop*. He knew only one person who owned a shop.

"Mary?" John croaked, his eyes wide, his voice splitting in two different directions.

Richie and Beth nodded at the same time.

"Jesus." He took a step forward and then an immediate step backward. "Is she all right?"

"She's holding it together..." Beth said, one hand on the back of her neck and her eyes on the floor. "But it's pretty bad, and she didn't call anyone. No friends or anything."

John thought helplessly of all the friends she'd had over at her beautiful house just last weekend. She hadn't called a single one of them. Why?

"She's alone?"

"Yeah. The cops are going to wrap things up for the day pretty soon, but it's a crime scene."

And then Mary would be alone at a crime scene, unable to even clean things up. She'd have to leave everything the way it was.

"God. She lives above the shop."

"Yeah. They broke through her front door, but the cops got there in time and the perps fled. She wasn't harmed. Just freaked out."

"Were they apprehended?" he asked in a voice that didn't quite sound like his own.

Beth pursed her lips. "No. They went out the back while the cops came in the front. They gave chase but lost them. They saw enough to do a rough identification, though, and the vandalism matches a few others that happened up in Williamsburg last month."

John nodded, trying to absorb the information in a clinical, practiced way, the way he did the details of any case. But he found that he couldn't. Mary, alone, scared, her shop wrecked.

"Shit. Maybe I should call Estrella." He pinched his eyes closed.

"John." Richie's sharp, rarely used tone had John startling. "Beth didn't come down here to tell you to call your mother. You need to *go*."

Beth nodded.

John didn't think this was the best time to point out that he and Mary were just friends. Her shop had been broken into badly enough that Beth was here, in his office, and Mary was there, alone.

"Yeah. Yeah, all right." He turned a circle and grabbed his bag.

"Do you have appointments this afternoon?" Richie asked. "Court?"

John pressed heavy fingers to his forehead. "No court. But I'm supposed to meet with Sarah about that sex trafficking case and then Weathers asked me to consult with him on a B and E. And the rest of the day was going to be prep for court next week."

"I'll let Sarah know you had a family emergency, and I'll take over the B and E consult. The rest you're just going to have to catch up on this weekend."

One of the main differences between being a public defender and working for a private defense firm was the hours. John and Richie generally worked a tight eight to four schedule, occasionally coming in early or leaving a bit late. But for the most part, they had their weekends. John would gladly give up his weekend to cut out early and make it to Mary.

"All right." John nodded dimly at Richie, grateful for the clear instructions, and followed Beth out of the office. She gave him a ride in the squad car down Court Street. John and Mary's places of work were only a five-minute drive away from one another. A fifteen-minute brisk walk. So close and yet so far.

He jumped out of the squad car and just stared at the outside of Mary's shop. The security gate was still pulled down, but her large front window was a spiderweb of white cracks. He could see from the scattered glass on the ground that the impact had come from the inside of the shop.

Though it usually glowed, today the lights seemed to be mostly off inside. The shop looked dull and listless, a normally vibrant soul asleep in a sickbed.

"They came in through the back," Beth told him. "We can access it through this alley."

She led him through to where the back entrance of Mary's shop was propped open. There were two cops smoking back there and yellow crime scene tape that Beth pulled up to let John duck under.

He stepped into Mary's storeroom and groaned. Boxes and boxes of goods were toppled and torn. There was a thin covering of down feathers over almost everything. Glass crunched under his feet. Not a thing had gone untouched. He couldn't even begin to estimate the cost of these kinds of damages. He hoped to God she had insurance.

"She's upstairs," Beth told him. She pointed the way through the decimated shop to the interior access door to the stairs that led to her apartment. John winced when he saw the damage to the inside of the shop. It was even worse than the storeroom. Every bit of upholstery sliced open, shelves yanked off the walls, leaving gaping, ragged holes in the drywall.

John walked up the same stairs he had last weekend, a bag of beer and lemonade in his hand at the time, his stupid heart beating nervously at the idea of seeing Mary in her natural habitat. Now his stupid heart was beating nervously at the idea of seeing Mary dejected and frightened.

Her front door was propped open as well. He frowned at the signs of forced entry against the locks. She'd have to get a new door.

That was when he heard it. Her sparkly laugh. It sent a shiver down his spine. He jumped, pleasantly surprised, like looking down at his hand and seeing an unexpected butterfly resting there.

He moved toward her kitchen, noting that nothing looked out of place or destroyed in her actual home. Good.

He wasn't sure what he'd been expecting. Mary with the lights out. Tears on her cheeks. Her shoulders hunched. Maybe even, indulgently, he'd imagined her hair a shade or two darker than normal. Everything dimmed by her shock and fear.

But no. Of course not. Mary sat at her kitchen table with a detective, her head thrown back in laughter, her sunny hair in a high pile on her head and a fancy, decorated T-shirt splashing color across John's eyes. She was not huddling in a corner, jumping at shadows. She was radiant light itself, and John should have known. He just should have known. Why did he keep expecting himself to be able to handle being around her? He should know by now that there was no immunizing himself to her. This pull was elemental, expansive.

She looked up, saw him there in the doorway and immediately rose up. Her jaw dropped open for a second and something flashed in her eyes. "John!"

"Beth—Officer Herari—told me what happened. I came to make sure—"

John cut off because Mary was across her kitchen in half a blink of an eye. She fit herself perfectly under John's chin, her hair like warm satin against his throat. Her arms came hard around his ribs in a single, solid band. She was pressed to him in a long, fierce line, only his messenger bag keeping their hips from lining up.

He dropped his arms around her, holding her closer than he'd ever thought he might be allowed to. He couldn't help but drop the weight of his cheek against her hair. He flattened his hands on her back and gave her a quick squeeze, and then another, when her nose turned in toward his sternum.

Her breath stuttered just a little bit, and when she pulled back from him, John saw it. Just a split second of fear and pain that she couldn't hold back anymore.

She stepped back from John, one hand firmly on his shoulder. "I'm so glad you're here," she said in a clear, low voice.

"Ms. Trace," the older detective said as he rose up from his seat at the table, his eyes bouncing back and forth between Mary and John. "I have everything I need from you right now. I'll be in touch with you tomorrow."

"Thank you so much for everything," Mary said, stepping away from John and following the detective to her front door.

They exchanged words that John didn't listen to. He was

still fighting his way through a full-body buzz from where she'd tossed herself against him. Didn't she know she was precious cargo? She shouldn't go slamming herself into unexpected men, like a ship on the sea. He traced a hand down the line of his chin to his throat, where her hair had been pressed. That hair was a hell of a weapon. Nothing had ever felt better or more dangerous against him.

She appeared in the doorway to the kitchen, and his fog immediately receded, because those were tears in her eyes.

"Mary."

"Oh, John," she said with a shudder, crossing the room to him again. This time, he dropped his messenger bag aside and met her in the middle. His hand came to her hair as her nose pressed hard into his sternum. "It was so terrible."

"Do you want to tell me about it?"

"Maybe later," she whispered. She looked up at him then, and John's heart stumbled. He'd been foolish to think that tears would dull Mary's light. If anything, the high emotion on her face almost heightened it. It was like the sun catching droplets of rain from the side, each drop its own gorgeous prism.

He talked himself out of tracing away the teardrops with his thumbs. Too risky. "Are you all right?" He had to know.

"I'm okay. Just shaky. And exhausted. I barely slept last night anyway. And then as I was drifting off, I heard them—" She took a deep breath. "My bones feel like they weigh a hundred pounds."

"You should take a nap. I could go out and bring back something for us to eat." He was being presumptuous assuming he could stay with her for dinner, but she just nodded.

"Okay. Yeah."

They separated from the hug and she took a few steps

toward her bedroom. She paused and peered down the hallway. "Actually, I think I'll come with you to get the food."

He blinked at her and she was back at his side. He'd never seen her flit quite so fast. He understood all at once. She was terrified to be here alone. And he didn't blame her. Her door was kicked in and she probably hadn't lain down on her bed since she'd bolted out of it after hearing the break-in. She wasn't eager to curl up alone in her unlocked house and he didn't blame her.

"Mary," he said after a second. "Maybe I could drop you somewhere. You could stay with someone tonight? Fin? Via?"

She was shaking her head. "No. No. They have Kylie and Matty. Enough on their plates. Their lives. I don't—" She shook her head even harder. "Maybe a hotel instead."

He thought of Mary alone in a huge hotel room. Somehow, even though he knew that the class of a fancy room would suit her better than his humble apartment ever would, the idea of her being alone tonight wasn't at all palatable.

"Come to my place," he told her, without taking a second to think about all the ways that invitation could be misconstrued.

Her brow furrowed.

"It's nothing fancy, but it's clean. And you'd have company. And I don't have kids or a life. I mean, I have a *life*, but nothing you'd be interrupting. I have to get brunch with my dad tomorrow, but frankly, I'd be thrilled if I had an excuse to cancel. And first thing tomorrow we'll get someone to fix your door so you won't have to worry. And you could just have a break. Be in a different part of the city and relax. Not that Bed-Stuy is, like, an amazing vacation destination, but still, it might be nice to—"

"Okay."

He blinked down at her. "Okay?"

"Okay, I'll come. Let me just grab a few things."

"Okay, you'll come to my place?"

Now she was the one blinking. "Well, am I invited or not?"

"Invited."

"So, let me get my stuff."

He picked up his messenger bag and arranged it over his shoulder for something to do. Mary was coming to spend the night at his place. Huh. He'd thought for sure she'd say no. It hadn't been an empty invitation, but he really hadn't thought there was almost any possible way she'd say yes. But she was packing a bag that very second. With things she'd need to spend the night with him.

Well, not *with him*. But at his house and— Oh, *crap*. He had a freaking studio apartment. How had this slipped his mind?! A bed and a love seat, that's all she wrote. Not even a blow-up mattress. He pictured himself in some nineties rom-com where he and Mary would end up sharing his bed "platonically" only to wake up spooning and in love.

Yeah, right. *He* might wake up spooning and in love. And with a knee to the nads. *Crossed off the list, remember?* He pulled out his phone and quickly texted his next-door neighbors. They'd let him stay over once before, when his mother's heat had been out and she and Cormac had stayed in his place. Hopefully they could put him up again, or he'd sleep on the floor.

"Ready?" She had a small overnight bag on her hip and a sad half smile on her face as she stood in the doorway. It was the half smile that did away with his reservations and worries. If she needed company and a place to stay, John was going to serve it up to her on a silver platter. No, a golden platter.

"Ready."

They walked to the train side by side after making sure with the cops downstairs that it was all right for her to leave and that they were going to secure her shop tonight. On the walk, Mary called her employees, gave them a quick rundown of what had happened and explained she wouldn't be needing any help for the weekend. They sat quietly side by side as the subway screeched and accelerated and slid into stop after stop, each one accentuating just how far they actually lived from one another. Two different dimensions.

John didn't let these thoughts get him down as the two of them jogged aboveground in his neighborhood. She was in flats, which he realized now, she rarely wore, because he could look down and see the top of her head. He felt an expanding tenderness for the fact that her hair was messily twisted into a bun. She'd managed to make it look fashionable and delicate all the same, but she'd also been frazzled and tired enough to leave parts of it messy.

This, more than anything, illustrated to him just how trying this day had been for her. "All right," he told her. "Let's see. We've got crappy pizza, mediocre burritos or insanely good Cuban."

"I think the crappy pizza sounds good, since you sold it so well." She crossed her eyes at him. "Just joking. I choose Cuban. Can we get it to go?"

He nodded and the two of them walked the few blocks in silence. He could practically feel her fatigue spiraling off of her like heat from a light bulb left on too long. It was still a bit too early for the dinner rush, so they were in and out with their to-go bag pretty fast. John was grateful that this place was too expensive for him to regularly patronize because there was no one working there to recognize him with this gorgeous blonde ray of sunshine. There was no one to rib him about who the pretty girl was, to reveal loudly and obnoxiously—the way they would have done in the burrito shop—that he never brought pretty girls around here.

John clung to the fact that the man who'd farewelled them at the Cuban joint had barely acknowledged John and Mary. The man's eyes hadn't goggled at the idea of the two of them having dinner together. Maybe it wasn't so outrageous.

They walked back to his house, and John's heart started to bang. "It's a walk-up," he told her in a voice a little more cracked than normal. He took a deep breath as he started up the stairs to his apartment.

All right, John, he coached himself. *You cannot be ashamed of your home. You worked hard to make it here. You live on your own in a clean apartment. She knows you're not a Rockefeller. Don't do yourself the disservice of apologizing for your life. There's nothing to apologize for. She wants to be here.*

He took another deep breath and didn't linger in front of the door. He merely unlocked it and let her into his life.

"OH, NO, YOU DON'T," John growled as he bent down in front of his door and scooped something up from the ground.

Mary was relieved to hear that his voice was back to a more normal pitch than it had been for the last few minutes. She'd begun to wonder if he'd been regretting bringing her here. Mary wanted nothing more than to just get inside his house and crash.

"Oh," she laughed as John straightened up and stepped in the door, holding it open for her. He had a wiggling, black-and-gray-striped ball of fur in his arms. At first glance the cat looked to be struggling, but when Mary looked closer,

she saw that the little beast was actually just wiggling farther into John's arms, attempting to get comfortable in its
throne. "I didn't know you had a cat!"

"You're not allergic, are you?" he asked immediately.
"Crap, I should have mentioned."

"No! I like cats." To prove it, Mary leaned forward and
scratched the kitty under the chin. To her delight, the cat
tipped its head back, luxuriating.

"Oh, good." John kicked the door closed behind them
and then set the cat on the ground. "Well, this is Ruth. She's
a little…forward, so feel free to ignore her if she's getting
on your nerves."

Ruth? He'd named his cat *Ruth*? For some reason, this
information made helium rise inside of Mary. She wanted
to laugh hysterically, hug John again, cry a little.

She needed to eat and crash out.

"Well," he said again, stepping over Ruth carefully.
"This is it."

Mary finally took a look around, trying not to appear
overeager to finally see John's home. It was small. Just one
room with a bed along the far wall and a kitchenette tucked
in the opposite corner. There was a kitchen table and, under
one window, a love seat with a coffee table in front.

Her first impressions were homey, clean, man-space.
She immediately loved all the touches of Estrella around
the apartment. There was a colorful, mismatched afghan
she'd obviously crocheted for John. And a series of paintings along the wall, some of her earlier work that Mary
had never seen before. The bottom half of one of his windows was covered over in a stained-glass windowpane that
Estrella had obviously worked hard on. The overall effect
was nice. It wasn't a curated space by any means, but it

wasn't depressing either. It was neat and intentional. Very John. She liked it.

"So, uh, make yourself at home. Gah! Ruth!" He did a quick little dance step to avoid his cat.

She covered her mouth with one hand so he wouldn't think she was laughing at him, even though she kind of was.

John's phone dinged in his pocket, and as he set their food on the table and unwound himself from his messenger bag, he checked the text.

"Oh, good. My neighbors texted me back. I'm gonna run over there and get things squared away."

What he was getting squared away, she had no idea. She was still standing on his front mat, taking in his apartment.

"Here," he said, striding over and lifting her bag off her shoulder. He set it on the love seat. "I probably should have mentioned that I don't have air-conditioning."

She saw his look of chagrin for only a moment before he turned to the window in the kitchen and propped it open with a box fan, flicking it on. He strode to the window above the bed, put one knee in the middle of the comforter and did the same with another box fan.

"But it's actually pretty comfortable at night with the airflow. You should be all right. Okay. Um. Bathroom's there, let me just…" He strode to the bathroom and poked his head inside, obviously checking to make sure it was clean. He nodded his head. "Yeah. So. I'll be right back."

And then he was scooting around her, out his front door. Mary heard him knock on the next door down and then the sound of his voice and another voice from the other side of the far wall. Thin walls in this building.

Mary looked longingly at the bathroom. She wanted

nothing more than an icy shower and her pajamas and a place to rest her head. But she figured that she'd wait until after she'd eaten. She washed her hands and set out their dinner. She found only four place settings of dishes in his cupboard, all clean, though a little chipped. She set the table with two of them, folding paper towels neatly underneath the silverware. She fished two beers out of the fridge. There was a small, stubby candle in the drawer next to the bottle opener, so she lit it, setting it in the middle of the table. She wished there was a flower she could set out, but this would have to do. She smiled as Ruth twined around her feet, roughly rubbing her little furry face against Mary's bare ankles.

He was right about the cross-breeze from the fans. The cool air felt heavenly and the white noise from the rushing breeze made Mary feel as if John's home were safely tucked into a cloud, floating above Brooklyn, high above any intruders or ruined shops.

Oh, God. Her beautiful shop. All that waste. The meaningless destruction of something so beautiful.

She felt a crack deep within her and knew that her tears weren't done. But she didn't want to cry right now. She wanted food and rest. So she went to her knees and scooped Ruth onto her lap.

Ruth made an alarmingly loud sound that Mary supposed was a purr. She laughed and poked at Ruth's flicking tail, scratched at her ears, absorbed the animal's warm, weighted comfort.

The voices on the other side of the wall stopped, and a moment later, John was back through his front door. "Everything's good over there. They said I can head over whenever you want to crash. I see that Ruth wasted no time in seducing you." His lips softened into a half smile at the sight of Mary on the floor with his goofy cat. Then his gaze flicked to the table and the smile tightened back into his usual expression of lined consternation.

He cleared his throat. "Table looks nice."

They sat down together, John filling up waters for them and cracking both beers open.

"What did you have to get figured out with the neighbors?" she asked.

"Oh. Just wanted to make sure I could sleep on their couch."

"Oh." She furrowed her brow and looked around. John had a small sofa and just the one bed. Of course there wasn't room for two in here. She wasn't sure why she hadn't picked out that detail immediately. "John, you don't have to do that. I could sleep on the sofa—"

"Mary." He frowned. "That thing is only three feet long. Just take the bed. The neighbors have let me sleep over before. They like me. I gave some free legal advice to their boy a few years back."

She glanced uneasily toward the bed, uncomfortable with booting him out of his own home. But he was thumbing through his cell phone, either oblivious to or ignoring her reaction.

He entered into a phone call, which surprised Mary a bit. He never made calls or texted when the two of them were together. She realized then how much she usually had his entire attention. The sudden loss of it threw into sharp relief the heady electric zing of having his full focus.

"Christo?" he said after a second. "Hey, it's John. Yeah. Right. Good to hear your voice too. How's Candy? No way, already? Hunter's a good school. Definitely. She gonna live at home? Probably for the best." He took a bite of food while he listened to the other man on the line for a minute, swallowing down half his water at once. "Listen, I called to see if there was a chance you'd break your no-work-on-Saturdays rule. Friend of mine got her house broken into last night and I was hoping to get her apartment secured by tomorrow. Nah, tomorrow is soon enough. With me, actually."

John's eyes met Mary's for a moment before they flicked away.

His cheeks went pink. "Yeah. No. It's not— Jesus, Christo."

Mary could hear laughter coming through the line loud and clear. John abandoned his dinner and rose up to stalk over to the kitchen window, looking out into the world. "Yeah, that should work. All right. I'll text you the address. Thanks, man."

John sat back down, digging into his food again, the tips of his ears and his cheeks still slightly pink.

"You just...handled that," Mary mused, setting her fork down.

"Oh. Right." John cleared his throat. "Sorry, I should have told you that my old friend is a locksmith and a carpenter, and he'll definitely get you fixed up."

"No apology necessary." Her eyes fell to the candle that sat between them. "I can't remember the last time someone just handled something like that for me."

"You've been running the shop on your own for a long time?"

Mary's eyes rose to his. This she could talk about, the history of the shop, not the way it was now, in shambles. "Almost six years. I inherited it, actually."

"Really?"

"Yeah. My aunt Tiff bought the building almost forty years ago. She lived in the apartment above and ran the shop below, just like me. She left the whole thing to me when she passed."

John blinked at her. She could see him filing away the information that she, in fact, *owned* that fancy Cobble Hill apartment, but thankfully that wasn't what he chose to comment on. "I'm so sorry for your loss. Was it sudden?"

Mary shook her head. "No. Cancer. We knew for a few years before she passed." She paused. She didn't have to tell him the rest, but for some reason, she felt herself wanting to. "She actually refused treatment there at the end. Her last year. She said that she'd rather live enjoying the time she had than hoping for a few more stolen moments." It was the choice that Naomi would never forgive her for. The choice that Mary had understood innately. "My mother seems to think that if Tiff had had a partner and a couple of kids, she might have chosen differently. Might still be with us." Mary shook her head. Being able to explain her mother's behavior didn't make it any less painful to endure.

"Wow," John whispered.

"Anyway. I still lived out in Connecticut in my hometown, but after I inherited the store and the apartment, it was a no-brainer to come here."

Plus, Cora's accident had happened and Mary had found that there was no way to stay away from Matty. But she didn't think that John needed to hear every sorry detail of how hard the last six years had been for her.

"Anyways, I took about six months to sort of revamp the shop and build up some inventory and renovate, and the rest is history."

"What did the shop used to be?"

"Oh, Aunt Tiff was a real free spirit. It was a hippie shop.

All the usual suspects. Incense, crappy essential oils, big turquoise rings."

"Tibetan carvings?"

"Exactly."

"Actually," John said as he squinted his eyes, "I think I'd been in there before. Sometime in high school. I was looking for a present for my girlfriend's birthday." Recognition sparked in his eyes. "Was your aunt blond? Like you?"

Mary nodded.

"Did she wear, like, muumuus?"

Mary nodded again, this time laughing and tearing up at the same time.

"I'm pretty sure I met her, then. She talked me into buying Julie this big necklace thingy."

Mary laughed again. "Tiff was quite the saleswoman." Her words were almost strangled, weighted down by the emotion they had to squeeze through to get out of her mouth. John had met Tiff. John and Tiff had spoken at one point. It was a gift to hear this story, like one more stolen moment with a woman whom Mary would never speak to again.

"I'm sorry," John said again, this time in a low voice. He slid his hand across the table and pressed his heavy fingers to Mary's forearm for just a sliver of a second.

"No, no, it's okay." Mary waved off his words. "It's just been a really long day."

They'd both eaten very fast, so John cleared their plates, found some clean towels and efficiently changed the sheets on his bed.

He tucked some clothes under his elbow and rocked on his heels, his hands in his pockets. "I just want you to know that this building is extremely secure. If you're worried, though, throw the dead bolts after I leave. And, as I'm sure you noticed, if you yell for me from my apartment, I'll definitely hear you next door."

He flashed her a quick, sheepish smile, and it made Mary want to weep. Even stuff that felt good felt bad. She was flayed open, tired and vulnerable and wanting every last drop of John's goodness right now. He'd sleep with her in the bed if she asked him. She knew it. He was just that kind of friend. He'd hold her hand if she wanted. He'd watch a movie and let her curl up on his lap like Ruth.

Different stages of life.

But it would all be because this terrible thing had happened to her shop. He was a good friend looking for any way to comfort her. She wanted John, wished very much that he wanted her too, but she wouldn't use this situation to her advantage. She refused to let the men who'd trashed her shop be responsible for her trashing her relationship with her new friend. Because if she took from him tonight, she was certain that things would be awkward tomorrow. She knew it.

And more than anything, she needed things to be okay when she opened her eyes in the morning. She wanted to feel refreshed and relieved to be where she was. Which meant that she needed to lean on John an appropriate amount right now. No matter the fact that his top button was loose and she really wouldn't have minded pressing her lips to that golden triangle at the bottom of his throat.

"Okay," she eventually said, somewhat scratchily. She wasn't sure if she was responding to what he'd said or if she was fortifying herself.

"You don't mind having Ruth around? She'll probably sleep up on the bed with you."

"Sounds nice."

He cleared his throat. "Okay. I'll come back in the morning. We'll get your door fixed." He lingered at his door for just a beat. "Good night, Mary."

"Good night, John."

CHAPTER TWELVE

TURNED OUT, SHE WAS both refreshed and relieved when she woke up the next morning. After John had left last night, she'd quickly showered, yanked her shorts and cami on and practically face-planted into the bed. She'd been out like a light. Around 2:00 a.m., a noise on the street below had woken Mary from a dead sleep, but then Ruth was there, stretched out along Mary's side, her tail flicking curiously, and Mary was soothed enough to fall back asleep.

But now it was 7:00 a.m., she had a full night's rest under her belt, the fog of yesterday starting to recede, and it was fully setting in just where exactly Mary was.

She was in John's apartment. John's *bed*.

It was such a strange intimacy to be in someone's bed without them. Almost as if they were there, or some shadowy ghost of them was there. Mary knew that John did not lay behind her on the other pillow, but she caught the faint strains of deodorant and detergent and aftershave, and she felt his presence anyhow. This was the ceiling that John looked at each morning. Those were the bonging, reverent tones of the church down the street that John listened to upon the turn of each hour. Here were John's worn cotton sheets, so soft after so many years of use.

It was like she was swimming in a sweatshirt of his, or wearing his reading glasses for a moment. It was delicious and disorienting.

What she wanted to do was make a cup of coffee in his decades-old Coffee Mate she'd spotted on the counter. She wanted to bring that coffee and sit for a while in John's bed. She wanted the sheets to pool around her hips. She wanted to pretend that John was just out grabbing some breakfast for them. That he'd be back in a matter of minutes. That he'd slide under the sheets with her and drink half her cup of coffee.

And because she wanted to do those things, Mary got out of bed instead. She knew that daydreaming any longer was bound to be bad for her health and bad for her relationship with John. So, she roused herself, brewed some coffee and took another quick shower. She changed into the dress she'd brought, and by the time the coffee was ready, her hair was already wispily drying, that was how warm it was today.

Mary sipped her coffee and picked up her towels from the bathroom sink. She wondered if he had a hamper or something she could put them in. Maybe some small part of her acknowledged that she wanted to snoop just a little bit, but most of her just wanted to not impose mess on her host's hospitality. Mary swung open the one door that he hadn't introduced her to, and sure enough, it was John's closet.

Her mouth fell flat open. She set her coffee down and pressed one palm to her racing heart. She didn't know why it hadn't occurred to her before. She didn't know how she'd missed this detail, so glaringly obvious now that it stared her in the face.

In John's neat, organized closet hung three crisply white button-downs. There, on a hanger, was his single midnight blue tie. Folded up on a pants hanger hung two pairs of black slacks. To the right were three small shelves where perhaps ten T-shirts were neatly folded, along with two or three pairs of leisure or workout pants and two pairs of shorts. On the ground was one pair of nice leather sneak-ers, one pair of running shoes and one pair of sandals that she could not, for the life of her, picture him wearing.

There were two more drawers where she imagined his underwear and socks to be, and she did not investigate to verify. She'd invaded his privacy enough. Mary stuffed her towels into the hamper and closed the door of his closet.

It was so clear to her now. God, she felt so stupid. And she'd internally accused *him* a million times of being judg-mental! John didn't dress this way because he was elitist and boring. He didn't wear the same pair of wingtips every day because he was clinging to the wingtip brotherhood that Mary had cruelly imagined him to be a part of. No. He dressed this way because he was a public defender and living in New York City on a public defender's salary, and didn't have money to burn on shoes and clothes and frivolity.

Mary looked down at the colorfully printed Diane von Furstenberg dress that she wore. Swishy, loud, flowery print. She'd bought it one day on a whim, because she'd felt like shopping. And then she'd judged John because he wore black and white every day.

Black and white never went out of style. They always made him look professional. He could wear it to work, on a date and, yes, even to a block party if he didn't mind look-ing a little overdressed. He wasn't boring. He was practical. And Mary wanted to kiss him for it.

JOHN KNOCKED ON his own door, still in his pajamas. He had his work shoes in one hand and yesterday's work clothes folded under his arm. He didn't particularly want Mary to see him in his faded blue pajama pants and undershirt, but he also hadn't wanted to change back into yesterday's clothes either. Maybe she'd be in her pajamas still and he wouldn't have to feel so bad.

Aaaaaaand, no such luck. Mary swung open the door— damn, she looked good in his apartment—looking freshly pressed and sparkly clean. She was all smiles and a hundred bright colors. John fought to not squint against the glare of her. The woman was freaking potent.

And nervous? John cocked his head to one side, still standing in the hallway, as he watched Mary's eyes track down his clothing, catch on his messy morning hair and skitter away.

"Morning!" she said, just a bit too brightly, even for Mary.

"Morning," he said back, his morning voice even scratchier than usual. "Bless you for making coffee."

"You want me to pour you a cup?"

Yeah, she was definitely nervous. She was standing in the middle of his living room holding one elbow and playing with the fabric of her dress with her free hand. Her eyes were on her pedicured toes.

"Uh, I'm gonna shower and change first, and then I'll grab some."

She nodded, turned on her heel and went to join Ruth on the love seat. John quickly showered and brushed his teeth. He was grateful he'd gotten a haircut this week because his hair parted perfectly and lay smooth. He quickly changed into his usual outfit, rolling his sleeves to his elbows and praying he wouldn't sweat through the shirt by noon. On a normal Saturday, one where he was headed to Estrella's house or getting work done at his kitchen table, he might have worn his old jeans and a T-shirt, but Mary looked like she was ready to strut down Fifth Avenue, and

John didn't think his ten-year-old jeans, white at the seams, would flourish by comparison.

He left the steamy bathroom and crossed to the kitchen area, pouring himself some coffee and going to sit with Mary on the love seat. It was a little bit too tight of a fit for two people and Ruth. The cat yowled at him when he sat on her tail. Ruth batted at his sleeve and rolled to her back, rubbing her face vigorously against his knee.

They both laughed, and John absently scratched at Ruth's belly. He was very aware of the fact that both he and Mary were staring at Ruth, almost as if they couldn't bear to look at one another. Why was this so intense? It felt like a morning after.

If it was just a feelings hangover, he could understand, Mary had had a hell of a day yesterday, but he couldn't help but feel like there was even more happening under the surface that he couldn't quite pin down.

He cleared his throat. "Are you hungry?"

"Yes," she answered immediately, making him laugh.

"All right, there's a few breakfast places around here and—" he squinted at the clock over the oven "—if we go soon, we'll probably beat the brunch rush. Oh, shit. Shitshitshitshitshit!" John stood up and strode across the room to the kitchen table, where he'd set his phone down when he came in.

"What is it?" Mary asked.

John groaned when he double-checked his calendar, even though he already knew what he'd find. "Shit. I'm so sorry, but I totally forgot to cancel on my dad. I had brunch plans with him. And now he's definitely already on his way to the place. It's too late to cancel." He looked up at Mary miserably. All he wanted was to have a casual breakfast with her. To stuff her full of hash browns and eggs and or-

CARA BASTONE 183

ange juice. He wanted to fortify her against the world. He
wanted to watch her sip coffee in that beautifully colorful
dress of hers and know that she'd changed into that dress
in *his* apartment that morning. Was that too much to ask
of the universe? Apparently.

Mary cocked her head to one side. "What's the big deal?
Do we not have time to get there or something?"

John felt something lift off in his gut. *We?* "You...want
to come along?"

"Oh." She instantly went bright red. "I didn't mean to
invite myself. I just thought— I'm hungry! I'm not thinking straight."

He chuckled at her flustered expression, her pink cheeks.
"No, that's okay. It just hadn't occurred to me that you'd
want to join us. But sure, yeah. It's a good brunch spot in
Brooklyn Heights, and then we can head over and get your
door fixed after."

"If you're sure I won't be intruding?"

John vehemently shook his head. If she was volunteering her company, he was accepting it. Time spent with his
father wasn't exactly the easiest, and John was extremely
eager to see how having a Mary Trace buffer would affect
the quality of it. Although...

"I should probably warn you..." He cleared his throat.
"I've never brought anyone to meet my father before, and
he'll probably think that we're together. No matter what
we say."

Mary traced a line of gray fur on Ruth's chest, her eyes
cast downward, her cheeks still pink. "I don't mind that."

John's mind instantly and ferociously examined that
phrase, turning it over, catching every possible light against
every possible surface. She didn't mind someone thinking

they were together? She didn't mind his father being obtuse and stubborn?

Or—*God*—she didn't mind the idea of the two of them actually being together? John's knees went jelly, and his fingers were cold in the pockets of his trousers. Was this an opening? His moment to tell her what he really wanted? What he'd tried to get himself to stop hoping for since the moment she'd walked out of that restaurant all those weeks ago?

"I mean," she continued with a shrug of one shoulder, "parents are going to believe whatever they want regardless of what you tell them. I've already told you how my parents are. Trust me, one suspicious father is nothing I can't deal with for the length of a single brunch."

Oh. The thing in his stomach that had lifted off touched back down to earth. Right. She'd meant that she didn't mind dealing with his dad. She wasn't over there fantasizing about being with John. She wasn't going to pretend, as John might have, that the two of them really were together, leaving his apartment on a hot July morning to do their due diligence with a monthly Saturday brunch with his father. She'd probably already forgotten the fact that she'd slept in his bed last night, or at least, she was glazing over it in her mind. She certainly wasn't marveling over the stunning newness of it, turning over last night in her heart like a stone, trying to figure out if it should be polished to a high shine or tossed back into the river.

He cleared his throat. "If you're sure, then we should get going."

"All right!" she said brightly, popping up and striding over to her bag. Her overnight bag. John nearly groaned aloud when he watched her pack her things up. His father was never going to believe they were just friends, not when she showed up on a Saturday morning at his side, an overnight bag on her hip. He was going to be denying Mary's place in his life for months with his father.

They walked to the train, and John waved through the window at his barber as they walked past.

"Is that where you get your hair cut?" Mary asked, stopping to look in the window.

"Uh-huh."

She studied the faded photos of which haircuts they offered up in the window. She pointed to one of the photos. "Is that the one you get?"

He laughed. "I don't actually choose from these photos. I just sit my ass down, pay the man fifteen bucks and leave when he's done."

She turned and studied his hair. John did everything he could not to shift on his feet, not to mess around with his hair. "It's a nice cut," she finally decided.

"Probably not the most fashionable way to wear my hair," he said, although he wasn't sure why he did.

She gave him a funny look, kind of like the one she'd given him when he'd first seen her that morning. Nervous, a little confused. "You don't care about that, do you, John?"

"No," he answered honestly. "It's important to me that I look presentable. But no, I'm not reading *Men's Vogue* in my spare time."

She laughed. "*Men's Vogue* is not a thing. And you always look very nice. Presentable. Your haircut isn't trendy, but it's classic. Never goes out of style."

He cut a look at her colorful dress, looking like it was just seconds from having been unwrapped from a department store bag. "You'd tell me if I start to look out of style or out of date?"

She cut a look back at him. "If you want me to."

"I want you to. How I look is important in that it's one of the main things that a jury assesses about me. At least at first. I have to strike a balance."

"You want to look like you take the whole thing seriously, but you also want to look like you're on their level. Not above anyone."

"Exactly."

They jogged down to the train and rode in companionable quiet. When she started fiddling with the zipper of her overnight bag, John had to fight the urge to take her hand in his. "You all right?"

She sighed. "I'm just sick over my shop. It took me so long to get it all fixed up just the way I liked it."

"We'll get it back to the way it was, Mary." And as soon as he said it, he knew he wasn't spinning a false hope. If he had to come by the shop after work every day for six months, he'd help her restore things.

"It's not that, really." She fiddled with the zipper more. "It's more that I'm trying to figure out *why* it happened. It doesn't even seem like anything was stolen. It's just this meaningless destruction."

She was zipping her bag an inch open and then closed over and over, and John just gave in to gravity. He reached over and took her nervous hand, sandwiched it between his two palms.

"I don't know what happened with your shop, Mary, but as a lawyer, I've had the opportunity to get into the minds of a lot of people who've done a lot of things." He sighed. "Have you ever seen a little kid stomp on a tulip? Or kick over someone else's sandcastle? Or have you ever seen someone smash a glass when they were angry? Sometimes it's just as simple as that. Again, we don't know anything yet about what happened or who did it, but I know that you might never have an adequate answer for why. Sometimes people just need to destroy something."

Her hand pivoted between his palms and her fingers laced with his. Suddenly, John wasn't just riding the train with Mary. He was speeding underground, every one of his fingers touching every one of Mary's with his other hand cupped over top, protecting this moment from the rest of the world.

"But they were coming up to my apartment, John. They kicked open the door right as the police got there. Were they—" She cut off for a second. "Were they coming for me?"

She was asking him if she was the something beautiful that was next on their list of things to destroy.

"Mary," he said carefully, turning on his seat so that he held her eyes as well as her hand. "I thank God that I don't ever have to know the answer to that question. Because the cops came, and you're safe here now. If they catch the people who did this, if they see their day in court, you might get some of your answers. But I really think it's important to concentrate on all the things that did happen instead of all the things that could've."

"What do you mean?"

"I mean that you responded correctly. You called the police, the police came and protected you and your shop. And now the cops do their job and you do yours. We move forward, get things back on track. That's what we can control."

She raised an eyebrow at him. "And if they catch the guys, then some defense attorney will do their job. Maybe even a public defender like you."

He fought off a wince. The system, all societal systems really, was so broken that oftentimes John felt his clients to be as much victims of circumstance as were the victims of the crimes in question. But there Mary sat, her store a smashed ornament on Court Street. "Mary."

She shook her sunny head of hair. "And that's the way it should be, I suppose." She sighed. "If they weren't defended, I might always worry they were wrongly convicted. And that's even more unfair than having your shop destroyed for no reason. I just want the right thing to happen. But nobody knows what the right thing is, do they?"

John blinked at her. She didn't want vengeance, he realized, the way so many victims of crimes wanted. No. She wanted justice.

She fell quiet and leaned her head back against the metal wall of the train, her eyes closed. She tightened her grip on his hand and John did the same. How could he make this woman feel safe again? How? A new door would help logistically, but he knew that this was so much more complicated than just getting a new security system installed. This was about Mary having faced something very ugly and trying to fit it into how she understood the world.

The train screeched into the station and Mary slid her hand out from John's. He shoved his hands into his pockets as they filed off, side by side.

"Look, Mary, are you sure you want to do this? Brunch with my father? It's pretty much guaranteed to be a weird time."

She nodded resolutely as they came aboveground. "I'm starving," she insisted with a smile.

John took a deep breath and led her into the restaurant.

JOHN APPARENTLY SPOTTED his father in the far corner almost immediately, and Mary expected John to lead the way through the restaurant. Instead, he pointed the direction and walked slightly behind her, one hand at the small of her back. It surprised Mary that he did this. He'd never struck her as a small-of-your-back guy before.

Then again, a month ago, she wouldn't have thought he was a sleep-on-the-neighbor's-couch kind of guy either, yet he'd gladly given up his space to make her comfortable. Which, she supposed, was exactly what he was doing right now as well. He was guiding her through the restaurant as a gesture of kindness, solidarity, maybe even protection? John might not be the most tactful guy in the history of the world, but Mary had never been more certain that he deeply cared about her well-being.

John Whitford Sr. rose up from his seat, tucking his phone into his pocket when they approached. His news-caster smile, which Mary was familiar with from all the campaign posters, was firmly in place. Not a millimeter changed in his expression, yet Mary was certain that she was seeing surprise on his face. His eyes darted from Mary to John, to John's hand at her back, to the bag on her hip. And then those eyes went back to Mary and just stayed there for a long second.

"Well, hello," he said, stepping around the table and holding out a hand. Mary was insanely relieved when all he did was shake it; she'd been dreading a back-of-the-hand kiss. "This is a surprise."

"This is Mary Trace. Mary, this is my father."

"Please, call me Jack," he said smoothly, adjusting his blue suit coat before he sat back down at the table.

"Nickname?" she asked, setting her bag down and sitting at the four-top.

"Only to those who know me best." Jack winked.

Mary smiled a little woodenly. He was just so smarmy. Nothing like John in the least.

She looked up at John and saw he was still standing,

staring down at the table in consternation. "There isn't a third place setting. I'll get the server."

And leave her there with Jack? Without thinking, Mary reached up and tugged at John's hand, her fingers automatically finding the warm part of his palm. "The server will be back in a moment," she reassured him.

When they'd been at the bar and she'd been trying to shake off his friend Hogan, John had read her eye contact exquisitely. He did the same thing now, his eyes searching her face. He nodded curtly and plunked down in the chair next to her, across from his father.

Jack cleared his throat. "I would have made the reservation for three if I'd have known…"

John waved his hand through the air. "It was unexpected for us as well."

Us. His hand on her back through the restaurant. John wasn't doing a very good job of explaining to his father that they weren't, in fact, together. The thought was giving Mary underboob sweat.

The restaurant was semi-fancy. It had golden lights and big-leafed ceiling fans spinning lazily. There was a river view out the back windows, and Mary's eyes followed a barge as it plodded its way downstream, the city fanning out beyond it. She wasn't sure if it was the heat, or the hell of a thirty-six hours she'd had, or the memory of her hand laced with John's, but Mary felt slightly dizzy.

She needed a second.

"I'm going to run to the restroom real quick."

She smiled at both men, pushed her chair back and moved quickly, and she hoped, gracefully to the restroom. She grabbed a paper towel, wet it and stepped into an open stall. Mary slapped it over the back of her neck and took a deep breath.

What a strange world. On a normal Saturday morning, she'd just be opening up her shop right now. Instead, she'd slept at John's house and was having brunch with his father. She looked for a second at her hands. Almost indulgently, she laced her own fingers together, the way she had with John on the train. He'd more than held her hand. He'd gripped her with one hand and sheltered her from the world with his other hand.

And touching was such a slippery slope, wasn't it? Because only moments later, he'd put one of those warm, calm palms at the small of her back. And moments after that, she'd slid her hand back into his, guided him down to his chair.

This was getting out of hand.

It was confusing to sleep in a man's bed and hold his hand and meet his father. And Mary wasn't even letting herself think about the two hugs they'd shared in her kitchen. She hadn't, even in the deepest parts of last night, allowed herself to mull over how it had felt to look up from her conversation with the detective to see John unexpectedly standing there, looking as curmudgeonly as always.

Talk about slippery slopes. Mary could practically feel herself clicking into skis, adjusting her goggles, pushing off down a black diamond.

"He said we're in different stages of life," she firmly reminded herself. "He doesn't look you up and down. He's not attracted to you."

Deciding that she'd feel better after she ate, Mary washed her hands, glared some sense into herself in the mirror and headed back out to the dining room. As she approached, she saw John and Jack in some sort of heated discussion. John leaned forward across the table while Jack leaned lazily back, a smug expression on his face. They cut off the moment they saw her and Mary was one hundred percent positive that conversation had been about her. No doubt John defending the innocence of their friendship. She could only imagine what he'd said.

As she slid into her seat, she couldn't help but smile down at the black coffee and fresh-squeezed orange juice that had been delivered to her place. John had the same at his. "Thanks," she told him.

"You're welcome."

They ordered breakfast, and when Jack handed over his menu, Mary felt his focus shift to her.

"So, Ms. Trace. Tell me about yourself." He turned those dark eyes on Mary, so unlike John's, and Mary couldn't help but feel as if she were on the witness stand. There was something in Jack's gaze that was complicated. He was reserving his judgment of her based on her answers to his questions, and he wanted her to know it.

"Jack—" John started.

Mary cut in. She wasn't scared of Jack Whitford. She'd been raised by Naomi Trace, for shit's sake. She knew how to deal with judgment when it sat down at the breakfast table.

"Well, I own a shop in Cobble Hill that does very well for itself. I've lived in Brooklyn for six years. I was born and raised in Connecticut, although I did my undergrad at Rutgers."

"And you're friends with my son." He stressed the word *friends* in a subtle yet accusatory way.

"Actually, I was originally friends with Estrella. She's the one who introduced us."

Just as she'd expected it might, the mention of his ex-wife altered whatever line of questioning he'd been headed down. He blinked at her for a moment. "Right."

"Whitford," a voice said over Mary's shoulder, and Mary craned her neck to see a very attractive man behind her. She blinked in confusion when the man's face was pointed toward John and not Jack.

It had never occurred to her that someone would refer to John as just "Whitford." It didn't suit him at all.

"Willis," John said in a voice as dry as it was gravelly. He wasn't happy to see this man. He cleared his throat. "Jack, Mary, this is my colleague Crash Willis. Crash, this is my friend Mary Trace and my father, John Whitford."

Mary noted that this time Jack didn't offer his nickname. He merely shook hands with this Crash person and eyed him appraisingly. "Colleague? You're also a public defender, then?"

Crash shook his head, coming to stand around the side of the table where Mary wouldn't have to crane her head to see him. "No. An ADA." He clapped a hand on John's shoulder. "John's worst nightmare."

John slid his eyes over to Mary and gave her a look so droll, so dismissive of Crash, so confident, that she almost aspirated her orange juice. She'd known that John was attractive, but didn't he know that a look like that was panty incinerating? No, she was certain that he did not know what effect this casual confidence had on Mary as he leaned back and said something snide to Crash.

The three men began talking and Mary found herself in a brief, potent daydream. She'd once imagined John scowling his way around a courtroom, dramatically pointing at the opposing counsel, passionately advocating for the wrongfully accused. But now she realized how ridiculous that assessment had been. John wasn't the type to strut and dramatize. No. He was too good for that, too confident in his own skills. John's main weapon, she was sure of it, would be ultimate, careful competence. He would lead the jury by the hand, calmly, confidently, without spoon-feeding them. He'd expect them to make the right decision, to side with him, because where else would anyone in their right mind side?

She imagined his midnight tie against his white shirt, his wide shoulders and wingtips, and his presence. John wasn't graceful, exactly. He took up too much stocky space for that. But he was incredibly self-contained, aware of his space and energy. And wasn't that almost the same thing?

Mary desperately wanted to observe him in court. To hear the rise and fall of that two-toned voice of his. She also knew just how dangerous that could end up being. This crush of hers would eat her alive if she ever got to see him work a room like that. Even now, him leaning irreverently back on two legs of his chair, some sly remark on his lips, Mary's feelings for him threatened to come tumbling forward. She desperately wanted to hold his hand again.

After a few minutes, Crash excused himself, his eyes lingering on Mary for a moment in a curious way, and then he was gone.

"Interesting guy," Jack said to John. Though he'd said only two words, Mary was certain that he'd actually said a mouthful to his son, à la Naomi Trace.

"Sure," John replied, craning his head as he looked around the restaurant. "Food's taking a long time."

"Seems to have his head on straight."

John didn't seem to be able to restrain his sigh this time. "Yup." He popped the *P*.

"Has a next step in mind for his career."

Ah. That was where this was heading. Compliments to this other guy's career were apparently digs on John's career. John didn't even bother responding.

Mary cleared her throat, finally drawing the men's attention away from one another and back to her. "Did it surprise you when John went to law school?"

Jack's eyes slid back to John. "No. But it surprised me when he decided to become a defense attorney."

John's loose confidence from moments before was dissolving into stiff-backed reserve. Mary intimately recognized the pose. It was what children did to block the judgment of their parents.

"And here we are again," John sighed in a near-sour tone.

"Why would it surprise you that he wanted to be a public defender?" Mary asked. To her, it made perfect sense that he'd land in that arena of the law.

"It wouldn't surprise me *now* that he wanted to do that," Jack told her, swirling his coffee in his cup. "But back then, I'd thought he might want to follow a little more closely in my footsteps. There were quite a lot of open doors he turned his back on."

"Jack," John muttered exasperatedly.

"John doesn't like open doors," Jack informed Mary cattily. "He gets pleasure from slamming them closed."

Mary looked back and forth between them, cataloging everything about Jack that she'd known prior to this brunch and everything she was learning at an alarmingly fast pace. She tilted her head to one side and took a sip of coffee, measuring Jack. What he was really saying hit her like a bolt of electricity.

"Hold on, you think John became a public defender just to spite you?" Mary asked incredulously, her amazement winning out over her propriety. Perhaps she'd only known John for half a summer, but she already knew just how ridiculously off base that assessment was.

Jack's eyebrows flipped upward at her tone. His mouth

twitched with a slight smile that Mary wasn't sure was altogether good-natured. He said nothing.

"There's no way that's true," she insisted. She felt John
shift beside her and she glanced at him but couldn't interpret his expression. She'd expected his eyes to be on
his father, but instead they were fairly well glued to her.
Mary studied him for a second, attempting to gauge if she
was making things better or worse. She couldn't tell. John
looked just as mixed-up as she felt.

"Why do *you* think he became a public defender?" Jack
asked with all the trap-laying of a seasoned lawyer. She
couldn't begin to guess what he thought of her, but Mary
knew that in the last few minutes, she'd sealed the coffin
on her first impression with Jack. There was nothing she
could say now that would change his opinion of her. She
also knew that with just the asking of that question he was
implying to her that she didn't actually know the answer.
That he knew better than she.

She straightened her back and set her coffee down, her
eyes on John's for a long beat before she turned back to
Jack and answered his question.

"Well, I don't know John well enough to really answer
that question in full. Decisions like that are generally layered. But come on, what the heck *else* was he supposed to
do with that huge, bleeding heart of his?"

As soon as the words were out of her mouth, Mary
understood the full truth of what she'd said. Jack's eyes
widened just a touch, and she felt her heart mirror his surprise. Because she was realizing—almost in real time—
that John, who'd once seemed so cruel and hard-hearted
to her, actually had the biggest heart of anyone she knew.

She thought of the cuddles he gave Ruth, the patient
game he'd played with Jewel. The man was a reluctant

vegan because animal cruelty trumped bacon in his play-book. He worked endless hours defending the lives of peo-ple who couldn't afford fancy lawyers. He truly believed in the system. He believed in the innocence of his clients. He saw the good in people. He'd dashed across town to hug her in her kitchen; he'd slept on his neighbor's couch for her. He'd held her hand on the train and called his friend to fix her door. She wasn't sure how she hadn't seen it be-fore. But frowny, scowly, grumpy, foot-in-mouth John was actually dangerously *sweet*.

She turned to look at him and wasn't surprised to see his eyebrows in a downward V as he looked back at her, the tips of his ears a rosy pink. He opened his mouth and closed it.

Jack started laughing and drew Mary's attention back to him. "I do believe you've struck John dumb. Not sure I've ever seen that happen before."

Mary cleared her throat, a little unsure of what to say next, off-kilter from her own realizations.

Jack smiled that smarmy smile as their waitress finally brought their food. He waited until she'd left to toss out his next topic of conversation.

"My son insists that the two of you are not involved," Jack said quasi-casually. "So, tell me, Mary. Why are you single?"

John groaned, but Mary just laughed. "Too young to be tied down," she answered playfully, although a splinter of regret wiggled its way between each word. Actually, she was single because the opposite was true. Too old for any-one to want to tie her down. For one anyone in particular. She smiled at Jack, hoping he couldn't see the rawness her own words had caused her. "Just a lone wolf, I guess."

John took the opportunity to jump in and change the subject. The rest of the breakfast, though by no means comfortable, flowed a bit easier, mostly thanks to John's constant corralling of his father into legal subjects and away from personal ones.

Still, by the time the two of them finally exited the restaurant, Mary couldn't help but dramatically sag against the side of the building.

"I warned you," John said with a shake of his head, a little twinkle in his eye. He reached out and plucked the duffel from her shoulder.

CHAPTER THIRTEEN

THE INSTALLATION OF Mary's new door went smoothly. Despite his familiar tone with John on the phone the night before, Christo was extremely professional with Mary. And after he installed the door, he even went around to all of her other doors and windows, making sure that she would be safe to sleep there that night.

He talked her through a quality security system to purchase and even agreed to come back and install it tomorrow if she wanted.

With a wave and smile, he was on his way back to his wife and kids, and then it was just John and Mary there alone again.

Though she'd slept well the night before, and it was only five o'clock, Mary felt fatigue starting to descend. The detective had called her that afternoon and told her that she could start cleaning up her shop Monday morning. She was both antsy to get started and preemptively exhausted at the thought of all the work there was to do.

"You all right?" John asked as he stood in the doorway between Mary's kitchen and living room, his hands in his pockets, his sleeves rolled to his elbows, concern in every line of his face.

"I'm fine. Just…overwhelmed."

She poured two glasses of lemonade and put one in John's hand as she walked past him to go sit on her couch.

John followed her and set himself down in the armchair. He leaned forward, his elbows on his knees. "Do you, ah, feel safe enough to sleep here tonight? I mean, without the security system installed yet?"

"No," she answered with a humorless laugh, figuring that John most likely knew her well enough at this point to know whether she was telling the truth or not.

"Do you want to sleep at my place again?" he asked in a voice that was much lower than his usual tone.

Yes.

"Oh, no, that's okay," Mary said in a rush. She didn't want him to ask her that. Couldn't handle him asking her that. Not when the answer was such a big fat, sparkling *God, yes.* Not when she was one hundred percent certain that in order to get herself to fall asleep in her big bed tonight, she was going to be pretending that she was in John's bed. One night had been an experiment. Two nights was suicide.

"Are you sure?"

"I've been texting with Tyler and Fin. Kylie's at a sleepover tonight, so they agreed to come sleep in my guest room. I'll have plenty of company."

"Right." John took a long drink from his lemonade, his eyes avoiding hers. "Great. That makes sense."

"They should be here in half an hour or so. Will you stay and have dinner with us?"

His eyes finally landed on hers again, and she was both warmed and shaken by how familiar his gaze had become to her. Those icy blues no longer seemed cold and distant to her; they seemed bright and defined by their almost unknowable depth.

"No," he said resolutely. "No, I think that if you're all right, then it's time for me to get back to reality."

He finished the rest of his lemonade in one huge gulp and rose to put his glass in the dishwasher. Mary was still sitting on the couch and sipping her drink, mulling over his definition of reality. The last day and a half certainly had an unreal quality to them, defined by pulsing, uncommon emotions. Everything from the fear during the break-in to the giddy euphoria of John's proximity had made her heart race. Maybe he was right. Maybe none of this was how real life was supposed to be. Real life was predictable and even.

Mary's real life didn't involve Ruth and it certainly didn't involve John's bed.

Maybe he was right. Maybe it was time to at least attempt to go back to normal.

She sighed and stood and met him at her front door. She refused to linger over the cheek kiss she gave as a goodbye to everyone special in her life. It was brief.

"Thank you, John, for everything." She opened her mouth to say more, but he shocked her by pulling her to him in one fierce, firm hug. It didn't last any longer than her cheek kiss had.

"There's no thanks necessary, Mary. Truly."

And then he was down her stairs and gone.

A FEW MORNINGS LATER, while Mary was vacuuming out broken glass from the rug at the front of the store, she heard a loud banging on the back door. Her fingers went cold and sweat popped down her spine. She scurried immediately to the counter where the register lived. John's friend Christo had installed security cameras on the exterior of the store, something she'd never had before, and the feeds fed directly to a small screen below the register. Mary let out a shaky, relieved breath when she saw it was just Estrella standing there, a picnic basket over one arm.

"I'm sorry I knocked so loud," Estrella said when Mary swung open the door for her. "I've never used this big metal door before."

Mary grimaced. "The front door is still out of commission, as you saw."

She didn't like thinking about the white spiderweb of cracks that rendered the glass door unusable.

Estrella stepped into the back room, her eyes on Mary, not on the mess that had been only partially cleaned up. She set down the picnic basket and simply held her arms out.

Mary went into the embrace without a second thought.

Estrella stroked Mary's hair and called her a sweet love while Mary cried. It didn't last for long, but it was one of those surprisingly potent cries, where each tear felt like it released a gallon of pent-up emotion. She'd barely realized how much she'd needed that, hadn't even hoped for that kind of release. When she stepped back from Estrella, she felt a hundred pounds lighter.

"I've missed you, Estrella."

"I've been keeping my distance over the last few weeks," Estrella said, smoothing her jean skirt. "I think I owe you an apology for the blind date situation."

Mary smiled. "It's okay. You were just trying to find a happy ending for people you love."

"I was being nosy and hopeful and we both know it." She glared at Mary.

Mary burst out laughing. "It's really okay."

"Are you sure?" Estrella's eyes searched hers. "Because you didn't call me when all of this happened." Estrella looked around at the store, and Mary was actually comforted by the pain that she saw on Estrella's face. The woman loved this shop almost as much as Mary did.

"It was a really crazy few days. I didn't really call anyone."

"You've handled all of it on your own?"

"Actually..." Mary kicked some broken glass away from
her feet. "John was here. He helped me through most of it."

There was a telling beat of silence, but Estrella seemed
to be committed to butting out of the situation. "Ah. I see.
All right, well, I brought you good wine and good cheese
and good bread. Let's have a picnic."

Mary laughed. "It's 10:00 a.m.!"

"All the better. If you can't drink wine in the morning
when you sit in the wreckage of your beautiful shop, then
when can you?"

Mary considered that a very good point. A few minutes later, they were arranged on the floor on a blanket
Estrella had brought, spreading goat cheese over baguettes
and sipping wine from plastic cups. Mary used the food
and drink as an excuse for why she wasn't adding to the
conversation, but really, it was because it was soothing to
hear Estrella chatter about the future of the shop. She had
all sorts of big ideas for how they could use the break-in
to start fresh, changing this or that, refocusing on certain
areas. Mary didn't agree with half of Estrella's vision, but
it was just so good to hear someone else dreaming and
planning and TLCing her shop.

It was a stark contrast to her parents' reaction. They'd
been horrified, of course, and Mary had had to talk them
out of coming in from Connecticut. But their reaction had
also been—surprise, surprise—judgmental. As if they
weren't shocked that it had happened because, after all,
Mary had been the one to choose to move to the big city,
where things like this happened every day. She had told
herself that they just hadn't understood the context.

John was lucky.

His mother fed Mary bread and fruit and cheese and wine and then packed up the picnic and set herself to work. The two women worked side by side for a few hours before Sebastian and Tyler showed up as they had yesterday as well. A few hours after that, Kylie was there, her bag tossed to the floor and determination on her face. She loved this shop as much as Mary and Estrella did, and the girl had seemed to take an almost personal offense to the destruction of it.

An hour after that, Via and Fin showed up, dinner in hand for all the workers. And after that, John. As they all had the day before, the group worked until well after the sun went down.

Mary fell into bed that night, exhausted, aware that she was going to have to do the whole thing again tomorrow. But not hopeless. Not the least bit hopeless.

IF SHE HADN'T been in the middle of a crisis, John might have truly considered going on another Mary fast. The first one hadn't worked well enough. The crush he'd been so deftly attempting to two-step around had finally sunk its claws in. Good and deep. A full-time dance partner.

It took Mary five straight days to get her shop back in order. And John was there five nights in a row, after work, Monday through Friday, to help. It relieved him to see that though she hadn't initially called any of her friends to come be with her the day after the break-in, they all showed up in spades to help with the reno of her shop. Sebastian and Tyler spent the most time, followed closely by Via and Fin. Kylie and Matty did their fair share as well.

But there was only so much that people who weren't Mary could really do. The actual cleanup of the shop wasn't going to take nearly as long as the paperwork that came with it all. John watched as Mary slowly got buried in the particulars of her insurance company. It was all made even more complicated by the fact that so much of what had been destroyed had been original pieces of artwork. Insurance would cover a lot of the damages, but not all. Mary was going to take a financial hit for this act of random cruelty.

It was the following Sunday night when John and Mary found themselves sitting at her kitchen table, wading through booklets of paperwork she'd printed out, John working from her laptop as well.

He figured that he probably had the highest tolerance for desk jockeying out of all of her friends, so he'd been the one to take on this particular aspect of aid. Meanwhile, down below, her shop was generally put back together. Just that morning Sebastian had overseen the installation of her new plate glass window in the front and Mary had started fresh with her late summer window display that afternoon. She'd reopen the store on Monday morning. Only a week and a half after the break-in. She'd be on quite a limited inventory for some time, but she'd be back to work at the very least.

John took another forkful of the room-temperature spaghetti and vegan meatballs in a glass casserole dish that sat on the table between them. A gift from Via, it had been heated up an hour ago, and he and Mary hadn't even bothered with dishes, just him eating from his end and her eating from hers.

John studied Mary for a long moment, her sunny head bent toward her phone as she looked something up on the insurance company's website, her face in repose. She'd worn a sundress again today. John wondered what she wore come wintertime. He hoped he'd be around to see it.

"Beer?" he asked her, knowing that Tyler had fully stocked her fridge that afternoon.

"Hmm? Oh, sure. I think I need a break, to be honest."

He'd been hoping she'd say that. John cleared the paperwork to one side and grabbed two beers from her fridge.

Mary looked absently out the window as she set her phone aside. He realized that there'd been no notifications barking from her phone all day. She hadn't texted anyone or taken any calls. He wondered if she was still searching for the right dating app. He'd been with her every night of the last week, but maybe she was waiting until things died down with her shop before she got back on the dating horse.

"You've been so sweet, John," she told him, breaking his reverie as she accepted the beer he held out to her. "Coming over here after work. Helping me with all this. So sweet."

He frowned. She'd never called him sweet before. Honestly, no one but Estrella had ever called him sweet in his entire life. He thought back to the brunch with his father that she'd endured last weekend. She'd said he had a huge, bleeding heart. She'd said it with absolute certainty, like she'd bushwhacked into the land where John's heart reigned and seen it with her own two eyes. He'd been mulling it over ever since then.

"I just want to make sure you're okay," he said, clearing his throat.

"I know you do." She seemed almost sad about that, looking out the window. After a minute, she looked back at him. "So, why *did* you choose to become a public defender?"

His eyebrows rose when he realized that she too had been thinking about that brunch with his dad. He lowered his eyes to his beer, took a long, thoughtful drink and leaned back in his chair. "Because the people who can't afford their own lawyers are disproportionately charged, sentenced and imprisoned." He paused. "I saw a map once, of New York City, and it marked areas based on wealth disparity and rate of incarceration. Lot of big old red zones in Brooklyn." He sighed. "I was in high school when I saw that. And, of course, I knew who my father was, even if he wasn't acknowledging me yet. He was already the DA of Manhattan at that point. The only interactions I had with him were watching him on the television giving half answers to reporters outside of courthouses about the black and brown people he'd just put behind bars."

Her eyebrows were the ones rising now. "So, he was right? You did become a public defender to spite him?"

He laughed and shook his head. "No, but I felt the weight of my bloodline on my back. I…believe in karma and I guess I wanted to somehow balance out some of what I'd seen my dad do. Even then I'd already gone to see him in court, even though I didn't introduce myself. And he's good at what he does. Really good. I just knew that I could be that good too, but that I could be on the team of the little guy. But it bothers me when he claims that I did it for him, because really, I made that decision for Estrella more than anyone."

"What do you mean?"

"My mother was the one who taught me to care about justice. About doing the most you possibly could for the people around you. To care about what was right or wrong. To never give up in the face of some all-powerful issue that you might never have a chance at correcting. It wasn't just my dad leaving us that made her that way. She was always taking me to marches and town hall meetings and protests. She was always petitioning the city for this or that. And meanwhile, making dinner for the people on our block who'd just gotten back from the hospital or had relatives visiting. You know, Cormac really did start out as our tenant. He'd just gotten out of rehab and his life was a mess. He'd had a fair amount of legal trouble himself, which, now that I'm thinking about it, probably motivated me toward becoming a public defender as well. He needed people on his team, just like so many people who'd reached a low point. He had next to no money and no real family to speak of. He once told me that my mother had let him live with us rent free for six months until he got back on his feet. Just to help him out."

"Wow."

"And then, once he'd started paying rent and had a good job working construction, they fell in love. A lifetime kind of love. But she wouldn't have ever had the opportunity for that kind of love if she hadn't taken a chance and opened her door to him in the first place. Those were all things that I learned just from being her son."

Mary was quiet for a long moment. "I can see why it would bother you that your dad assumes the public defender choice was in reaction to him. Kind of a conceited assumption."

John chuckled. "Well, my dad is kind of a conceited guy. He has a lot of trouble seeing an issue for anything beyond what it means for him."

"You don't have that problem." She lowered her chin to her palm and smiled. Her face was friendly, but John felt pinned in place by her expression.

"Not usually. No." His voice was slightly hoarse. He cleared his throat. He wanted to change the subject. "You know, Mary, I've been wondering about something my dad brought up at that brunch."

"Oh, yeah?" She straightened and dropped her eyes to her beer, as if she already knew what he was going to ask.

"Yeah." He cleared his throat again. Okay, he was just going to ask it. He'd been wanting to know pretty much since the day that he'd met her, and he hadn't been able to figure it out just from getting to know her. He was going to have to flat out ask at some point, so why not now? He ignored the hollow banging of his heart and just jumped right in.

"Mary, why *are* you single?" John cleared his throat again. "I mean, I know my dad is an asshole for asking that the other day, but it actually sparked a curiosity in me. It doesn't, ah, really make sense to me that you haven't met someone."

He could only imagine that her answer would be laden with someones she'd dumped for some reason or another. He couldn't imagine reality being any other way. Because once a man actually got a chance with Mary Trace, John couldn't imagine him doing anything but holding on to it with both hands. And superglue. A nail gun, if necessary.

Mary twisted her mouth to one side and stared out the window again. "I kinda thought that Estrella would have laid it all out for you already."

"Hmm? You've talked to Estrella about it?"

Mary blushed a little and nodded, twisting her beer one way and another. "Remember at the block party? When you asked if I was desperate?"

John groaned and knocked his forehead against the table with a comical whack, making Mary burst out laughing. "Please don't remind me of that," he pleaded. "That was the second worst thing I ever said to you."

He looked up just in time to see a vulnerable expression flit across her face, but then she sequestered it immediately behind a smile. "It's okay, John. You wanted to know why your mother was pushing the issue so much. If I wasn't totally desperate for dates, then why the heck was she foisting every man in Brooklyn into my lineup, right?"

He nodded, still feeling an uneasy, humiliated chagrin at his own clumsy rudeness.

"Well, the answer is that about two weeks before that, Estrella came over to my shop around closing time and we ended up having dinner together up here in my apartment. She asked me the same question that you just did. And though we've been casual friends for a long time, it was the first time we'd ever had a real heart-to-heart like that. It…affected her, I guess."

Mary twiddled with her beer some more and John stayed quiet.

"I told you that I came back to Brooklyn after my aunt died. I didn't mention that it was right after my best friend died as well."

Her eyes met his, and John's heart constricted. He leaned forward across the table, wanting to take her hand but scared to break the spell. "Oh, Mary," he whispered.

"It was terrible. She was killed in a car accident. Drunk driver hit her. She was Matty's mom. Sebastian's wife."

"Oh." John blinked. "I guess I didn't realize that Via wasn't Matty's mom."

"They make a good family," Mary agreed. "The three of them. But yeah, Cora and Seb were married. When Aunt Tiff died, Cora wanted me to come to Brooklyn, but I wasn't sure if I could handle coming here and taking on the store. I was working at an interior decorating company in Connecticut, still trying to make my mother happy in at least one regard." Mary smirked. "But after Cora died, I realized that here was where I needed to be. Sebastian and

Matty were so lost without her, and I had an apartment and a shop just waiting for me. I just had to come and do the hard work and claim it. So, I did. I threw myself into getting the shop off the ground, and I threw myself into their lives. Both Tyler and I did. That's how he and I became friends. And for a long time, it was just Tyler, Sebastian and I. A trio."

She smiled fondly, and John had to ask. "Were you ever, ah, *with* either of them?"

Mary laughed and rolled her eyes. "That would be a no. Sebastian had been my best friend's husband and a total mess besides. And Tyler is…not quite my style. Lovely, wonderful, perfect for Fin, but not for me. I don't think either of us ever even entertained the idea."

John nodded, feeling foolish for the swamping relief of knowing that she'd never been kissed by either of her stupidly good-looking best friends. "So, you're saying that for a long time dating just wasn't on your radar?"

"Yeah. I was just too hurt. Losing Aunt Tiff was like losing a parent and a best friend all in one. And losing Cora was like losing a best friend and a sister all in one. I felt friendless and family-less."

"Even with your parents?"

She made a face as she weighed her answer, tipping her head from side to side. "I'm the odd one out with my parents. If anything, my relationship with my mom got even worse after Tiff died. Tiff was really the referee between us. Even more than that, she was the translator. She understood us both so well that she could explain us to the other one. We've never quite gotten back to that point, my mother and I, being able to understand one another."

Mary sighed. "So, yeah. I had the shop to tend to and Sebastian and Matty to take care of. And then when things started getting better with them, I had Tyler and Sebastian to keep me company. A few years after Cora died, I did start dating again. This guy named Doug."

Doug. What kind of shit-stupid name was Doug? Doug sounded like a telemarketer. He sounded like he wore dirty socks too many days in a row. Doug sounded like a boring, lifeless prick.

John cleared his throat, a little surprised at his own internal vehemence. "Ah, what was Doug like?" He didn't give a shit what Doug was like, but he had to say something.

Mary cocked her head to one side and thought for a minute. "The life of every party. Gregarious. Friendly. Great first impression."

Oh. Great. Literally everything that John wasn't. "Uh-huh."

"Cora would have sniffed him out immediately."

"Sniffed him out for what?"

"For being disingenuous. She had a bloodhound nose for that kind of thing. And a zero-tolerance policy. She would have known right away that I shouldn't have wasted my time on him." Mary sighed. "I thought he was great, however. He was just so *fun.* And it had been a long time since I'd had any fun. And it had been a long time since I'd had somebody who thought I was the most special, out of everybody else. Cora and Tiff, they were both such persistent cheerleaders. They both thought I was the crème de la crème. They gave me such confidence on a daily basis. I hadn't realized I'd missed that until I had Doug in my corner."

John took a long drink of beer. "So, what ended up happening?"

Mary sighed. "He was sleeping with someone else." Her eyes dropped. "A woman in her young twenties. Though he's my age. They're still together. I see them around Cobble Hill sometimes and… You know, I wish it didn't bother

me, I really do. But it just does." Her eyes stayed down. "I'm
not naive. I know that it's considered weird in our culture to
be a woman and thirty-seven and childless and never been
married. But I wasn't interested in either of those things in
my twenties. A lot in part because of how much my mother
pressured me to *get* interested." She laughed, somewhere
between humor and disdain. "Cora had Matty, so I had my
baby fix whenever I wanted it. And then, out of nowhere,
both Tiff and Cora were gone, and life happened, and grief
happened, and then Doug happened, and here we are, six
years later, and I'm finally starting to think about wanting
a partner and find out I'm over the hill."

I was expecting someone younger.

If there'd been a dagger sticking out of her kitchen floor,
John would have gladly tossed himself onto it. What an absolute asshole he'd been. He hadn't realized, until this second, how personal that comment must have felt to Mary.
He'd known it was a stupid thing to say, but she was just so
gorgeous, so undeniably perfect in his eyes, that he hadn't
thought there was even a chance that a comment like that
might actually stick to her. But there, with the first words
he'd ever said to her, he'd shredded through one of her
most tender insecurities. She'd been left by her boyfriend
for a younger woman, and John's words had made her feel
as if there was something wrong with her for looking for
love in the latter half of her thirties. Which, honestly, he
didn't think there was anything wrong with that no matter what the reason. But certainly not when the reason was
dealing with the deaths of the two most important people
in one's life.

God. No wonder she'd left the restaurant. No wonder
Tyler had given him a hard time at the party. No wonder

she'd crossed John off her list. He considered it a holy miracle that she'd even let him back into her life as a friend.

But that was just who Mary was. She was not a grudge-holder. And less than two months after he'd told her she was too old and stabbed her straight through the heart of her self-consciousness, she'd defended him to his father, asserted the existence of John's apparently huge heart.

She was the one with the heart. Even after everything she'd been through, she was still handing that heart out in handfuls, welcoming people into her life, smiling at block parties and cheek-kissing her friends.

Shit. John felt a crack run down the center of his chest, like the first telltale sign of an earthquake. He pressed the heel of his hand to his heart, trying to hold himself in one piece. This couldn't be happening to him. He couldn't crack open for Mary. He couldn't fork over his entire heart to her right at that moment, over spaghetti and paperwork. Not at the exact same moment he'd realized just how badly he'd screwed everything up.

He'd known that he'd been rude enough for her to lose interest in him immediately. He hadn't realized that he'd deeply wounded her. So, what was he supposed to do now, his stupid, beating heart in one hand and Mary's in the other?

He couldn't fall in love with her right now. He just couldn't. It was insanity. It was a road to nowhere.

It was unstoppable.

John took a deep breath he hoped didn't sound as shaky as it felt. He still held the heel of one hand over his breastbone, trying to keep his heart where it belonged, in his own chest. "Mary, I just want to be clear here. I should never have said—"

She held up a hand, stopping him. She'd never done that

before. It was a forceful gesture that belied the seemingly easy smile on her face. "Let's not talk about that. Yeah. It's been a rough week and a half. And my brain is fried from all the paperwork and the conversation. Let's just not re-hash the night we met. Okay?"

He closed his mouth, opened it, let his eyes slide from her face to the hand she still held up. That hand was certain, steady and telling him in no uncertain terms that what was done was done. Of course it was. How many chances did John expect to get with the world's most lovely creature? He'd had it, and he'd blown it. And now all he could do was staple his chest closed and keep his heart in its home. All he could do was try not to hurt her again.

He nodded and cleared his throat. "All right."

She dropped her hand. "I think I'm done with paperwork for the night. I was thinking of watching a movie," she said brightly. "You're welcome to stay if you want."

"No," he said gently as he shook his head. "No, I should go." Always he was telling her no when he just wanted to say yes, yes, yes. But just as when she'd invited him to stay and have dinner with Tyler and Fin last weekend, he'd known that it was time for him to go home and remember who he really was. What his life really was. To refamiliarize himself with the constraints on his actual world. So much of the time he spent with Mary had a Technicolor, dreamlike quality to it. It wasn't good to stay there too long. It made his real life seem too drab and harsh by comparison.

He wanted nothing more than to sit next to Mary and watch a movie on her couch. Which was why he dragged himself up, said a quick goodbye and hauled his ass back to Bed-Stuy. An hour later, his hair wet from the shower and Ruth on his lap, John finally let out a deep breath, the one he hadn't quite been able to catch sitting at her kitchen table with her. And it was then, in the safety of his own solitude, that he let his chest fully crack open. That he let himself feel it. Truly feel it.

CHAPTER FOURTEEN

THE NEXT FRIDAY, Richie and John packed up a little bit earlier than they might have normally done and walked to Cobble Hill from the public defender's office. They'd been invited, by Tyler of all people, to an impromptu party at a bar around the corner from Mary's shop. They were going to celebrate her shop's return to glory and all the hard work that Mary had put in over the last few weeks.

Richie had jumped on the invitation surprisingly fast. "I'm sick of seeing Hogan at Fellow's every Friday night," he explained to John as they weaved their way through the traffic on Court Street, ignoring the honking horns. It was the height of summer, but New York was rewarding good behavior with a surprisingly fresh night. There was a breeze and low humidity, but John knew that by next week, this would only be a fond memory. Even the sidewalks would sweat while the city baked from the inside out the way it did every August.

"I thought people generally liked being in the proximity of their crushes."

Richie rolled his eyes and stepped aside to let a flock of pretty women in high heels scuttle past. "That's only if there's a possibility of the crush being requited. It's hopeless in my case. And Hogan gets a kick out of winding me up."

John frowned. "You think he knows how you feel?"

"I know that he knows. It's an ego boost for him."

John frowned, disliking Hogan even more than before. "That's screwed up. You're a person. He shouldn't treat you like that."

Richie shook his head and tossed his arm around John's shoulders. "If only all the straight boys were as nice as you, John."

John cocked his head to one side. "Must be something in the water lately. You're calling me nice, last week Mary called me sweet and the week before that she said I had a big heart."

Richie's eyebrows rose. "And this surprises you?"

"I'm more used to being categorized as a dick, to be honest."

"Yeah, but that's only how you come off, John. It's not who you really are. Anyone who really knows you figures that out pretty quickly. Hey, Beth!" Richie called suddenly, waving as he spotted their friend across the street, two blocks down from the bar.

She waved and waited for them to cross the street to her. "You guys headed to Mary's party too?"

"Are you?" John asked in surprise.

"Yeah." Beth bounced on her toes. "I've been stopping into her shop since the break-in to make sure she's doing all right, and she invited me to come along."

John couldn't stop his incredulous chuckle, the shake of his head. "Jeez, is there anyone that woman can't charm?"

Beth gave him a funny look. "She's good people."

"Yeah."

For some reason this put John in a sour mood as they stepped through the door of the bar. Everyone loved Mary. It was almost unavoidable. He'd never even stood a chance, apparently. The fact that the bar was sexily lit and serving up sixteen-dollar cocktails and the dance floor was filled to the gills with Brooklyn's version of glitterati made him even more sour. Seeing Beth Herari, a cop whom he deeply respected, buying expensive drinks on a cop's salary all because Mary was so damn lovable somehow just pissed John off.

The woman was a siren. John was sick of smashing on the rocks.

He wished he could fall in love with someone who stirred tolerable, manageable feelings in him. He didn't want this nervous-boisterous-hysterical-more-more-more desire for Mary. He didn't want his stomach to swoop down to his pockets when he caught a flash of her sunny hair across the bar. He didn't want the bass of the music to fade away as he let himself be drawn toward that sunny flash. He didn't want to immediately lose track of Richie and Beth as he shouldered his way through one corner of the dance floor. He didn't want the fastest route to Mary to be a straight line. He wanted to be detached enough to float over to her eventually, cool as a cucumber. Instead, he was suddenly standing in front of her, not seconds after he'd entered the bar, his breath in his chest, looking down at her while she looked up at him.

"Hi!" She tossed her arms around his neck and didn't kiss his cheek. Instead she pressed her cheek to his, and his nose somehow found its way into her hair.

She must have come up on her toes to hug him because a second later she was back to her normal height and beaming up at him.

"Whatcha drinkin'?" she asked.

"Oh." John frowned and squinted at the bar. He happened to catch the eyes of both Sebastian and Tyler, who were leaning against the bar and watching his interaction with Mary. "I haven't decided yet."

"Whatever it is, put it on my tab, okay?"

He frowned harder. "Uh—"

"Seriously, John. I couldn't have gotten through this without you. Let me at least buy you a drink."

"Okay," he agreed, knowing there was no point in arguing with her. And knowing that there was less than zero chance that he was going to put anything on Mary's tab.

"Oh. Beth's here!" Mary stepped around him and weaved her way through the crowd.

John stood there a moment longer, looking down at the space where she'd just been. He gave his head a shake and headed toward the bar. He shook hands with Sebastian, who looked like he was restraining a smile, and then Tyler, who looked torn between amusement and suspicion.

"All good?" Sebastian asked, clapping John on the back.

John had actually spent a fair amount of time with these two men over the last few weeks and he liked both of them. Except when they were teasing him over his apparently obvious reaction to Mary's proximity.

"Yeah," John said gruffly, catching the pretty bartender's eye. "Long week, though. You?"

"Pretty good, pretty good," Sebastian said a little distractedly.

"Yeah. Me too," Tyler chimed in, sounding just as vague.

John paid for his beer and turned back to face the dance floor, the way the other two men were. He immediately understood their distracted manner. Via and Fin were on the dance floor, cutting two very good-looking rugs.

"Where's Matty tonight?" John asked.

"Got a babysitter for him," Sebastian responded, tearing his gaze from his girlfriend. "Actually, Kylie is looking after him."

"Can you believe that?" Tyler chimed in, looking a little bemused with the development. "Eight months ago, I wouldn't have even trusted her to be at home on her own. And now she's looking after your kid."

"She's come a long way since Thanksgiving," Sebastian agreed. "And I gotta admit, it's nice to be out on the town with you and Mary at the same time. I don't actually remember the last time that happened."

"She seems happy," John said, unable to keep himself from finding Mary in the crowd, laughing at something Beth was saying and lighting up her corner of the room.

"It takes a lot to keep Mary down," Seb replied. "She's been through a lot over the last few years. As traumatic as these last few weeks have been, they weren't anything that she couldn't handle."

"She's strong," John agreed. "When you first meet her, you kind of think that someone that happy must be out of touch or naive. But she's not. She works hard to be happy. I respect that."

Tyler's beer came down on the bar as he turned to John. "All right, I'm just gonna say it. You avoided answering at Mary's party, but come on, it's obvious. You're into her. She's in— Mmph!"

Fin, possibly with the accuracy of a clairvoyant, had appeared at Tyler's side in just enough time to clap a hand over his mouth, tugging him toward the dance floor. She hissed something that sounded suspiciously like "Let them figure it out!"

But John couldn't be sure. He cleared his throat and finished his beer a lot faster than he'd anticipated. He chanced a quick glance at Sebastian, who looked about as uncomfortable as John felt. "He has a big mouth," Sebastian said after a beat. "But he means well. And he wants what's best for Mary."

"So do I," John said carefully.

Thirty quiet, awkward seconds passed.

"Look, man," Sebastian said. "If you—"

"Who the hell is that?" John interrupted as soon as his eyes zeroed in on the redheaded male model talking to Mary. John might not have cared if not for the fact that Mary seemed about three shades duller than she usually did. She seemed almost to have shrunk in on herself, one hand gripping the other elbow and her eyes on this stooge's chest instead of his face.

A woman with beautiful black hair down her back tucked under the redhead's arm and Mary seemed to wilt even further.

John put the pieces together just as Sebastian answered.

"Aw, shit. That's Doug. Her cheating ex."

"And that's the woman he left her for?"

"Yeah. *Shit.* I told Mary that we should choose another bar, but she insisted on this one. It's one of her favorites, and she said it would be like Doug won if she avoided it."

The guy, Doug, was giving Mary a casual wave and pulling his girl to the other side of the bar. He passed by John, and John had to resist the juvenile urge to stick out one foot and make Darling Doug face-plant on the parquet.

John's eyes went immediately back to Mary, who was now talking with Richie, her mouth pulled down and her eyes sad.

"This," John said in a voice he pretty much only used in a courtroom, "is completely unacceptable."

And he meant it. With every beating centimeter of his cracked-open heart. Seeing Mary with her light this dimmed was a crime against nature. Against the universe. It defied the laws of physics and made John's skin crawl.

Doug, he couldn't care less about. Doug could jump in

a lake. It was Mary that John was concerned about, and before he thought twice about it, John slapped his empty beer bottle down on the bar and strode through the crowd with one thought and one thought only pulsing through his mind along with the beat of the music. He was going to turn Mary's light back on if he died trying.

WELL, THAT SUCKED.

It was only a matter of time before Mary ran into Doug in the bar he considered to be his home turf. It just blew that it had to be on *this* night, when she'd been so determined to have a good time. Her shop was put back together and glittering again, she was caught up on her insurance paperwork and all of her closest friends were here, celebrating with her. It should have been a night for the ages. Instead she was just feeling defeated.

These were the moments she missed Cora the most. Cora would have told Doug to take a long walk off a short pier. She would have intercepted him before he'd even approached Mary. She would have told him that the bar was closed for him tonight but try again later, ding-dong.

Instead, Mary had been caught unawares when she'd heard his voice in her ear. She'd been unable to think of anything to do besides play nice when she'd turned and seen Doug and Anna. And now all she felt was the dizzying absence where her good mood had just been. It had been a hard two weeks, so there were plenty of bummed-out feelings to rush in and set up shop.

Richie, sensing her change in demeanor, leaned in to ask her something, but the music was too loud and she couldn't hear him. Beth too was looking at Mary in concern. Mary glanced over one shoulder and watched as Doug pulled out a barstool for Anna, boxing her in against the bar the way he used to do with Mary.

It hit Mary that it wasn't just Cora that Mary was lonely for. She was lonely for a partner. She wanted someone who knew the whole story. Her whole story. She wanted someone who was going to crawl into bed with her tonight. Someone who would lower the stakes on her sadness and discomfort. Because what would this fleeting feeling really matter if there was someone who could roll his eyes at Doug? Who made sure her drink wasn't empty. Who looped an arm around her neck from behind and whispered in her ear. Who wanted to leave with her.

She just wanted someone to want to leave with her.

"Mary?" Richie was saying, obviously concerned, leaning toward her.

She shook her head, horrified when the backs of her eyes started to tighten. No. Not now. No crying right now.

"Mary," a different voice said into her ear. An exhilaratingly familiar voice. A two-toned voice. A voice made up of two voices mixed into one. A man with so many different facets he couldn't be contained by one sound.

He didn't loop an arm around her neck the way she'd just been fantasizing about, but he did put two of his heavy fingers on the inside of her elbow and press in, just a bit, to get her to turn toward him.

And turn she did.

She'd never seen this look on his face before.

Oh, Christ. She knew that look. That was a you-might-not-know-it-yet-but-I'm-kinda-the-man kind of look. That there, ladies and gentlemen, was a knee-knocker.

Mary gaped up at him. What was happening? Was he about to kiss her?

The hand that was on the inside of her arm trailed down

until palm met palm. He gave her a gentle tug that had her half stepping into him.

"Dance with me," she watched his lips say.

Dance with him? With John? Never in seven million years would she think that John Modesto-Whitford was a bar dancer.

"Oh," she said, thrown off by his unexpected mood and still conscious of Doug on one side of the bar. "I— I don't know." She dug her heels in.

He didn't tug her again. Instead, he let her hand drop, but he held her eye contact. Those formerly icy eyes of his were backlit with some confident determination. For just a moment, she could see his resemblance to his father— in a good way. She could see that buried somewhere inside John's gorgeous heart was a man who knew how to get what he wanted. And what he wanted, apparently, was Mary on the dance floor.

That intoxicating stare still glued to hers, John took one step back and then another. He was five feet out from her, on the edge of the dance floor, his eyes reeling her in. A familiar song played, the beat dropped, John's feet stepped to one side, his shoulders hit on the downbeat, one finger came up, he pointed at Mary.

Her mouth dropped open.

He was dancing for her, in a room full of people, tempting her to come play with him. He pointed at the ceiling next, back to her, his hips getting in on the rhythm. He was a sexy-dorky dancer, confident and—*gah*—smiling.

It was the smile that did it. He had a smile that utilized every single one of those lines on his face, this time for good. It was like every inch of his face smiled, not just his mouth. Sure, his teeth flashed and his lips widened, but it was his smiling eyes, his squinched-up nose, his ears lifted a quarter inch that really did Mary in.

Unexpected, a laugh of pure joy bubbled up out of her. Mary threw her hands over her mouth, laughing with radiant happiness as she watched John two-step for her, his eyes still on hers.

It wasn't a choice, really, it was just what happened next. Mary took four little steps and ended up in John's arms, the momentum of her impact spinning them one hundred and eighty degrees. He took her hand and spun her out and then back in so that she landed against him again, their hip bones clacking and their unabashed grins only six inches apart.

She remembered how much she loved this song and threw her arms around his neck. His hands were firm at her hips and back, guiding her against him. She'd danced with both Tyler and Sebastian before, but never like *this*. It wasn't indecent, definitely PG-13, but he held her closer than he ever had before, the sexiness offset by the grinning, ebullient joy emanating from him. She knew then, she just *knew*, that John wanted nothing more than to be close to her. At this moment at least, she was getting what she wished for, a man who wanted to be next to her.

God, that felt good. He dipped her a little, swung her a few feet farther into the crowd, away from the edge. The other people on the dance floor were simply blurs of color and clothes. Only John was in high-definition. The ever-present shading on his jaw, the undone top button of his shirt, the springtime blue of his eyes, the visible heartbeat in his throat.

It was there that her eyes bottomed out. On his pulse point. On the physical evidence of John's heart. The grumpy-sweet heart she had such an unbelievable soft spot for. She planted a palm against his throat as the beat to the song intensified, all the dancers really caught up in it now. He hadn't taken his eyes from hers for minutes, but now his gaze truly searched her.

She finally tore her eyes away, only to rest her cheek on his sternum and experience his heartbeat from the main source. His heart hammered under her cheek. He wanted her. He'd crossed a crowded room to be closer to her. He held her.

And with every speeding beat of his heart, every slide of his feet, every press of his hands at her back, John gave Mary everything she needed.

THERE WERE SOME nights that made John feel like a middle schooler again. In a good way. And this was one of them. His and Mary's moods had apparently been infectious to their friends, and the rest of the time in the bar, even with Dud Doug's presence looming in the corner, had been a deliciously good time. Now it was past midnight and the group had left the bar, walking in a large, too-loud crowd down the sidewalk toward Mary's house.

John just smiled to himself as they all chattered loudly, laughing hard and leaning on one another.

Mary had invited everyone back to her place for a nightcap, and she led the group at the front. John was the caboose, locking her downstairs door after him and watching everyone file up her stairs to her apartment.

He felt the tug to be close to her. He'd wanted to walk next to her on the way home. But he knew just how obvious a move that would be.

The ten minutes of delirious dancing they'd shared had been hands down in the top three experiences of John's life.

It was no surprise to him that all their friends had pretty much gotten a contact high.

He was almost, *almost* positive that she'd felt the exact same way. That she'd clutched him as tightly as he'd clutched her. That, tonight at least, she was kinda giving him a green light.

John mulled over this green light. He'd been given green lights before, of course. But usually in a club, on a dance floor, when all there was next to do was get the heck to one of their houses and take their clothes off.

Mary's green light had been in her smile, her cheek over his heart, the way she'd lingered at his elbow while the group had laughed and joked and bought more drinks.

Now they were back in her apartment, Mary passing out drinks and filling bowls with pretzels, and John couldn't tell if the green-light moment had passed or not. He figured it would be a hell of a lot easier to figure out if there weren't so many friends sitting in between them on the couch.

And it would probably be easier to figure out if Tyler weren't suspiciously looking at John pretty much every time John looked up. John couldn't help but shake his head and muffle his laughter into his hand. Yeah, didn't seem like tonight was the night. Unless he outwaited everyone else, but that seemed dangerously forward.

Besides, Richie and he had been at work at 7:00 a.m. that morning. Richie's eyes were closed as he leaned back in the armchair, a beer listing in one hand.

Mary swooped over and righted the beer, squeezing Richie's knee. "You wanna sleep in the guest room tonight?" she asked Richie. "You look mighty sleepy."

And there was John's answer. He highly doubted that Mary was planning on having John stay over in her bed if she was inviting Richie to sleep in the next room over.

The disappointment he swallowed down was eased by the surprising amount of relief that came with it. He didn't want things to move too fast with Mary. He didn't want to ambush her. Tonight had been the first night that he'd felt something shift between them, and to try to sleep with her would almost be doing that shift a disservice. He didn't want to whip the tablecloth off the table just to watch the china smash on the floor. He didn't need to rush her. Or himself. Or the moment.

It meant that this green light he'd been getting wasn't for sex, and it wasn't for tonight. This green light was a green light for possibility, for hope, for maybe. And that was good enough for John. More than good enough.

He wouldn't have minded, though, an opportunity this evening to put his cards on the table, but he didn't particularly want to put his cards on the table in front of Tyler.

"No, no, you sweet, wonderful woman," Richie said, blinking his tired eyes up at her. "I think I'm just gonna catch a cab back to my neighborhood."

John inwardly nodded. That was his cue. There was no way that Richie was actually catching a cab. The two of them were MetroCard people. Which meant that Richie was going to get on the train at 1:00 a.m. alone, and John didn't like that. Richie was thin and trendy in his tailored suits and had been pushed around on the train before. But never when John was with him. Which was why John stretched, finished the glass of water that Mary had presented him with a few minutes earlier and rose to his feet along with Richie.

"I'll share with you," John said with a yawn.

Richie looked mildly surprised, as did Tyler and Sebastian, but John ignored all three of them and just went to put his cup in the dishwasher. When he turned, he was alone in the kitchen with Mary, who was standing a few feet away, her back against her countertops.

She was worrying her bottom lip between her shiny, white teeth, and her eyes were stuck somewhere around the top button of his shirt. Her body language spoke of nerves and uncertainty, but it was nothing like she'd been with Doug in the bar. Everything about the hands she fluttered around the skirt of her dress and the skate of her hair over her shoulders said *I like this*.

"I'm gonna head out," he told her unnecessarily, considering he'd just announced the same thing to the entire living room. *I want to stay*, his eyes said.

"I guess it's getting pretty late," she replied. *What just happened between us at the bar?* her eyes said back.

"Crazy night, huh?" *I don't know, but I liked it.*

"The good kind of crazy." The strap of her sundress fell over one shoulder and John reached forward to slip it back up her arm. He took longer than strictly necessary, smoothing it over her soft skin with his heavy fingers.

The voices in the other room crescendoed into a playful argument, and once again, they were reminded that they weren't alone.

She frowned. "I needed a good kind of crazy night, to be honest. I'm going to visit my parents tomorrow afternoon through Monday, and I'll need all the fortification I can get."

"I wish you didn't have to dread going there so much," he said in a low voice. *I wish I could come with you*, his eyes said.

"I know," she said softly. *God, me too*, her eyes said back.

He smoothed the strap of her sundress one more time, and Mary quickly rose on her toes to kiss his cheek. She placed her hand in the middle of his chest to steady herself and John knew instinctively that she was seeking his heartbeat again, the way she had when they'd been dancing.

Little did she know that she didn't have to hunt it down, that it was already hers.

CHAPTER FIFTEEN

NAOMI TRACE'S ATTIC was not the kind of place that had secrets. Every single item was perfectly labeled in a perfectly sized storage Tupperware. Besides, the things she stored up there only took up half of one wall anyhow. The woman was infamous for ruthlessly tossing away keepsakes. Mary had clear memories of her mother nodding briskly at an A-plus essay Mary had brought home and then promptly tossing it into the recycling, seeing no reason to keep it.

Which was why Mary was surprised to find herself in the attic on Sunday morning, her mother pointing to which clear plastic boxes she wanted Mary to shuffle around.

"That one there. No. Wait, it's the one next to it. Yes."

Mary blinked at the perfect label that ran along the side of the box. "Photographs," it read.

She was surprised to see that her mother kept a miscellaneous box of photographs in the attic because Naomi was strictly a photos-belong-in-photo-albums sort of person. Mary had thought that all the photos her parents owned were currently neatly shelved alongside their John Grisham and Agatha Christie collections in the living room.

But here she was, staring down at a plastic shoebox filled to the brim with old photos.

"Here," her mother said impatiently, gesturing for Mary to hand over the box. Then she reached her hand out and firmly helped Mary step out of the maze of other boxes.

Mary had a flashback to her childhood. Slipping at the edge
of a pool and falling into the deep end before she could
swim. There was the sun, too bright through the water,
the white-bubbled panic slipping out of Mary's nose and
mouth. And then there was her mother, a firm hand under
Mary's armpit, yanking her up and out of the water, pushing her wet hair back from her face. "You're all right," her
mother had said. Firm, clear, comforting.

"Come, sit," Naomi said now in that exact same tone
of voice.

Mary was a little mystified. Her mother was perched on
top of one of the larger storage boxes, moved to the side
just enough for Mary to have room as well. This was unusual. When her mother had asked her to help her in the
attic, Mary assumed that there was some baking utensil or
end-of-the-summer decoration her mother wanted brought
down. It hadn't occurred to her that her mother had wanted
to sit in the warm attic and look at forgotten photos.

Mary sat down. Naomi was already digging through
the box.

"Wait!" Mary stilled Naomi's shuffling fingers with a
hand and reached in to pull out some old Polaroids she'd
never seen before. "Is this the day I was born?"

"Oh, don't look at those. I look like I'd been baking on
the side of the road for a week."

But Mary was stunned. Her mother never looked less
than perfect and here she was, so young it was almost painful to look at her, her blond hair messily pulled back, her
cheeks red, her eyes swollen, staring at a little bundle in her
arms in utter amazement. She'd never seen so much emotion on her mother's face before. Mary dug through and
found two more. All of them were obviously taken within
the same few minutes. Because there was Mary's wrinkled,

mutinous face poking out from the hospital-issued pink-and-blue blanket, there were Mary's parents beaming for the camera, looking like they'd been through the ordeal of a lifetime. And then, lastly, there was a photo of Naomi asleep with Mary on her chest. Naomi's hair was sticking out every which way, her mouth gaping open she was sleeping so hard.

"I can't believe you let someone take these," Mary mused. Naomi did not approve of candids.

"I didn't *let* anyone take them. Tiff insisted." Naomi sniffed.

"She was at the hospital the day I was born?"

Naomi nodded. "She told me I'd treasure these photos one day."

"And now they're in a box in the attic," Mary said drily.

"Well, I didn't throw them away, did I? Here, put them back in. It's not what I'm looking for."

Mary did as she was told, but she watched her mother carefully. It was true that her mother hadn't thrown the photos away. In a house with not an extra ounce of fat on its bones, maybe that really did mean that, in a way, her mother treasured these photos. It just also meant that her mother couldn't bear to display a photo where she didn't look Hollywood-ready. Mary reflected on all the photos in frames downstairs, family portraits taken by professionals, all of them. And even the ones in the albums were all particularly flattering to her mother.

There was a series of photos lining one hallway of her mother's pageant days. Glamour shot after glamour shot of Naomi looking utterly stunning, even with her outdated coif of a hairdo and sparkly, outrageous gown. The only photo they had of Naomi showing any emotion other than a beatific smile was the single photo of the Miss Connecticut crown being placed on her head. Tears streamed down her face as she stared in shock out at the crowd. Mary had seen plenty of media representations of pageants in which the winner delivered a sort of practiced shock in order to endear herself to the crowd. But anyone who looked at that picture would know that Naomi truly hadn't expected to win the title.

"Here," Naomi said, shoving a small stack of photos into Mary's hand. "This is what I wanted to show you."

Mary thumbed through the photos. They were of her mother and father at various events. A couple shots from some barbecue, a few from school events of Mary's. Mary was in early high school in these photos, her swim team sweats in one photo, a homecoming dress in another photo. Then there were two of her mother on her own, candids. Her slicing carrots for a salad in one of them and her in the driver's seat in the other. In neither photo was she aware she was being photographed.

"Tiff took these ones too." Mary knew instinctually.

"Tiff took pretty much every photo in this box." She sniffed again. "She just loved taking bad pictures of me."

Mary squinted up at her mother in surprise. "You think these photos are bad?"

To Mary's eye, her mother looked relaxed and natural in the candids, as lovely as always. In the posed ones at the school events, her mother looked just how she'd remembered her looking from that time period. Nothing bad about it.

"You don't see the crow's-feet and the turkey wattle?" Naomi asked caustically, pointing at the virtually nonexistent flaws in each photo. "My hair was starting to change texture, and I had no idea how to style it yet. Hence that hairstyle. I'd started to gain weight too. Hadn't yet joined Weight Watchers."

"Mom..." Mary trailed off, shocked at her mother's harsh appraisal of herself, at the realization that her mother kept a box of ugly photos tucked away in the attic.

"I wanted you to see these, Mary. Do you have any idea how old I am in these photos?"

Mary's stomach dropped out, through her feet, through to the second floor of the house, and kept on going down to the kitchen and straight into the basement.

"I see you've upped the ante and decided to start harassing me with visual aids." Mary was proud of herself for keeping any of her anger and outrage and pain out of her voice.

"I'm not harassing you, Mary. I'm trying to show you something. I wasn't that much older than you in these pictures."

These pictures, where, in Mary's eyes, her mother looked utterly lovely. Yes, she looked forty years old. But she *was* forty years old. Where the hell was the crime in that?

Her mother stood suddenly, grabbing Mary's hand and practically dragging her down the attic stairs. They wound up in the hallway with the pageant photos. Naomi pointed with a manicured, shaking finger at the beautiful twenty-year-old girl there. "You know the story, Mary. You know how your father and I met."

"Dad was a dorky broadcasting guy up in the booth that day," Mary said in a voice shaky from her adrenaline, from her disbelief at what was happening. "He fell in love with you during the competition and found you in the dressing room after you won. Brought you a bouquet of crappy daisies and asked you on a date."

"Your father was *not* dorky," Naomi claimed. "He was just...less fashionable than some other men. But he was kind to me. And sweet and smart."

"Mom!" Mary took her mother by the shoulders. "How come you can't defend yourself the way you just did Dad? He was *totally* a dork. A computer nerd. You are beautiful in these pictures." Mary held up the plastic box. "Why can't you see reality?"

"You have no idea, Mary," Naomi hissed. "You have no idea how long it took for us to get pregnant. You have no idea what it's like to really watch your body change with age. You have no idea—"

"You were twenty-five when you got pregnant! What do you mean it took you a long time?"

"All our friends were pregnant already. Your father and I took years, Mary. Do you know how humiliating that was? How happy I was when you were finally here?"

"No, Mom. I didn't know any of that. Because you've been hiding the evidence in the attic like a crazy person." Mary shook the box of photos. "I really can't believe this is happening. You think that showing me these photos of you at age forty is going to scare me into running out and getting married and knocked up? You think I don't know what it's like to watch my body change as I age? You think I'm the exact same as I was in my twenties? You think I haven't changed my style and my beauty care regimen and my exercise routine? I'm aware of my age, Mom. It just doesn't affect my happiness."

Naomi pinched the bridge of her nose. When she spoke, it was with a shaky, synthetic patience. "Your father fell in love with me because of my looks, Mary. At first, at least. When we'd been married and been through life together, he loved me for different reasons. He's loyal and faithful and sweet. But it was this that got him. This." She pointed again at the beautiful girl in the pageant photos. "And I'm begging you to keep an open mind."

"An open mind?" Mary asked in confusion. "An *open mind*? You've got to be kidding me. You're telling me to have an open mind? You're the most closed-minded person in my life!"

Naomi reeled back. "I'm not closed-minded. I'm realistic. And it wouldn't kill you to get your head out of the clouds."

"Mom, I don't have my head in the clouds. I started a business over from scratch. A successful business. I've almost doubled my savings in the last three years. I've picked up and rebuilt in just a few weeks since the break-in. I have valuable relationships."

The doorbell rang and both Naomi and Mary jumped. The two women froze, eyeing one another.

A flash of guilt crossed Naomi's face.

"Who's at the door?" Mary asked suspiciously.

"I asked you to keep an open mind. Please, Mary."

"Mom. Who. Is. At. The. Door."

"I'll get it!" her father yelled as he came up the basement steps, oblivious to the civil war that was breaking out in his own home.

"Mom—"

"Carver!" her father said in surprise at the front door, two rooms over. "What a surprise! Come in!"

"Sorry," said a familiar voice that made Mary's stomach plummet. "I didn't mean for this to be a surprise. Naomi invited me for lunch."

Mary took her mother by the elbow and dragged her up the second-floor stairs to the room where Mary was staying.

"Carver Reinhardt? *Carver Reinhardt?* Is this a joke? You invited my high school boyfriend here as a setup?"

"Open mind," Naomi replied in a voice that was significantly less sure of herself than it had been for the last few minutes.

Maybe that was because Mary was actually letting her fury and outrage show on her face. She was done holding it back. She turned to her overnight bag and began stuffing her belongings back into it.

"What are you doing?" Naomi asked. "You're *packing*?"

"I'm leaving. I'm going out the back door, and I'm getting on the train, and I'm going home."

"Mary, you have a guest! You can't just—"

"No. You have a guest. And I suddenly understand everything. I see exactly how little you think of me, Mom. How little I matter to you. I'm nothing because I don't have a man or children. To you, I'll always be half a person until I have those things."

"Mary—"

"No. Don't tell me that I'm wrong. I know I'm right. Otherwise you wouldn't have invited Carver Reinhardt into my childhood home in some sort of sick setup."

"Oh, forgive me for setting you up with a handsome, successful man."

"I do not forgive you. For any of this. And I won't be returning until I have an actual apology from you. Until you understand that I am a person. Full and complete. And so was Tiff. And if I choose to be buried between strangers, that does not make my life less significant than yours. This is beyond fucked up, Mom. I love you, but this is untenable. If you ever want to call me or come to Brooklyn, I'll take the call. I'll never turn you away. But I will not be calling you, and I will not be coming back here. Not until you apologize for this."

Mary zipped her bag with a flourish, kissed her mother on the cheek and sneaked out the back.

THE NEXT DAY as he strode down the hall toward his office, John's mind was deeply mulling the details of Hang Nguyen's case. Her trial had been in full swing for the last two work-days, and after Hang took the stand this afternoon, things would come to a close. He knew better than to have high hopes, but what he did know was how hard he'd prepped for this case. How many extra hours had gone into it. And how much he truly, deeply believed in her innocence. He'd just come back from a meeting with her where they'd gone over her testimony, and if John did say so himself, he thought that her quiet, polite, eloquent honesty had a good chance of pushing her into the jury's hearts.

John had his eyes on the email he was reading on his phone. It wasn't the motion in his office that suddenly drew his eyes upward. No, it was the sudden *lack* of motion. John had the immediate impression of deer frozen in the head-lights as he, one hand on the doorknob to his own office, looked up and absorbed a tableau of *oh, shit*.

Because Richie Dear was halfway crawled over top of his own desk, his shirt partially unbuttoned, his hair and reading glasses equally askew. And underneath Richie was a man. A man by the name of Crash Willis.

John took in the scene before him, outwardly placid, inwardly befuddled. Crash Willis? Richie was making out with *Crash Willis*?

John said nothing aloud, just let his eyes fall to the floor, where he saw a mess of papers and office supplies that had obviously been swept aside in the heat of the moment.

"You better not have broken my stapler again," John said, almost nonsensical in his battle to understand what-ever the hell was happening in front of him. "I had to buy the last one with my own money."

"Ah. I'm…gonna go." Crash's voice was shockingly

hoarse. Devoid of all bluster and irritating smugness that was usually sewn into the very fabric of his being.

John had the wherewithal to step into the hallway, give the two debauched men a moment to right themselves in their place of work. He heard a few rushed, intimate whispers, the rustle of clothing, and then Crash was practically sprinting down the hall, the back of his neck an electric pink.

John stepped back into his office and shut the door behind him. "Crash Willis?"

"Oh, shut up," Richie said, sitting on his desk with his legs swinging in childish circles, one hand sliding down his face.

Richie looked just as chagrined as he did pleased with himself. Rumpled and confused and...thrilled.

"Richie," John tried again, striding over and taking his friend by the shoulders. "Crash Willis."

Richie laughed. "I know, John. I was there."

John folded back into his own squeaky swivel chair and rested his temple on his closed fist, studying his best friend. "You're what? Sleeping with the enemy?"

Richie's feet swung in wider circles. "We haven't quite gotten there yet, but I sure as shit hope that's where this is heading."

John groaned. "First a cop and now an ADA? What, do you have some sort of Darth Vader fetish or something?"

Richie laughed, and it was full of relief. John wondered if Richie had thought that he'd actually be mad at him over something like this. Richie looked so relieved that John was joking with him.

"Crash isn't on the dark side. He's just a douchebag. A little lost."

"I didn't even realize he was gay," John mused.

"Yap. I've known since he started working here." Richie studied his fingernails for a few seconds. "He doesn't hide it. You'd know that if you ever did more than trade barbs with him."

John frowned. What a weird freaking morning. Because here he was, feeling guilty about being a dick to Crash Willis.

"I...thought you had feelings for Hogan Trencher."

Richie frowned, like he couldn't believe that John could be this dense. "Hogan's straight, John. Get over it."

John was quiet for a minute, musing inwardly on how complicated it would be to have feelings for someone who didn't, couldn't ever, have feelings for you. He wasn't exactly sure what was going on with Mary, but at least he knew that she found him to be handsome. There was that little nugget to cling to. He momentarily considered a world where Mary wouldn't ever even find him attractive. How painful that would be. It was in that moment, no matter how John personally felt about Crash Willis, that he decided to be happy for Richie.

"Are you two dating?" he asked.

Richie grimaced. "I like him. He likes me. He's not fooling around in anyone else's office for now. Is that enough of an answer, Mom?"

John stared unseeingly out their shoebox-sized window. "Crash Willis," he said again. "Well, I'm happy for you, Rich. Mazel."

"Oh, John, you sentimental sap."

Richie's voice dripped with sarcasm, but John could read between the lines and see how much his approval meant to Richie.

"Besides," Richie said, sitting on his chair and swiveling toward his desk, "now you and I are even."

"Even?" John exclaimed. "For what?"

He put his foot on the side of Richie's chair and swiveled him back around. He'd never in his life been caught necking in the office.

Richie had a sly smile on his face as he clicked a pen with annoying slowness. "For that show you put on at Mary's party."

John frowned. "There was no show."

"Oh, for the love of God, John, there was a show. A freaking *hawt* show."

John folded his arms over his chest. "We were just dancing."

"*That* wasn't dancing. That was foreplay."

John grunted. "Foreplay implies there was play. And there was no play. I went home with *you*."

"Foreplay doesn't imply immediate play. And don't tell me you don't have plans to see her again soon. Don't tell me you left her house without securing a playdate."

John grunted again. He actually had left the house without securing a date. A fact that now seemed like a grossly incompetent oversight. Why hadn't he shot his shot that night? Why hadn't he laid it all out on the table for her? For God's sake, the woman had pressed her cheek to his heartbeat. She'd smiled into his smile. He should have asked her on a date. He should have trusted the signs. John eyed Richie. "You, ah, think she was interested?"

Richie's chin dropped two inches as he shot John a look dry enough to turn a grape into a raisin. "John" was all he said.

John's foot bounced. "It's just weird is all," he eventually said. "I've spent so much time convincing people that there was nothing going on between us. My mom. My dad. Her friend Tyler."

"Convincing?" Richie asked pointedly.

"Yeah. Everyone was skeptical."

"John, have you ever stopped to really think about what that actually means that no one believed you? Not your mother, your father or her friend Tyler?"

"What do you mean?"

"I mean that there's a reason you have to *convince* them that you two weren't together."

John cast his eyes down, frustrated and embarrassed. "Because my feelings for her are so freaking obvious."

"No. Well, yes. But, jeez, you're dense. That's not what I'm talking about. So, listen closely because I'm only going to lay this out once. Nice and clear." Richie clicked that pen again, faster this time. "All these people, including myself, think that you and she *make sense together*, John. When they ask if you're together, what they're really asking is *Why not?* Because they look at you and they think, *Yup, there are two people who could really make a go of it.*"

John stared at Richie. His friend was rarely this fired up outside of a courtroom. And apparently he wasn't finished. Richie barreled on. "I truly think that you might be the only person on earth who looks at the two of you and thinks you're not good enough for her. People aren't thinking about you having to save money to take her out to a fancy birthday dinner. They aren't imagining her in her Tom Ford shoes avoiding the loose nails in the floor of your tiny apartment. They aren't wondering why in God's name she would slum it with you. You're the only one who asks those questions."

John marveled inwardly at how well his best friend knew him. He opened his mouth to speak, but Richie kept going. "The rest of the world looks at you and thinks, *Look at those two bighearted, kind, hardworking people. Don't they make a handsome couple?* So, why in God's name can't you see it, John? Why? You're the only one left fighting this thing when you're the one who actually wants to be with her. And don't deny it, John. I've seen it on your grumpy-ass face. You look at Mary like all the light in the world originates from her. Stop telling yourself you can't have her. Just stop it already."

John just stared at Richie.

Richie glared back.

"Wow," John eventually said. "I was gonna wait until she got back from Connecticut. But… I guess I'll go call her?"

"Good." Richie nodded his head, swiveled back to his desk and made several decisive swipes with his pen on whatever paper was in front of him.

John stepped out into the hallway and strode all the way down to the window at the end of the hall. Brooklyn sprawled out a few floors below. He watched people scurrying from place to place, guzzling water and trying to stay out of the blazingly direct sunlight.

"Hi," Mary answered on the first ring.

"Hi," he answered slowly, partly because his stomach was swooping and partly because she sounded different than she normally did. "I was going to wait to call you until you got back to Brooklyn. I didn't want to interrupt your family time—"

"You're not interrupting. I came home yesterday. Unexpectedly."

He frowned. She sounded dull. Hurt. "Is everything all right?"

"Ugh. Yes. I just had a fight with my mother, and I needed to get back to reality before she got too far into my brain."

"I'm sorry, Mary. I've definitely been there with my dad before."

John wanted to know more. He wanted her to unload on him so that he could help carry some of the heaviness he could hear in her voice. But he had to be in court in twenty minutes, and he assumed that she was at work as well. Besides, maybe that was better done in person?

He took a deep breath.

"I was calling because I was hoping to see you this week. Are you free anytime? I could just pop by the shop."

She paused, his stomach plummeted.

"Will you make me dinner instead?" she asked.

His stomach took off like a Fourth of July firework. He actually felt a little ill with how fast it swooped. Making someone dinner was a date-like thing to do.

"I know it's presumptuous to invite myself over to your place," she said. "But it's been a hell of a couple weeks, and I just want a beer and something simple to eat, and I want to pet Ruth."

John blinked. He…kind of couldn't believe his ears? Because this was Mary Trace on the other end of the line. She was asking for Ruth. And for a simple meal. And his studio apartment. She was asking him for a whole lot of things that he could absolutely give her. What a freaking world.

"I— Yes. Of course. Anything." He cleared his throat. "What day are you free?"

"Thursday."

John felt a bite of disappointment. It was only Monday and that felt like an interminably long wait to him. He imagined a movie star happening into her shop tomorrow, falling in love with her on sight and whisking her away to Ibiza.

No. It was just three days. He could be patient. And besides, this was his moment. This was what Richie was talking about. John had an opportunity to tell Mary exactly what he was hoping to have happen between them.

And that was all he could really do, lay it all out there for her. If he was lucky, she'd want something similar to what he wanted. But he was never going to know if he didn't take this chance. If he didn't treat Thursday like the stroke of heavenly opportunity that it really was. He could be bummed that he wasn't going to see her for half a week, or he could treat this as if the cosmic cogs of kismet had all ticktocked into perfect sync in order to create this little window of a moment.

Thursday. What *couldn't* happen on a Thursday? Thursday was a gift from God.

"Perfect." He checked his calendar. "Eight o'clock work for you?"

"It does."

"See you then, Mary."

"See you then, John."

MARY HUNG UP the phone and stared unseeingly down the cereal aisle.

"This ain't your living room, honey," a woman said at Mary's shoulder, muscling past her with her grocery cart and giving Mary the stink eye for blocking the way.

Mary shook her head. Right. She was in public. Her heart was galloping, she had underboob sweat and she was in public.

The last twenty-four hours had been a mess. Mary had yo-yoed from outrage to pain to everything in between.

Mary pushed thoughts of her judgmental mother from her brain and thought instead back to Friday night. John's confident hands at her back, her cheek over his heartbeat.

She grabbed cereal off the shelf and tossed it into her cart, moving to the next aisle. She thought of John smoothing the strap of her sundress over her shoulder, the weight of his hand at her collarbone.

"John likes me," she told herself.

I was expecting someone younger.

Different stages of life.

Interestingly enough, when Mary heard those two phrases this time, they were in her mother's voice in her head, not John's. Those two simple sentences didn't paint a very flattering picture of how John felt about her. But she was done letting those handfuls of words outweigh everything else. The way he'd smiled at her on the dance floor. His hand at her back when she'd met his father. His fingers laced with hers on the train. He'd given her his bed, for goodness' sake.

And the hug. She could finally let herself think of the way he'd held her in her kitchen after the break-in.

It had been medicine, that hug.

Maybe she'd even known then, that things had changed between the two of them. Because those kinds of hugs were rare. And he'd given her two of them.

John liked her. Maybe, technically, she wasn't quite sure if Thursday was a date or not. And maybe, technically, she still hadn't seen his eyes track her up and down the way they had that waitress, but he'd danced with her like he'd wanted her. And that was enough for her. For now, that was enough.

CHAPTER SIXTEEN

IT WAS WEDNESDAY night at 5:00 p.m. that John was nearly brought down to the sidewalk in a sweaty, joyful hug. Hang Nguyen's mother, Cuc, was sobbing into John's shoulder and leaning her whole weight on him.

"Mom!" Hang said, trying to pry her mother off of her lawyer, but it was no use. "I'm so sorry, Mr. Modesto-Whitford."

"It's okay," John said, a blisteringly big smile on his face as he patted Cuc's back. "I know exactly how she feels."

Hang broke into a smile herself, still nervous at the edges, tight with emotion even as she blinked with relief. She gave up on trying to pry her mother away from John and just plunked herself down on the nearest bench. "Oh, my God," she muttered into her hands. "I can't believe it's over."

"It's officially over," John repeated, his smile threatening to helicopter him straight into the ominously gray cumulonimbus that was creeping up from the edge of the horizon.

Cuc said something to Hang in Vietnamese.

"Yes, Mom. You're right. Come sit." Hang patted the bench beside her and finally Cuc released John's neck only to give her daughter's neck the same treatment. The two women hugged and cried, and John gave himself the small pleasure of soaking it in. There were so few moments like this one as a public defender. When the world quieted and the only thing buzzing through his veins was good news.

All charges dropped. The jury had found Hang Nguyen innocent on all counts. This good-hearted young woman would not be serving time she didn't deserve to serve. She would not be spending time and energy and worry inside the walls of that courthouse. She would sleep well tonight.

And so would John.

The three of them walked to a meeting room in the public defender's office, where he explained things in full to them, walked them through the next steps. They spoke for another twenty minutes, exalting in their shared victory. And then the mother and daughter went on their way. He left a note for Sarah on his way back to his office. She didn't accept presents of any kind from her staff, but she had a hell of a thank-you card headed her way.

Richie had already left for the night, so the office was quiet and hot as John sat there, buzzing, looking at the ceiling.

He'd won.

Hang had won.

He'd fought tooth and nail and saved years of this girl's life. This, right here, was worth every late night, every moment of worry. Every taunting comment from his father.

There was a knock on his door and John lifted his head just as Crash Willis stepped inside.

"Willis."

"Whitford." There was a long pause and then Crash gave him an unexpected smile. "Reynolds told me about your win just now. Congrats."

John's eyebrows rose. "That's…generous of you."

Crash's eyes flickered over to Richie's desk. He took a deep breath and gave a shrug. "I think we got off on the wrong foot all those years ago. I'm not a bad guy. And for the record, I didn't mean to crash your breakfast with your father the other day. He's kind of a personal hero of mine, and I just...couldn't help myself."

"My father is a personal hero of yours."

"He's an exceptional lawyer."

Well, he figured that Crash's apparent idolization of a man with an uncompromising hardline on crime was Richie's problem. All John had to do was play nice. He surveyed Crash's face, which looked like he was smelling something bad and pretending he wasn't. John internally sighed.

"I take it you're here, in my office, attempting to make amends, because you have a crush on my best friend."

Crash's cheeks went electric pink, but he didn't drop eye contact. "I think my odds with Richie are gonna be drastically improved if you and I aren't enemies."

John could respect that logic. Especially as his mind flicked momentarily over to Tyler. He actually might have to follow Crash's logic himself pretty soon. "We're not enemies. And as long as you treat Richie well, then we're not going to have any kind of problem."

Crash wilted a little bit, but it seemed to be with relief. "You're not going to whisper in his ear about what a snake I am?"

"Richie's a smart person. If he wants to date an ADA, that's his business."

"You say ADA like your father isn't the most famous district attorney in the United States."

John shrugged. "Justice is supposed to be blind. I try not to inflate my father's ego too much."

"Fair enough," Crash said after a moment, as if what John said actually made sense to him. "Congrats, though, on your win today. I mean that. There are too few days when I feel the way you looked when I walked in here."

John stood, draped his messenger bag over his body and held out a hand to Crash. "True."

The men shook hands and parted ways in the hallway.

The adrenaline from the win still buzzed in John's veins and even the interaction with Crash was buoying him. He was happy for Richie, to have found someone who liked him enough to make amends with an enemy on his behalf. He was blindingly happy for Hang and her mother, who he hoped were going to celebrate tonight.

There was sparkling water in his blood, and suddenly, John wanted to celebrate tonight. He wanted a freezing-cold drink. Or two. Or three. He wanted to share this bubbling, blazing feeling with the world. He didn't want Ruth to be the only being who knew just how freaking happy this made him.

He pulled out his phone. Without too much thought, he called Mary.

"Hi!" she answered, this greeting sounding significantly sunnier than her last one had.

"I know we don't have plans until tomorrow, but I had some good news, and I'm over the moon." *And I just wanted to hear your voice.* He could hear those words in his head as clearly as if he'd said them out loud. He wondered if Mary could as well.

"Oh," she said softly, and he could sense the pleasure there. There were people talking in the background, and he guessed that she was at a bar or restaurant. "Wanna come tell me the good news in person? I'm out with Beth Herari. Richie's here too, actually. That wasn't planned, though."

"At Fellow's?"

"Yup."

Of course Mary would be at John's regular watering hole, rubbing elbows with John's world. Of course, after half a season of being intertwined in his life, she was threaded through almost every single aspect of it.

He laughed. "I'll be there in five."

John's spirit was on roller skates as he strode down the long city blocks that divided Brooklyn Heights from Fort Greene, deftly sidestepping shoppers who were cruising the Fulton Mall, mostly, he figured, for the free air-conditioning. It was August and the city was doing that charming thing it did midsummer, where it became the mouth of hell, each building absorbing the heat of the sun and spitting it back onto the population for hours after sunset.

But John didn't care. He was buoyant. He was a human glass of champagne. He was a fresh start and a fresh breeze, and he was on his way to meet Mary Trace in a bar.

"Hey, John!" someone called to him when he stepped through the door at Fellow's. He waved but didn't stop, scanning the area for a bright, sunny head of hair. He spotted Richie, leaning too far over the bar to hear something Marissa was saying, and then there was Mary. Laughing hard at a story Beth was telling, her hair lit up like a beacon and her dress falling off one shoulder.

The bar was crowded for a Wednesday. He shouldered his way through his colleagues, his eyes on Mary.

She looked up, as if his gaze had called to her, and her smile fell away. She looked elated to see him, but there was more to this expression. She looked as charged as he felt. As if seeing him cross a bar on a single-minded mission was *really* doing it for her. John would have done this same strutting, striding walk for hours if it really was all it took to put that look on her face. Her hair fell over one eye; her teeth caught at her bottom lip.

John was twenty feet away, ten, five, one. He stepped around Beth and into Mary's side. She twisted on the barstool to face him as one of John's hands went around to her lower back. His other hand slid up to her cheek, her chin resting on the pad of his thumb. Her eyes swallowed him alive as, stars in his bloodstream, John leaned forward and planted a good, hard kiss on her cheek.

It didn't last for more than a few seconds, and if it had been between two different people, it might have even been platonic. But because it was Mary, John shivered against her. As brief as it had been, the corner of his mouth had touched the corner of hers. She wore mint ChapStick that he hoped he'd taste on his lips in the few moments before Gabriel led him through the pearly gates one day. He knew he'd surprised her because she was breathless when he pulled away, her eyes wide, her fingers tangled in the collar of his shirt.

"Hi," he said, six inches from her mouth. The very same mouth his body was begging for him to lean down and taste.

"Hi," she whispered, more air than word. Her thumb drew a circle in the stubble just under his chin and there was nothing in this entire bar but for Mary's eyes. There might not have been anything in this entire *world* but for Mary's eyes.

"Whoa," he heard Richie say behind him.

He tore his eyes from Mary's and acknowledged his friend.

"I take it you won your case," Richie said.

"That I did."

"Really? Is that the good news? Tell me about it!" Mary's hand, still tangled in his collar, relaxed and slid down over his chest. She smoothed it around to his back, pulling him against where she sat on her barstool as the crowd behind him bore down on them. "Want some of my beer? Or should we get you one?"

John's heart led a six-mile parade down the streets of Brooklyn. Because Mary was pulling him into her side, waving down Marissa to make sure he got a drink. And then she was gasping in joy and excitement as he explained about the case he'd just won. Richie bought another round, and they all toasted Hang Nguyen and her bright future. The bar got even more crowded, and John was practically pasted into Mary's side.

"Save my seat," she said to him, her lips at his ear as she slid down to go to the bathroom. John parked himself onto her barstool and swallowed down half his beer in one go as she evaporated into the crowd. Both Richie and Marissa made wide, pointed eye contact with John. Beth tactfully looked away, sipping from her beer innocently.

A few weeks ago, John might have been uncomfortable about the fact that his friends were watching him cuddle and flirt with Mary. But tonight? Nothing mattered tonight but making Mary smile. Nothing mattered but fanning the burning, liquid electricity in his gut. Regrets were not a concept he even vaguely understood right now.

He just shrugged at his friends, impulsively ordered another round for the group and laughed.

A moment later, there was a hand on his shoulder, but before John could stand to give Mary her seat back, she was gracefully sliding against him, planting herself onto the triangle of barstool between his legs.

"Let's just share," she suggested over her shoulder, her hair brushing his chin as he leaned down to hear her.

John scooted back an inch on the stool, braced a forearm across the front of her hips and hoisted her more securely against him.

He knew, that with her plush ass firmly planted between his spread legs, there was going to be no hiding how much he wanted her. But, he wondered, what was the alternative? *Not* having Mary wiggle herself into his lap? Hard pass.

She didn't protest at having his arm around her waist, so he left it there, reveling when she leaned her weight into him, her back against his chest. He was lost in the slip of her dress off her perfect shoulder. He was wholly engrossed in the mystery of where the hell her bra strap was. Was she wearing some contraption under the pink dress that didn't require straps? Was she bare? Her shoulder was certainly bare, and it took every ounce of fortitude in John's being not to nuzzle her there.

She kept the conversation lively with Beth and Richie, and he could feel her voice reverberate through her chest and into him. Every laugh, every movement of her hands pushed her against him until John felt like he might go insane. He was more aroused than he could ever remember being. This erotic dance she was doing against him was so different, so much more intense, than anything he'd ever done on a dance floor. This wasn't an intentional grinding of two bodies against one another, the promise of a make out in a cab on the frantic ride back to one of their places. No, this was so much more exquisitely torturous than that.

He had the soft scent of her skin filling up every lungful of air he took, the gentle tickle of her hair under his chin, the intoxicating tug of her fingers at the wrist of his sleeve as she absently played with the button there.

Beth and Richie started laughing about something together, and Mary took the opportunity to tip her head back and catch John's eye. "You're awfully quiet back there," she said with a sly smile on her lips.

It hit him all at once. She was doing this on purpose.

The little minx! She knew exactly how every minuscule press and lean and jiggle was affecting him.

Well. Two could definitely play that game. He felt his eyelids lower in both competition and satisfaction.

John cleared his throat and adjusted his arm across her hip bones, bringing her infinitesimally closer to him.

With his free hand, he brushed her hair back under the guise of clearing the way for him to whisper in her ear. But he took the opportunity to let the pad of his thumb linger at the back of her neck. He held her gently, firmly in place while his nose just barely skimmed the upper shell of her ear.

"Guess I'm just enjoying the company."

He was obliged to watch her pupils dilate as she licked her lips.

"Another round?" Marissa shouted over the noise of the crowd.

Richie made a face at them, testing the waters to see if they were going to stick around for that long. Maybe if Mary had been a different, less earthquaking woman, John would have been anxious to get out of the bar with her and get on with their night. But right now, with her warm and vibrating in his lap, there was nowhere else in the solar system that he wanted to be.

"Sure!" Mary shouted back.

Their beers came, and John watched, point-blank, while Mary slipped the lime out of the neck of the bottle and sucked it clean. When she licked her lips, John licked his own lips. When she took a sip from her beer, John looked away, let out a long breath and took a deep swallow of his own beer, hoping to cool some of this fire inside him. So far, she was definitely winning the painfully delicious game they were playing with one another.

John looked down. Two of their legs were hidden in the shadow underneath the overhang of the bar and John took the opportunity. He laid his palm over his own knee. He couldn't see her face, but he felt Mary's awareness circle down and land right there. To the hand he'd placed just an inch from her leg.

John leaned forward, pretending to be straining to hear something Richie was saying, but really he was taking the opportunity to bend Mary over, just a tiny bit. He tightened his hold at her waist and moved his hand from his own knee to her knee, as if he were bracing her against the shift in balance. He answered Richie, careful not to shout in Mary's ear, and then leaned them both back, adjusting her against him but leaving his hands where they were. One palm on her opposite hip and one palm over her knee, his fingers stretched down to her bare calf. Her dress was short, so he was skin on skin.

Her fingers tugged at the button at his wrist, one gentle nail tracing a path on the skin under his sleeve. His own fingers stretched in response, his thumb drawing a circle on the inside of her knee.

She pushed back into him, just slightly, her ass into his unmistakable hardness, and did she…? Yes, she'd definitely just opened her legs a tantalizing half inch. John let out a breath and could practically watch it wash over that exposed patch of golden shoulder. He wanted to follow his breath with his lips, his lips with his tongue, his tongue with his teeth. He couldn't help but shift his hips forward a barely there centimeter, pressing himself into her softness.

His beer was half-drank and long forgotten on the bar next to him. One needed a free hand to drink a beer and his hands were currently *ocupado*. Exactly where they'd been born to be.

John slid his hand just an inch up the inside of her leg, still basically on her knee, just the smallest bit under the hem of her dress. If Richie and Beth were to look down, they might raise an eyebrow, but it wasn't indecent. Still, John felt Mary melt back against him, her leg shifting, pushing against his, opening an amount so small that if his hand hadn't been there, he might have missed it.

She ran a hand through her hair, fluffing it, pulling it up off the back of her neck, and when it fell, John realized that they were sitting so close that her hair fell over his own shoulder. He felt the warm, silky weight of it tumbling down his arm, cascading everywhere as she leaned forward to laugh with Beth.

That sheet of her hair was too much temptation. He slid his hand up from her leg and brushed her hair down her back, smoothing it. He wanted to see her hair wet. He wanted to see *her* wet. He wanted a long luxurious, soapy shower with Mary. But he also wanted a quick late-for-work shower with her just as badly. He wanted to watch her brush her teeth while she wore a white towel in that twist thing that women did. He wanted to race around a kitchen with her, make sure she left the house with at least a cup of coffee and a muffin. If she even ate muffins.

He slid his hand back to her knee and maybe half an inch farther up her leg than it had been before. "What kind of breakfast do you usually eat in the morning?" he couldn't help but ask, muttering into her ear. He wanted information, anything he could learn about her. He wanted his morning-time fantasy to be as accurate as possible.

She tipped her head back and eyed him, her eyes at half-mast. "You planning on feeding me breakfast, John?"

Boi-oi-oi-oing. If he hadn't been sprung for the last half an hour—which he had been—he certainly freaking would be right now. John might not be as smooth as some of her Maserati-driving silver foxes, but he was pretty sure she'd just asked him if he was going to take her home tonight. If he was going to sleep the night with her, then feed her in the morning to keep her strength up. John had always been a die-hard fan of morning sex, but casual hookups in his world were generally done in the dark of the witching hour, the heat vampirically turning to dust in the morning light.

But with Mary? Gah—yeah. He'd morning sex her until they had to sleep again. Until there was nothing to do but hurriedly slug back coffee and orange juice and bagels on the way to work, and send her on her way with the memory of him between her legs.

Her question lingered between them.

"Couldn't let you go hungry."

Her eyes darkened further, her tongue wetting her lips. He followed the movement with his eyes, and without him telling it to, his hand was now a full inch and a half under the hem of her dress.

Her eyes were on his mouth, he was sure of it.

"I'd make sure you were taken care of, Mary," he told her.

She swallowed and made a small sound that he barely heard over the shouting crowd all around them. Under the bar, her ankle hooked around his and John figured it might be time to leave. There was savoring a moment, and then there was letting it pass by. He was not letting Mary pass him by, not when she had two fingers teasing the inside of his wrist and her sunny hair trapped between their bodies.

Because he was a good friend, or maybe because he really was tired, Richie suddenly yawned and threw some cash on the bar. "I'm gonna head out. Beth, want a walking buddy to the train?"

Beth and Richie quickly waved goodbye and disappeared through the crowd. Now it was just John and Mary all alone in this crowded, pulsing bar. There was an empty barstool where Beth had just been sitting, and Mary slid down, off the one she was sharing with John. But she didn't step away from him. Instead she turned in the circle of his arms and pushed herself into him, her soft breasts pressing into his chest, the tips of her hair tickling the forearm he had barred against her lower back.

"Wanna be my walking buddy?" she asked, her head tipped up to his, her eyes on his lips.

John lifted his hips, pulled out his wallet and tossed money on the bar. If it was the wrong amount, Marissa would tell him about it next time he saw her, but for now, he needed to be outside, in the night, with Mary.

They got jostled as they pushed their way through the crowd, but neither of them seemed to care. John led the way, his hand back, laced with Mary's. When they finally made it out the door of the bar, they both laughed into the muggy air.

"Somehow, I was expecting a breath of fresh air when we finally got out of that sweatbox," Mary said, shaking her head.

"Not in Brooklyn in midsummer," John said with a laugh. As hot as it was outside, he felt the absence of her weight against him, and he gently tugged her forward. She leaned into his side. "Cab?" he asked. "Train? Walk?"

"It's only ten blocks."

Somehow, they'd decided to go to her house without either of them having to discuss it.

"Can you walk it in those heels?" He looked down at the electric-blue skyscrapers that were precariously strapped to her feet.

"I can do lots of things in heels, John," she said with a sexy, laughing look on her face, backing away in the direction of her apartment.

He gulped. He got a sudden flash of Mary standing naked in nothing but those heels. Another flash and then there she was, digging those heels into his back. He didn't let her get far before he was beside her again. They walked so fast they both breathed hard. Their fingers laced, as much to keep a connection as to tug one another along, as if they were both nervous the other might change their mind at the last second.

Mary's shop was tucked in for the night, glowing sedately behind its brand-new security gate. She jammed her keys into the red door beside the gate, the one that led up the stairs to her apartment. They practically sprinted up the stairs after he locked the bottom door behind them. And then there was just her lone door at the top of the stairs. The last real obstacle that John could foresee tonight.

She jabbed with her keys, missing twice. Her hands shook, the lock wouldn't give, John couldn't wait.

His hands on her hips from behind, he pushed with one set of fingers and pulled with the other. Mary spun, her back against the door, her head falling back.

His eyes on hers, his hands still gripping her hips, John moved in slow motion. She was glowing, golden, nervous perfection vibrating between the brackets of his hands. He lowered his head and finally, *finally* fit his mouth to hers. The first touch was a bit askew, and he re-placed his mouth, this time sliding perfectly into the landscape of her lips. She gasped, her lips softening even as her hands tightened in his hair. He grunted at the sharp pull, pinned there against the softest lips he'd ever kissed. Mary's mouth painted the illusion that he could just keep on sinking in, that she was bottomless, that there were oceans of silky heat just waiting for him to explore.

He kissed at her bottom lip and tugged it gently down. She complied prettily, her mouth coming open under his, and then John couldn't help but swipe his tongue inside. He tasted the mint from her ChapStick and lime and fresh human woman.

She was all plush, tart sweetness, her tongue meeting his and stilling him. For a moment, they just pressed against one another, as if they were testing to make sure the other was real. But he couldn't wait forever. His tongue slid against hers and she moaned breathily. He made a broken sound in response and her hands came to the sides of his face, clutching him like she was solely in charge of holding him in one piece.

He tested her, pushing and tasting, and she chased his tongue with hers. She made a sound of frustration that made him smile. The shape of the smile faded immediately, as his mouth was otherwise occupied, but the feeling remained. He clutched hard at her hips, and their heads tipped from one side to the other.

He was dizzy on her, huffing too hard and too fast whatever exquisite toxin she was pumping into him.

"John," she gasped, her head knocking gently back onto the door. He lifted his head to better see her expression, and it was only then that he realized he'd lifted her. Somehow his hands had fallen down from her hips to her ass and now those electric-blue heels were digging into his lower back as he pinned her against her own front door. Her weight felt so good, as if only with her in his arms could he be positive that she wasn't going to flitter away, a dream at dawn.

She was here. So real. Panting his name as her fingers

dug into his shoulders and her head tipped back against the door.

Holy God.

He planted his forehead on the door just over her shoulder and looked down her body.

"Fug," he said blearily as he realized that her dress had gotten hiked up to her hips and it was her hot-pink panties that were smashed against the zipper of his slacks.

"Inside," she panted and leaned forward to suck on his neck, punctuating it with a brief, sharp bite that jolted him.

Her words only made partial sense to him. He stared down at those hot-pink panties and then back up to her face. "Inside?" he asked, just as bleary as before. "Right now?"

She laughed and leaned forward to tug on his bottom lip with her teeth. "Inside *my apartment*."

"Ah." That made more sense. He let her slide down his body and took the keys that were still clutched in her hand. John studied her hand for just a moment, saw the imprint of a house key against her palm and realized that that, right there, was proof of how badly she wanted him. Bad enough to leave the outline of a key where she'd gripped it too hard. If it hadn't been weird, he would have taken a photo of it. Instead, he kissed it and smoothly unlocked her door.

They were barely inside before she was tugging at his midnight tie, pulling at his buttons, throwing her purse in the direction of the couch, stumbling with the force of her throw.

Stumbling...

Shit. John put hands on her shoulders and steadied her, eyeing her. He'd seen her drink four beers while he'd been sitting with her, but she'd been at the bar when he'd gotten there. He'd had five drinks tonight. And no dinner. Which was about twice as much as he usually had if he was going to hook up with someone. And this wasn't someone. This was Mary.

"Shit," he cursed, raising his hands up to his hair and tugging. *"Shit."*

"What?"

"Mary, we're drunk."

She frowned, shook her head and then laughed when she tipped slightly to the side. "Maybe just a little bit."

"A little bit is too much if we're really gonna do this."

She eyed him, trying to figure out if he was bluffing. She must have read the sincerity on his face because she stepped back, her hands on her hips. "Shit," she echoed him.

Suddenly, a look of horror came over her face. She took two steps back from him and stood in front of her door. She threw the dead bolt and then the chain lock. Slamming her back against the door, she tossed her arms out in a T. "You're going to go, aren't you? You can't leave! No. Don't go."

The idea of him leaving was obviously panicking her. Whatever lusty beast inside him that had gotten its feathers ruffled at the idea of missing out on sex was instantly soothed. Because he couldn't make love to her while they were drunk. But staying? Well, staying was absolutely something he could give her.

"Am I invited to stay?" he asked quietly.

"Yes."

He shrugged his shoulders and held his arms out for a hug. "Then I'm staying."

His arms were suddenly full of Mary, and they both stumbled backward.

"You're going to kill us both with these heels," he laughed and went down on one knee in front of her to divest her of one heel and then the other. When he looked back up at her, her eyes were dark, and her lips were bitten red.

"Promise me you'll do that again when I can actually show you how sexy I find it."

"I promise." His voice was pure gravel. There were about seven hundred places he wanted to kiss her right now, but in order to save both their sanities, he simply placed a chaste kiss right on her kneecap before he stood up.

"Water?" he asked.

"Sure." She swayed into the kitchen, yawning and stretching her arms up over her head as she went.

John took off his shoes and followed her into the kitchen. She put a glass of ice water in his hand and leaned against the opposite counter, hoisting herself up. They held one another's eyes as they both drank deeply, John finishing his entire glass and her getting about halfway there. They set their glasses aside, and Mary pulled her knees apart a scant inch. John caught a glimpse of hot pink and he groaned, twisting his head to one side.

"Play fair, Mary."

When he looked up, her knees were pressed together again, but her eyes were impishly pleased with herself. She yawned again.

"Are you sure you want me to stay?" he asked. "You seem tired."

"Aren't you tired?" She cocked her head to one side.

"Well, actually..." Now that she mentioned it, he was tired. It was a couple hours later than he usually stayed up on a work night.

"Bedtime?" she asked, sliding down from the counter and holding out a hand to him.

"Mary..."

"I won't try anything." She lifted her fingers in the Boy

Scout pledge. "Let's just lie down for a little while. I'm sleepy."

He watched her walk down the long, dim hallway that led to her bedroom. She disappeared through the door, a lamp flicking on a moment later.

John dragged a hand down his face, feeling like he was in some sort of soupy, delicious dream. He knew exactly how he'd gotten this far into the evening without realizing he was drunk. Because Mary made him feel drunk even when he was dead-ass sober. Her presence, her spirit, her demeanor, it helium-ed him. He was used to feeling loopy and spinny when he was near her.

"There in a sec," he called down the hall before he deviated to the bathroom. He did his business and carefully tucked and zipped everything back into place. Just one more way of telling himself that his clothes needed to stay on tonight. John washed his hands and splashed his face with cold water, laughing when he saw his expression. "What a dork," he muttered to himself good-naturedly.

But all the chuckling lightness was immediately bootheeled when he stepped into the doorway of Mary's room and saw her curled up on the bed. She was over top of her covers, still in her pink dress, her legs bare.

She lifted her head to look at him and patted the pillow next to her. John walked around to the side of the bed she'd indicated and, painfully aware of every tiny movement, slid onto the bed next to Mary.

Instantly she closed the gap between them, one of her legs looping over his and her face nuzzling into the crook above his shoulder. One of her palms found one of his palms and soon her deep, even breathing dragged him under.

CHAPTER SEVENTEEN

THE FIRST THING Mary saw when she opened her eyes was gray morning light filtering over her hand. Wait. No. That was much too large to be her hand. She wiggled her fingers and the large, broad-palmed, blunt-fingered hand she was looking at moved a tiny bit. Ah. There was a man's hand resting on top of hers.

The rest came in a cascade of memory and information. John striding through the bar to get to her. The cheek kiss. His infectious joy. Sharing the barstool with him. The pressing, the tracing of circles on his wrist, his hand on her knee, holding hands as they basically sprinted home.

The kiss against her door.

Mamma Fracking Mia, THE KISS AGAINST HER DOOR.

Hands down, no question, the absolute best kiss of her entire freaking life. The second his mouth had touched hers, she'd been gone, every ounce of her focus on his lips. The building could have fallen down around them and she wouldn't have noticed. He was a good kisser. John Modesto-Whitford: scowler, sayer of rude things, sweet, kindhearted, kisser of the lights out.

Seriously, if the man had sex the way he kissed, she wasn't sure she'd make it to see the morning light.

But wait, she was already seeing the morning light. It was brightening by the second.

How cute was it that he hadn't let them sleep together last night? Mary had wanted to. She was certain that if they had, she wouldn't have a single regret this morning. But still, it just added to his sweetness. The man truly *considered* her. Even when the raging boner she'd been pressed up against had to have been weighing down the pro column, he'd still talked both of them into waiting for sobriety.

And now sobriety was here.

She stretched a little and yawned. Yikes, sobriety was here, but so was her morning breath. Maybe she could sneak out of bed and brush real quick without waking him up. But when she stretched one leg out, the hand on her hand clamped down, ran up her arm and found a home around her waist. He'd been loosely spooning her, but now he was tight against her. He grumbled, low in his throat, but Mary wasn't sure if he was awake or not. Well, one part of him certainly was awake, and it was as hard as it had been last night. He pressed hot and insistent into her ass and thigh.

But seriously, she was going to have to do something about this breath. She slid out from under his arm and tip-toed to the bathroom. First things first, she peed, and then she moved to the sink.

Mary almost screamed.

Natural light filtered in through the window, lighting her harshly from the side. It had been a long time since she'd fallen asleep with her makeup on and, good Jesus, it was a grim state of affairs on her face right now. She looked cracked and smudged and wrecked. And not in a good way.

She scrambled for makeup-removing pads and moisturizer, rubbing at her skin almost frantically. Now, with the makeup removed and her face lotioned up, she looked red and shiny. Her pink dress, which had seemed so pretty the night before, was wrinkled. The chic style of it made a mockery of her makeup-less face, pink as the inside of a strawberry.

God.

Mary tore her eyes from her reflection and quickly brushed her teeth, hoping that when she looked up, her color would have gone down a little. But alas, she still looked pink and puffy and…old.

Mary brought a shaking hand to her mouth. Her hair was frizzy and lank, her skin lined and swollen from too little sleep and too much beer. There was none of her usual sparkle. The harsh morning light was only getting harsher.

She looked down at herself, pulling the neckline of her dress away from her in order to peek down at her body. Her chest had those lines it sometimes got when she slept on her side and her breasts pulled, all night, to one side. Her underwear was hot pink and ridiculous. She was wearing sorority-girl underwear. Why had she thought this was cute on her? This was clearly for college students.

"Oh, God," she whispered. There was nothing for her to change into in here. Nowhere to run, nowhere to hide. John was either asleep or just waking up in her bed. He thought he'd be waking up to the Mary of last night, polished and put-together and confident.

Instead he'd be waking up to this Mary. She felt as if her mother had somehow made a deal with the devil and had Mary waking up to the fate she'd always envisioned for her daughter. She looked in the mirror and didn't see Tiff's Mary. She didn't see Cora's MFT. No. She saw Naomi's busted-ass daughter, old and silly and ridiculous.

"Oh, *God.*" Regardless, she had to go out there. She couldn't hide in here all morning. It was only 5:00 a.m. Maybe she could scuttle him out the door before the light got too bright and he saw what he was really dealing with.

She took a deep breath, feeling lower than she had in years, and padded back into her bedroom. He was on his back and rubbing at his face when she came in. He cracked one eye when he heard her, a sleepy smile blooming over his face.

"Hi," he said softly, reaching for her.

She let him take her hand, because how in the hell was she supposed to keep from reaching out to him when he reached out to her? It was like a law of the universe. He tugged her forward, and she sat on the edge of the bed, facing away from him.

"Did you sleep well?" she asked, casting about for anything to say that wasn't *Could you please leave so that you don't find out I'm secretly a hag and run screaming from my apartment?*

"Mmm," he answered. Apparently he was too cute and dozy in the morning to string sentences together. He curled against her, and she melted when his hand traced down her spine. Maybe that was why she didn't have it in her to protest when he gently tugged her down and folded her into him, his mouth landing on her exposed shoulder, his hand spanning her tummy as he kissed his way to her neck.

Did he have to be so cuddly and sexy in the morning? He was making this a hundred times harder than it had to be. Why couldn't he have been awkward and aloof, anxious to get the hell out of her house the way some men were? It would have been so much easier if they could just have a good old-fashioned awkward morning after.

But he showed no signs of awkwardness as he grumbled something unintelligible into her collarbone and traced a hand down to her knee.

"John," she whispered, her eyes closed tight.

"Mary," he whispered back, and she could hear the happiness in his voice.

When she didn't answer, he paused in his ministrations and sat up, balancing his head on one hand.

She winced. She really didn't want him to get an eyeful of what she looked like right now. Things were safer when he'd had his face buried in her neck.

"Are you all right?" he asked.

"Um—" She cut herself off because she had no idea what to say. He was looking at her the way he always did. With his brows in a V, his complicated eyes layered with concern and caring. Why wasn't he recoiling from her? "I just feel a little off. Now that we're, ah, sober."

He went perfectly still. Mary got the strange feeling like she'd just dumped a bucket of ice water over his head, but she wasn't exactly sure why.

He was silent for a long moment, and then he cleared his throat. "Things are looking different to you in the morning, huh?"

That was exactly right. The biggest "thing" looking different was namely her.

"Sort of?" she said. His eyes were tracking around her bedroom, catching on this and that. After a moment, his gaze landed on her face and skittered away. He sat up and rolled to the other side of the bed, dragging a hand over his face.

"Right," he muttered. "Right."

He stood up and went to the bathroom. Mary sat up as well. She wanted to change her clothes, but God forbid he come back midchange. It would be just her luck if he caught her pulling the underwear out of her ass right about now. No, thank you.

She sat on the edge of her bed and cupped her elbows, feeling utterly wretched.

"I just want to make sure I'm clear on this, all right?" He spoke from the doorway and she stood and turned, the bed in between them.

His eyes, for the first time ever, cast down her body and back up. She'd been waiting and waiting for him to do that to her, to be the recipient of that appraisal, but now that it was happening, she hated it. With the morning light beaming in on her, her hair in a rat's nest and last night's dress wrinkled and loose, she didn't feel sexy and desired. She felt diminished and exposed.

"You're saying," he said slowly, as if he were painstakingly gathering each word, "that you wanted to sleep with me last night, while we were drunk. But now, in the morning light, you're feeling differently?"

That was exactly how she was feeling. She didn't answer aloud; apparently her face did that for her.

His eyes widened as he took in her expression. "Wow," he whispered, taking a step back from her. "Wow. I'm such an idiot."

He turned on his heel and disappeared from the doorway.

Mary stood there for a moment, a frown on her face. Wait. Why had he just called himself an idiot?

She strode after him, even though she wanted to pull her bedcovers over her head and not come out until the next day.

"What do you mean?" she called after him, seeing that he was already at her front door, toeing into his wingtips. "What do you mean you're an idiot?"

"I— You— Shit." John tried and failed to get a sentence out. "I'm an idiot for thinking that dancing at your party…sharing a chair with you…that those things were a green light. That it was all an indicator that maybe you wanted... *Shit*."

He bent and tied one shoe and the next, his fingers as dexterous as his words apparently weren't. He stood when his shoelaces were in a crisp knot, his hands jammed in his pockets.

"Mary, it is totally fine, more than fine, for you to change your mind about who you want to sleep with. I'm sorry if I'm guilting you. I'm trying not to. I'm being a dick. I'm just mad at myself for thinking... Shit. I'm gonna go."

"Wait." She held a hand out in a stop sign as her world tilted and his words filtered into her brain in a seemingly random order. He thought she'd changed her mind about *him*?! Oh, God. He thought that the "morning light" had shown poorly upon *him*? "Wait, John."

"No, I'd rather go. It's okay, Mary. I understand. Beer goggles happen to the best of us." He gave her a grim look that was probably an understanding smile in his mind. "You don't have to apologize. And frankly, I don't think I can handle you being sweet to me right now. So. Yeah. I'm gonna go. I have to go."

He undid her locks, pulled open the door and pounded down her stairs. She heard her bottom door close, and then all was silent in her apartment.

"Beer goggles?" she said aloud, to no one. The thought was so ridiculous she laughed, but the sound was incredulous, bitter, horrified. "He thinks I had beer goggles for him? He is an idiot. He's an idiotic, sweet, sexy, perfect... *Shit*." She replayed their conversation in her head and realized how it all would have sounded to someone who was dealing with his own insecurities. She had just figured that how she'd been feeling about herself was so loud and insistent that there was no way in hell he'd been misinterpreting her meaning.

And now John was getting on the train thinking that she regretted kissing him, being with him, cuddling him on the barstool.

She glanced at the wall clock— 5:10 a.m. If she left now, she could still catch him before work.

CHAPTER EIGHTEEN

WELL, HE WAS back in Ruthlandia.

Not that bad a place to be, if he was being honest.

He wanted to curl in on himself, to look around his studio apartment and take it apart piece by piece in his head, comparison by comparison. Rejecting Mary's judgment of him was difficult, like deep breathing through a charley horse. Part of him wanted nothing more than to admit that she was right. That he was a broke, shabby public defender, and she was right for changing her mind about him.

But no.

He scratched Ruth under the chin and balanced his cup of coffee on his knee.

Succumbing to that kind of self-hatred was a disservice to Estrella, to the way he'd been raised. It was admitting that his father was right. That money mattered more than anything else. John hadn't let his self-worth be bought by his father, and he wouldn't let it be sold by Mary.

"Just because I'm not what she wants doesn't mean I'm not good enough for her," he informed Ruth, who merely arched a feline eyebrow and gave a rather pointed yowl. "Even if her mattress is a damn cloud and her room looks like a page from a West Elm catalog."

He stood up and strode to stand in front of the box fan. It was too hot in his apartment to sit in one place.

"You don't care about West Elm, do you, Ruth?" he asked

her as she plowed her forehead into his ankles. "That's why you're my best girl. All you need is food in your bowl and water— Oh, crap." He strode over and filled up her water bowl, plopped a fresh can of food down for her.

He stood in front of the box fan and watched Ruth eat her breakfast. His insides hurt. He was haunted by thoughts of Mary's bedroom. The expensive, decorative baubles twisting in the sunlight at her window, the framed art photographs he was willing to bet were originals, her heaven-soft duvet cover that wasn't made of any material John had ever encountered before.

He winced and dragged a hand over his face, trying like hell not to feel like an idiot for thinking he had a real chance with her.

In an attempt to trick his mind into another direction, John pulled out his phone and opened his email. There at the top of the stack was the unanswered email he'd received from his father last week.

Come spend time with me, son, his email had implored.

You're too rich for comfort, John's non-reply had said back.

John sighed. Why was it always about money? "Whaddaya think, Ruthie?" John asked, setting his phone back down on his kitchen table. "Should I shelve my dignity for a week and let my father take me on a bonding vacation?" Jack would certainly pay for it if John told him he couldn't afford to go.

His head snapped up at the tap-tap on his front door. John groaned, pressing his fingers against his suddenly pounding forehead. He knew, without having to look, exactly who was at the door. Even her knock was sweet. Two little taps, polite knuckles. God, he wasn't ready for this. Her words earlier this morning had almost been a kindness. They'd cut him down to ribbons, but at least he knew, without question, where she stood on the matter. He didn't want her sweetness, her reason. He didn't want her to be nice to him right now. And he knew, without question, that if he opened that door, she was going to be unbearably sweet to him.

Ugh.

With any luck, she'd heard him asking Ruth for her opinion on financial matters. Wouldn't that just be the cherry on top.

Two more knocks, these slightly louder than the last.

Deciding that he wasn't so much of an asshole that he could hold his breath and pretend he wasn't home, John stepped around Ruth and dragged his ass over to the door. With grim surrender, he swung open the door.

She stood there, an unexpected expression on her face, her hands on her hips. Her hair was piled up messily on top of her head, still wet from a shower, and she wore no makeup. She was in red shorts and a white T-shirt and perfectly white sneakers. She looked like she'd just thrown some clothes on to run down to the bodega, but here she was, all the way across town, standing at his door.

Apparently even piles of ribbons were capable of stomach-swooping. He wished like heck it didn't affect him to see her standing there in his doorway. But of course, it did.

John frowned at her. Mary frowned back, her eyebrows knitting forward like her forehead muscles were straining from the position.

"Mary—"

"*You're* not attracted to *me*." She cut him off, her expression morphing from surly to stubborn.

"*What?*" It was probably the only thing she could have said that truly shocked him. One hand on the door, practically blocking her from coming inside, John just blinked at her.

She shoved forward, knocking his arm askew and coming into his house. She kicked off her white sneakers to reveal tiny, pink socks. She tossed her purse down next to her sneakers and whirled on him, her eyes narrowed.

Thoroughly thrown off and befuddled, John muscled Ruth back from the open door and closed it behind them. He turned to Mary and mirrored her position. Hands on hips. A scowl for the ages.

Surprisingly, he broke before she did. "You think I'm not attracted to you?"

She stalked over to his kitchen, poured herself a glass of water, chugged it down to empty and slammed the glass down. "I know you're not attracted to me. That's what the whole problem is. Has always been."

In the courtroom, he was notorious for being a quick thinker. He'd been captain of his debate team in high school. He drove Estrella nuts when they watched *Jeopardy!*, always saying the answers before the contestants did.

But staring at Mary standing in her stocking feet in his kitchen, glaring at him, John's mind was completely blank. He had no idea how to respond to her utterly insane statement.

He settled on a second *"What?"*

Still glaring at him, she held up her fingers and listed the incriminating evidence. "You never look me up and down the way you do every other woman on earth. Besides last night you've never tried to kiss me, but we were drunk so that barely counts. And if we'd gotten naked this morning, you would have seen me all in the bright light, and you'd have to come face-to-face with my age. I… I couldn't handle that. Not when you already think I'm too old for you."

There were too many threads to grab hold of in what she'd just said, too many issues to address. He went for the most glaring one. "Too old for me? This is about what I said on our blind date? Mary, for God's sake, are you ever going to let me live that down?" He stalked forward, his blood boiling in his veins.

"John, it was *humiliating*. I did my hair, chose an outfit, walked into that restaurant feeling like a million bucks. And ten seconds later, I felt about two inches tall." She threw her arms into the air. "It would have been three inches, but I was so *stooped with age*."

He took three more steps forward and took her by the shoulders. "You think you were the only one who was humiliated, Mary?" He squeezed her shoulders once, firmly, and then stepped back from her, pressing his fingers to his forehead in deference to the headache. "You want to know how I felt? I'd scrambled across town to be on time for the date, so I was still in my work clothes, sweaty and smelling like fried chicken because one of my clients works at a Crown Fried Chicken and it was the only place she could meet me. So, then, there I am, in a fifteen-dollar haircut, twenty-nine dollars in cash in my wallet, at a restaurant expensive enough for me to have to charge dinner to my credit card, on a date set up by my mother. My *mother*. God bless her, Mary, but what man in his right mind isn't humiliated by a date set up by his mother?" He paced away from her, still pressing his fingers against the headache. "My mother is a lot of things, but reality-based is not one of them." He turned to her. "You know how she described you to me? A beautiful, bubbly blonde who loves to chat about movies and music. She said you liked going to the beach and pilates. She said you were thinking about starting business school."

"That's all true—"

"She made you sound like you were about twenty-five years old, Mary. I thought to myself, *John, the rumpled work clothes and cheap haircut won't matter to a twenty-five-year-old. She'll be impressed that you even have a full-time job. That you made it through law school. If it's a match, hopefully you can start taking her to happy hours at more affordable restaurants, and she'll be impressed that you know how to life-hack your way through this fucking city.*"

He paced again. "You say you felt like a million bucks? Mary, you *looked* like a hundred million. A billion. My first date in six months, and I'd been expecting a softball. Someone who I could maybe impress with a law degree until I could get comfortable enough to flirt with her. But in walks this—" he waved his hands in the air, searching for the words "—sophisticated creature in some sort of dress...heels...your hair..." He trailed off, not adept enough to actually describe how she'd looked. "And then you saw me across the restaurant and smiled at me with that fucking smile of yours."

"What's wrong with my smile?" Mary croaked.

"Nothing. There's absolutely nothing wrong with it. It's the best fucking smile in the universe. But you know what that kind of smile says to a man like me across a restaurant? It says, *I will devastate you, you poor schmuck.* And then there you were. The most gorgeous woman in the entire restaurant, on the entire block, in the entire goddamn borough, and you were sitting down to dinner with me. Fried-chicken suit and all." He pressed at his forehead again, trying to smooth away the ache. "I said the first thing that came to mind. It was fucking stupid. I immediately regretted it. I had no idea it would shape our entire relationship."

"You…you mean that you meant that *literally*? You weren't calling me old? You were saying that you were literally expecting someone younger?"

"It's not an excuse. It was a rude thing to say, and I wanted to staple my mouth closed the second I said it. But yes. I meant it literally. I don't care about our age difference, Mary. It's negligible anyways. Only six years."

"But…" She looked deeply confused. "I heard you tell Tyler that we're in different stages of our lives. Like I was three moves away from winding up in an old folks' home."

"*That's* what you took from that statement? Oh, God." He threw his arms up at the universe. "I have the worst freaking luck for you to have overheard that. No. That is not what I meant. I was standing in your beautiful kitchen, staring at your hanging collection of copper pots when I said that."

"What do my pots have to do with anything?"

"I have one cast-iron pan, Mary. *One.* And I use it for literally everything. I have one sharp knife. Four cups. Two mugs—"

"So?!"

"So? What I mean is that you're in this place in your life where you can host dinner parties in your two-bedroom apartment. I mean, my God, you had a candle the size of my forearm next to your gigantic bathtub. You probably drink red wine in that bathtub and listen to audiobooks. Mary, I don't even have air-conditioning! My big splurge last year was *Ruth*. A rescue cat! We're at *different stages of our lives*. That's what I meant. You're a put-together, affluent woman. I'm still scrambling to pay off my student loans. It has nothing to do with age. It has everything to do with who we are."

He was starting to deflate. He'd never expected to lay it all out like this to Mary. He'd never even wanted to.

John strode over to his couch and plunked down. He lowered his forehead to his fingertips and rubbed at the ache.

"Not attracted to you?" In for a penny, in for a pound. He might as well clear it all up now. There was nothing else to lose. Their friendship was most likely shot to shit. All he was going to get from her were a few tipsy kisses last night and a goodbye in a few moments once she'd said what she came to say. "You want to know why I never look you up and down? Because it *hurts* to look at you." He leaned back on the couch and closed his eyes, his face tipped up toward the ceiling. "Being around you is like being parched while there's a glass of lemonade sitting right there, within arm's reach. I have to talk myself out of gulping you down pretty much every second we're together. I'd never be able to sip. That's why I don't look you up and down."

John felt a soft, light touch at his arm and his eyes flung open. She'd padded over without him realizing it. She stood next to the couch, her eyes on her own fingers, which played with the sleeve of his shirt.

"You're in a T-shirt," she whispered. "And shorts."

"I was going to go for a run before work. Before it got too hot outside," he defended himself. "You're in shorts too."

"I've never seen you in anything but your fancy clothes. And your pj's once."

He blinked. If he was interpreting the expression on her face correctly, then she was looking at him rather softly. It was confusing. Weren't they fighting? Wasn't she just about to say goodbye?

With one pink-socked foot, she nudged at his shin. "You have hairy legs," she whispered.

He looked down at his legs. Looked back up at her.

She took a deep breath. "This is how I look without makeup."

"There's no need to brag, Mary."

She laughed and rolled her eyes and went pink in the cheeks. "This is a big deal for me, John. To stand here in laundry-day clothes and wet hair and no makeup and no sleep. The world isn't kind to pretty much any women when it comes to how they look. But especially not 'women of a certain age.' Ain't that right, Ruth?" Mary scratched at Ruth's head where she twined between her feet, but when she straightened again, her face was deadly serious. "My mother *constantly* reminds me how old I am. How time is running out for me. Dying alone is right around the corner. It's been getting harder to ignore her. And I hate to think it's because she's right." Mary shuddered. "I'm not naive. The world isn't as accepting of you if you're over thirty-five and single. Hell, even Sebastian and Tyler, two of the most open-minded guys I know, partnered up with people a decade younger, or more, than them."

She took a deep breath and nudged at his shin again with her toes. "So, yeah. This is it. This is what I look like with no makeup on. After too little sleep. Thirty-seven and a beer too many. Whatcha see is whatcha get."

Her bare legs were close enough for him to knock his knee against hers. If he reached up, he could loop a finger through one of her belt loops. Instead, John tried to calm his tumbling mind and piece together everything she'd just said to him. Her age, her mother, his apparent lack of attraction this morning.

"You're telling me all this because…" He was pretty sure he already knew the answer, but he really, really didn't want to misunderstand.

She took another deep breath and the sight of her nervous had him reaching up to take her hand, gently leading her to sit next to him on his tiny couch.

"Because when you asked me if things felt different in the morning light, I wasn't lying," she said. "But I didn't mean what you thought I meant." She looked away and reached down to skim her hand over Ruth's arching back. "I meant that, like I said, you were about to see me in the bright morning light, and I thought you already had such an issue with my age that you wouldn't be able to ignore it all spotlighted like that. I get that I misunderstood that now. But think of it from my point of view. Last night I felt sexy and loose. This morning I felt hungover and ugly." She turned her head to face away. "I didn't want you to see me that way."

John's throat closed over the words he tried to say. He took a deep breath and tried again. "I thought you turned me away because you'd seen the situation in the *metaphorical* morning light and decided that you didn't really want me."

"I know you thought that," she said, turning back to him, though her eyes stayed cast down. "But by the time I'd put the pieces together, you'd already left. We really misunderstood each other."

"Misunderstanding doesn't begin to cover it." He impulsively reached forward and took her hand. It was the same hand that had had the imprint of a house key across her palm last night. It was the hand that had borne the evidence of how much she'd wanted him.

How could he have let that get lost in the mud of his own insecurities? How many times had he told himself that money wasn't everything? And then, at the first sign of choppy water, he'd assumed that she'd changed her mind about dating a working-class public servant. *He'd* made the situation about money. Not Mary.

He quickly kissed her palm and then placed it flat against his beating heart, knowing that she liked to feel his heartbeat. "Mary, do you know what Richie told me about you the other day?"

She shook her head, her eyes still down.

"He told me that I look at you like all the light in the world originates from inside you."

Her eyes flashed up to meet his.

"And he's right," John continued. "What he said made instant sense to me because that's actually how I feel. To me, Mary, you're radiant." He touched her hair with his free hand. "You're sunny and bright. But it's not just your hair or your coloring. It's your mood that shines through."

Her eyes fell again. "I know I'm a happy-go-lucky type of person, but I'm not always upbeat. There are times that I'm seriously down."

"I know that. I've seen some of them. You know what I thought the first time I saw you cry? That it was like water caught in sunlight. It's not about whether or not you're *happy*, Mary. You always glow with this internal light. You can't help it. It's your spirit. Your determination, your kind heart. The laughing, the smiling, it adds to it, but it doesn't define it. I can't define it either, really. Shit."

He turned his head away to gather his thoughts, and when he looked back, Mary was staring right at him, obviously trying to figure out if she believed what he was saying or not.

He barreled on, determined to get the rest out. "I think you're the most beautiful person I've ever met, and it has very little to do with clothes or makeup or whatever. It's you, Mary. It's your whole thing that you have going on.

That's the best I can describe it. It doesn't have anything to do with age. I don't want to date a twenty-five-year-old. Not even the twenty-five-year-old version of you. I want you, as you are right in this moment. With the sum of all your experiences making you who you are. I wouldn't shave a single day off your life. This is who you are. And you are what I want."

Mary blinked at him for a long moment and then shocked him when she burst into tears. She covered her mouth with one hand but looked up at him with red, watery eyes, tears practically pouring down her cheeks. Apparently, Ruth was concerned as well, because when John tried to lean toward Mary to hold her, suddenly there was a twenty-pound ball of yowling fur in the way, putting her paws on Mary's shoulder and staring her in the face.

Laughter mixed with Mary's tears, and she settled the cat on her lap. "It's okay, Ruth. It's okay."

"What's happening?" John asked nervously, having just poured his entire heart out and now desperately unsure if it had been well received or not.

Mary brushed at her tears with the shoulder of her T-shirt. "I always knew that people like you existed. That there was a man like you out there, and that I deserved him. But my mother almost, *almost* had me convinced that I was wrong." She held up two fingers a centimeter apart to show how close she'd come to succumbing to her mother's beliefs.

"Someday," John said, "if I ever meet your mother, I'm bringing a foghorn to drown out every single thing she says to you."

Mary burst out laughing. "Then she'd just take it upon herself to email me her opinions and complaints."

"Seriously, it sounds like your mother has a very skewed view of the world." Taking a deep breath, John scooted forward and shooed Ruth off Mary's lap. "I'd really like to be the person who counterbalances all her whacked opinions."

Mary laughed again and then stood up all of a sudden. John felt like she'd ripped Velcro off one whole side of him. He'd been about to kiss her, but she was striding away into the kitchen, gulping more water from her glass, and then into the bathroom. She left the door open, and he heard the sink running.

"So," she called through the open door. "You like me for the sum of all my experiences, huh?"

"And more," he called back, wondering if he should keep sitting on the couch like a dope or if he should stand up and go to her.

She answered that question a moment later when she came striding out of the bathroom and toward the couch.

John was hit all over again by the sight of her long legs in those short red shorts. He liked her in a simple T-shirt with her wet hair in a messy knot. She looked like she had much more important things on her mind than how she looked, which he knew was the case even when she was in her fancy sundresses and high heels. Even so, this look felt private. Like in her casual clothes, she'd dressed for the honesty of this moment. Guest list: two. Well, three if you counted Ruth.

He grinned in surprise when instead of sitting back down on the cushion beside him, she plunked directly into his lap. Her long legs fell off to the side, and her arms went around his neck.

"I like *you* for your hairy legs," she informed him crisply.

He laughed. He liked this rascally version of Mary. She seemed so light. So free. Free of insecurity, he realized.

Regret threatened to tidal wave him that he'd contributed to that insecurity with his stupid-ass comments about her age and their stages of life. But he swerved the feeling. He didn't want to get bogged down in regret. Right now, he wanted to match her mood.

"There's a hairy chest that goes with the hairy legs," he told her.

Her eyes widened and she leaned forward, tugging the collar of his shirt a few inches and trying to peer down his spine. "And a hairy back as well?"

He laughed harder. "Not yet. But maybe someday. I can only aspire."

She laughed too, cuddling into him. She was warm and smooth, and John fully succumbed to that humming zing that happened when two people touched with intention.

He glanced at the clock over his stove. It was 6:00 a.m. Could all this have possibly happened before an even remotely reasonable hour this morning? He had to be at work in an hour. Two hours at the latest, if he really pushed it, and he was willing to scramble for the rest of the day. Which he obviously was. Mary had to open her shop by nine.

They didn't exactly have endless time to luxuriate with one another. But was he going to reject this moment for something as trivial as not quite enough time? He most certainly was not. He didn't need this to be a sweeping, dizzy, sexy twirl off the dance floor of a Friday night. He didn't need a weekend to sprawl out in front of them in order to enjoy Mary. He didn't care that they both had work today. Or that it was just any old Thursday. To him, that was perfect. Because he didn't want Mary to exist in the sexiest, most relaxed parts of his life. He wanted Mary in every part of his life. Including Thursday mornings before work.

She was sprawled in his lap, one of his arms holding up her back and the other looped under her knees. She had one hand flat on his chest and one arm around his neck.

She used her nose to draw a line from his forehead down between his eyebrows.

"Do you still have a headache?" she asked in a whisper.

"How did you know I had one?"

"You always press your fingers against your forehead when your head aches."

He pushed his face forward, pressing his nose against hers, nuzzling into her neck. "No. It went away right around the time I realized you weren't leaving."

"I'm not leaving," she confirmed, tipping her head to one side to give him clearer access to her throat. He didn't kiss her exactly, just sort of walked his mouth up the long, smooth column to her ear.

"Mary."

"Hmm?" She leaned back into his arm, giving him her weight and the impression that he'd just turned her into liquid caramel in his arms. He liked liquid-caramel Mary, loose and warm and open.

"I have a very important question to ask you." His voice was even more shredded than usual. It didn't surprise him.

She used her nose again to draw a line, this time up a tendon in his neck and all the way to the corner of his jaw. "What's that?"

"Were you wearing a bra last night? Under your dress?"

She smiled and pulled back from him. Her eyes were dozy and heavy but still alert. "Why?"

"Because I spent the entire time at the bar trying to figure out where the hell your bra strap was."

She laughed. "It was a strapless bra. Nothing too fancy, to be honest."

He grunted. "Doesn't have to be fancy to get the job done."

"And what job is that?"

"Driving me out of my mind, apparently."

She laughed again. "I take it you were a fan of the dress?"

He grunted. "I have a major crush on that dress."

"Confession—I have a major crush on your bed. I think it's the greatest bed of all time."

He blinked at her for a moment, confusion settling in when he realized how sincere she was being. "My bed?" He glanced over her shoulder at the piece of furniture in question. It was so ordinary in comparison to the extravagant five-star ordeal she slept in at her house. "Really?"

She nodded. "It's safe and warm and smells like your aftershave."

He leaned forward and took a quick sip from her lips. "I'm safe." Another sip. "I'm warm." Another longer, more lingering sip. "I smell like my aftershave."

She shivered each time their mouths connected, and on the last one, she chased him forward, spoke against his lips. "Let's be naked now."

"Yeah," he agreed immediately, rising up with her in his arms.

She squeaked and gripped at his shoulders. "John!"

"I've got you." And he did. He felt the same way he had when he'd lifted her against her door the night before. The weight of her was reassuring, comforting, thrilling all at once. Something about holding Mary's body up with his body made John feel more a part of the human race than any other thing he'd done in his life.

The light was full now, but it still had that pre–7:00 a.m. magic that shadowed certain things and made other things glow. John wanted to collapse onto the bed in a pile, but more than anything, he knew that seeing was believing and he needed to see Mary on his bed. He set her down and stood back.

Mary immediately flopped backward, stretching her arms above her head, mussing the covers and making an *mmm* sound like she'd just tasted something delicious.

John took one step back and then another, until he was far enough away to get the whole frame crammed into his memory. The image of those red shorts on his boring, blue bedspread. Yow. That was so freaking hot.

Someday, he'd like to watch her strip out of her clothes while she lay on his bed, but then she looked up at him, reaching her hand out for him, and the distance part of the morning was officially over.

CHAPTER NINETEEN

JOHN STOOD FIVE feet away with one hand tugging down the bottom half of his face. Mary took a mental snapshot of the man who was looking at her like she was literally everything he'd ever wanted.

Mary knew that insecurities ran deep, and they weren't anyone's duty to dispel but her own. But still, the look on John's face right now certainly helped. He wasn't wishing her to be anything different than the person she was.

She reached her hand out to him, for him, needing him. And as she'd known he would be, he was there immediately. Palm to palm, fingers threaded and then, yes, his mouth on hers. John put one knee on the edge of the bed and leaned over her, taking deep draughts of her mouth. He tasted her fully, slowly, as if they had all the time in the universe, as if the light weren't changing that very moment, as if the world weren't marching on all around them, as if the two of them weren't changing and growing and aging even as they clutched at one another, as if this moment had its own set of orbiting planets, its own gravitational force, its own history.

He shifted his weight and sheltered her, the bed dipping as he planted a hand and took even more from her mouth. His tongue was both soft and overbearing at once and Mary reveled in it, how perfectly John that combination was. Sweet and obliviously intense. He tasted delicious, like toothpaste and fresh coffee and how much he wanted her. She felt his breath fan out over her cheek and it wasn't steady.

She thought of how he looked from afar, broad shoulders, hands in pockets, black and white. Steady. Substantial. Unshakable. But his hand was trembling as he laid it over her hip and stomach. His fingers shook, just slightly, as he slid them down and then back up, catching under the bottom hem of her shirt, under fabric, to touch her bare skin. His fingers flexed at the dip of her waist, pressing into her softness, testing the line between her body and the rest of the world. The edges of her.

He leaned back, one knee on the bed, one foot on the floor, and his eyes were bleary as his pupils grew and shrank. He gripped the bottom of her shirt in both hands and determinedly pulled it up. She'd thought he'd yank it right off, but halfway there, he made a strangled noise and fell down on her again, his mouth opening against her hip bone, his stubble rubbing at her navel, his forehead planting at the V of her ribs.

She let out a half laugh, half groan because joy was rising in her as fast as her arousal was. She grabbed her own shirt and yanked it off, and John looked dazed when he tipped his head and saw her nothing-special bra. Beige colored, because her shirt was white and she'd wanted it to be invisible. Even so, his nostrils flared like she'd just revealed the finest lingerie. He gripped her ribs with one hand and yanked at her bra strap with his teeth.

She laughed fully now. "What is it with you and bra straps?"

"They've never lost their mystique," he told her in a gravelly voice. "Ever since I was a kid, it's never failed to amaze me that sometimes, depending on what a woman is wearing, you can just casually see part of her underwear. Bra straps are freaking hot."

"I'm sorry I robbed you of bra straps with my strapless bra last night."

"Don't be. That was hot too, a little mystery. Bras are girl-magic. So hot."

As if to prove it, John's hands were suddenly everywhere. Cupping her breasts over top of her bra, gliding and pressing, in almost-chaste second-base action. But then, in the blink of an eye, he tipped her to one side, flashed his hand behind her back and unhooked her bra smoothly. He didn't pull it away yet, though.

"Wow," she commented. "Most men fumble the clasp a little bit."

He smirked at her. "I'm a bra expert, Mare." Then he promptly tipped his head to one side, somewhat sheepishly. "My high school girlfriend held me at second base for about a year and a half. There was nothing to do but learn how to remove a bra really well."

Mary did that laugh-groan-gasp thing again. Because she loved learning about his dorky past. And he'd called her Marc, the way only those closest to her did.

She craned up, needing to kiss him, and he obliged instantly. His lips were firm, his sweeping tongue soft and reverent. He groaned into her mouth, and Mary felt it down to her lungs. She deepened the kiss, their teeth clacked lightly and Mary grabbed at his hair. His hand slipped under the loosened cup of her bra, and they both made a sound akin to pain. When she opened her eyes, it was to see John's clamped closed, the fringe of his black eyelashes almost disappearing. He pulled away from the kiss, his eyes coming open as his thumb strummed across her nipple, and Mary arched for him.

He sat back on his knees and tugged the bra away.

"Mary," he whispered. "Jesus Christ, you're gorgeous."

She lay topless on his bed, her body burning under his bright gaze. She dropped her eyes and saw that he was tenting his basketball shorts indecently. She lifted one leg and planted the flat of her foot against his thigh. Her knee fell to the side and his nostrils flared as she opened herself to him.

He briefly covered his eyes with one hand. "You trying to get me to fuck you with your shorts still on?"

Mary went tight and liquid between her thighs all at once. "Is that an option?"

He laughed, but it was pained, harsh. He reached down and undid her shorts, tugging them away. "Someday. For now, let's keep things simple."

His fingers tangled in the sides of her white underwear, but he didn't move them. Instead, he fell forward and started kissing at her chest. Mary gasped for air when he sucked one of her nipples into his mouth, almost harshly. He scooped at her breasts, rounding them, pillowing them, burying his stubbly face in her softness. He started an unfamiliar rhythm. A tug-scrape-smooth using his lips and teeth and tongue against one nipple and then the other. Mary felt a string pull tight inside her, and she opened her mouth, chasing the feeling as she stared unseeing at the sunlight and shadow on his ceiling. His rhythm was methodical, purposeful, the way some men went down on a woman with a specific goal in mind.

Her hips started to buck underneath him. She hooked a leg around him and began to grind herself against his body, any part of his body, seeking friction at all and every cost.

"John," she gasped, tossing her head to one side as her fingers ached from how hard she gripped his comforter. *"John."*

He was going to make her come with nothing more than his mouth at her breasts, his strong hands caging her in.

At the last second, he pulled away, roughly pushing open her legs and tugging the seam of her underwear to one side. John ducked his head and tongue-kissed her between her legs, ending on a seeking suck that, like a star pulling tight in the moments before explosion, had her trembling on the edge of something world-ending. He slightly softened the suck, flicked his tongue, and Mary was gone.

She screamed his name, grateful he was pinning her thighs down because her entire body shook violently. Her world tumbled, dragging Mary along with it. She gasped for air, but it didn't help the rainbow of spots that appeared in her vision as she said his name over and over again.

He kneaded at her wetness softly with his tongue and lips, as if making certain to press out every single aftershock. When she was finally able to look down, she saw immediately that his gentle mouth was at direct odds with his blazing eyes. Black and white, two-toned voice, rude and sweet, two men at once. He watched her with a look she'd never seen before from him.

She reached down and grabbed a handful of his shirt, yanking hard enough to stretch the fabric. He heeded. As he came up onto his knees, she sat up with him and they both ripped his shirt off. She barely had time to see the thatch of hair across his wide chest, his strong arms where they plugged into round shoulders and smoothly arcing collarbones. She barely saw it because he tumbled her backward.

He pressed her down with his weight, both hands cradling the back of her skull, tangling in her hair. "Let me, Mary," he said. He bent his head and bit lightly at the pulse in her neck, but then his eyes were back on hers, and she was swimming in them, tumbling, lashed to him and spinning, just the two of them. "Let me," he said again, part command, part plea.

"Condom," she gasped, and he scrabbled at his nightstand drawer, grappling for a moment, before he brought an unopened box to his mouth and tore it gracelessly open. Condoms flew in an arc over the bed and onto the floor, but thankfully there was one in easy reach. Again, he was on his knees over her, shoving his shorts and boxers down to midknee.

He bounced free, his shaft almost touching his own stomach he wanted her so badly. Mary gasped, needing more oxygen than the hot, close air this room was providing her. His shaft was blunt and wide. Mary took the opportunity while he was tearing the condom open to sit up and get a better look. But she didn't have time to do more than that. His hands came down, and he firmly slid the condom on.

He barred a forearm across her lower back and dragged her hips up to his, tossing her backward onto the bed, cradling her head with one palm as he came over her.

"Yes," she whispered, reveling in his obvious desperation for her, like he couldn't go another second without her heat. "Yes."

With one dexterous hand he pulled her panties to the side and firmly slid a finger, and then another, inside of her, opening her up for him. She hooked a leg around his waist. Mary gasped, huffing air, as John pushed the head of his shaft up against his fingers, docking himself an inch inside of her.

His attention went from between her legs to her face. "Yes?" He crooked his fingers inside of her, rubbing at her G-spot in a crazy-making motion.

"Yes."

"You're gonna let me, Mary? You're finally gonna let me."

Again, his words were a mixture of plea and command, and the combination had a rush of wetness making her ache between her legs. "Now," she begged.

John pressed his hips forward, and his hardness pushed into her in the same motion that he removed his fingers. The push and pull of it was unlike anything she'd ever felt before and Mary straight-up screamed as he buried himself to the hilt inside of her.

She was clawed against him completely, her ankles crossed at his lower back, her hands in fists at his shoulder blades, her forehead jammed into the crook of his neck. "John."

He lifted his head to study her face, his expression softening at whatever he saw there. "I'll never get enough of you saying my name like that."

He dropped his mouth to hers and started grinding his hips against hers. He went even deeper and had her gasping, her fingers scratching over his back. His pelvic bone found her clit, and she moaned.

He swallowed down her sound as his tongue tangled with hers, pulling out halfway and pushing back in. Mary somehow went tight and loose at the same time. He picked up the pace, but he was never sharp; his strokes were almost round, dragging decadently against the right places. Her fingers slipped against his back, the hot air bearing down on them, both of them dizzily panting each other's carbon dioxide. His stubble scraped her cheek as his face slotted in beside hers, the bed creaking beneath them, his breath in her ear. He still had one hand in her hair and the sharp sting of his tight fingers had her gasping in pleasure. He'd held her in place like this once before, when he'd whispered in her ear at the bar. She should have known then that he'd be this bossy in bed. God, she loved it.

"Can you come like this?" he asked her. "With me on top?"

"Sometimes. But usually it's better if I'm on top."

She'd barely gotten the sentence out before he was gripping her at her waist and rolling them. She was disoriented for a moment, the room spinning around her while she got her balance against him. She planted her hands at his chest and blinked down at the sight.

"Jeez, you're hot," she informed him. He wasn't cut exactly, but he was strong and extremely well formed. His normal clothes made him look put-together and contained, but looking down at him now, bare chested, Mary was very aware that she had a completely uncivilized man inside of her. She glanced back, saw that his shorts and underwear were still bunched halfway down his legs, and it made her clamp down on him. He hadn't even been able to wait to get completely naked. Why was that so freaking sexy?

He jutted his hips up under her, his hands tracing her waist, molding her breasts, tangling in her hair, tugging her down for a kiss. "Show me how you like it," he muttered against her mouth.

She reached up and planted a hand against the wall over his head, bracing herself for the deep grind she started up almost immediately. She took him deep and then deeper. He swore and lifted his head only to bang it back down on the bed. She didn't bother with putting on a show for him, or with teasing. Mary went straight for the gold. She found herself with her head tipped back toward the ceiling, one hand tangled with one of John's, bracing her. She clawed at the wall as she grinded her hips back and forth on him, shamelessly using his body for her pleasure.

He was speaking gibberish, his voice pure gravel as his free hand grabbed a handful of her ass. His hips jutted up into hers but not too invasively. He'd asked her to show him how she liked it and now he was obviously paying attention, absorbing the motion, learning. She was quickening, tightening, chasing orgasm, and it broke over her magnificently.

He realized she was coming and gripped her hips with both hands, grinding her down on him as he cursed out the universe.

Mary let herself be putty against him for just a few seconds as he kissed at her neck and pushed up into her from below. She tipped her head to one side and spoke into his ear. "Now show me how *you* like it, John."

His eyes searched hers for just a moment before he was gripping the condom and pulling out of her, rolling out from under her and pressing a hand down on her lower back to keep her belly-down on the bed.

He canted her hips up and tugged her underwear to the side again, this time pressing into her easily, as ready as her body was to accept him again. It wasn't the deepest penetration, but it was by far their most intimate position. He was stretched out over top of her, his hand tangled in her hair and his cheek pressing against hers. He gave her some of his weight but not all of it. Mary was pinned between him and the bed, forcefully adored, nothing to do but accept the pleasure he was pistoning into her. Her breasts and clit were erotically abraded by the fabric of the bedspread as he worked himself into her, his speed picking up, his chest plastered to her back.

Mary could feel his heartbeat banging against her shoulder blade, and she squeezed her eyes shut, relishing how alive he was, how alive *she* was. His fingers came up and clamshelled over her hands, his leg hair scraping her calves. He sheltered her and took from her and gave to her all at once.

"John," she whispered his name again and again.

She was naming the moment, and for her, its name was John. There was no other word for this feeling, this catapult into a new life. His name meant a million things in that moment. It was the man stiffening against her as he finally succumbed to his own pleasure, it was his heartbeat at her back, it was the electric friction every place they touched. It was everything she felt for him, all at once.

JOHN GASPED FOR life as he lay on his back, every muscle in his body turned to pudding. She panted into his ear and he loved it, her body half on, half off of his. The heat was oppressive in his apartment, and their skin slid against each other without either of them moving. If John could have swallowed the moment whole, he would have. Everything was perfect. John had never known a perfect this perfect.

He shifted against her and his attention was drawn down to the basketball shorts and boxers that were still bunched around his knees.

He'd put her facedown and fucked her half-dressed. Jeez.

"I probably should have mentioned that I haven't had sex in a long time and it was going to be, ah, vigorous. I'll make it prettier next time," he promised breathlessly, kicking his shorts and underwear off.

"That was plenty pretty, John," she said, just as breathlessly. He reached down and peeled off the condom, tying it off and throwing it in the trash can next to his bed. He jumped when he felt her touch between his legs.

"Can I?" she asked, lifting her head to look in his eyes.

He cleared his throat. "Sure."

He was still half-hard, and it might not go down with her fingers dancing over him like that. She nudged his shaft to one side and then the other, obviously in a playful, curious mood.

Her fingers circled him; she pushed down and tugged back up. "You're uncircumcised."

He cleared his throat again. "Yeah."

"Hot."

"Yeah?"

He caught her eye and she blushed. "Totally. I can't explain it. There's just something more…animalistic about it. Ruder. I like it." She was fully pink now, and John was delighted.

"Mary?"

"Hmm?"

"That was the hottest sex of my life. Seriously. Jesus. I mean, wow."

She nuzzled into him, and she kept her hand between his legs, though she wasn't playing anymore, just holding him, almost companionably. Not that one companion generally cuddled another companion's dick, but still. It wasn't explicitly sexual the way she held on to him. "Me too," she whispered. "With a bullet."

He tried to keep his proud masculine preening contained on the inside. "And on a Thursday morning before work."

She stretched and rolled onto her back, taking her hand with her. "Got anything for breakfast?"

"I can make you a smoothie. Or we can grab something from the coffee shop by the train."

"Mmm." She clapped a hand over his mouth. "Don't talk about the outside world. The outside world doesn't exist anymore. We fucked it away."

He laughed. "If you say so." He played with her hair, amazed that he was allowed to. That he'd been inside her just minutes before. Yesterday after work seemed a million years ago. He'd never have imagined, upon striding into Fellow's last night, that he would be here now, Mary wrapped around him. A thought occurred to him and this thing was still so new that his stomach flipped when he asked her, "You still want to get together tonight?"

"Definitely," she answered immediately, making him smile.

"I'd say we should go to your house for the air-conditioning—" his hand absently scooped and tumbled her hair "—but I don't usually like to leave Ruth alone at night, and I already did last night."

At his words, her entire body tightened against his, her face buried just above his armpit, her legs clamped around him, her fingers digging into his hips.

"Are you okay?" He looked down at her in alarm, having no idea what the heck had just happened.

She nodded against him, and when she looked up, her eyes were wide and her lip was between her teeth. "I'm okay," she answered, sounding strained. "Ask me later. I can't talk about it now."

But that look on her face was just about all the answer he needed. He was pretty sure, almost positive, that talking about not wanting to leave Ruth alone had just kicked her over the edge and into love with him. He searched her gaze and saw that she was overwhelmed, giddy, terrified. He leaned forward and gently kissed her, hoping to soothe her. He knew the feeling.

"Ask me later too, okay?" he said softly, and this time it was her eyes searching his, trying to figure out if he was saying what she thought he was.

She blushed and buried her face, and John gave her one last cuddle before he sat up on the edge of the bed. He cleared his throat. "I think we should take a freezing-cold shower together so that we don't get heatstroke before we even go outside," he suggested over his shoulder.

She gasped and then her hands were gentle on his back. "Oh, my God, John. I scratched you to hell back here." Her fingers gently traced the lines that her nails had apparently scored into him. He flexed his back, feeling around.

"I like it," he told her honestly. "It feels good. It'll make me think of you all day."

She hooked her chin over his shoulder and straddled him from behind, her legs along his legs, her wetness smashed against him. "That's how I feel about you between my legs. I'll feel it all day."

He groaned and looked at the clock. "Shit. Work. You can't say stuff like that to me when we're gonna be late for work."

"We'll take a quick shower," she promised, her hand snaking around to his front and gripping him again, this time pumping him with much more intention than her playful touch from before.

He stopped protesting and instead reveled in the feel of her delicate but firm grip. He looked down at his lap and grunted at the erotic sight of her gorgeous hand gripping him so tightly. She slid around to his lap, slipping off her underwear and swiping a condom from the floor on her way. She sheathed him with it as she straddled him. He sat on the edge of the bed and she sat on him, lifting up and taking him in in one long, wet slide.

This time wasn't any prettier than the last time, he figured, but he couldn't find it in him to care. She rode him hard, artlessly, and it was hands down the sexiest thing he'd ever seen. He leaned back on his palms and just watched, letting her get herself off on his body any way that she wanted. When she shuddered hard, calling his name and clamping down on him rhythmically, he banded an arm around her waist, securing her, and drove himself upward in several short, intense strokes before he was coming hard, sharply, woozily. Perfection.

They sagged to the side, and he took a long moment to gain his breath back before he was lifting her, carrying her to his shower.

"You love carrying me," she muttered into his shoulder.

"I do," he agreed. "It makes me feel…"

"Like a man?"

"Not quite. It makes me feel human. I can't explain it. Connected to you. Protective. Like I'm the one thing in between you and the rest of the world. I love it."

He set her down carefully in the shower and her smile nearly knocked his metaphorical socks off. He'd told her she was radiant and, boy howdy, he hadn't been lying. The woman was incandescent.

A second later, though, before he could twist on the shower, she stiffened, clapping a hand over his mouth even though he hadn't been talking.

"Shh!" she hissed. "Do you hear that?"

John cocked an ear and heard the familiar, benign tones of his neighbors talking. "My neighbors?"

"I forgot how thin your walls are." She had both hands pressed to her flaming pink cheeks. "Oh, God. *John.*"

He couldn't help but grin. "Are you reflecting on the number of times you just screamed my name?"

"I can't believe this. I haven't even met them yet!"

"Mary, it's New York. Hearing your neighbors have sex is a citywide experience. Practically a rite of passage. Besides, they're not exactly celibate. I'm sure they don't begrudge me returning the favor."

"But I was *loud.*"

He laughed, charmed and so freaking in love with her.

"I know. It was the best. I hope you're like that every time. Lets me know I'm doing well."

"It lets everyone on your entire floor know you're doing well."

He laughed again and turned on the shower, laughing harder when she yelped and twisted away from the cold spray. "There are worse things, Mary. There are much worse things."

CHAPTER TWENTY

JOHN ROUNDED THE corner off the elevator and paused when he saw Richie and Crash talking in the hallway outside the office door. The two men cut off their conversation as John approached and a smug, shit-eating grin exploded over Richie's face.

"Crash," Richie ordered in a bossy tone. "Do this with me."

Richie doo-wop stepped to one side, shucking his arms with his feet. And then to the other side. He looked over, saw that Crash was abstaining from the dance move and frowned. "Crash!"

Sighing, Crash joined in the dance step, looking half chagrined at dancing in his place of work and half pleased that Richie was bullying him into goofiness. "Why are we dancing?"

"We're celebrating John. Who did something very naughty last night. I can see it all over his face."

John laughed and covered said face with one hand, attempting to step around the dancing men and into his office, but Richie got in the way.

"Am I wrong?" Richie teased. "Just tell me I'm wrong, and I'll stop dancing."

"Can I stop dancing anyhow?" Crash asked from behind them.

"Never!" Richie demanded, leaning around John and looking Crash up and down. "I like when you dance."

John turned in time to see Crash go an immediate electric pink. He stopped dancing and scratched the back of his neck with one hand, looking completely unsure of what to say next and altogether very un-Crash-like.

A thought struck John. The Crash Willis that John had known was not dancing in the halls. He wasn't blushing or flirting at work. He was a smarmy, smug kiss-ass, hell-bent on needling John at every turn. But that version of this man had apparently exited the building. John wondered if maybe, just maybe, coming to John's office to be an asshole to John for all those years had been the only reason Crash had been able to invent to come to John's office in the first place. AKA Richie's office.

It didn't make John like Crash any better that years of snide comments and douchebaggery had been an attempt at getting closer to Richie, but at least John could sort of understand the logic of it. People did all sorts of ridiculous things when they wanted someone they weren't sure they could ever have.

"Can I carry on with my workday?" John asked Richie, who was still barring the open door to the office.

Richie narrowed his eyes. "You're not going to give me any details?"

"Not a one."

"Which means that things were really serious and you don't want to disrespect her by gossiping."

John narrowed his eyes right back at Richie and slightly nodded his head in Crash's general direction. "Maybe you can sympathize?"

Richie's eyes narrowed even further and John heard the

unmistakable sounds of Crash shuffling from one side to the other.

"Welp," Richie said, a smile breaking out over his face. "I suppose the public's not going to defend itself."

He stepped aside and swept his hands toward the door, waving John into work. John knew that as soon as Crash left, he was going to get an earful for that insinuation. He also knew that he was going to have to come up with the most tepid version of the facts surrounding his relationship with Mary. He didn't want to actually give up any of the dirt, but Richie was known to steal all of John's writing utensils and bogart the air-conditioning unit until John told him what he wanted to know.

It was a good night was what John decided on. *We hooked up. We're seeing each other again tonight.*

There. That would quell Richie's insatiable curiosity. And then John could get to work.

Richie shooed Crash off to work, whispering something in his ear that made him go electric pink again, and then closed the door to their office, whipping around and narrowing his eyes at John.

"Give it up. I get that you didn't want to spill in front of Crash. But come on. It's just you and me now. Gimme every dirty detail before I explode from curiosity."

It was a good night. We hooked up. We're seeing each other again tonight. John opened his mouth. "I'm such a goner," he said instead and pushed his fingers against his forehead. It was just a habit, though, because there was no headache brewing there. No tension. No fear or anxiety. Nope. The only thing rising inside of John at that particular moment was joy.

"Is that a good thing or a bad thing?" Richie asked, his arms crossed over his chest and his back against the door.

John dropped his hand and sighed. "It's a good thing. It's a freaking *great* thing."

"Yes!" Richie did three quick karate punches and a sloppy roundhouse kick that came shockingly close to John's nose in their cramped office space. "Yesyesyes! Finally! I knew it. I *knew* last night was the night. I will gladly accept flowers, gift certificates, a night out on the town, you pick."

John laughed and shook his head at his irreverent friend. "I'm sorry. You want me to get you a gift because things with Mary finally started happening?"

"Hey! Who dragged Beth out of that bar last night? I opened up a lane for you, John. That's invaluable in fragile moments like that."

John considered his friend's words and then bobbed his head from side to side, conceding the point. "You'll get a nice thank-you card in the mail."

"Cheapskate."

John shrugged. "Tigers don't change their stripes. Especially when they suddenly have a beautiful woman to take out for dinner every once in a while."

"You have to know by now that she doesn't care about your money situation. She's into you for you. I can tell. I have a sixth sense about these things."

John sighed and the joy didn't stop rising within him; it just rose at a much more sedate pace. "We haven't really talked about all that yet. But I'm starting to understand that this is likely my issue much more than it's Mary's. And yes, I'm also beginning to understand that she's really into me. Because of who I am. That's part of why I'm such a goner." John dragged his hands over his face and let his fingertips grip at his jawbone for a long minute, elongating his face in glee and surprise. "I seriously cannot believe this is happening."

"Believe it, baby," Richie said, a wide, gleeful grin on his face. "You deserve it."

THEY SPENT THAT night together as they'd planned to and then the entire weekend as well. It was Sunday afternoon when John realized how far off the deep end he'd really gone with Mary.

Because he was literally herding a cat. While he wore oven mitts.

He was chasing Ruth around his apartment, attempting to jam her into her kennel for the cab ride over to Mary's. Ruth was an easygoing personality, unless it came to getting crammed into a confined space, which John considered fair. Annoying, but fair.

She'd nearly scratched the oven mitts to ribbons by the time he'd loaded her in. He strapped a backpack on, filled with stuff that Ruth would need to spend the next few days at Mary's house and a few changes of clothes for himself as well.

He was not, by any means, moving in with Mary. But there was a heat wave coming. It was going to be over a hundred degrees for at least four days and Mary had put her foot down. John could stay at his house if he wanted, she'd informed him. But she and Ruth were staying where there was air-conditioning.

He'd also considered that to be fair. Mary had already proven that she had no problem sleeping hot and naked in front of his cheap box fan. And besides, in the hottest parts of the summer, he usually took Ruth and stayed in his old room at Estrella's, where there was an ancient window unit that made life tolerable. He'd had to shelve a surprisingly small amount of pride in order to hail the cab that was going to whisk him and Ruth away to a fancier life with a gorgeous woman.

Who wore a sundress down to her toes, her hair in damp waves down her back. She bit into a slice of watermelon when she greeted John at her door and popped a bite of the icy fruit into his mouth before she kissed him.

"Mmm," he murmured, feeling like he was in the best part of a great dream, the part right before everything went wobbly and stopped making sense.

"Hey, Ruthie!" Mary took the kennel from John and set it down. John closed the door.

"I'm warning you, she's usually very grumpy after a cab ride in her kennel."

"She's entitled. No one likes to be handled." Mary let the cat out and clicked her tongue, like Ruth was a dog. "Come on, girl, come see your area."

To John's amazement, his cat actually followed after Mary.

"Her area?" he called, setting his bag down on the floor and following after them. He stopped stock-still in the doorway of a small room next to the bathroom. He hadn't even known this little room was there. "Your laundry room has air-conditioning," John said tonelessly.

The fact that she even had a laundry room was mind-boggling to John. But that she paid to keep it cool in the summer? Jeez.

"It's central air," Mary replied, on her knees next to Ruth, showing her a shiny new litter box and tall cat castle that Ruth was already getting her claws blissfully stuck to.

John blinked down at the mouse with a jingle bell that Ruth had started batting around.

"You got Ruth a bunch of toys. And a litter box. And a castle."

Mary looked up at him. "I assumed you were going to bring food for her. But yeah, she needs a little apartment if she's going to stay here for a few days. I wanted her to be comfortable."

John knew that Mary was actually saying, *I wanted you to be comfortable, John.*

He looked down at the small, portable litter box he'd brought, clutched in his hands. He took a deep breath and decided then and there that feeling inadequate was a waste of energy. "You're the sweetest woman of all time."

It was only when Mary flushed with pink relief and pleasure that John saw just how nervous she'd been to show him her purchases. She'd wanted to welcome him without damaging his pride.

He set the travel litter box aside, strode to the kitchen, washed his hands and whirled on Mary, picking her up by the hips and setting her on the kitchen counter. He stepped between her legs, getting tangled up in the skirt of her sundress and loving it.

"I'm serious, Mare." He nuzzled at her neck, her hair, one cheek against hers. "I'm not exaggerating. You are literally the sweetest person I've ever met. I'm never getting over you."

He hadn't meant to say the last part out loud.

She stiffened in his arms for just a moment, and he cursed himself for saying too much too fast. Wasn't *I'm never getting over you* the same thing as saying *I'm going to love you forever*? They weren't there yet. They weren't even close to—

"Good," Mary told him fiercely, her fingers tangled in

the hair at the crown of his head, pulling him back an inch so she could glare at him. "That works just fine for me."

And then her fingers were scrabbling at his shirt. He had the feeling that she was trying very hard not to tear any buttons.

Everything in John pulled tight, almost painfully. He was frozen in a block of time, the world spinning on without him.

Good.

She wanted him to love her.

Good.

And it was just so freaking *good*.

John animated all at once, breath in his chest, his heart racing to catch up with everything it had just missed. He pulled his arms from around her waist, grabbed his white shirt at the center and gave it a good yank. Buttons flew everywhere as he destroyed it, ripped it off his shoulders.

"Your shirt!" she yelped. "You wrecked it!"

"I have others."

Her hands were palms down in his chest hair, her fingers gripping too hard at his shoulders and collarbones. He loved the way she touched him. Like he could take it. Like there was no breaking him. *Good.*

"John, you wrecked one of your shirts for me." When she landed her forehead against his shoulder in what appeared to be overwhelmed reverence, John guessed that at some point she had snooped in his closet and seen how few clothes he actually owned. She must have seen how scrupulously he cared for his wardrobe.

"My birthday is in a month," he informed her. "You can buy me a new one. Any color you want."

That—if her tongue in his mouth was any indication—had been exactly the right thing to say. John groaned against the wet-hot slide of her mouth pressed to his. She tasted like watermelon. He was lost in the feel of her. The warm silk of her hair. The insistent stroke of her hands against him. He heard his belt and zipper before he quite registered what she was doing. He grabbed his pants before they fell and pulled the condom out of his pocket that he'd optimistically placed there before he'd left his apartment. There were about a thousand more crammed into his backpack.

Mary took the condom from him and sheathed him with it as his hands slipped under her dress and found her underwear. Those were gone, her dress hitched up and then they were smashed against one another, him slipping and sliding against her wetness as they kissed and kissed and kissed.

When he held her still and pushed inside, they both braced and groaned and panted against the utterly exquisite rightness of it. What a strange thing it was that bodies wanted to do when in love, John mused for a moment. That more than sleeping or eating or any other basic need, at that moment John wanted to be inside of Mary. And it made sense to him. Because her body was the most sacred, most special place on earth. He wanted to be where Mary was. Exactly where she was. So close he was part of her. She bit hard at his bottom lip and clawed at his back, loving him fiercely, and he knew she wanted exactly the same thing as he did.

WHEN THE HEAT WAVE subsided back into the low nineties, John and Ruth moved back to his apartment, but Mary pretty much moved with them. They were spending almost every single night together.

It was overwhelming to her, not the speed or intensity with which they were starting their relationship, but how obvious it now was that she'd been utterly starving for this kind of love. Both she and John were gorging on one another, relishing the company, the affection, the sex.

They'd incubated together for a week and a half when Estrella invited Mary over to her house for a Sunday dinner.

John hadn't mentioned to his mother that he and Mary were actually together now. They figured they could tell her together at the dinner.

Mary found herself unexpectedly nervous as she knocked on Estrella's door that night. It wasn't that she suddenly expected Estrella to disapprove of her. It was that everything in Mary's life was changing so quickly. She'd had a hell of a summer—the blind dates, the break-in, Johnjohnjohn. And now this, her relationship with Estrella was about to change as well.

Estrella, one of her closest friends, was about to become the mother of the man she was seeing. That was new. And scary.

Mary took a deep breath that stalled when Estrella's door swung open. But it was just John standing there, grinning at her, munching on something crunchy. His eyes looked lazy and relaxed and utterly thrilled to see her. They'd woken up together that morning, but Mary had spent the day at the shop and he'd had a ton of work to catch up on. It felt like they'd been separated for days. John pulled her in off the doorstep and hugged her tightly against him.

"Damn, you look lovely."

She'd better look lovely. She'd spent an extra hour on her appearance for Estrella. She'd straightened her hair, done her makeup, practically hauled her entire closet off its hangers before she'd decided on this one perfect, peachy dress that showed off her shoulders and her calves.

John crunched in her ear.

She laughed and pulled back. "What are you munching on?"

"My mother made tortilla chips and guac. Seriously, you'll never be the same after you eat her chips and guac. By the way, there's way more people here than we thought."

He took her hand and tugged her back through the house to the kitchen and all the way through to the back porch that Mary hadn't even known was there. Mary peeked out, gasped and then yanked John back into the kitchen. "There's a dozen people out there!"

"Like I said. More than we thought." He frowned down at her quizzically.

"Let's wait to tell her."

He frowned even more, that beloved V carving its place on his face. "Until when?"

"We'll wait out everyone and tell her when it's just us. Later tonight. I just don't want to do it in front of everyone."

The V eased as soon as he realized that she wasn't hoping to wait indefinitely to tell his mother. "Okay. Sounds reasonable."

They dropped hands and stepped out onto the porch.

"Mary!"

Estrella, salt-and-pepper hair in a messy bundle on top of her head and a loose sundress flapping around her knees, practically bowled other guests aside.

Mary found herself wrapped up in a warm, firm hug. "You look beautiful!" Estrella crowed into Mary's hair before she'd even released her. "Radiant and happy and perfect. I'm so glad you're here. Now the party is perfect."

Tears sprang to Mary's eyes as this woman, this good mother, poured support and positive feeling into her. This woman who held nothing back from Mary. Who hadn't held it against her when she'd initially rejected John. Who'd shown up at her shop with a wine and cheese picnic and helped Mary rebuild. Who thought Mary was the tippiest top of any mountaintop.

This was what a mother's hug and acceptance were supposed to feel like. And Mary truly hadn't felt that since Tiff had passed. Estrella loosened the hug to step back, but Mary held on tight and the embrace continued. Two tears rolled down Mary's face before she stepped back from the hug and wiped the tears from her face, her eyes blurred and all the other guests at the party disappeared into a smudge of color.

"John and I are together," she told Estrella. She heard John's intake of breath and then his warm hand was at her waist.

"I thought we were waiting," he said, but his words were basically turned into a groaning *oof* as his mother cuffed him around the neck and dragged him into a hug that looked rather painful. Estrella pecked at the side of his head with forceful kisses.

"I knew it!" she crowed through tears. "I knew the two of you were a love match. I knew it from the day I met Mary, but I didn't want to push. She wasn't really dating, and then before I knew it, she was dating that horrible Doug. But then! The window! The opening! And I kicked you through straight to her, my boy. And you're such a good boy. You did such a good job."

She released John with such force he stumbled backward and then Estrella pounced back onto Mary. "I told you he was a nice boy. Clumsy but sweet. Oh, Mary. And you're such a good girl."

"Estrella." A deep voice came from over Estrella's shoulder, and then there was Cormac, prying a sobbing Estrella off of Mary's neck. "Let the girl take a breath."

In fact, taking a breath was the first thing Mary did

once Cormac had successfully pried Estrella off of her. She gasped for air and sagged back into John, who wrapped both arms around her waist and laughed into her hair.

"Sorry," Mary said as she turned to him. "Your mom is such a good mom. I got overwhelmed. I didn't want to hide it."

"Fine by me, baby," John murmured, brushing her hair back from her face and kissing her gently. "I'd been trying to figure out how I was supposed to keep from flirting with you until the rest of the guests left."

"Oh, my God," Estrella said through more tears. "They're *canoodling*."

"Can this count as your birthday present this year, Ma?" John asked with an easy smile on his face.

"Slippery slope, son," Cormac admonished with a smile that matched John's. "Next year she'll be demanding a wedding for her birthday. The year after that, grandbabies."

Both Mary and John stiffened.

"Right," John said with a laugh. "Socks it is, then, Ma."

The rest of the evening passed much less eventfully with good food and cold drinks and even a light breeze once the sun went down. It turned out that Mary actually knew most of the people from when she'd met them at the block party.

When it was just the four of them, John, Mary, Estrella and Cormac, Estrella's eyes filled with tears again. Mary perched on John's lap even though there was plenty of available seating.

"I won't pressure you," Estrella started, and John groaned. "Ma..."

Estrella waved a hand through the air, striking John's disapproval from the record. "I won't pressure you, but I just want you to know, Mary, that I love you. And that you are welcome in my house and in my heart, and I couldn't be happier."

Mary burst into tears herself.

On their way home, the train rocking them back and forth and into one another in a way that was soothing only to New Yorkers, Mary tipped her head up from John's shoulder and squinted at him. "You're really lucky to have a mom like the one you have."

John nodded. "I've learned that over the years." He cleared his throat and looked momentarily nervous. "Ah, I'm more than happy to share the wealth, Mary. Anytime you need a mom, you should hit up Estrella. Nothing would make her happier." He kissed Mary's palm. "Or me happier, for that matter."

Mary settled her head back on his shoulder and sighed. It had been so long since she'd felt like this. Like she was part of a unit. She'd never once felt this way with her parents. She'd felt like this with Tiff and with Cora. And now with John and Estrella. And Ruth, of course.

She knew that the time was coming when John would have to meet her parents. The thought sat heavily in her gut. Her mother hadn't reached out since the Carver Reinhardt debacle. It wasn't altogether unusual to go a month without a check-in from her folks, but the silence felt particularly loud right now. Mary had made it clear that she wouldn't be reaching out to them.

Whenever her mother called, whenever it was time for Mary to visit again, she'd have John. And it was important to remember that.

This time, she had John.

CHAPTER TWENTY-ONE

Two weeks later, the end of August was bearing down on them and the weather hadn't let up one bit. Mary had gotten distracted in her cool storeroom that morning, sighing over the fall decorations she wouldn't be able to put up in her shop window for another month at least. October couldn't come soon enough for her. She was tired of underboob sweat. She was tired of her summer wardrobe. She was tired of having to eat her weight in fruit popsicles just to make sure she didn't succumb to heatstroke.

She was also excited about weathering a new season with John. This summer had spanned on for years, it felt like. Though, so had her connection to John. They'd been together only a few weeks, not even a real month yet, but Mary felt like the strength and quality of their relationship was so much more substantial than that. She was anxious for time to catch up with her feelings.

She spent the day in her shop, relishing the air-conditioning and helping customers. Though the end of summer was usually a little slow retail-wise, she'd noticed a surge in customer interest since the break-in. Maybe the way she'd rearranged the shop was catching more eyes off the sidewalk, or maybe people who'd heard about the break-in were stopping by to see how things were going. Either way, Mary's business was doing well enough that any second she wasn't with John, she was busy in her shop.

Mary helped a customer choose between two sets of handblown glass tumblers and carefully wrapped and packaged them for him. She was dimly aware that he was an attractive man and that he was probably flirting with her, but her mind was elsewhere as she handed him his purchase and gave him a bright smile.

She noticed that his eyes had strayed to her left hand, a look of confusion on his face as she merrily sent him on his way. With a defeated shrug, he was gone.

When Mary looked over at the door, it was a double take. She was surprised to see John standing off to one side of her shop, just past the entrance, his eyes pinned to her.

Her insides turned to a slow-moving wildfire. She knew that look he was giving her. That was his I-know-what-Mary-looks-like-naked look.

Another customer with a question pulled her attention away, and it was ten more minutes before the shop was empty. Kylie was sorting through inventory in the back room, finally back on a regular work schedule post break-in.

John, hands in pockets, strolled quasi-casually over to her. She leaned across the counter to him, her elbows planted, and accepted a quick-hot sip of a kiss.

"What a lucky woman I am," she told him easily, almost thoughtlessly. "To have such a broody, handsome boyfriend."

She froze for a moment, shocked at herself.

She hadn't meant to call John her boyfriend. They hadn't quite discussed it yet, what they were to one another. Did John even have girlfriends? The word sounded so juvenile. Fun, exhilarating, but juvenile. She was positive they were monogamous simply due to the amount of sex they were having. The man would have to be addicted to sex, Red Bull and Viagra if he were going to somehow be having more sex with someone else on the side.

His brows pulled down in that V that she'd come to love so dearly, and his lips twitched in a smile so slight, a stranger wouldn't notice it. But Mary did. "I was just thinking the same thing," he said in his two-toned voice.

"You were just thinking how lucky I am?" she asked innocently, widening her smile and batting her eyelashes. "How sweet."

He laughed. "I was thinking how lucky *I* am." John slipped his hand across the counter and grabbed hers, doing that palm-kissing thing he always did with her. The man had a serious thing for her palms. "Remember that day Estrella and I came to your shop?"

"When she dragged you in by your ear?"

"I came willingly!" he insisted. "I told you that I knew I needed to apologize. And apologize I did."

Mary squeezed his hand. "It was actually a very good apology, by the way." She cocked her head to one side. "That apology was the first thing I truly liked about you. Not every person can apologize and mean it the way you did."

"I already liked everything about you," John admitted, those light eyes eating up her entire expression. "I felt like such an ass for what I'd said on our date, and then I felt like an ass for witnessing you ask that guy out when you obviously wanted to do it privately. Remember that guy? *James.*"

She laughed in surprise as a look of disdain crossed John's face. "You remember his name?"

The tips of John's ears went pink, but he shrugged. "It was a memorable moment. And he stuck in my head because I couldn't for the life of me believe that anyone in their right mind would reject you, for any reason. Married or not."

Mary laughed again. "John, you'd rejected me not two days before that!"

He shook his head adamantly. "I stupidly pushed you away, but I certainly didn't reject you." He kissed her palm again. "The point is, I was jealous of that guy, flirting with you so easily. And he didn't have his mother there with him." John shook his head with a little laugh, looking down at their laced fingers and then back into Mary's face. "I wanted to *be* that guy."

"I wouldn't want you to be that guy," Mary replied immediately, vehemently. "Because then you wouldn't be you. And there's no one else like you. Seriously, I've looked. I've had thirty-seven years to search, and you're the only one I've found."

John's eyes dropped back to their hands and Mary took the opportunity to really look at his face. Sometimes, when his eyes were on her, that iceberg blue was the only thing she could see, she missed the forest for the trees. But now she took great pleasure in observing the inky black frame of his hair and eyebrows. She relished the cut of his jaw, highlighted with blue-black stubble, the way his ears lay so flat against his head. Jeez, she was gone for him.

"So. Boyfriend, huh?" His eyes flicked up and she froze, flushing deeply.

"I...thought so? I mean, obviously it's not a decision that can be made unilaterally, but yeah. It rolled off my tongue so easily I think because it suits what we are to one another." She cleared her throat. "Right?"

He was full-on grinning now, the way he had on the dance floor. It was the kind of smile that changed his entire face. "I can't believe MFT just asked me to be her boyfriend."

Mary laughed and warmed and smiled all at once. She'd told him about Cora's nickname. She loved so much that there was someone on planet Earth who called her that again. "So what if I did?"

"I haven't been a boyfriend since undergrad. I might be bad at it."

"I'm not particularly worried." A thought occurred to her. "Although maybe *you* should be. Boyfriends tend to meet parents."

He gave her a look that was so patently Estrella that Mary nearly laughed aloud. "I'll be thrilled to meet your mother. I'll tell her all about my cougar fetish."

Mary threw her head back and roared with laughter. "Oh, my God. She'd have a heart attack. It would serve her right for laying into me about my age this much."

Mary sobered and absently leaned forward to kiss John again, barely registering that she was seeking comfort from him. "It really is going to be terrible, John. Meeting her. I'm going to be humiliated the entire time with the way she speaks to me. You're going to see what a pushover my dad is. Ugh. Let's just skip it."

"Mary." His hand went up to her cheek, pushing her hair back. He opened his mouth to say something, but the bell over the door jingled, and they both looked back to see who was coming into the shop.

It was Via and Matty, chatting with one another and grinning about something. They both looked extremely sweaty and Mary saw that Via had their softball stuff strapped to her back. Via was volunteering for Matty's summer Coach Pitch league, and their practices took place in a park only a few blocks from Mary's shop.

"Hi, guys!" Mary called, thrilled to see them.

Via looked up, her eyes taking in the way Mary and John leaned toward one another, the grip of their hands. "Hi."

"Water," Matty croaked, dramatically clutching at his throat. "Preferably Gatorade."

The adults all laughed at his antics. "I have water and lemonade up in my apartment. You're welcome to it."

"Let's get some and bring it down for the girls, Matty," John suggested, nodding his head toward the stairs up to Mary's apartment.

"Which girls?" Matty asked. "Them?" He pointed at Mary and Via. "They're definitely ladies."

The adults laughed again, and John held the door for Matty, saying something to him with a smile as he followed him up to the apartment.

"Ooooh," Via teased softly, leaning her petite frame against the counter much the way John just had, her eyes sparkling. "Mary's got it bad."

Mary blushed and smiled. "That obvious, huh?"

"You two seriously seem over the moon for each other."

Mary took a deep breath. "I think we are."

Mary and John had spent time with her group of friends twice over the last month. Tyler's skeptical deep freeze of John had lasted about seven seconds once he'd realized how sweet John was to Mary. How lucky he obviously felt. John didn't fit seamlessly into the group. He didn't have a ton to talk to Sebastian or Tyler about, and honestly, he'd seemed at his most comfortable tossing a Frisbee with Matty out back. But still, to Mary it had been perfect. Because as compatible as she'd been with each person in her friend group as individuals, for a long time she'd felt like the odd person out. The only single one. The one who'd had more of a connection to Cora than she had with Via or Fin. A relic of the past.

Not that she didn't love Via and Fin. Not that she didn't value their friendships deeply. She did. The same way she did with Tyler and Seb. Her best friends. The two people who'd been there in her darkest times. Who'd helped her start her shop. Who'd helped her rebuild her shop. But somehow, having John there, as odd a fit for the group as she herself was, made Mary finally feel like she fit. Because no matter what, John was going home with her. He wanted to go home with her. He checked her drink level to make sure she wasn't thirsty, literally and metaphorically, and at the end of any gathering, they held hands on the train, on the way to one of their houses, wherever Ruth currently was. It was a fresh, potent heaven that Mary had barely let herself hope for.

Via, still smiling over teasing Mary, paused for a second and twiddled her fingers on the counter. "Listen, while Matty's upstairs, I wanted to bring something up to you."

"Shoot." Mary didn't often see Via look nervous.

"We're headed up to White Plains this weekend to spend time with Art and Muriel."

Art and Muriel were Matty's grandparents on Cora's side. They'd met and interacted with Via plenty of times since she and Sebastian became an item, but to Mary's knowledge, this would be Via's first time in White Plains. AKA Cora's childhood home. That might be…a lot.

"Wow."

"Yeah." Via let out a deep breath. "I'm really nervous about it. But also, Matty asked to go see Cora's gravesite. And he really wants me to be there too."

Something twisted inside Mary, but not in a bad way.

"That makes sense. You're his other parent. He wants you to be with him."

"I know. It's silly, but I really don't want to be stepping on anyone's toes about it. I've never attempted to replace Cora or anything like that. And part of me would really like to go to her gravesite and pay my respects, you know? She is the reason that I have a real family now. Seb and Matty are everything to me. But I guess… I was just wondering…" Via cleared her throat, many layers of emotion all swirling together in her throat. "If you're not doing anything this weekend, if maybe you might want to join us?"

"You want me to come with you guys to Cora's grave?" It surprised Mary simply because she would have thought that might be something their family wanted to keep very private.

"If it's too painful or too private for you, please, feel no pressure at all. But Seb mentioned that you used to take Matty there when he was a toddler, when it was too hard for Seb to do it himself. And it just got me thinking about family and how hodgepodge all of our families are. And how grateful I am that you were there for Seb and Matty before I knew them. And—"

Emotion thick in Via's throat cut her off. She let out a long breath.

"And you'd love to have your friend there with you," Mary guessed softly. "Both to support you and maybe to take some of the intensity out of the moment?"

Mary could only guess what it might be like to visit your partner's deceased wife's grave for the first time. Especially when it had become so clear that Via and Matty were as close to mother and son as two people could really get. Mary figured that if her presence there would tone down the symbolism in Via's mind a little bit, that if it were a group of people there, and not Seb and Matty bringing Via to, like, introduce her or something, it might be a little bit easier. Well, Mary could make that happen.

"Yes," Via said quietly, clearing her throat. Her eyes flicked to the ceiling, where they could hear Matty's and John's footsteps as they started descending the stairs. "Seb thought it would be a good idea too. If you want to, that is."

"I'd be honored," Mary answered immediately. She'd have to refigure the shift schedule at the shop for the weekend, but that was small potatoes, really. "Can I bring John?"

"Of course!" Via squeaked, both with relief and pleasure. "I really like John!"

"Oh. Good," he said from behind her, a pitcher of lemonade in one hand and glasses in the other. "I really like you too."

Via turned bright pink and just laughed at herself.

"I found cookies," Matty informed the group, holding up a box of Girl Scout cookies that Mary didn't even remember purchasing.

"How in God's name did you find those?"

"They were in the back of your cabinet."

"He literally got on his hands and knees and disappeared into the cabinet," John said, laughing. "The kid is like a bloodhound."

"Let's check the expiration date on these, shall we?" Mary reached down and laughed. "Yikes. Two years old. I think we'd better skip it, my dude."

Matty's face fell.

"There's that bakery down the block," Kylie said, emerging from the back of the store and wiping her dusty hands on her trousers. "If you need a cookie fix, Matty."

Matty took a gasping gulp of air after he was finished

demolishing an entire cup of lemonade. "Yes. I do. I need cookies. Will you come too?"

Kylie smiled at him, her red hair in a style that she'd only recently started wearing, a sort of complicated braid crown that suited her fox-like face. She was beautiful, Mary thought. And happy. And so was Matty. So many harsh things had happened in these kids' lives and here they were grinning at each other about cookies.

"Can I take my break, Mary?"

"Of course."

"I'll go too," Via decided, her eyes bouncing back and forth between Mary and John. She leaned across the counter, kissed Mary on the cheek, and then the shop was empty again.

"Via wants me to come with them the first time she ever visits Cora's grave," Mary said without preamble.

"Wow." John's eyes grew wide, his expression somber. He knew the gravity of the ask. Mary had explained to him the complicated web that held Mary, Sebastian, Via and Matty all together. The hole that Cora had left behind, the balm that Via had become for all of them. Not a replacement, but a beautiful addition to lives that had been missing Cora for far too long. "Wow. Do you want to?"

Mary nodded. "Yes. It's been a while since I've been there. And I'd love to make things easier for Via, for all of them, if I can."

John's somber expression softened infinitesimally. "Sweetest person on planet Earth," he told her.

Mary smiled. "Will you come too? For the weekend? It's just up in White Plains. We could get an Airbnb or something. Maybe Estrella could watch Ruth? Oh! We could invite Fin and Ty and Ky to come too. They don't have to do the whole cemetery thing, but they could hang out with us in the meantime. What do you think?"

John nodded. "I think," he said carefully, "that White Plains isn't very far from Connecticut."

She frowned. "You want to meet my parents."

"Well. No," he answered with his patent honesty, making Mary laugh. "But I wonder if maybe we shouldn't end the standoff with your mother. It wouldn't have to be a huge deal. We could just pop in for an hour. Get things moving again."

"I'll think about it," Mary promised. The weekend would be emotional enough without adding a trip to her mother's house. But maybe he was right. Maybe it was time to see if things could be repaired. Mary had always been the odd man out at her parents' house. But maybe John would be the odd man out as well, just like with their friends. And they could be odd together. Emphasis on together.

CHAPTER TWENTY-TWO

As MUCH AS John didn't understand the desire to ever leave New York City, he had to admit, all that cement sure seemed to trap the heat. As soon as they left the city limits, the sizzling temperatures just sort of sedated themselves, tumbling down into the manageable eighties range. That was nice.

John and Mary rode the Metro-North with Tyler, Fin, Kylie, Via, Sebastian, Matty and his dog, Crabby. Sebastian's truck was apparently in the shop, otherwise some of them would have driven with him, but John, a native New Yorker to his bones, was infinitely more comfortable on a train than he was in someone else's pickup truck.

They hadn't all been able to get seats together, but they were scattered in twos and threes up and down the train car, and John had to admit, that just like other times he'd spent with this group, he felt like he was part of a scrum of chattering middle schoolers on a field trip. They were laughing at one another's jokes, giddy at fleeing the hot city, at traveling in a flock. It was fun.

Matty was pretty much the mayor of the train car. He walked up and down the aisle, checking on all the members of his group, even talking with some people he'd never met before. He obviously considered himself to be Crabby's ambassador, explaining to anyone within earshot that Crabby was a good dog who'd never bite anyone and they'd had to pay extra for him to get a ticket on the train car. Also, that no matter how good a dog he was, his dad had insisted that Crabby had to stay parked between his feet the entire time, otherwise Matty would have brought him around to meet people.

John was just as charmed as the rest of the train car, and he finally fully understood why this trip had been so important to Mary. As much as each couple was separate from one another, they were also all meshed and bonded in a hundred different ways. Seb and Tyler had grown up best friends. Same with Via and Fin. Kylie was closest to her brother, but now that he and Fin were together, they seemed to be a real family unit. Kylie and Matty both loved Mary to distraction, obviously as comfortable with her as they were with their guardians. The most obvious part was how much each and every person in this group loved Mary. They were protective and indulgent, lighting up when she was near. She did that to people. Lit them up.

Of course they would want Mary near at a time like this. Who wouldn't?

They got off the train in the White Plains station and the group split up. Matty, Via, Seb and Crabby waved goodbye and hopped in a car with Matty's grandparents. The rest of the group walked the quarter mile to their Airbnb, chosen for its proximity to the train station. All of them had had work on Friday, so it was Saturday midmorning that they settled into their rooms at the Airbnb, the commute having been about only two hours total. The cemetery visit was set for tomorrow, so all of Saturday stretched out before them.

An hour after they arrived, John found himself in a hammock, a beer in his hand and Mary plastered along his side.

"Why are you frowning?" she asked him, her fingers tracing his eyebrows.

"It's so quiet," he complained. He was made nervous

by the rolling stretch of green grass below them, by the lack of traffic noise. It was probably his imagination, but he thought the sky to be a disconcerting blue out here in the suburbs.

Mary laughed. "Would it make you feel better if I slammed a few car doors and shouted at some passerby?"

He laughed too. "Infinitely."

John fiddled with Mary's golden hair, took a long sip of his beer and decided to tell her the real truth about why he was frowning. "I was supposed to go on vacation with my dad this weekend."

Mary stiffened. "What? Oh, my gosh, John. I didn't mean to mess up your plans!"

"You didn't," he reassured her. "I'd already said no a couple of weeks ago. It's just funny, knowing that he and Maddox are off somewhere bonding, and I'm not there. Not that it's the first time it's ever happened. They vacation together every year or so, and have since Maddox was a kid. But it's the first time since we reconnected that I've been on vacation somewhere else at the same time. Usually I'm too busy working myself into the ground to give it much thought."

"Why did you say no to the trip?"

John was quiet for a while, gathering his thoughts. "Honestly, there were a lot of reasons. Wanting to spend time with you was probably the most obvious one." He paused. "Mary, I'm sure it's quite clear to you, but I don't have a ton of money. Don't get me wrong. I'm good with money. I'm responsible. But New York is expensive, and public defenders don't get loan forgiveness until the ten-year mark. I've got a ways to go yet."

She snuggled closer to him, but he could feel her tension. "I know that."

"Right. Well. My dad is very rich. And whenever he invites me to do something with him, it's way too expensive for me to ever pay my own way."

"So you have to decide if you're gonna skip it or let him pay for you."

He squeezed her close, unsurprised that she'd instantly understood. She was smart like that. "Exactly. Can you guess how many times I've ever let him pay for me?"

"Zero?"

"Yup." John sighed, long and hard. "I'm starting to rethink my stance on that, however. You're helping me."

"Me?"

"Yeah. Our differences. What you can afford versus what I can afford. I thought I might never be able to get over it. But with you, I don't take it as personally as I do with my dad. I don't know. I'm finding myself less and less threatened with the whole thing. You don't measure my worth by my bank account. So, I've been starting to wonder why *I* do, you know?" His hand sifted through her hair. "For a long time, I figured that my dad was trying to buy my forgiveness with his gifts and trips and trust funds. But now I think he's just trying to figure out a way to spend some time with me."

Mary smoothed his T-shirt down. He'd planned on wearing his usual slacks and button-down, but she'd recently started talking him into more casual clothes on the weekend. She'd shown him how to do something called a French tuck with his shirts that supposedly made his plain clothing look a little more fashionable. John cared about that just about as far as he could drop-kick it, but still, it made Mary happy.

"Have you thought about inviting him to do something you could afford to do? I dunno, a baseball game? Or even, like, a weekend out on Far Rockaway? Something like that?"

He kissed her forehead. "Yeah, actually, when I told him I wasn't coming out to Colorado this week, that's exactly what I did. I floated the idea of a weekend in Toms River. Whale watching from the ferries. Something we both like."

Mary cranked her head back, a smile on her face. "You're into whale watching?"

"Not that I've done a ton of it, but yeah. Whales are cool."

She laughed and buried her face against his shoulder. "You're cool."

He was the one laughing now. "We both know I'm a dork."

"You're a hot dork. Which makes you cool."

"Whatever you say."

"Lawn bowling?" Tyler shouted from the back porch over to the lovebirds in the hammock. "Just found a kit in the garage!"

"What the hell is lawn bowling?" John asked.

"I'll teach you, city boy," Mary said, rolling from the hammock and tugging him upward.

They passed the rest of the day in lazy luxury, playing lawn games, going for a walk around the neighborhood, grilling their early dinner on the back patio.

John was just trying to decide whether or not an after-dinner nap would disturb his sleep cycle when Mary slid onto his lap. She was biting her bottom lip, looking nervous about something.

"If we were going to go, now would probably be the time."

"Go..." A light flicked on in his head. "To Connecticut?"

"Yeah. I just looked it up. It's only a thirty-minute cab

ride from here. Which would put us at my parents' house in time for their nightly *Downton Abbey* slash glass-of-brandy ritual."

John blinked at her. "That's a thing?"

"They're in their early sixties and live in suburban Connecticut, John. It's not like they have a hopping nightlife."

He stood up, setting her on her feet. "Yes. Let's go. If you're inviting me, I'm accepting."

He wasn't sure why her reconciliation with her mother was so important to him. He just knew that it was clear how much it had been weighing on Mary, and he wanted to do anything he could to help lift that weight off of her.

They were in a cab and on the highway when Mary turned to him. "I kind of feel like I'm copping out, being the one to reach out to them. Show up on their doorstep."

"Because you laid down an ultimatum?"

She bit her lip and nodded. "Yeah. And then I had all these fantasies about my mother showing up in Brooklyn and saying she was wrong."

John didn't know Mary's mother, but he knew people, and he figured that the odds of that panning out the way she'd hoped had been vanishingly slim. "Whether or not she admits she was wrong, you know the truth. I know the truth. She can't take that from us."

Mary studied him. "Something you've learned as a public defender?"

John sighed. "Unfortunately, yes. But also as my father's son. You know, he never apologized to Estrella? Even after he finally acknowledged me as his kid?"

"Wow."

"Yeah. Estrella says it's because she was the love of his life, and to apologize is to recognize everything he lost when he walked out the door."

Mary burst out laughing. "Jeez. To have Estrella's confidence."

John chuckled as well. "I think she might be right. But either way, she's taught me not to wait around for apologies or for closure. No one can validate your story but you, Mary."

He thought of the morning she'd shown up at his house in red shorts, the morning they'd put everything on the table. He picked up her hand and positioned her fingers so that her thumb and pointer were only a centimeter apart from one another.

"You once told me that your mother had you this close to scrapping everything you knew to be true about the world, about yourself."

Mary nodded solemnly.

"But just remember," John continued. "That she never got you to here." He pressed her fingers together. "She might have brought you to the edge, Mary, but you never went all the way to her side. You never let her take it all. You held strong. Holding strong at a centimeter is just as admirable as holding strong at a mile."

Mary's eyes were glazed with tears when they pulled up in front of a neat, suburban lawn. The house was brick and squat and smaller than John had been expecting. The yard was well kept, the garage door closed, the blinds drawn. Everything perfectly tucked in for the night. He looked up and down the block at each house and saw more of the same. It was a nice neighborhood. He could picture Mary growing up there. Her sunny head bouncing as she hopscotched down the sidewalk. Her grinding the gears of her father's car as she learned how to drive in that cul-de-sac.

Mary took a deep breath as they stood on the front porch and reached for John's hand. He was about to tell her that they didn't have to do this, that they could just turn around and head back to White Plains, when she reached forward and rang the bell.

A few moments later, the porch light flicked on, there was some scuffling behind the door and then there was an older man, his white hair in a low ring from ear to ear, a small snifter in one hand, his plaid pajamas a strange juxtaposition to the balmy summer evening.

"Mary!" Her father's glasses winked in the porch light as he stepped barefoot onto the porch and gathered his daughter up in a huge hug, gripping her so tightly his brandy snifter almost tumbled from his hand. "Oh, my girl, I didn't think— I wasn't sure— Oh, Mary, I'm so glad you're here."

When he stepped back from her, John got the distinct impression that her father was swallowing down tears as fast as he was his surprise.

"Come in, come in." He shuffled both of them into the house, his gaze barely even flicking over to John, as if he didn't care who the strange man in his foyer was, he only had eyes for his daughter. "Naomi!"

"Dad!" Mary jumped, as if him shouting across the house for his wife had shocked her.

"Naomi!" he shouted again, agitated and excited and still clutching Mary's shoulders with one arm. He obviously didn't want to let her go. "I didn't know she was going to do that, Mary. The blind date thing. I didn't think she was going to spring that on you. And then when she told me what you'd said, that you weren't going to come around here anymore, well, I didn't blame you. I've spent the last month trying to figure out if I should go to Brooklyn, but I didn't want to invade your space. But I've been so scared that everything was ruined. I didn't know when I'd see you next."

The man's eyes filled with tears as he hugged his daughter again. John might have felt out of place or uncomfortable at witnessing this show of obvious vulnerability, but he truly didn't even think his presence had registered for Mary's father.

"Mary!" And then there she was, the infamous Naomi Trace. She was beautiful, of course, even more beautiful than John had pictured her. She had short, stylishly cut and dyed blond hair, and a surprisingly colorful silk robe that she clutched around her neck and covered her down to her toes. He'd never seen so much silk in one place before outside of old Hollywood films. "What are you doing here? At this hour?"

Naomi's eyes flicked to John, and she patted self-consciously at her hair.

"You told Dad that I wasn't going to come around anymore? That's it? That's all you told him?"

Naomi's eyes bounced away from John, over to Mary, and then back to John. "I—"

"Was there more?" Mary's dad asked, one hand still on Mary's shoulder.

"Yes, there was more!" Mary threw her hands up in the air. "I said I wasn't coming back here *unless she apologized to me.* But I made sure to tell her that I would always answer a phone call from you two. That I would never turn you away. I wasn't cutting you out! Either of you!"

Mary's father turned to his wife, his face as white as chalk. Without another word, he turned and walked out of the foyer.

Naomi took half a step after him, stopped, patted her hair again and turned back to Mary. "You might have called."

"Well, I'm glad I didn't, so you didn't have time to reframe your story for Dad!"

"Mary!" Naomi admonished with a surprising amount

of self-righteousness, considering she'd just gotten caught in a rather egregious lie by omission. "Can we not do this in front of a guest?"

Mary pinched the bridge of her nose in a rare show of frustration and pain. It snapped something inside of John. Nobody got to make Mary cave in on herself. Not Dud Doug and not her mother. He was at her side in a second, his arm around her waist and his lips at her temple.

Mary breathed deeply through her nose, leaning into John. "Mom, meet John Modesto-Whitford. John, meet my mother, Naomi. He's not a guest, for the record. He's my boyfriend."

"You brought a man to meet us?" Naomi asked carefully, a strange light in her eyes as she looked back and forth between John and Mary.

"She's torn between celebrating the fact that I won't die a spinster and reaming me out for bringing you over when she's wearing her after-dinner robe," Mary translated, turning to John.

Naomi pinched her lips together before she stepped forward for a handshake. "Well, I have to admit this isn't exactly how I pictured meeting Mary's beau."

"Well, I pictured you calling me to apologize for your behavior, so I guess we can't all get what we want, can we, Mom?"

Naomi blanched and took a step back. "I'm going to change my clothes and get your father. Mary, why don't you bring John into the sitting room?"

Mary grabbed John's hand and dragged him through a dining room, the kitchen and then back to a darkened living room area, where an episode of a television show was paused on the screen.

Mary collapsed onto the couch and dragged John down with her. "Holy crap," John muttered.

"Yeah." Mary pinched the bridge of her nose again. "I never imagined she would lie to my dad like that. I mean, I was starting to wonder why he wasn't texting or calling, but I never thought…"

"Okay." John rubbed at his forehead for a moment, then dropped his hand, realizing that Mary knew his tell and not wanting to imply that any of this was too stressful for him. He organized his thoughts in his brain. "Mary, I want to be whatever you need right now. If you need me to sit stoically by your side, I'm there. If you need me to hold your hand and laugh at their jokes and pretend everything is just dandy, I'll do it. It'll be really hard for me not to defend you, because that's kind of my knee-jerk reaction, but for you, I'll—"

"Are you nuts? Defend me! It's been six years since I had Tiff defend me to my mother's face. I'm dying out here. What's the point of dating a public defender if he won't even defend you to your mother?"

John burst out laughing. "Fair enough. Defending you it is. And then we leave."

"Perfect."

Mary sagged onto John's shoulder, her palm pressing against his sternum for just a moment in that absent way of hers, seeking his heartbeat out. God, he loved that.

They both straightened, however, when a few moments later her parents came into the room. Her father plunking hard into an armchair on one side of Mary, and Naomi perching prettily on the edge of the chair next to John. They'd both changed out of their pajamas, and Naomi looked as if she'd taken the time to gather herself together, but Mary's father looked like he was about ten seconds from bursting into tears.

"John, I didn't get a chance to introduce you before, but this is my father, Trevor Trace. Dad, this is my boyfriend, John Modesto-Whitford."

Trevor leaned across Mary and gave John a brisk handshake. "I'm sorry that you have to be introduced to Mary's family in such dramatic fashion."

Naomi laughed uncomfortably from her chair. "It doesn't have to be dramatic," she said in a stilted, singsongy tone of voice, as if she were warning her husband and daughter not to embarrass her.

John nearly rolled his eyes. As far as he was concerned, she'd already embarrassed herself with the way she'd been treating her daughter.

"So," Trevor said as he cleared his throat, apparently determined to make the most of Mary's visit. "How did you two meet?"

John took his opportunity, lacing his fingers with Mary's. "My mother is a good friend of Mary's, and an artisan who works with Mary's shop."

"She set you up?" Naomi asked pointedly, and John was sure she was thinking of her own attempt to set Mary up.

"No," John said, shaking his head. "She tried, but those things never work out. Mary and I found our way to one another on our own eventually, without any meddling."

Naomi pursed her lips and sat back. "How long have you been together?"

"Just a month or so," Mary said casually. "But we had feelings for a while before we got together."

John couldn't help but turn to Mary and smile, unfolding her fingers to kiss her palm.

"Have you thought about what the future holds for you

two?" Of course this was Naomi's next question. John should have guessed.

"Naomi," Trevor warned. "Don't go there."

"It's an innocent question!"

John defended the innocent on a regular basis and he knew, in every molecule of his being, that there was absolutely nothing innocent about the question she'd just asked.

"What the future holds for us?" John mused. *Prospect Park to watch the leaves change colors. Thanksgiving at Estrella's house—and hopefully not here. Sweating over what to get Mary for Christmas. The joy of watching Mary bundle herself into winter gear. Rejoicing when spring comes again because then summer will be around the corner and we will be able to celebrate our one-year anniversary.* "Oh, just being together, mostly."

It was a dumb answer, obtusely evasive, and he doubted it would hold Naomi at bay. But he refused to give her what she was fishing for.

Naomi cleared her throat. "Are your parents together, John?"

"Translation," Mary said, propping her chin on her hand, "what are your thoughts on marriage?"

Naomi glared at her daughter but didn't refute the claim.

Now John was the one clearing his throat. "No, my parents aren't together. But maybe it would help answer some of your questions, Naomi, if I just came clean about something. I'm crazy about Mary. I think she's the most wonderful person on planet Earth. And the idea of getting to spend time with her, grow with her, fills me with nothing but happiness. That's what I see for our future. Us. Together."

He said most of that right into Mary's eyes. She went pink in the cheeks and bit her bottom lip.

"And children?" Naomi asked, her hands clenched together so tightly they were white at the knuckles, as if she already knew the blowback she'd get for this question.

"Mom!"

"Naomi!"

Naomi winced at both Mary's and Trevor's admonishments, but her eye contact remained steadily linked with John's. He'd never felt more grateful to have been raised by Estrella than he was in that particular moment. Maybe his mother was a bit too nosy for her own good, but she'd never have subjected anyone to a conversation this blatantly intrusive.

And that was what ultimately got John. That Naomi felt she had the right to invade into Mary's life like this. This was so much worse than Estrella pulling strings behind the scenes, even though it sounded like Naomi had done some of that as well. It never failed to amaze John what some people would do ostensibly in the name of their children. Looking at Naomi right now, her back stiff, her hands clenched, her face set and lined, he realized that she truly believed she was right for asking these questions. That she was doing this for Mary's own good.

"Wow, personal question," he said, holding her eye contact, hoping to get her to at least acknowledge with a facial expression that she was vastly overstepping. But nothing. She was completely stoic. He decided to go another route and mildly shock her. "Mary and I haven't talked about kids yet. We're pretty new. But knowing us, if we did decide to have a kid, I think we'd just, you know, try pretty hard to make one."

Mary made a snorting noise and covered the bottom half of her face with her hand. Naomi flushed and pressed her lips together. John felt that he might have won that round.

He'd illustrated how inappropriate her question was by providing her with an inappropriate answer.

But apparently Naomi was not to be outdone. "And if the natural way doesn't work? She's almost forty, you know. Are you opposed to medical intervention for pregnancy, John? It can be a long, painful slog."

John's mouth dropped open. He hadn't met this woman twenty minutes ago, and she was already pumping him for information on whether or not he'd be willing to jack off into a cup? Was there no line she wouldn't cross?

"Mom!" Mary jumped to her feet. "For the love of God!"

"You have to have a plan for this kind of thing, Mary," Naomi said, though she was starting to lose her cool. She looked far less confident than she had just moments before. "That's just reality."

John was about to jump in, but Mary got there first. "You're saying the word *reality*, Mom. But what you really mean to say is *fear*. You're terrified of me turning into Tiff. Of me making the same choices that she did."

Naomi's face went ash white. "Don't even say that out loud."

"I'm not trying to be melodramatic here. But don't you get it, Mom? You can't bully me into living my life on your terms. That doesn't make me any safer from the boogeyman. Tiff made a hard choice at the end of her life. One I admire, not because it glorifies dying single, Mom, the way you seem to think it does. But because it was a full, independent choice she made, free from outside influence."

Mary took a deep breath and John just gaped at her. Apparently she didn't need defending in the least. She was doing just fine on her own.

Naomi's mouth opened and closed. She looked utterly gobsmacked.

"You don't want me to live in regret, I get that. You don't want me to miss my chance at having a fulfilled life. I get that too. But you don't get to decide what fulfills me. And, newsflash, having a kid out of fear of *not* having a kid never made anybody very happy. Maybe you know something about that?"

"That is not why we had you, pumpkin!" Trevor spoke up finally, reaching forward and taking Mary's hand, guiding her back down to the couch. "We had you because we wanted a child. We wanted you. The day you were born was the happiest day of either of our lives."

Mary blinked at her father, then turned and blinked at her mother. "Then why don't either of you treat me with respect?"

Her words sucked the oxygen out of the room.

"Mom, you've belittled me and ragged on me for as long as I can remember. In my twenties, I wasn't accepting enough dates, you didn't like Cora, you wished I wouldn't spend so much time with Tiff. In my thirties, you wanted me to get over their deaths like that." She snapped her fingers. "You demanded that I date, but men who were too old were not family material, men who were too young were embarrassing. You beat me down on every occasion you could, hoping to break me into wanting exactly what you want. But neither of you stopped to see what *I* wanted. You've only been to my shop four times in six years. And I built it from scratch. You know how hard that is? You haven't been there since the break-in. You barely offered any support to me at all on that front. And, Dad, you never stand up for me. Maybe once a year you'll say one little thing on my behalf, but you never actually stand between me and Mom. How am I supposed to interpret that? These behaviors, they are not respectful. And I was right to tell you that I won't be coming back until you apologize. Because even now, Mom, I finally bring a man home and you're still not happy. It's so clear to me now. If I get married, you'll be telling me I'm too old to wear white or a certain cut of wedding dress. If I have a kid, you'll always be reminding me that I'm older than the other mothers and what a shame that is. There's no way to please you! And shame on me for thinking that there ever was! Because either you accept me, love me for who I am, Mary Freaking Trace, or you don't get to have me in your life anymore. The end!"

Mary stood up, took one wobbly step toward the middle of the room, and John was instantly at her side, steadying her.

"Mary!" her mother called after her.

But Mary didn't stop. She went all the way to the front hall, where she shoved her feet into her sandals and flung open the front door. John didn't even have time to tie his shoes before he was out, after her, into the night.

CHAPTER TWENTY-THREE

THE RIDE BACK from Connecticut went by in a blur. Mary was quiet as she watched the darkened highway speed past her windows. John held her hand across the back seat, but he could apparently sense her need for quiet.

She didn't speak at all until they were latched behind the door of their Airbnb bedroom, across the house from Ty and Fin and Kylie.

"Do you see why my age has been a sensitive subject for me?" she asked, finally breaking the quiet between them.

John let out a breath that sounded like a tire being popped. "Good God, yes. I totally understand. That was awful. She's an undeniably hard person, Mare. I think it's gonna take me a year to process everything that just happened." He flopped backward onto the bed, his arms flung out above him. Rolling his head to eye her across the dim room, he squinted. "I think I need to apologize even more for saying—"

She laughed and held up a hand. "We're past that, sweetheart. You've made it exceedingly clear how you actually feel about my age. How you feel about me."

Mary bit her lip and turned away from John, taking out one earring and then the other, slicking her dress over her head and staring at herself in the dim light. She looked shadowed and mature and confident. She replayed certain parts of the evening in her head.

"Did you mean what you said tonight?" She turned to him in just her bra and underwear and watched his eyes get stuck on many interesting parts of her body.

"Yes," he answered huskily. "I'm not sure which part you're referring to, but I meant everything. Every word."

She stalked toward him, threw a knee over his hips and pinned his hands next to his ears. His lips quirked and his eyes heated. "What about the part about having kids?" she asked, her heart tripping against her ribs. "Did you mean that too?"

John's brow pulled down into a V, and she knew him well enough now to know that he was thinking, not judging. "Mare, what will be, will be. If kids are in the stars for us, I'm not worried about making a family with you. It'll pan out somehow."

"That's how I feel." She cocked her head to one side. "I've never been too worried about it. Which I think worries my mother most of all. As a woman, apparently it's my God-given duty to worry myself into a raisin over my own fertility."

"Don't do that," he said with a smile. "I'll love you when you're a raisin, but I don't want you to worry yourself into one."

Their eyes got stuck on each other as John's words sank in. It was the first time either of them had said the word *love* to one another. But the moment wasn't scary. The moment felt good. The moment felt warm. There was central air pumping through the room, but Mary felt the heat rise between them. She felt lit from within, churning with a glowing heat that she wanted nothing more than to share with him.

"I'll love you when you're a raisin too," she said in a low voice. She still pinned his hands to the mattress, and she gave them a little extra push to let him know that she wanted him to keep them there as she unbuttoned his shirt.

He was breathing fast, flexing his hands, looking like he wanted to touch her every single place he could. But he didn't lift his arms except to help her peel his shirt off. "Mary," he whispered.

She slid down his body and worked him free of his pants next, roughly shoving his boxers away like they were a personal offense to her. John moved his hands but only to clutch at his own hair, the strands of black spiking up between his fingers.

Mary tossed her bra and underwear away, planted her knees on the bed and bent over him. She loved this man, and her body demanded that she show him. She took his hardness in one hand and swallowed him down in one big gulp, holding him against the back of her throat and drawing his eyes to hers.

He said something that she didn't hear before she kept at him, working him in and out of her mouth, again and again. He spoke again and grunted. Suddenly, she set him free and let every inch of her skin slick across his as she crawled up his body.

"You have to be quiet," she admonished him with a smile on her face as she pressed in for a kiss, giving him all her weight. "There's other people in the house."

"Quiet," he agreed, almost nonsensically, his eyes on her mouth.

She slid against him again, opening her legs and pinning him with a hug, her mouth pressed to his. He made a small, almost restrained noise, and she reveled in the fact that she was definitely peeling him apart little by little.

The conversation with her parents tonight had been emotional and intense, but also freeing. She'd understood, for the first time ever, that there was no use changing herself for them. Either they were going to figure out how to love

her or they weren't. She couldn't make them. And in the meantime, she had this big, broad-shouldered, mean-faced, sweet-hearted man who wanted to leave with her. Would go anywhere with her, she knew. This man who was clutching at every part of her he could, who was trying to get his bleary eyes to focus as he gasped for air.

Mary reared up and spread her legs over his hips, teasing him with her wetness. They'd decided to forego condoms just last week, and she couldn't have been more grateful for the decision than she was at that very moment. When she sat herself down, took him in one inch at a time, the look on his face was worth it. It was worth every moment, every misunderstanding, every bit of doubt she'd had to wade through. Because here she was, right now, fully seated on a man who, she just knew, had decided she was everything he'd ever wanted.

She started to ride him, but he grunted and she fell forward, her palm over his lips and her mouth at his ear. "Quiet," she demanded. She reveled in the role reversal. Usually she was the one screaming her head off during sex.

They rolled halfway, a tangle of limbs, no clear position, and the bed started to squeak. John stood, arms banded around her, keeping her linked to him, and cast around for a quiet place to keep this party going. Mary looked too. There was nothing. Not even a dresser. Just a director's chair under the window that was not going to hold them.

"Bed," she demanded. "We'll be quiet."

He fell back onto the bed, and she ground herself against him, attempting to fuse them. Her fingers and hands everywhere and the same with his. They twisted onto their sides, and then him on top. They got a little too vigorous, the bed squeaked and they brought it back to a frantic, grasping glide against one another. Somehow the lack of a

thrusting plunge was even hotter than if they'd been able to have sex the way their bodies were screaming at them to do. Mary felt that every inch of her was consumed with him. His quiet, restrained breath, his teeth clamping onto her shoulder, his heavy fingers in her hair, clasping her hip.

She tightened her legs over his back and held him in place, working herself against him barely a half inch at a time, the pressure unbelievable, his flavor in her mouth, his whispered name on her lips as she catapulted herself over the edge.

She tightened hard onto him, against him, and moments later, he was rigid against her, pulsing within her, their bodies slick and aching from how tightly they'd gripped one another.

He let himself sag, full weight onto her, but when he lifted his head, the kiss was surprisingly light. Intense, but light. It was all flavor. All loose. The kind of kiss that can only happen after sex. No anticipation to speed it up, all connection, just long, slow tasting.

After a few long moments, John pulled himself off of her and padded to their attached bathroom. He came back with a warm washcloth that he pressed between Mary's legs. She stretched and smiled with her eyes closed.

"Just in case it wasn't clear," she said, opening her eyes again, "I'm in—"

"I'm in love with you," he interrupted her, his brows down in that V. "Big-time. Sorry to interrupt. I just would always kick myself if I wasn't the one to say it first. I just want you to know that even before you loved me back, I was in love with you. I'm pretty sure it's impossible to know you and *not* be in love with you."

Mary lunged up and wiggled her way onto his lap. "Did you just tell me that you loved me big-time?"

He laughed. "Guess so."

"Couldn't have said it better myself," she decided, kissing him one more time. "Love you. Big-time."

He laughed at himself. "Told you I was a dork."

"You're not a dork any more than I'm a snob."

John flopped next to her and sifted her hair through his fingers. "Who would have thought that we'd fit together so well?"

"Your mother."

They both groaned and laughed. "And me," Mary whispered after a moment. "I had a sneaking suspicion we might be a good fit."

"So did I." He paused. "I wanted to tell you about my suspicion that night of the fake date, when I walked you home. But then you said that you'd crossed me off your list, and I figured I'd save myself the heartache."

Mary groaned again and clutched him close. "I can't believe I said that. Especially when I was, like, four seconds away from catching feelings for you."

"I'm pretty sure I loved you then. Or was just about to. Even when I didn't think I had a chance. I was already committed to being in your life. As a friend, but still. Being in your life was important to me."

Mary's eyes teared up, and she pressed her forehead to his. They fell asleep just like that.

THOSE WORDS OF John's stayed in Mary's head on repeat as they stood in front of Cora's well-kept grave the next day. Being in your life is important to me.

That phrase alone meant almost as much as him telling her he was in love with her. Because there were so many kinds of love. And death had stolen so much of it from Mary too soon. More than she wanted kids, more than she

wanted marriage, she just wanted John to *be there*. She wanted him to want to be there.

He wanted that too, she was sure of it. Wasn't that how he'd answered her mother's question last night? When asked about the future, all he'd had to say was that he wanted to be with her. In her mind, it was better than a marriage proposal.

She transmitted these thoughts toward Cora's gravestone, psychically greeting her best friend. Mary and John stood back from Sebastian and Via, who had Matty tucked between them. Mary wanted to express solidarity while also giving their family a bit of space.

Mary hadn't expected to feel connected to Cora's gravestone when she first started coming here, because Cora wasn't actually there. The idea of being trapped in a box for all eternity had been Cora's version of hell, so she'd been cremated instead. Sebastian, Matty and Cora's parents had spread her ashes in the backyard where she'd grown up. So there was nothing marking this spot as Cora's besides her name. Even so, Mary liked to think she could feel her friend there. Tall, blonde, bossy, brightly crude, loyal, Mary's most fervent champion.

Mary watched while first Sebastian approached the gravestone, laying a palm against it, and she could see his mouth moving as he spoke some secret words to Cora.

A moment later, Matty joined him. Sebastian swept Matty up into his arms, being pretty much the only adult in the world large enough to actually lift the gigantic kid. He walked back to Via, kissed her on the lips and headed back toward the main road, where Tyler, Fin and Kylie were all waiting.

Mary squeezed John's fingers, stepped around Via with a little pat to her shoulder and laid the bouquet of purple tu-

lips she'd brought so that they were propped against Cora's name. "I met a guy," she whispered to her friend. "You'd like him. He's rude and protective of me. Just like you." Mary smiled, brushed at her tears. "He helped me stand up to my mom. Finally. Can you believe that? Even you and Tiff never quite got me to do that. I told my folks that they needed to respect me in order to keep me in their lives. I'm pretty much expecting a call from my dad any minute. He's never been one to hold out on me. But my mom? I don't know. I wouldn't be surprised if it takes her a couple of years." Mary traced the script of Cora's name with one finger, hoping her friend could hear her. "But you know what? For the first time, I kind of feel like I have the years to give. Somehow, being with John, it's kind of turned off the ticking clock for me. I've got time, Cora. I've never felt like that before."

Mary laid her palm flat against the top of the gravestone. "Love you forever, Cora."

She rose and walked back to John, taking his hand as the two of them left the cemetery. Mary glanced back just once to see Via still standing there, looking down at the headstone.

The train ride back to the city was a surprisingly festive one. It was almost as if everyone had shed a weight back in White Plains. Tyler and Fin were cuddled up against one another. He was laughing and shaking his head as she gave him the bad news about something she was reading on his palm. Matty, Kylie and Crabby were crammed into a bench seat together, both plugged into a movie, looking as comfortable together as siblings. John and Mary sat together facing Seb and Via, and that was where the relief was most tangible.

Mary felt that as disappointing as that conversation with

her mother had gone, she'd already set it down in Connecticut. There was nothing more to do than to live her life the way she wanted to. She could only hope that her parents would come to see it her way. And if they didn't, she was lucky enough to have Estrella.

There was some sort of giddiness emanating off of Seb and Via as well, and when Via rose to go to the snack car, Mary made sure to catch her.

"How was it today?" Mary asked. "Not too scary?"

"It was all right," Via confirmed. "It's complicated, how I feel about her. But more than anything, I'm so grateful for Seb and Matty. For the life I have with them." Via paused, looked around and then pulled Mary out of the concessions line by her elbow. "I, uh, told Cora that I'm going to ask Seb to marry me."

"What?!" Mary squawked, instant tears rising to her eyes. "Oh, Via, I'm so *happy* for you guys!"

"Me too," Via said, her cheeks pink as she shed a tear herself. "And I'm terrified. And excited. And all mixed-up. But yeah, mostly happy."

"Do you have a plan? When? Where?"

"No. Not yet. Just whenever the moment is right, I think. Maybe sometime in the next three months or so. Before Christmas."

Mary squeezed Via into a tight hug and hoped that her friend could feel just how happy she really was. "That's just perfect."

They got back in line, both of them flushed and loopy with Via's news, and Via stocked up on snacks for the kids. Mary took her time to choose, so Via went back to their seats first. A moment later, there was Seb at her side.

"Hey."

"Did Via forget something? She nearly bought out the entire snack car."

He smiled. "She really doesn't like the idea of Matty or I going hungry ever. We're lucky she makes such healthy food or me and the kid would plump up Violet Beauregarde–style."

"You're lucky to have her."

"I sure am." He shifted on his feet and looked behind him. When he turned back to Mary, something tripped up her spine. She wasn't a clairvoyant like Fin, but she was definitely getting a déjà vu–style vibe. "I'm gonna ask her to marry me. I talked about it with Cora's parents this weekend."

Mary eeped, squawked and then forcibly threw her hands over her own mouth so she wouldn't spoil anything. She was so bad at secrets.

"What?" Sebastian asked, reading her reaction.

"I'm just so happy for you!" She threw her arms around Seb's neck to hide her expression from him. "That's amazing! Incredible! I had no idea you guys were thinking about that! I'm flabbergasted!" Okay. Maybe she needed to dial it back a touch.

Seb laughed and patted her back. "Yeah, I've been thinking about it for a while. Wanted to take it slowly, make sure that Matty was comfortable with the direction everything was headed. But then I caught him online the other day."

Mary's brain broke. No. Nonono. Matty was too young to be looking at naughty stuff online. Matty was her little baby boychkin. She couldn't hear this—

"He was googling ring bearer pillows," Sebastian said, half laughing, half bemused.

Mary burst out in relieved laughter. "Oh, thank *God*."

Sebastian chuckled as well. "I asked him what it was for. And he told me he'd just started thinking about weddings recently and was curious about it. I took that as a sign that he was ready to start talking about the future with Via. He told me I should get a move on. So. Here we are."

"Do you have a plan?" Mary asked. She cleared her throat, trying not to sound rehearsed. "When? Where?"

"No plan," Seb said, shaking his head. "I think I'll know when the moment is right. Maybe sometime in the next six months."

Mary nearly swallowed her tongue. "Maybe sooner?" she croaked.

"Maybe." Sebastian squinted at her. "Mary, you're acting weird. Do you know something…?"

"No! I know nothing! I have to pee! Two Coronas with lime and a bag of pretzels." She thrust her money into Seb's hand and skedaddled out of the snack car, back to where they were all sitting. Safety in numbers.

She practically collapsed onto John's lap, pressing her lips to his. "Help me," she groaned. "Save me from myself."

He laughed. "What do you need?"

She gave him the CliffsNotes version and he agreed to help her field any more awkward questions.

Luckily, they made it back to Grand Central unscathed. They piled onto the subway together, and all of them, unwilling to part ways, immediately jumped on Via's invitation to feed everyone dinner.

When they came aboveground in Seb and Via's neighborhood, Mary pulled John back to walk behind the group. She liked seeing so many people she loved all clumped together, talking and laughing and evolving before her very eyes. And she loved, most of all, having John there by her side as she did it.

They walked quietly together, skipping over uneven squares of the sidewalk.

"I think the heat finally broke," John noted, lifting his head to the late afternoon sun, looking for once like he enjoyed its bright glare.

Mary nodded. "And soon it'll be fall. My favorite season, I think. So bittersweet. So determined to remind everybody that everything is always changing."

John nodded. "Plus, Estrella makes the most incredible walnut stuffing at Thanksgiving. That's why I always look forward to the fall."

"And then winter. Will you take me skating in Prospect Park?"

John grimaced. "I'll death-grip the wall and inch along while you skate."

She laughed. "And then ball games in the springtime. You like the Cyclones? We usually do a big birthday ball game celebration for Matty."

"Sounds great. And then it'll be summer again. Our time. I don't think I'll ever get through a hot summer and not think about this one. My favorite summer I've ever had."

Mary flushed with pleasure. "And then it'll all start over again. The whole cycle."

John kissed her temple. "That's right," he agreed. "Time. We've got nothing but time."

* * * * *

If you loved Flirting with Forever,
don't miss a single book in the
Forever Yours series by Cara Bastone,
available now!

Just a Heartbeat Away
Can't Help Falling

ACKNOWLEDGMENTS

Part of me will probably always be amazed that this is my actual job. I get to spend time with these characters every morning, hot cup of coffee in my hand, dog at my feet. I'm proud of myself for making this dream of mine a reality and I'd like to take a moment to acknowledge all the people who this truly, truly couldn't have happened without. To Tara Gelsomino, my patient agent, who always knows how to make a good manuscript even better. You are the person who somehow gets my work from my desktop out into the world. I can't even begin to explain how many hats you have to wear to be able to do that. Thank you. Jess Verdi, you were the first person to believe these characters had what it took to stand up off the page. I can never, ever thank you enough for the chance you took on me. To Allison Carroll, my truly brilliant editor, do you kind of feel like we knew one another in a different life? I could not have written this book without your encouragement, your eye for detail, your vision and your perpetually amazing innate understanding of what I'm trying to say. To Bonnie Lo for combing through this manuscript and making it sparkle. To Michele Bidelspach for bringing this manuscript on home. To the entire HQN team, including all the people who will continue to shepherd this project well after I've written the acknowledgments page. To my proofreader, whoever you will be, you're the bomb. Those who design the cover, you're my heroes! To Ed Menchavez for consulting with me on what it means to be a public defender in this complicated world. Thank you! To my Ambro Fam and my Sands Fam, who knew pretty much nothing about the romance world but have all found ways to support me in this journey, thank you. I can't imagine how an author could do this without all these people in her corner. And most of all, to Jon. Who can't stop telling people how proud he is of my accomplishments. Who thinks I'm a badass. Who takes long walks with me and discusses tropes, plot devices, character arc. Who gently tells me when it's time to take a break. Thank you, thank you, thank you.

Jillie's a bestselling horror writer who wants to be left alone in her isolated mountainside cabin. Matt bought the abandoned ski resort next door and plans to reopen it. These uneasy neighbors battle over everything...

Read on for a sneak peek at
Her Mountainside Haven,
the next book in the Gallant Lake Stories
by Jo McNally.

"And your secluded mountainside home with the fancy electronics is part of that safety net? And your hellhound?"

Jillie chuckled, looking up to where Sophie was glaring down at Matt from the deck. "Don't insult my dog. She's more for companionship than protection. Although her appearance doesn't hurt." She shuddered and pulled her jacket tighter.

God, he'd kept her standing out here in the cold and dark while he grilled her with questions. She'd already hinted that it was time for him to go. He scrubbed his hands down his face.

"I'm sorry, Jillie. You must be freezing. Go on up. Once I know you're inside, I'll take off."

"And you were on your way to dinner. You must be starving." She hesitated for just a moment. In that moment, he *really* wanted her to invite him up to join her for dinner, but that didn't happen. Instead, she flashed him a quick smile before turning to go. "Thanks again, Matt."

Let her walk away. Way too complicated. Just let her walk away. She was all the way up to the deck when he heard his own voice calling out to her.

"The old ski lift is working well, but I need to give it a few test runs, just to get acquainted with the thing. If you want a ride up to that craggy summit you like so much, I'll be heading up there Sunday afternoon. It'll just be us. No workers. No spectators."

Her head started to move back and forth, then stopped. She looked down at him in silence, then gave a loud sigh. "Maybe. I'll let you know. I've…I've got to go in."

He watched her and Sophie go through the door. She turned and locked it, then gave him a stuttering wave. For someone obsessed with privacy, it was interesting that this entire wall, right up to the peak of the A-frame roof, was glass. He lifted his hand, then headed to his car. He wasn't sure what surprised him more. That he'd asked Jillie to ride to the top of the mountain with him, or that she'd said maybe. As he turned the ignition, he realized he was smiling.

Don't miss
Her Mountainside Haven *by Jo McNally,*
available February 2021 wherever
Harlequin Special Edition books and ebooks are sold.

Harlequin.com

Get 4 FREE REWARDS!

We'll send you 2 FREE Books plus 2 FREE Mystery Gifts.

FREE
Value Over
$20

Both the **Romance** and **Suspense** collections feature compelling novels written by many of today's bestselling authors.